"The only thing that matters now is our newly formed false union, my dear Lady Matthew."

"Then you will do it?" she asked.

He nodded slowly. "Under certain conditions."

"Conditions? What conditions? I am willing to pay you handsomely."

"Possibly, but I am not overly concerned with your money."

"That is absurd. Why on earth not?" Not that she particularly cared right now. It was difficult to concentrate on anything beyond the proximity of his body to hers.

"It doesn't interest me."

Her voice faltered at the look in his eyes. Her heart thudded in her chest. The moment the words formed on her lips, she knew the question was a mistake. Or an invitation. And did not care. "What *does* interest you?"

"Any number of things, my dear," he said softly. "But they shall have to wait."

VICTORIA ALEXANDER

Her HIGHNESS, My Wife

AVON BOOKS
An Imprint of HarperCollinsPublishers

This is a work of fiction. Names, characters, places, and incidents are products of the author's imagination or are used fictitiously and are not to be construed as real. Any resemblance to actual events, locales, organizations, or persons, living or dead, is entirely coincidental.

AVON BOOKS
An Imprint of HarperCollins*Publishers*
10 East 53rd Street
New York, New York 10022-5299

Copyright © 2002 by Cheryl Griffin
Excerpts from *The Lady Is Tempted* copyright © 2002 by Cathy Maxwell; *Her Highness, My Wife* copyright © 2002 by Cheryl Griffin; *Shadow Dance* copyright © 1989, 2002 by Susan Andersen; *The Woman Most Likely To . . .* copyright © 2002 by Alison Hart; *Untie My Heart* copyright © 2002 by Judith Ivory, Inc.; *She Went All the Way* copyright © 2002 by Meggin Cabot
ISBN: 0-06-000144-5
www.avonromance.com

First Avon Books paperback printing: August 2002

Avon Trademark Reg. U.S. Pat. Off. and in Other Countries, Marca Registrada, Hecho en U.S.A.
HarperCollins® is a registered trademark of HarperCollins Publishers Inc.

Printed in the U.S.A.

10 9 8 7 6 5 4 3 2 1

Prologue

. . . and so, my dearest daughter, do not regret fleeing Avalonia. These are dangerous times and you
leave at my insistence. I shall rest easier knowing you
and your child are safe.

I have included letters of introduction to three
women, members of some of England's most powerful families and the daughters of old friends. They
will assist you and I urge you to call on them.

Do not hesitate to use whatever means necessary
to ensure your survival. Understand, the symbols of
heritage have no more significance than that which
we assign them. Do not cling to tokens at the risk of
your safety. Remember, your true heritage lies in
your heart.

Pray, dearest Sophia, for the soul of your husband, for the safety of your father and brothers and
for the future of your country. Face whatever lies
ahead with courage and strength. And know, my dar-
ling, no matter where you are my love is with you.
Always . . .

The words resounded in Sophia's head. She had no need to read her mother's letter again; every line was engraved upon her heart.

She glanced at her daughter sleeping in the nearby cradle and saw in her mind's eye the child's father, killed a mere six months ago in the turmoil that engulfed the tiny kingdom of Greater Avalonia. She'd loved him without restraint, without hesitation, thankful, until now, that they'd found such a love, unexpected in a marriage born of political necessity rather than affection.

No. She gazed out the window at the rolling hills of this patch of England that had become her sanctuary and her home. Regardless of what end he had come to, regardless of what fate befell her, she was lucky to have known, however briefly, such happiness. Now she had a new husband, a good man, and a new life, and if passion played no role, perhaps it would grow in time.

Sophia turned her attention, and her pen, back to the paper before her.

Dearest Mother,

Her mother was wrong. Regardless of Sophia's circumstances, she would not abandon her sacred obligation.

The Ladies Hutchins, Helmsley and Cranston were kind and gracious and have extended the hand of friendship.

She would never relinquish the heritage it was her sworn duty to protect.

*Yet I shall do what I feel I must, dear mother, as her-
itage is the tie that binds the past to the future. . . .*

Sophia was a hereditary princess of the Kingdom
of Greater Avalonia. And she would fulfill the single
most important responsibility inherent in that position until the day she died.

And beyond.

Chapter 1

"*D*id you miss me?"

The lilting tone with its subtle accent drifted into the stables he'd rented for a workshop on the outskirts of London, and for the span of a pulse beat, Lord Matthew Weston froze.

He'd never thought to hear that voice again save perhaps in his dreams, late at night when his mind was free to remember what he refused to consider in the light of day.

It took every ounce of strength he possessed not to look up from the work before him on the rough-hewn table. After all, hadn't he rehearsed this scene in his head a hundred times? A thousand? He'd practiced the right words, the proper manner. He'd be cold, aloof, indifferent. And why not? Her reappearance in his life was of no consequence.

He hadn't counted on the blood rushing in his ears or the thud of his heart in his chest.

"I scarce noticed you were gone." His voice sounded light, disinterested. Perfect. As if she'd been gone no more than an hour or so. As if he were far too busy to notice her absence.

For a long moment she was silent. His muscles ached with the effort of not acknowledging the significance of her presence and the strain of waiting for her response.

At last her laugh echoed through the stable and rippled through his blood. "I see you are still tinkering. It's most comforting to know some things in this world do not change."

"The world is constantly changing." Matt picked up the mechanism he'd been working on and studied it, as if it were much more important to him than she was. As if he didn't care enough to so much as glance at her. But he did care. More than he'd expected. He drew a breath to steady his nerves. "Constantly evolving. Nothing stays the same."

He straightened and glanced toward the wide-open doors. She was little more than a silhouette against the bright afternoon sun. Not that he needed to see her. He knew her face as well as he knew her laugh or her touch. In spite of his best efforts, everything about her was engraved in his memory as it had once been on his heart. "Nothing at all."

She laughed again and his jaw clenched. "Come now, that is far too philosophical and entirely too serious for a summer's day. Philosophy should be reserved for long, cold winter nights when there is little more to do than comment on the state of the world around us."

"Should it?"

"Indeed it should," she said firmly and stepped farther into the stables. "Odd . . . I don't remember you as being at all serious."

A teasing note rang in her voice and he was at once grateful *she* was not at all serious. Regardless of the countless times he'd gone over this very conversation in his head, right now he wasn't prepared to discuss serious matters. In truth, he wasn't prepared for *her*.

He placed the apparatus back on the table, picked up a rag and wiped the grease and grime from his hands. "I am surprised you remember me at all."

"Oh, I remember you quite well. How could I not?" She moved closer, away from the glare of the sun, and he could see her clearly now: the delicate shape of her face, the tilt of her nose and, even in the shadowed stables, the vivid green of her eyes. "Why, it has scarce been a year since we—"

"Fifteen months, three weeks and four days," he said without thinking, surprised to realize he knew exactly how long it had been since he'd last seen her. Last kissed her.

"Yes, well, time passes far too swiftly." She trailed her fingers along the edge of his worktable and glanced at the assorted bolts and screws, odds and ends strewn across the surface. All part of his attempt to refine a device of his own design to effectively heat the air required to lift a balloon without blowing himself up in the process. "Are you still sailing the heavens?"

The phrase caught at him. *Sailing the heavens* was the whimsical term she'd first called his efforts at ballooning and then what they'd shared between them. It had seemed so fitting once. Not just for his work but for the way she, and she alone, had made him feel. *Sailing the heavens.* He pushed aside the sentiment.

"I am indeed. Even now, I am preparing for a competition of sorts. A design contest, really. I have some innovations that may prove quite profitable."

"It's dangerous, you know." She glanced up at him. "This business of flying."

"That's what makes it exciting. The risk. The gamble. It's the best part of living, knowing your very existence is at stake." *Or your heart.* He ignored the unbidden thought and shrugged. "The most interesting things in life have an element of danger to them."

She shook her head; her voice was somber. "A woman in Paris died just last month. Her balloon caught fire and she plunged to her death."

"Madame Blanchard. Yes, I had heard of it." He had met the lady while in Paris last year. She was the widow of a balloonist and had taken up where her husband had left off. "A pity but not surprising. She was given to aerial fireworks and furthermore employed hydrogen for her balloon. Given the flammable nature of the gas, her demise was inevitable."

"Inevitable?" Her gaze met his and concern showed in her eyes. "As is yours?"

"Are you worried about me?" He raised a skeptical brow. "It's a bit late, don't you think?"

"I would hate to see you meet the same fate."

"Why?"

"It would be a shame. A waste." She looked away. "I do dislike waste."

He leaned toward her, the intensity in his voice belying his slow smile. "And would you grieve for me?"

Her gaze snapped back to his and her brows pulled together indignantly. "Of course."

He laughed and straightened. "How gracious of you, considering how little regard you had for me a year ago."

"Fifteen months, three weeks and four days," she said under her breath.

"However, you needn't concern yourself. I have no intention of losing my life. Not in the immediate future, at any rate. Besides, at the moment I am using heated air rather than hydrogen. The lift is not as great, but inflation is far quicker and the risks are fewer."

"Oh, indeed, that is ever so much safer." Sarcasm dripped from her words. "A fire to heat your air, on board a mere basket, beneath a taffeta balloon, towering over the treetops is scarcely more dangerous than . . . than a stroll in a park."

"You seemed to enjoy it." He studied her, wondering if she would rise to his bait or if her emotions were as fiercely under control as his. Or if indeed she cared at all. "And enjoyed Paris as well, if I recall."

She brushed aside the pointed reference to the past. "I assume, as you are still involved in this questionable pursuit, that you have not yet managed to acquire the funds needed for investment in a ship?"

So she did indeed remember something about their time together. He'd told her of his dreams and his plans to use whatever profits there were to be made from ballooning to buy a share in a ship and from that to make his fortune.

"Not yet." He gestured at the paraphernalia on the table. "But, should I win this competition, I will."

"And if you do not win?"

"Then I shall start over." His voice was matter-of-fact. "I have before, I will again."

"No doubt." She wandered the perimeter of his work area, pausing to examine the wicker gondola off to one side.

At once the absurdity of the situation struck him. A myriad of unanswered questions hung in the air between them, yet their conversation was as nonchalant as if they were mere acquaintances. As if they'd never shared blissful days and glorious nights lost in one another. Never made promises, vows of ridiculous concepts like *always* and *forever* that apparently only he had fully intended to keep. As if she'd never ripped his heart from his chest and left him alone and empty.

How odd, to be with her now with so much unsaid. So much pride would not allow him to say.

"How are you really, Matthew?" She glanced up at him. "Or should I say Lord Weston?"

He leaned back against the table, crossed his arms over his chest and considered her thoughtfully. He'd never told her of the title he was entitled to by birth, yet now she knew. How interesting. Still, what he hadn't said about himself paled in comparison to what she had not seen fit to reveal.

"No one has ever called me Lord Weston. The title is actually the Lord Matthew Weston or Lord Matthew, although I cannot recall the last time anyone called me Lord Matthew either. It is not a title I choose to use. I much prefer to be addressed as Captain, although that's not entirely accurate either, as my days of naval service are long past. Regardless, formality between us seems somewhat absurd." He unfolded his arms and braced his hands behind him on the edge of the table. "If I remember, we disregarded proper forms of address from the beginning, using our given names without regard to title or position. Matthew. Tatiana. Or, if you prefer . . ." He met her gaze and allowed a touch of triumph to show in his smile. "Princess."

Surprise flickered across her face.

He raised a brow. "You didn't think I'd learn the truth?"

Princess Tatiana Marguerite Nadia Pruzinsky of the Kingdom of Greater Avalonia raised a royal shoulder in a casual shrug. "I should have, I suppose, I simply did not think of it."

"I daresay there are any number of things you did not think of." He narrowed his eyes, anger he thought long gone rising within him. Still, his voice was controlled, his manner cool. "I'm certain it never occurred to you that disappearing from my bed, our bed, in the middle of the night—"

"It was closer to dawn," she murmured.

"—leaving nothing but a tersely worded note—"

"You thought it terse?" She frowned. "I thought it was a bit simple, perhaps, but it said what was necessary to say."

"Did it?" Sarcasm tinged his words. "All it said was that you had responsibilities and obligations you could no longer ignore. It further said you intended to—"

"Enough." She thrust out her hand to stop him. "I know what I said. And, possibly, it was not . . ." She searched for a word. "Sufficient."

"Sufficient?" In spite of his intentions, his voice rose and he nearly choked on the words. "It was bloody well anything but sufficient. It left more questions than answers and was scarcely the kind of note you leave a man you claim to—"

"Very well, it was not at all sufficient," she said quickly, "although it did seem so at the time." She cast him a pleasant smile. "Do accept my apologies."

"That's it, then?" He pulled his brows together. "Nothing more from you than *do accept my apologies*?"

"My sincere apologies."

He glared in disbelief. She was offering him no

more than the kind of apology one gave for a minor social faux pas.

"My *most* sincere apologies."

Is that all she thought the pain she inflicted on him was worth? *Most sincere apologies?*

"You may stop looking at me like that now, Matthew." Impatience sounded in her voice. "I am deeply, deeply sorry. It was a horrid thing to do. Thoughtless and inexcusable, and I truly regret it. There, now. I hope that satisfies you, because that is the end of it."

"The end of it?" He shook his head. Maybe it was. Still . . . "Don't I deserve more?"

"Perhaps. But I have not more to give you." She turned and stepped away, then whirled back to face him. "I am sorry, you know, it was a dreadful mistake."

"All of it?"

"No," she snapped. "Not all of it, you annoying man. Only the way I left you. And that is all I intend to say for the moment. I will not be interrogated about this."

"Is that a royal command?"

Her eyes narrowed slightly. "Yes."

He stared at her for a long moment and couldn't resist a slight laugh. "You are indeed a princess. I never would have guessed. It came as quite a shock."

"I am certain it did." She studied him warily. It was apparent that she did not intend to say anything further regarding her past actions, and for now he would let it go. For whatever reason, she had appeared once again in his life, and right now it may well be more important to find out why she was back than why she'd left.

"I see you no longer travel alone." He nodded toward the stable yard. A good half dozen or so men on horseback waited patiently. They were not uniformed, but it was apparent by their bearing that they were military. Some sort of royal guard, no doubt. They were accompanied by a single woman, also on horseback. "It's an impressive assembly."

She smiled ruefully. "It is a burden of position, to be always accompanied, to have constant companionship. It is not—"

"Why are you here?" he said abruptly, the question as startling to him as to her, perhaps more.

"I . . ." She paused for a moment, obviously considering her answer. "I need your assistance."

"My assistance?" Surprise swept through him, and an odd touch of disappointment. "Whatever for?"

"Well, you see . . ." She bit her bottom lip thoughtfully and his stomach tightened at the familiar habit. "I am writing the history of my family, the House of Pruzinsky, and—"

"You're doing what?" Disbelief sounded in his voice.

"I am writing the history of the royal family," she said in the firm manner of a governess, contradicting everything he knew of her. "It is something of a scholarly endeavor, and—"

"That's the most ridiculous thing I've ever heard. I don't believe you for a moment." He laughed. "You're not the type of woman who could ever be interested in anything scholarly. Frivolous or meaningless, perhaps, but never intellectual."

"Frivolous? Meaningless?" Indignation snapped in her eyes and she stepped toward him. "I will have you know I was an excellent student as a girl. My tutors could not praise me enough. I speak six languages.

I am not only familiar with the works of Aristotle and Descartes, but I understand them. I can list the names and major accomplishments, in order, of the emperors of Rome. I am well versed in Shakespeare and know complete scenes from a good number of his plays by heart."

She moved closer, too absorbed by her defense of her intelligence to notice she was now a scant foot away from him. But he did notice.

"I can recite the names and dates of rule of every monarch for the last five hundred years of every significant power in Europe, including your own country."

Near enough for him to reach out and—

"I know, and comprehend, the underlying reasons, as well as the obvious causes, for the major conflicts and wars among the nations of the world, including the complaints of those clever Americans who were intelligent enough to tell your barbaric country precisely where it could put its taxes and its tea!"

She stared up at him. Fire shot from her eyes. Passion shadowed every line of her body. Her blond hair moved in silken emphasis with every bob of her head. She was fervent and fascinating and abruptly he realized he'd lied to himself. For fifteen months, three weeks and four days he'd told himself he wanted nothing more to do with her. He'd sworn he didn't care, perhaps he'd never cared. He'd promised himself, if he ever saw her again, he would treat her with the disdain she deserved.

Now he realized he wanted her as much today as he had a year ago. Nothing had changed that. Not her leaving. Not his broken heart. Not even his pride.

"And furthermore . . ." She glared up at him. He

was a good half foot taller than she. He straightened, the movement bringing his body to within inches of hers. She was too caught up in her tirade to note their close proximity. Her scent, a subtle blend of exotic flowers and vague hints of foreign spice, wafted around him, and his stomach twisted with memory and desire.

"I well understand the flammable properties of hydrogen, as well as the basic principles of lighter-than-air flight. And I know most of the learned men in your field consider balloons filled with hot air to be considerably *more* dangerous than those filled with hydrogen because of the constant threat of fire to the balloon itself."

"Aerostat," he said absently, gazing into her green eyes and remembering how they'd darken in the throes of passion.

"What?" She shook her head with confusion.

"Aerostat. Remember?" His gaze dropped to her lips. Full and ripe and lush. He hadn't forgotten the feel of those sweet lips against his. He drew a deep breath and met her gaze. "We call them aerostats, not balloons."

"Yes, of course. And I knew that too." She stared up at him, eyes wide with . . . what? Apprehension? Desire?

Heat flashed between them. His gaze locked on hers and he struggled to breathe. To remember to breathe. "And those of us who fly them are aeronauts."

"Indeed. I knew that as well." She swallowed hard.

Without thinking, he lowered his head. Her chin rose. He couldn't seem to stop himself. It was as if he were guided by an unseen hand. Of fate or destiny. Or, more likely, desire. Demanding and undeniable.

His mouth moved closer to hers, even as he acknowledged kissing her, wanting her was entirely different than loving her. Loving her was a mistake that, this time, could well destroy him.

A mistake he would not make again.

His lips brushed hers and he whispered against them. "What do you want, Tatiana?"

"I want . . . that is, I need . . ." She sighed, and her breath mingled with his. "I need a husband."

He stilled, his lips still lightly touching hers, her words as shocking as a splash of cold water. "What?"

"I need a husband. I need you"—she drew a deep breath—"to pose as my husband."

"To pose—" He jerked back and stared down at her. "No!"

"Do hear me out before you say no." She tilted her head in that beguiling manner that haunted his dreams. "Do you not want to know why I have made such a request before you say no?"

"Not particularly," he said sharply. "Besides, I have already said no."

"Not as far as I am concerned." She waved away his refusal. "You simply cannot say no until you know why."

"I can and I have." His voice was firm.

She huffed in annoyance. "This is not at all gallant of you."

"Do forgive me." He swept an exaggerated bow. "I would not wish to be ungallant."

"Excellent." She beamed. "I knew you would change your mind."

"I have not changed my mind." Admittedly, though, he was intrigued by her persistence and could not ignore a touch of unwanted curiosity.

"Come, now, Matthew, I . . ." She stopped and

stared, an expression akin to horror on her face. "You are not married, are you?"

"Not at the moment," he said mildly. "And you?"

Her relief was palpable. As well it should be. She apparently needed him as her husband now, though it was a position she had once paid no heed to at all.

She shook her head. "I have not married . . . again."

Again. The simple word hovered in the air. *Again.*

"So . . ." He picked up a short cut of pipe and hefted it absently in his hand. "Tell me why you propose this ridiculous charade."

"It is an interesting story." She turned away from him and paced, as if she needed time to choose the right words. "A half century ago, my aunt, the last hereditary princess before me—"

"Hereditary princess?" He raised a brow.

"A princess who is in line for the throne," she said offhandedly.

"And you are a hereditary princess?" he asked slowly. "You can inherit your country's throne?"

"After my father, if both my brothers were to perish, then yes." She glanced at him. "They are extremely healthy and not at all prone to accident. I have no doubt my brother Alexei will be the next ruler of Avalonia, and that is as it should be. I have no desire to rule. Ever."

"I see." He hadn't realized the importance of her position. Perhaps her note about responsibility was sufficient after all.

"At any rate, Sophia—that was her name—fled the country with her infant daughter after her husband was killed in an insurrection. She took only a handful of belongings." She paused for a moment as if debat-

ing precisely how much to reveal, and Matt wondered idly what those belongings were.

"A few months after her arrival, she wed the Earl
of Worthington, in effect abdicating her position and
essentially severing ties with her home. She never
sent her mother, my grandmother, more than a single
letter. Aside from that, there is nothing known of her
life from the time she left Avalonia to the moment she
married the earl. It is that story I wish to document."

"Why?"

"Why?" She looked at him curiously, as if the answer were obvious. "Sophia was a member of the
royal family of my country. One of a select line of
hereditary princesses. Whether the choices she made
in her life were right or wrong, she cannot be allowed
to be forgotten." Determination lifted her chin. "I will
not permit it."

"I see." He supposed it made sense in a convoluted, feminine sort of way. "What I don't understand
is why you need me."

She heaved a long-suffering sigh. "I cannot go
blithely around England demanding information
about a lost princess. Not as myself anyway. It simply
would not work." She lowered her voice in a confidential manner. "You may not be aware of this, but
many people are quite intimidated by royalty."

"Really?" He stifled a smile.

"Indeed they are." She nodded seriously. "However, Lord Weston and his wife, Lady Weston, Avalonian by birth—"

"Lord and Lady Matthew."

"Are you certain? It doesn't have the same impos-
ing sound to it."

"I am certain."

"Very well, then. Lord and Lady *Matthew* can certainly retrace the steps of the Princess Sophia and meet with those who knew her. They will be much more willing to respond without censoring their words or being the least bit uncomfortable. Their comments will be honest and candid." She flashed him a triumphant smile. "Now do you understand?"

"Not really." He shook his head. "It seems like a great deal of trouble for a bit of insignificant information."

"It is not insignificant. And I thought it was a brilliant idea," she said loftily.

"It's ridiculous. Aside from everything else, in my adult life I have never been known as Lord Matthew. My brothers have used their titles, but I have not spoken to them or anyone else in my family for the past decade. My sudden appearance as—"

"Perhaps you should." Her tone was prim.

"Should what?"

"Speak to your family. Perhaps it is time. Ten years is an exceedingly long time, and it does seem that regardless of—"

"Enough," Matt said firmly, ignoring the fact that he had been thinking much the same thing of late. He simply didn't know how to go about it or how he'd be received. He certainly didn't like to hear it coming from her. "My relationship with my family is not the issue at the moment."

"No, I suppose not." She glanced around at the assorted debris that made up his work. "Did I mention I am willing to pay you a great deal of money for your help? Enough to purchase a ship, if that is what you wish."

"You did not mention it, but it makes no difference as to whether or not I will help you." His tone was hard.

"And will you?"

He fully intended to refuse. "I don't . . ."

She gazed at him hopefully, her green eyes wide with anticipation, and his determination faltered.

He tried again. "I can't . . ."

She chewed her bottom lip and his mouth went dry.

"What I mean to say . . ." He sighed with resignation. "I will consider it."

"I can ask for nothing more at the moment." She cast him a brilliant smile, and he wondered if he'd ever really had a hope of turning her down. "I should like to proceed as soon as possible. If you would call on me tomorrow, we may make the arrangements." She pulled a folded paper from the cuff of her pelisse and handed it to him. "This lists the names of three ladies Sophia mentioned in her letter. They apparently provided her shelter and assistance. I believe even the closest is some distance away. You will want to plan our travels accordingly."

"If I agree."

"If you agree. It also has the address of the house we are residing in, much more circumspect than a hotel. I wish to keep my presence in England discreet." She handed him the paper.

"I will call on you tomorrow to give you my answer," he said in a no-nonsense tone that even he didn't believe.

"As you wish. Tomorrow, then." She nodded and started toward the door.

"One more thing, *Princess*," he said, surrendering to his curiosity.

She paused.

"How did you know all that? About the opinions of experts on the dangers of hydrogen versus hot air?"

She turned back and cast him an overly innocent look. "Why, my dear Lord Matthew, that was yet another lesson I learned as a girl. In the study of military history, I believe. One should know all there is to know about your opponent and never underestimate him."

"Are we opponents, then?"

"I have not yet decided." Tatiana flashed him a teasing smile, and once again his insides churned. "Have you?"

He stared for a long moment, then smiled slowly. "I don't know."

She laughed, turned away and sailed out the door to her waiting escort.

His immediate impulse was to turn her down flat. Of course, he could certainly use the money, even if accepting it would be something of a blow to his pride. In truth, he'd rather risk his life each day, living on his pension and his prize savings, working toward building his own fortune, than take her money. Still, some would say she owed him something. Why not money?

He watched a gentleman assist her onto her horse and ignored a twinge of envy. It was past time to admit, at least to himself, that he hadn't put her behind him at all. He still wanted her, more than he'd ever wanted any woman. What he didn't know was what else he felt about her. He'd long thought it was the abrupt, unexpected nature of their parting, the sense of a task unfinished, that had kept him from getting on with his life. Although he had rather thought he had gone on until now.

Regardless, there was no question that he had indeed loved her once. For a scant six glorious days he had loved her with the kind of intense emotion that strikes without warning and promises to last a lifetime. He leaned against the rough frame of the opening and watched the departing riders. Nothing but love could have hurt as much or lasted as long.

He lingered in the doorway until she and her companions disappeared down the road. And stayed staring, unseeing, long after that. It was obvious that she was involved in something beyond the writing of a family history. Regardless of her ardent defense of her academic accomplishments, she was not a scholar. Her explanation as to why she wished to retrace the steps of her aunt did not seem even remotely valid.

Accepting her proposal would allow him to finally put the past to rest, to finish that unfinished task. But this time, it would be on his terms, not hers. This time, if anyone left, it would be him. This time, his heart would play no role.

He turned from the door and unfolded the paper still in his hand. The address was in a well-to-do area of the city, not up to the standards of royalty, perhaps, but close enough. His glance slipped to the neatly penned list of women and his jaw tightened. Was this why she wanted his help? Did she realize the significance of the last name? Or was it simply some odd coincidence? Some quirk of fate designed to bring them together once again?

Whatever the answer, there was no question now as to his decision. He would indeed accompany her.

He would find out precisely why she was back and exactly what she really wanted. He would pose as her husband and allow her to be introduced as Lady Matthew. Why not?

After all, for one brief handful of days in Paris a scant fifteen months, three weeks and four days ago, she had earned it.

Chapter 2

*T*atiana walked toward the waiting entourage with a firm, steady step. She could feel Matthew's gaze bore into her back. She kept her shoulders straight and clasped her hands together to still their trembling. It would never do to let him know how difficult it had been to see him again. How hard it had been to act nonchalant and lighthearted, as if indeed she had nothing on her mind beyond a silly memoir of her aunt's travels.

When all she wanted to do was throw herself in his arms and beg his forgiveness. Confess her mistakes, her cowardice, her weaknesses.

He was as vibrant as she had remembered in both appearance and spirit. Tall and handsome, his brown hair kissed golden by the sun, his face and forearms tanned from his work out-of-doors. He fairly quivered with suppressed energy. There was an intensity about him, the way he spoke and walked and even simply stood and stared, that bespoke of a man who would make his mark on the world.

As he had on her.

"Well?" Captain Petrov, Dimitri, stepped forward to help her onto her horse. "Did he agree?"

"No, but he will." Tatiana allowed Dimitri to assist her into the sidesaddle and braced herself for the comments she knew would come. Katerina, Lady Kaminsky, the only other woman in the group, glanced from Tatiana to Dimitri and back, then cast the princess an encouraging smile and directed her horse to follow a few paces behind. Katerina too knew what lay ahead.

Dimitri swung himself up onto his horse and barked a brisk order to the riders. His well-trained men divided into lead positions or trailed behind, providing the illusion of privacy for their princess and their captain.

Dimitri edged his horse close to Tatiana's. "Did you tell him the truth? About the jewels?"

"Of course not." She settled herself in the saddle and ignored the censorious note in his voice. Dimitri and his cousin Katerina had grown up with Tatiana and, in spite of the differences in their stations, were still her closest—in truth, her only—confidants. He now served as a captain in the royal guard, and the widowed Katerina was her traveling companion.

"I fully agree with you on that point," Tatiana continued. "I shudder to think what the consequences would be if our enemies knew the famed Heavens of Avalonia were missing. It is best to keep my true purpose here undisclosed for the moment."

"Even from this man you claim to trust?"

"Yes."

"I still think this plan of yours is ridiculous, not to mention highly improper and possibly dangerous."

"As you have not hesitated to point out. Over and

over again. Nonetheless"—she met his gaze directly—
"I intend to proceed without interference from you or
anyone."

Dimitri shook his head. "Your father would not approve, nor would your brother."

"My father has been ill and Alexei has been far too
busy countering the efforts of our cousin to seize
power to concern himself with my affairs."

It was the truth as far as it went. Alexei, crown
prince and heir to the throne of Avalonia, had indeed
been forced of late to occupy his every waking moment with quelling the seeds of unrest sown by their
cousin, the Princess Valentina. It still rankled that Tatiana had been allowed no part in that. Indeed, she
had been sent away for her own safety, even though
her father was still ill and she would much preferred
to have stayed.

Alexei's latest letter, along with dispatches and official correspondence for Dimitri, had reached her in
France and told of his success in thwarting Valentina,
thanks to the unexpected help of their English cousin,
Viscount Beaumont. The king's health was much improved and all was again well at home. As for her
brother Nikolai, he would probably applaud her efforts, but he was traveling the continent and she had
no idea where he was. Besides, this was her quest,
and hers alone.

Although Alexei's recent trip to England this past
spring had been successful in reuniting the English
branch of the House of Pruzinsky, he had not located
the missing jewels. Tatiana was determined to succeed where he had failed.

"Regardless—"

"There is nothing more to be said on the matter."
Her tone was hard and unyielding.

"There is a great deal more to be said," Dimitri muttered, then sighed. "At least you have chosen someone to assist you who appears to be an honorable sort. From what I have learned of this Matthew Weston, he was considered an excellent officer, his naval career was distinguished and his family's reputation is impeccable, even if he does not acknowledge his heritage."

Tatiana vaguely remembered Matthew mentioning a rift with his family but until recently she had had no idea he was the youngest son of a marquess. It had simply not come up in the bare week—in truth, a mere six days—they had spent together.

"He is also considered quite clever, at least among those other idiots—"

Tatiana slanted him a sharp glance.

"Forgive me, Your Highness." Dimitri's lips tightened. "I meant to say *inventors* or *entrepreneurs* or . . . is *dreamers* acceptable?"

As annoying as the sarcasm in his voice was, she could not suppress a slight smile. "The path to the future has always been led by dreamers, and I daresay always shall be."

"So be it. As I was saying, he is thought of highly among his fellow *dreamers* who are possessed by the idea of sailing the skies. They are a competitive lot, yet they acknowledge Weston as a man with a great deal of promise."

"Thorough, as always, Dimitri," she said mildly. "Even if your investigation went beyond the limits of my request."

His brows pulled together. "You cannot think I would allow you to undertake this ridiculous quest of yours without—"

"You do not *allow* me—"

"I do not even know how you are acquainted with this man, or why you see fit to involve him, or the circumstances—"

"That is quite enough, Captain." Her voice was sharp, imperious and startling even to her.

Surprise washed across Dimitri's face. She never called him *Captain*.

"I have made my decision. You may accept it or not, but you have neither the power nor the authority to deter me." She studied him coolly. "I will, however, give you the choice of remaining in London as a precaution should I require your assistance or returning to Avalonia."

His eyes narrowed. "If I return home, you can rest assured I will be back in six weeks or less with orders from your father to stop you from this foolishness."

She lifted her chin slightly and met his gaze with a direct and steady stare. "Perhaps. But I am an adult of five and twenty years and fully capable of making my own choices in life."

"You are also a subject of the king, and if your father—"

"I am a hereditary princess of Avalonia." She emphasized each word in a deliberate manner he could not fail to understand. "I am third in line to rule. And here and now, in this place and time, I am your sovereign." She met his gaze and held her breath, knowing full well if he challenged her, the courage it had taken her so long to develop might well fail. "So what is it to be, Captain? Will you stay in England or run home to tell tales about the misadventures of your princess?"

He stared for a long moment. At last he blew a resigned breath. "You have changed, Princess. There is a sense of resolve about you I have not seen before."

"I have a purpose in my life now, Dimitri. I know what I want and I am determined to get it."

"It is more than that." He studied her carefully. "You have always been somewhat quiet, never given to demands or orders, but your manner is different now. You no longer hesitate to take matters into your own hands. It is as if you have at last grown into your position."

"Have I?" She raised a brow. Only this childhood friend would dare to be so presumptuous. "And is that good or dreadful?"

"I noticed it first perhaps a year ago." He continued as if he had not heard, as if he were trying to work out a puzzle. "At the time, I wondered if you had at last started anew and laid the past to rest."

"Along with my late husband," she said dryly.

"But in recent days, since you have made me aware of your plans, I have come to realize the change in your manner dated more precisely to the week in Paris when you disappeared. When we did not know where you were. If you had been abducted or killed or—"

"Dimitri." Her voice carried a warning he ignored.

His brow furrowed and he spoke more to himself than to her. "And you adamantly refused to discuss your absence. It was the first time I can recall you ever issuing a royal command. Of course, we were simply grateful you were unharmed, and it scarcely mattered where you had been. Whom you had—"

Realization lit his eyes. "I have been a fool. That is when you met this man, is it not?"

Denial was pointless. "Yes."

"I see." Dimitri considered her thoughtfully. She had known him her entire life and knew enough to brace herself now. "Then tell me, Princess." He leaned closer, his voice low, confidential, accusing. "Is it the Heavens you want, or"—his gaze searched hers—"the man?"

Her hand itched to slap his face. She summoned all her restraint and forced a cold smile. "You forget yourself, Captain. Do not let our friendship blind you to the fact that I can have you reduced in rank, imprisoned or even, if I so wish, shot."

"Forgive me, Your Highness." Shock colored Dimitri's voice. "I did indeed overstep my bounds."

"Yes, you did." She leaned toward him and lowered her voice. "I would, of course, never do such a thing, but you would be wise to realize that I could."

"Indeed I would." He paused.

"Yes?"

"May I speak frankly?"

Guilt washed away her brief sense of triumph and she sighed. "You always have."

"Perhaps, but you have never threatened to have me shot before."

"Never?" She smiled to lighten the moment.

"Never." He shook his head. "You wield your power now with a firm hand. You have not done so in the past. It is somewhat disquieting."

"I imagine it is. Like discovering a puppy has learned to bite." She reached out and laid her gloved hand over his. "You and Katerina are now, and always have been, my dearest—my only—real friends. But Dimitri, is it not past time that I use the power that is my birthright to take my life, my destiny, into my own hands?"

He stared at her as if she were speaking a language unknown to him. "You have responsibilities—"

"And have I not lived up to them? Have I not always, always done exactly what was expected of me? Without question or protest or hesitation? From my public demeanor to my most private relationships, have I not always been"—she searched for the right words—"for the most part perfect?"

"Princess, I—"

"Consider my life for a moment. Was I not betrothed as a child to the son of an ally of my father's for the purposes of politics? And even though Phillipe's country was no longer independent and the alliance between our families no longer necessary, did I not wed him anyway because my father, my king, had given his word?"

And did I not give him my heart as well? Tatiana removed her hand from Dimitri's and straightened.

"And was I not a good and faithful wife even as he had no understanding of such qualities himself?" Anger too long restrained surged through her. "Did I not pretend I was unaware of the indiscretions he took no pains to hide? Did I not ignore that I was the subject of gossip and pity and humiliation?" She tried and failed to keep a bitter note from her voice. "You knew, did you not?"

Dimitri's jaw clenched. His gaze met hers and he drew a deep breath. "I—"

"No." She waved away his response. "It is unfair of me to expect an answer. Your loyalty and desire for my protection would never have allowed you to be the bearer of such news. But I am well aware that you and everyone in the court, perhaps everyone in the country, knew of Phillipe's dalliances."

"He has been dead for nearly three years now, Princess," Dimitri said quietly.

"Yes. A tragic accident." But she, and no doubt most of the world, knew Phillipe's horse would not have thrown him had the creature not been panicked by the gunshots fired by an angry husband encountering Phillipe bidding his latest, and his last, conquest farewell. "And I did exactly what was expected, mourning the official, and so very proper, length of time. Yet even as such pretense ends, the anger lingers."

"Perhaps it is time to put the past behind you. To forgive or least forget."

"You misunderstand. My anger is not directed at Phillipe but at myself. Phillipe, was . . . I do not know." She shrugged. She had long ago accepted the truth of her husband's character. "Perhaps he could have been a better man married to someone else. As it was, he was weaker in nature than even I." She shook her head. "You see, while he was not my choice, I was silly enough to trust my heart to him."

"I did not know."

"Few did, and to my credit, such affection did not last long. Still, it is not easy to accept or forgive your own foolishness. And therein lies the anger."

"You were never foolish."

"Dear Dimitri, you have always been a poor liar, and I do appreciate it. I was extremely foolish."

He looked as if he were about to speak, then thought better of it.

"Yes?"

"A matter of curiosity, nothing more."

"Go on. What is it you wish to know now? I promise I will not have you shot." She grinned. "Today."

"Then it is perhaps worth the risk." He smiled dryly. "Still, as I have been chastised once already for my impertinence, I shall hold my tongue."

"And if you did not," she said slowly, "what would you ask?"

"Simply if you are still foolish enough to give your heart to a man who is not worthy of it."

"Your instincts are correct as always. It is a presumptuous question and you are wise to refrain from asking."

"I thought as much." He touched his fingers to the rim of his hat, nodded and directed his horse to join the riders up ahead.

It was an irony of their relationship. He was one of the few people in the world she counted as friend, yet that friendship could only go so far. Regardless of the frank nature of today's discussion and so many in the past, there were boundaries between princess and subject he would never cross. Boundaries she would never push.

Matthew had never treated her as royalty. He had treated her as a woman. A desirable woman. It had been a unique and thoroughly wonderful experience. Oh certainly she had usurped Katerina's position, claiming to be nothing more than a companion to royalty when she and the dashing lord had first met. And loved. Even so, today, knowing her true identity, he treated her no differently than he had last year. Aside from the chill in his manner, of course, and the touch of disdain in his eye.

It would be hard, if not impossible, to win his heart again. But in this too she was determined to succeed.

Katerina edged her horse to Tatiana's side. "My cousin does not look happy."

Tatiana uttered a short laugh. "I can scarce recall the last time he did look happy."

"His responsibilities weigh heavily on him. And he is concerned for you."

"I am well aware of that. And I do appreciate his concern. However—"

"However, he does not know as much as he thinks he knows: the true purpose of your quest. That, no doubt, is for the best." Katerina studied her. "And what of your Lord Weston? Was your reunion successful?"

"My Lord Matthew, actually. I do like the way the *my* part of it sounds. However, I cannot say I could term our meeting successful." Tatiana smiled ruefully. "He did not throw me out, but he has not agreed to my proposal." She met her friend's gaze with confidence. "But he will."

"Did you tell him about the Heavens?"

"Not yet."

"Did you tell him—"

"No."

"Perhaps you should simply tell him the truth."

"No." Tatiana shook her head. "I suspect he is not entirely certain as to his feelings about me at the present, which I think is a very good beginning. But he is not ready, and, to be honest, neither am I. I would wager he has spent a great deal of time hating me and I dare not give him another reason to continue."

"Would he?"

"I do not know." Even as she said the words, she realized there was much about Matthew she did not know. Yet it did not matter. Somewhere, deep within her, she knew all she had to about this man she had loved once and never stopped loving.

"I can scarce blame Dimitri for his concern." Worry showed in Katerina's eyes. "I too fear for you. It is a hazardous game you play with this man. Do not forget, when you left him he did not come after you."

"I have forgotten nothing." It did bother her that Matthew had not moved heaven and earth to find her, although she could hardly blame him, given the abrupt nature of her departure. Still, today he had known her true identity. He had obviously cared enough to discover at least that.

"You could lose much."

"But I could gain the world, and that, dear Katerina, is what makes it worthwhile." Matthew's words rang in her head. "And exciting. The risk. The gamble. Knowing your very heart is at stake. I have never known such excitement. Or such passion. Or such—"

"Love," Katerina said simply.

"Love." Tatiana nodded.

From the moment she had met the adventurous Englishman with the flirtatious manner and amused look in his eye, she had been unequivocally and irrevocably in love. Their days together were as sharp in her memory as if they had happened yesterday.

In the first moment of rebellion of her entire life, she had escaped the confines of companions and escorts and rank, slipping away from the Paris hotel that housed the Avalonian contingent. It was highly improper, more than a little dangerous, and she had loved every reckless minute. It was as if, having left the encumbrances of her title behind, she had left the position behind as well. She was not the Princess Tatiana, heir to the throne of Avalonia, but simply the woman: Tatiana Pruzinsky. And she reveled in it.

She would have thought that alone was responsible for her immediate attraction to the bold, brash stranger selling balloon ascensions in a Paris park, especially as she was feeling rather bold and brash herself, a completely different person from the quiet, dutiful creature she had always been. But even the giddy sensation of floating above the treetops, of sheer unadulterated freedom, paled in comparison to the intoxication of being in his arms and later in his bed.

And in his life.

She and Matthew had explored parts of the ancient city she would never have been privy to without his company on the ground and, even better, in the air. And more, they explored each other. Their hopes, their dreams, their very souls. She had never known absolute happiness before, had never suspected mere mortals could laugh so much, could share such joy.

Later, she would wonder how she had managed to reveal so much of herself without revealing her identity, and realized who she was to the rest of the world was not as important as who she was to him and to herself. She had never tasted freedom like this of both spirit and body, and she would never be the same.

When she had first left her companions, she had not planned to be gone more than a few hours, but an afternoon had turned to an evening, a night to a morn, nearly a week in all. A passage of time she had barely noted. It was not until she had vowed to love him forever that the unyielding sword of reality had struck with a relentless blow and she knew she could not stay with him unless she first settled the rest of her life. She could not abandon the responsibilities of her position to her country or her family as easily as she had slipped out of her hotel rooms.

Their days together were a glorious dream built on passion and desire and unexpected, unremitting love, but built as well on deceit. She could not bear to tell him the truth and she accepted now, as she did then, the cowardice of her actions. She had left his bed and his life with no more than a note about duty she knew full well was insufficient. A note that released him from further obligation to her. She had wanted to pour her heart out on that paper. Reveal the truth about herself and confess how much he had changed her life and how very much she loved him and vow she would return. But she did not want to make another promise she might not be able to keep.

Yet in the fifteen months, three weeks and four days since she had vanished from his life, the power of the love they had shared had not dimmed but had in fact grown stronger. Strong enough to finally overcome a lifetime of perfect behavior, of the weakness of not questioning the life laid out for her. When she had learned the jewels that were hers to wear and indeed to protect, as a hereditary princess of Avalonia, were imitation and the real gems had been long since lost, she had seized upon it.

If she could recover the jewels, she would fulfill her responsibility to her title, her family and her country. At least in her own mind. Why, had any princess before ever accomplished such a feat? Success would give her the courage and perhaps even the right to demand to be able to live her own life with the man she loved. Even abdicate her position, if necessary. How could anyone deny her? After all, what could be more significant than restoring the legendary Heavens of Avalonia, the symbol of her family's right to rule and her country's very existence, to their rightful place?

And while recovering the jewels, she fully intended to recover Matthew's love as well. She refused to consider the possibility of failure on either count.

Did she not already have something of a plan for finding the Heavens? Surely she would think of some way to win Matthew's heart as well. She had no doubt, given his actions today, that he already desired her. Perhaps that was the place to start.

"Do you know how potent an aphrodisiac laughter is?" Tatiana said without thinking.

"I have an idea," Katerina said softly.

"Of course. How thoughtless of me."

Katerina's marriage had been a love match on both sides. When her husband had died of a swift and violent illness, Katerina was devastated. She had become the princess's official companion while both women were still in mourning. For Tatiana, helping her friend find her way through her grief eased her own bitterness as well as an odd touch of sorrow that her marriage had been so disappointing.

"Is that how you intend to charm your way back into his affections, then?" Katerina asked. "With laughter?"

"Perhaps not entirely into his affections. But it may well be the first step to charming my way back into his life."

Tatiana cast her friend a wicked grin. "And his bed."

♛

Chapter 3

Ephraim Cadwallender leaned back behind his desk in the new offices of *Cadwallender's Weekly World Messenger* and blew a long, low whistle. "That's quite a proposition."

"Indeed it is." Matt balanced a glass of the excellent whiskey Ephraim kept in his desk in one hand and held a cigar in the other. The whiskey was the publisher's one true extravagance and well appreciated by his friends. The cigars were Matt's contribution to the evening.

"Are you going to take her up on it?"

Matt swirled the liquor in his glass. "Absolutely."

"For the money, of course," Ephraim said without a doubt in his voice.

"The money, old man, is the least of my reasons."

"The least?" Ephraim raised a brow. "I would think it would be the best."

"There are certain aspects of this that are considerably more important than money," Matt said slowly.

"What could possibly be more important than money?"

"To begin with, she's up to something beyond writing a family history. Her story is absurd and I don't believe her for a moment."

"Forgive me for mentioning the obvious, but what difference does it make?"

"It makes a great deal of difference." A dozen unanswered questions crowded Matt's mind. "She's not quite as clever as she thinks. It's apparent there is something she hasn't seen fit to tell me. I want to know what it is."

Ephraim blew a long breath. "I thought you'd had your fill of ferreting out secrets long ago."

"One never gets tired of ferreting out secrets; part of one's nature, I suppose." Matt chuckled. "In one way or another, I seem to be constantly trying to do just that. To uncover the secrets of the forces of physics and nature to control flight, in and of itself a secret until not more than half a century ago."

"Still, I scarcely think—"

"And I am certain"—he leaned forward and pinned Ephraim's gaze with his—"whatever Her Highness is up to, it has to do with my family."

"*Your* family?" Ephraim frowned. "The family you've had no contact with in more than a decade?"

"One and the same." Matt smiled wryly. "It seems one of the ladies mentioned in the letter that is the heart of this proposition is a member of my family. To be specific, my grandmother. Another lady is one of her oldest friends."

"I don't see why that should make you suspicious. Your family is rather well connected. I am extraordinarily suspicious, part of *my* nature, yet it doesn't strike me as being at all unusual that your grandmother's name, or the name of her friend, should come up."

"Think about it, Ephraim. If Tatiana is only interested in writing of the travels of a long-dead relation, why wouldn't she simply tell me of my family's involvement?"

"She doesn't know?" Ephraim said helpfully.

"It's a possibility. Indeed, it could be nothing more than an intriguing coincidence. However, she did encourage me to mend the rift with my family." Matt shrugged. "It was during the natural course of our conversation and might well mean nothing at all, but I don't trust her."

"So you will accompany her to protect your family's interests?"

"Exactly."

"But you don't especially like your family."

"You're wrong there. It is my family that does not especially like me."

"As far as you know," Ephraim said pointedly.

"As far as I know." Matt sipped thoughtfully at the whiskey. "However, my grandmother was always fond of me."

It was his grandmother who had taken the place of his mother when his mother died shortly after Matthew's birth. His grandmother who had taken his side during his escalating clashes with his father as he grew older. And his grandmother who had wept when his father secured an appointment for him in the navy and sent him off.

"And I was quite fond of her."

It was only in recent years, with the wisdom born of distance and experience, that he'd reexamined his younger days. He was indeed a wild youth, far more prone to trouble and scandalous behavior than his three older bothers combined. He could see now, where he couldn't then, a father's frustration when faced with a rebellious and uncontrollable child. He could understand now a father's desire for his son's future to be molded by something beyond indulgence and excess. Only now could he recognize and be grateful for a father's courage in sending a son into the world to make his own way and find his own strength. And he could at last accept the love required to do it all.

He'd learned of his father's death shortly before the war ended and wondered at the irony and desperate regret of it. When at last Matt had realized he could not forgive his father because in truth the older man had done nothing *to* forgive save force his youngest child to become a man they could both be proud of, it was too late. It was a debt he could not repay.

Until, perhaps, now.

"You've still not spoken to your brothers, then." Ephraim said as if it didn't matter.

"You know full well I haven't." Matt's tone was as casual as his friend's. "Nor have they spoken to me."

"And you have been so exceedingly easy to find since we left His Majesty's Service, refusing to use your title and flitting from England to France and back." Ephraim scoffed. "In the last three years, you've barely had a permanent address."

"Couldn't be helped, old man. The life of an aeronaut, and all that. And I did not flit."

Matt had long ago acknowledged to himself that he would like nothing better than to reacquaint himself with his brothers. But while he'd had no hesitation about confronting the enemy on a battle-scarred ship at sea, in the three years since the war had ended he had not been able to summon the courage to face his family. His departure from Weston Manor had been neither cordial nor sedate, and while he wanted to go home, he was not eager for the reception that awaited him.

"So you're doing this for your family?"

"I wouldn't say that."

"You wouldn't *admit* that. However, it seems to me a man who is willing to go to such lengths to protect his family is lying to himself about something," Ephraim mused. "Either how he really feels about said family—"

"Hardly," Matt lied.

"Or about the money."

"I'm not entirely certain I'll take her money."

"That"—Ephraim pointed his cigar and squinted through the smoke—"is perhaps one of the most asinine things I have ever heard you say. Why, in the name of all that's holy, not?"

Matt bit back a grin at the printer's indignation. "Pride, I suppose. I dislike the idea of allowing her, or any woman, to purchase me like a sack of grain."

"Well, she can purchase me. I'd take her money without so much as a moment of hesitation. In fact, if you're not interested, I'd be more than willing to volunteer my services. At those prices she can buy me and my pride. Do feel free to pass on my name." Ephraim paused. "She's not one of those horse-faced princesses, is she? The ones whose portraits can't quite hide the truth of their appearance? Knowing you, I assume she's attractive."

"Quite."

"Then you're doing it for the woman."

"Don't be absurd."

Ephraim studied his friend curiously. "There's a great deal you haven't told me, isn't there?"

"Not a great deal." Matt shifted in his seat, well

aware of just how much he'd kept from Ephraim. They had been friends for nearly a decade and had met when they'd served on the same ship. Each had saved the other's life on more than one occasion, and Matt had shared far more with Ephraim than with any man alive. Yet on the subject of Tatiana he'd never said a word.

"You said you made her acquaintance in Paris last year." Ephraim's voice was thoughtful. "And when you returned to England, you were in the foulest of moods—"

"Me? The foulest of moods?" Matt widened his eyes in feigned surprise. "I am never anything but jovial and even-tempered."

Ephraim ignored him. "—and spent a good six months in an impressive state of drunkenness."

"Hardly six months," Matt said in an offhand manner. "Scarcely more than four. And my condition had more to do with the fact that my work wasn't going well and I couldn't—"

"I stand corrected." Ephraim waved away Matt's comment. "Although that's not the impression I had then. At the time, you indicated that your melancholy, obvious anger and ongoing inebriation were to the blame or credit of a member of the fairer sex. However, you never revealed the details of what was obviously a disastrous liaison. As you had never before been the least bit reluctant to regale me with your amorous adventures, I assumed this was somewhat more serious than usual."

Matt puffed on his cigar, then grinned. "She quite broke my heart."

Ephraim's eyes narrowed knowingly. "That's what I thought."

"It wasn't as bad—"

"It was." Ephraim leaned forward. "And it was this woman, wasn't it? This *princess*?"

Matt met the other man's gaze and considered his answer. He hated to admit what a fool he'd been for not seeing Tatiana was not who she'd said she was. And more, for losing his heart to her. But now that she was back in his life with her outrageous and too-tempting offer, it was perhaps past time to take an objective look at what had passed between them. He shrugged. "I didn't know she was a princess."

"Didn't know?" Ephraim's brows drew together in mock astonishment. "What? She wore no crown? Had no royal retainers in her wake? Bore no trappings of monarchy? I've never met a princess yet who wasn't obviously a princess."

"And you've met so many."

"Not a one," Ephraim said with a wicked grin. "But I have a vivid imagination."

Matt laughed, pleased to note he could now see humor where there had been only anger and pain before. Odd, how time and distance changed one's outlook. Odder still, how long it took him to realize it. He drew on his cigar and sent a thoughtful smoke ring drifting toward the ceiling. "She told me she was a companion to a princess."

"Really? A princess pretending to be a commoner? In disguise, as it were?" A familiar light shone in Ephraim's eye. "How very intriguing."

"I know what you're thinking, and you can forget it right now." Matt aimed his cigar at him. "I have no intention of contributing so much as a single word about this for that scandal sheet of yours."

Ephraim paid no heed. "*My Adventures with a*

Princess in Paris. Or better yet: *A Revelation of Royal Secrets.* It's a damn fine title for a story."

"This is exactly why I never told you about her."

"Hah." Ephraim snorted in disbelief.

"Very well, not exactly." Matt shrugged in surrender. "I admit it was far more serious than any relationship I'd ever had with a woman. And frankly, it was damned painful at the end."

"Hence the drinking."

"Dulled the pain." Matt raised his glass in a toast. "It works exceedingly well."

"But you have gotten over her." Ephraim's statement was as much question as comment.

"Of course. She's just another woman. No more important than any other in the scheme of the world. Oh, certainly this one could rule her own country one day—a very small country, I might add, really rather insignificant—but I didn't know that at the time and it makes no difference now."

"Then you have put her in the past."

"Where she belongs," Matt said firmly.

"And it doesn't bother you that she's reappeared?"

"Not in the slightest."

"And you no longer mind discussing her?"

"Absolutely not." Matt didn't hesitate for an instant and almost believed his own words.

"Then why not write a story for me about your affair with her?" Ephraim leaned forward, his eyes gleaming with editorial excitement. *"Passion in Paris: A Royal Rendezvous."*

"Passion in Paris?" Matt grimaced. "Sounds exceedingly sordid."

"Doesn't it, though? My readers will love it. Circulation will soar. There's nothing the common man likes to read about so much as the foibles of royalty. Scandal sells papers and there's nothing better, unless"—Ephraim straightened—"it's a nice juicy murder. Is there any chance—"

"Sorry, old man." Matt laughed. "Besides, you know full well I am not fond of writing so much as a letter, let alone one of your stories."

"All you need to do is give me the details; I'll do the writing." Ephraim practically chortled with anticipation. "With my editorial flair and a bit of creative embellishment, it will be—"

"No." Matt's voice was firm.

"Why not?"

"It doesn't seem"—he searched for the word—"honorable, I suppose."

"Were her actions honorable?"

It was an excellent question. One Matt had never especially considered and one he had no answer to now. He hadn't understood the significance of her position before today, and it put a distinctly different light on her abandonment. "To be honest, I'm no longer certain, but it scarcely matters. It's my honor in question at the moment, and I will not betray her trust by allowing you to make our relationship public fodder."

"I'll change your names," Ephraim said hopefully. "I'll make it impossible for anyone to recognize you or her. It can be completely anonymous."

"Absolutely not."

"Pity." The printer thought for a moment, obviously unwilling to give up. "Still, consider for a moment what an excellent way it would be to wreak revenge on her. Get a bit of your own back. She did, after all, break your heart."

"It has healed and taught me a valuable lesson in the process."

"Oh?"

"Princess, lady or whore—the so-called fairer sex is not to be trusted." Matt pulled a healthy swallow of his drink and relished the slow burn of the liquor. "None of them."

"I could have told you that." Ephraim sipped his whiskey and considered his friend. "At least you can give me the details."

"Ephraim."

"Oh, not for publication." He heaved a dramatic sigh. "Although it does pain me to pass this by. But do allow me to indulge my personal, if not my professional, curiosity. How does one meet a princess posing as one of us ordinary folk?"

"I was engaged in hawking balloon rides in a public park as a way to provide a bit of extra funds. She said she'd always wanted to fly." For a moment, he was back to that glorious spring day and the presence of an enticing green-eyed creature with a demeanor that was at once reticent and daring.

She was an enigma to him when they'd first met. A woman obviously of proper breeding, yet without so much as a groom accompanying her for protection or chaperone. She'd explained it by claiming she was a widow, a companion to royalty, and had felt the need to escape the confines of her position. Even on that first afternoon he was too enchanted to do more than brush off the suspicious nature of her story. In point of fact, she was a widow and had indeed slipped the bonds of her rank, but it was there that the truth of her story ended.

"Excellent. *Passion over Paris* is a much better title."

Ephraim pulled on his cigar and let the smoke drift lazily upward in emphasis to the teasing note in his voice.

"What a shame you won't be able to use it," Matt said pointedly.

"And after you met," Ephraim prodded. "Then what?"

"Then . . ." Matt paused for a long moment, the memory of their interlude washing through him with a strength that was almost physical. A mere six days filled with passion and excitement and the adventure of exploring each other, body and soul. And more, the shocking tenderness of feelings he never suspected could be so intense, so overwhelming, so complete. He was a fool to have fallen so thoroughly under her spell. To have abandoned all logic and rational thought. To have surrendered his soul.

"Then?" Ephraim prompted.

But it was indeed all in the past and he was done with her. At least where his heart was concerned. As for the rest of her . . .

Matt cast Ephraim a wicked glance. "Then, old man, we did what lovers in Paris always do."

Ephraim stared. "That's it? That's all you're going to tell me?"

Matt leaned back in his chair, grinned and silently puffed his cigar.

"It's that blasted sense of honor of yours again, isn't it?" Ephraim scowled. "First pride, now honor. I'm bloody grateful I'm not shackled with anything so debilitating."

"Come, now, Ephraim," Matt said mildly, "I've seen you engage in behavior that could well be described as honorable."

"Keep it to yourself," the other man muttered.

Matt laughed.

Ephraim fell silent and the two men shared a companionable silence broken only by the subtle sounds of the sipping of whiskey or the smoking of cigars. It was late and Ephraim's handful of employees had long since left. The steam-powered printing press in the main room was quiet, but as the week progressed it would operate late into the night printing copies of the *Messenger* for its weekly issue on Sunday.

"So if you're not doing it for your family or for the money—"

"I've not decided that yet."

"Very well. Aside from the matter of payment, why are you doing it?" Ephraim narrowed his eyes. "I assume you are accepting her offer, aren't you?"

Matt nodded.

"Then why—"

"I have my reasons. Curiosity, I suppose, prime among them. I want to know what she's hiding and the real reason why she has again entered my life."

"Ah-ha, you do still care for her."

"Not at all."

"Prove it." Challenge sounded in Ephraim's voice. He pulled open a drawer and tossed a small leather-bound book on the desk. "Keep a journal of your time with her, your travels and adventures."

"I don't write."

"You can write letters. Write them to me. And when it's over, I'll publish them. And," Ephraim added, "pay you handsomely."

Matt shook his head. "I see no difference between this and publishing what passed between us once before."

"The difference, my friend, is that this time"—Ephraim drew the words out in a deliberate manner—

"there is no question of affection. It is a business arrangement between the two of you. A contract of sorts. Nothing more. If you will not accept payment from her, should you not get something of value from the arrangement?"

"Oh, I intend to get something. Satisfaction, if nothing else. However, you have convinced me to accept her money, for the time being. Regardless of pride, I certainly need it, and it will indeed put our arrangement on a solid financial footing. Besides, I can always refuse it later."

Why not agree to Ephraim's request as well? After all, didn't he owe this old friend far more in terms of loyalty and allegiance than he ever had to Tatiana? And hadn't Ephraim repaid him in kind through the years, whereas Tatiana had left him without a second thought?

"I shall make a bargain with you. I will keep your journal, but I will make no guarantee as to its ultimate use. Agreed?"

"I can ask for nothing more." Ephraim grinned. "Unless you'd care to share more of those reasons of yours for going along with this royal farce."

"I suppose you could call the entire incident unfinished and unresolved." Matt puffed on the cigar and considered his words. "Our parting was not entirely mutual. I woke up one morning and she was gone, leaving behind nothing more than a note about responsibility and a promise to free us both from any legal entanglement."

"Legal entanglement?" Ephraim's brows drew together.

"You see, my friend, in France, a legal marriage is not necessarily sanctioned by the church. It can also be nothing more than a civil arrangement performed by a local official." Matt studied the glowing end of the cigar. "A moderate bribe in the right hands can circumvent any requirements for public notice or eliminate the wait for performance of a ceremony."

"And you know all of this because . . ." Ephraim said slowly.

"When Tatiana asked me today to play the role of her husband, it was not simply due to my handsome face, witty manner and devilish charm." Matt grinned wickedly. "Although admittedly I am amply endowed with all that and more."

"And humble as well." Ephraim's murmur belied the growing realization in his eyes.

"Indeed. No, she asked me to pose as her husband because I have experience in the part." Matt savored the look on Ephraim's face. "I see you have ascertained just how foolish I was. Her promise to free me from legal entanglement referred to procuring an annulment in her own country. No doubt an easy act for a misguided princess."

"Then you're saying . . ." Ephraim's voice had an odd strangled quality about it, as if he couldn't believe or accept his own words.

"I'm saying exactly what you think I'm saying. It lasted less than a full day, but for that handful of hours"—Matt chuckled wryly—"I was indeed her husband."

Chapter 4

*T*atiana straightened her shoulders and raised her chin in the royal manner she had been taught from birth. A manner that trained her to ignore the fluttering sensation lodged somewhere between her heart and her stomach. She drew a steady breath and stepped purposefully toward the parlor where Matthew waited.

The residence she had arranged to occupy was large enough to house her traveling companions and staff, yet not overly grand, and was located in a neighborhood both fashionable and discreet. Most of the homes around the square were minimally staffed, their owners retreating to their country estates during the summer months. As such, there were few people about to speculate on exactly who was staying in the home of Lord Westerfield, long a friend of the Avalonian people and loyal to her family. Servants would talk, of course, but then when did they not?

She adopted a pleasant smile, welcoming yet not overly eager. It would not do to let Matthew know how important his agreement to her proposal was or, in truth, how important he was to her. She was fairly certain he was the type of man who did not especially value what came too easily.

Tatiana pushed open the doors and stepped into the salon.

Matthew leaned casually against the mantel on the opposite side of the room. His worn attire was not up to the standards of the well-appointed parlor, but his demeanor was as proper as if he were dressed in the first stare of fashion. Odd, how she had not before noticed the marks of good breeding in his bearing. He was as comfortable here as he had been in his stables. Or in the gondola of a balloon or, she imagined, the bow of a ship.

"Lord Matthew."

"Your Highness." He straightened, and his voice held the correct note of deference, yet there was a distinct gleam in his eye. Sarcasm, perhaps.

"How delightful to see you again."

"The delight is mine, Your Highness." He swept a perfect bow, and again she realized Matthew may not have participated in society as such in any number of years, but it was obvious he was born to it.

"I did not expect you at such an early hour. It is scarcely midmorning."

"Ah, but, Your Highness . . ." Now there was no mistaking the sarcasm in his tone, as well as his eye. Not simply the subtle way in which he emphasized her position, but the frequency with which he used the proper form of address. *Your Highness* had a distinctly pointed edge. ". . . every moment we are separated seems a lifetime."

"How lovely of you to say so." She wasn't entirely sure what polite game of words he was playing, but she could certainly play one of her own. She closed the doors firmly behind her. "And during those moments, that lifetime, did you miss me?"

The corner of his mouth twitched, as if he were trying not to laugh. "I scarce noted you were gone."

She smiled slowly. "That's precisely what you said yesterday, my lord. Surely you can some up with something more original."

"Indeed, I could." His brows drew together in mock consideration. "But what would it be, I wonder?"

"Well, you could say you missed me as . . ."—she thought for a moment—"as the blossom in the heat of the day misses the morning dew."

"I doubt it. I should never say anything so absurd." He shook his head. "Perhaps as the fox misses the hounds. Now, that I might say."

"It doesn't convey quite the right sentiment, though." She narrowed her eyes thoughtfully. "I should think *as the moon misses the evening star* to be much better."

"Far too sentimental. However, if it's sentiment we're after, *as the deer misses the hunter* conveys the proper feeling."

"Not at all." Her voice was sharp, but her smile stayed firmly in place. "*As the night misses the sun* is much more appropriate."

"But not as good as *as the horse misses the flies about his tail*." Satisfaction rang in his voice.

"Now, that is original, for everyone save the horse. You do have a way with words, my lord." Still, it would not do to let him believe he had won. She cast him a triumphant smile. "And regardless of how you choose to say it, it is sufficient to know you did indeed miss me."

His eyes widened slightly in surprise, and perhaps

appreciation, then he grinned. "Certainly, but only *as the horse*—"

"Oh, do leave the poor horse in peace." She crossed the room, seated herself in a French-styled armchair and gestured for him to sit on a nearby sofa. "Have you come to give me your answer, or do you have no other purpose here this morning than to be annoying?"

"Being annoying, Your Highness, is simply an unexpected pleasure." He ignored her invitation and instead wandered casually around the perimeter of the room, forcing her to turn her head to follow him, his movement as deliberately irritating as his words. "I have, however, given your proposition the consideration it deserves. In truth, I have thought of little else since we spoke. It is quite intriguing."

"I thought so." She nodded firmly. "I think uncovering the true story of the travels of the Princess Sophia will be most interesting, and something of an adventure as well."

"Adventure? Perhaps." He slanted her a sharp glance. "However, that's not the part that I find interesting."

"Really? Why on earth not?"

"For one thing, I'm not sure that I believe this nonsense about writing a family history."

She widened her eyes and lied through her teeth. "You mentioned that yesterday, but I assure you it is quite true."

He studied her carefully and she returned his gaze with an unflinching calm. After all, there was a certain element of truth to her claim. She did need to know exactly where Sophia had gone and what she had done. Sophia's flight from Avalonia coincided with the disappearance of the Heavens, and while it was possible there was no connection at all, it was more than likely the princess had taken the jewels. For their safety or hers.

"You don't lie well."

"Nonsense. I lie exceedingly well, but only for the very best reasons." She smiled in an overly sweet manner. "Although I will admit, before meeting you, I had little experience with lying and no need to do so."

"It's gratifying to know I bring out the best in you."

"I thought you would appreciate it," she said primly.

"Indeed I do." He paused and stared thoughtfully. "Regardless of the true purpose of your presence here, I must confess to a great deal of curiosity."

"About what, exactly?" She forced a light laugh. "I have already told you, my lord, I want nothing more than to write—"

"Not about that." He waved away her comment. "I am willing to accept your claim, for the moment. What has piqued my curiosity is why you feel it necessary to pose as my wife."

"I have explained that as well. People are often quite intimidated by royalty and not at all inclined to be candid." She sighed. "Goodness, my lord, did you not pay attention to anything I have said thus far?"

His eyes narrowed in irritation and she bit back a satisfied smile. With scarcely any effort at all, she could be every bit as annoying as he. And enjoy it every bit as much.

"I should think"—his words were measured— "given what has passed between us, the last person on the face of the earth you would wish to involve in a deception such as you propose would be me." His gaze trapped hers and the fluttering in her midsection returned. "I should further think you would hesitate to so much as cross my path, let alone ask me to play husband—"

"One would think so."

"—as you showed no reluctance in absolving me of that position. And did so without even the minor courtesy of informing me as to your intentions until such time as I could not raise a word in protest." His voice was light, but his gaze hardened. "I gather procuring your annulment posed no particular problem?"

"No, no problem at all." She gathered her resolve and drew a steadying breath. "In point of fact, I—"

"You needn't explain further; I scarcely need a detailed account." He continued his meandering, moving to a position somewhere behind her. She refused to give him the satisfaction of twisting in her chair, especially since he would not allow her to finish her explanation. Besides, she could listen perfectly well without looking at him.

"When I discovered your true identity, I realized how simple it would for the member of a royal family to rid herself of an impulsive, and obviously unwanted, marriage to someone of my position. The civil nature of our union, unsanctioned by any church, in a country in which neither of us were citizens, plus our use of a modest bribe to circumvent the usual requirements, all meant the legality of the marriage was no doubt questionable in the first place."

"Really? I had never considered that."

She could hear the shrug in his voice behind her. "It's of little consequence now. It is over and done with." Abruptly, he stepped directly in front of her chair and stared down at her.

"The only thing that matters now is our newly formed union." Matthew braced his hands on the arms of the chair, effectively trapping her, and bent close. "My dear *Lady Matthew*."

She gazed up at him, resisting both the urge to shrink back and the desire to strain forward. He was extraordinarily close. So close she could stare into the endless depths of his blue eyes. Eyes she had once lost her soul in and never found again.

"Then you will do it?"

He nodded slowly. "Under certain conditions."

"Conditions? What conditions? I am willing to pay you handsomely. Given that, I should think any conditions would be mine."

"Possibly, but I am not overly concerned with your money."

"That is absurd. Why on earth not?" Not that she particularly cared right now. It was difficult to concentrate on anything beyond the enticing rise and fall of his chest with every breath and the proximity of his body to hers.

"It doesn't interest me."

"Nonsense. You need . . ." Her voice faltered at the look in his eye. Speculation and . . . more. Her heart thudded in her chest. The moment the words formed on her lips, she knew the question was a mistake. Or an invitation. And did not care. "What *does* interest you?"

His gaze strayed from her eyes to her mouth and back. Without thinking, she shifted slightly until her lips were scarcely more than a whisper from his.

"Any number of things, my dear," he said softly, his breath mingling with hers. "But they shall have to wait." Abruptly, he drew back and straightened to loom over her. "At this point, what interests me most is whether or not you will accept my conditions."

"I see." She cleared her throat, ignoring the smug look on his face. The blasted man knew full well she wanted him to kiss her, and probably realized she wanted to kiss him back. "What are your conditions, then?"

"First of all, if you are to pose as my wife . . ." He stepped aside and again roamed restlessly around the parlor, examining an objet d'art here, a painting there, his attitude as casual as his words. ". . . you shall have to play the role in a realistic manner. If we are to fool the rest of the world, we shall have to be convincing."

"It would be ridiculous to do otherwise." She watched him cautiously and folded her hands in her lap. "How, pray tell, do you propose we do that?"

"To begin with, this"—he gestured at the opulent room—"will not do at all."

"Why not?" She furrowed her brow. "This is a lovely house, and quite well situated."

"However, it is not the house Matthew Weston— forgive me, *Lord* Matthew—would occupy. Not with the current state of his finances." He picked up an apple from a bowl on a nearby table and tossed it idly in one hand. "I live primarily on a small naval pension, most of which goes for the supplies necessary for my work, and my ever-dwindling savings."

"Yes?" She heard his words, but her gaze fixed on the mesmerizing motion of the apple. His hands, deft and sure, releasing and catching the scarlet fruit.

"Did I tell you I am trying to refine a heating system of my own design to greater increase control aloft and during ascensions?"

"No." His strong, tanned fingers captured the apple, enveloped its vivid flesh in an all-consuming caress.

"I can scarce afford to fund this project as well as a proper residence, so at the moment I am living in the cottage beside the stables you visited yesterday."

Without effort she remembered how those fingers had felt on her flesh.

"In truth, it's barely more than a roof and four walls, but it was included in the lease of the stables and serves my needs."

How his caresses had captured her body and seared her soul.

"Nonetheless, right now it is my place of residence. Where I live and where I expect . . ."

How all-consuming the passion had been between them.

". . . my *wife* to live as well." He caught the apple and held it still.

My wife to live?

The words jerked her to attention. Matthew grinned expectantly.

"You expect me to live in a . . . a"—she could barely choke out the word—"cottage?"

He shrugged. "If truth were told, it's not substantially better than a shack."

"A shack?" She rose to her feet. This was not at all what she had in mind. "You expect me to live in a shack?"

"The rooms we shared in Paris were not especially grand. They were rather shabby, if I recall."

"Yes, well, that was"—she groped for the right words—"not at all the same. That was under different circumstances entirely."

"Do you think so?" He frowned. "It seems to me,

then and as you propose to do now, you were pretending to be someone you weren't," he said pointedly.

She ignored him. "Still, my lord *Matthew*, I couldn't possibly—"

"If you are to be my wife, you are to be my wife in the fullest sense of the word."

"But surely you cannot expect me to—" She caught herself and stared. "What do you mean, *fullest sense of the word*?"

"I mean my wife has to live on my income." His grin widened. "It's extremely modest."

"I see." She bit her bottom lip absently. There were benefits to being in close quarters with him. He certainly could not ignore her presence in a—she shuddered to herself—cottage. And was that not exactly what she had planned? "It is not as if we will spend any significant time there. Indeed, our quest will take us to any number of places where I am certain Lord and Lady Matthew will be most welcome. Why, we shall be traveling much of the time. On the road, as it were, and—"

"Yes, well, that is another consideration." A thoughtful expression crossed Matthew's face.

"Another consideration?" She crossed her arms over her chest.

"I have only one horse, and he is better suited to pull—"

"A carriage?" she said hopefully.

"It's really a wagon." He shook his head in a regretful manner she didn't believe for a moment. "In truth, more of a cart."

"To go along with the shack, no doubt." She would put up with his living conditions, castle or cottage scarcely mattered, as long as she was with him. But she had absolutely no intention of traveling in a cart or a wagon. Still, it was not necessary for him to know that. "Very well."

"And there will be no servants," he warned.

"Of course not, given your modest income," she said brightly. "Is that it, then? Your conditions?"

"Not entirely." He studied the apple in his hand casually.

"Really? Whatever is left?" She ticked the items off on her fingers. "Thus far you have eliminated servants and any possibility of civilized living either during our travels or when we are in the proximity of London. It seems to me your requirements ensure I will indeed act as your wife in the fullest, as well as the most frugal, sense of the word."

He raised his gaze to hers and wicked triumph glittered in his eyes. "Not entirely."

She drew her brows together. "I don't see—" At once she did see, and all too well. The man was an annoying beast, but at least he still wanted her, and that was a start. And he had played right into her hands.

"You do not mean . . ." She widened her eyes in stunned disbelief. "You cannot possibly believe . . ." She wrung her hands together and paced to the right. "Surely, you do not expect that I . . ." She swiveled and paced to the left. "That you . . . that we . . ." She stopped and turned toward him. "That you think I would . . . Oh, Matthew, how could you?" She let out a wrenching sob, buried her face in her hands and wept in the manner of any virtuous women presented with such an edict.

"Good Lord! Your Highness. Tatiana." Concern sounded in his voice and she heard him step closer. "I didn't mean—"

"I know what you meant." She sobbed.

"I didn't realize you'd— That is to say, I didn't want—"

"You most certainly did." She dropped her hands and glared at him. "This is exactly what you wanted. Exactly the response you hoped for." She advanced toward him. "Are you happy now? Was my reaction dramatic enough for you? Was I as aghast, as offended, as *hurt* as you'd wished?"

"I never—"

"And was it satisfying, Matthew?" She stepped to within a few inches of him and planted her hands on her hips. "Or was there a moment of regret over your beastly behavior?"

"There is now." He glared down at her but held his ground.

"Hah. I doubt that. Your intentions with this and every other of your ridiculous conditions was to shock me and, furthermore, to put me in my place. Obviously as revenge for the wrongs I have done you."

"They were not," he said indignantly.

"Come, now. You don't lie nearly as well as I do." She cast him a look of disdain. "These stipulations of yours, especially the last one." She shook her head. "Did you really believe for a moment I would fall to pieces at the idea of sharing your bed? I am not a blushing virgin. I have been married."

"Twice, by last count." His eyes narrowed dangerously. "Or have I missed another marriage or two?"

"Not yet," she snapped. "But the day is still young."

"Excellent. Then you will no longer need me."

"However, at this particular moment, I do still need you."

"Do you?" An odd intensity underlaid his words.

"Yes," she said sharply. "And if you think your silly conditions will dissuade me, you do not—"

"Know you?" he said pointedly.

She stared at him for a long moment. He was wrong, and it was discouraging to realize he did not understand that. In their few short days together he knew her better than anyone alive. Knew the truth of her heart and soul that she had never revealed to anyone but him. He simply never knew the details of her life that were at once significant and yet so inconsequential.

She drew a deep breath and stepped back, forcing a casual note to her voice and her manner. "Now, then, regarding your conditions."

"Yes?"

"I quite understand your position and I must compliment you on such clear thinking. If indeed we are to be convincing, it is necessary to play our parts as thoroughly as possible. Therefore"—she lifted a shoulder in a casual shrug—"I accept your conditions."

"All of them?" He raised a brow.

"Why not? If I remember correctly, sharing your bed was not an unbearable hardship. We had rather a remarkable time together. In truth, it was the most exciting . . . well, *adventure* of my life. Besides, whether you are willing to admit it or not, you are far too honorable a man to insist that I do anything against my will."

"Are you certain?" That wicked gleam had returned to his eye and he resumed tossing the apple still in his hand.

"I am."

"Don't be."

"Excellent." She reached out and caught the apple in midair. "Surprise and uncertainty are the very blood and bones of adventure. And I am now confident our masquerade will indeed be an adventure." Her gaze met and meshed with his and she bit into the apple.

She could see the struggle in his eyes and, even better, the moment when he lost. When his gaze slipped to her mouth. She chewed deliberately and swallowed, licking the apple juice from her lips.

"It should be a most"—his gaze met hers and he smiled—"satisfying adventure."

The look in his eye was determined. Challenging.

He grabbed her hand and brought the apple to his mouth, biting it as she had, his gaze still locked with hers. For the first time she wondered if she was up to meeting such a challenge with such a man. The woman she had been most of her life was not. The woman she was now had yet to be tried.

He chewed and swallowed, his hand still on hers. Her fingers loosened and the apple dropped unheeded to the floor. For an endless moment they froze, as if time itself had stopped. Electricity arched between. Heat flowed from his hand to hers. The very air between them sizzled.

"When do you wish to begin?" His voice was forced, as if he could barely get the words out.

"As soon as possible." She struggled to breathe.

"Tomorrow, then?" He made no move to release her.

"Early, I should think." She made no effort to leave.

"Very well." He drew a deep shuddering breath and let go of her hand.

She brushed aside the odd sensation of loss, stepped away and nodded, fighting to ignore a yearning that threatened to overwhelm her.

"Shall I call for you, then? Here?" At once he was as composed as if nothing had passed between them.

"No," she said quickly, her outward manner as serene as his.

His expression tightened. "Of course not, Your Highness. You couldn't possibly wish to be seen leaving with someone of my menial position in society."

"Nonsense, my lord." Where did the man get such ideas? She heaved an exasperated sigh. "I do not want to be seen with anyone. Only a few of my most trusted advisors know of my plan and I wish it to remain that way. This is not precisely a proper sort of adventure."

"No, I suppose not." He shrugged as if it were of no consequence. "I shall wait for you, then, at the cottage." He nodded and turned to leave.

Without thinking, she started after him. "My lord. Matthew."

"Yes?" He turned back.

"I just . . ." She had no idea what she wanted to say. But she couldn't let him go. Not now. Not yet. Not with this tension between them. She stepped closer. "I . . ."

"Yes?" he said again.

"I do appreciate what you're doing for me."

"Do you?"

"Very much so. Particularly given how you feel about me."

"And how do I feel about you?" His expression was unfathomable.

"It is obvious that you are still angry with me."

"Is it?"

"Yes. It is also apparent that you don't fully believe what I am trying to do."

"I have made no secret of that." He studied her curiously. They were but a long stride apart. "Is there anything else? Any other observations you wish to share? About my *feelings*?"

"No. I do not . . ." She stopped and considered him. "Yes. In truth, there is." She straightened her shoulders and met his gaze directly. It was past time to issue a challenge of her own. "I quite believe you would like to kiss me."

"Would I?" He laughed. "What makes you think so?"

"Everything about you." She swept a wide gesture in his direction. "Your manner. Your so-called conditions. The words you do not say as much as those you do." She cast him a smug grin. "The very look in your eye."

"The look in my eye, you say? How interesting. But perhaps you're right. I daresay I've never kissed a princess before." She started to protest, but he raised a hand to silence her. "Not knowing she was a princess, at any rate. I do recall once kissing the companion to a princess."

She rolled her gaze toward the ceiling. "You are annoying, my lord."

"Flattering of you to say so yet again. But I would much prefer to discuss your earlier observation." In one swift move, he stepped close and pulled her into his arms, gazing into her eyes. "Is this the look you were speaking of?"

"Yes." She stared up at him. "That is it exactly."

"I see." He drew his brows together thoughtfully. "Do you think I should do something about it?"

"I think"—she raised her chin defiantly and resisted

the urge to wrap her arms around him—"you would be the worst kind of fool if you did not."

"I would be the worst kind of fool if I did." His tone was abruptly serious. His blue eyes searched hers.

Disappointment stabbed her, as sharp and unyielding as his gaze. "And we certainly would not want that."

She pushed out of his embrace and turned away. He grabbed her elbow, spun her around and jerked her back into his arms. "Yet, I have been a fool before."

Without pause, his lips crushed hers, his kiss hard and demanding, punishing and unrelenting. And she reveled in it.

He raised his head and glared. "This means nothing to me, you know."

"It means nothing to me as well." She threw her arms around his neck and pulled his lips back to hers.

His mouth over hers softened, opened. She clung to him, melted against him. Passion too long unfulfilled and not for a moment forgotten welled between them.

He drew his lips from hers and feathered kisses along the line of her jaw to a point beneath her ear. She tilted her head and closed her eyes and lost herself in his touch, known for far too long only in her dreams.

He murmured against her skin. "I shall not fall in love with you again."

"Nor do I expect you to." Her words were scarcely more than a sigh.

"And should you fall in love with me"—his mouth trailed down her neck—"I shall be compelled to break your heart."

"I can expect no less." Her hands clutched at his shoulders and she shivered with the delight of his lips at the base of her throat. "Indeed, it is your turn to do so."

"As long as we understand one another, Your Highness."

"Oh, we do, my lord, we do indeed."

His lips met hers again, and for a long moment she knew nothing in the world save the joy of at last being again in his arms. Finally he released her, slowly, with a reluctance she prayed wasn't entirely due to lust.

She stepped back and struggled for a semblance of composure. "Until tomorrow, then."

"I should be going." He paused as if he wished to say something more.

"Yes?"

He shook his head, then turned and strode toward the doors. He pulled them open and glanced back. "I warn you, this adventure of yours has no more significance to me than a business arrangement. And as such I will attach no more emotion to it than that."

She widened her eyes innocently. "I assure you I do not intend to allow my feelings for you to change in the slightest.

"Excellent." Again, his expression was unreadable. "We shall make quite an interesting pair, Lord and Lady Matthew. A gentleman whose best quality is the ability to be annoying and a princess with a tendency toward lie—"

"I prefer the term *misstatement*," she said firmly.

He laughed and turned to go.

"Matthew?"

He paused.

"Will you miss me?"

He grinned. "Only as the horse—"

"Good day, my lord," she said firmly, suppressing her own laugh.

He took his leave and she stared unseeing at the doors that closed in his wake.

Working her way back into this stubborn man's heart would not be easy. Finding the missing Heavens might well prove to be the easier of her quests.

But not the most important.

Chapter 5

Matt threw open the door of the cottage and stared down the road as he had a dozen times or more in the hour since dawn. Where was the blasted woman? She should have been here by now. She was the one eager to get this farce under way. This was her adventure, not his.

Perhaps she had changed her mind. Come to her senses and realized just how absurd this so-called adventure was. This mission of hers to retrace and document the travels of a fleeing princess half a century ago. He snorted with disdain. He could have come up with a better story without trying. Still, it served her purpose, whatever her purpose was. It was obviously more important to her than a silly history of her family. But what could be of such significance that she would come to him for help?

Unless she chose him only because of his grandmother's involvement.

He turned away from the door and ran this hand through his hair. The question of why Tatiana had reappeared in his life had haunted him through the endless hours of the night past, just as it had the night before. He'd tossed and turned and scarcely slept more than an hour or so at best. Even when exhaustion had claimed him, he'd had no peace. His slumber was fraught with unanswered questions and all-too-vivid memories.

Matt absently paced the length of the room, acknowledging in the back of his mind how often he'd walked this same stretch of floor trying to puzzle out a problem. Those difficulties were typically of a mechanical nature. This was different. This was personal. And far more difficult.

At some point in the long, restless night he'd wondered if perhaps Tatiana's true intentions had little to do with a long-dead relative and everything to do with the man she'd asked for help. If possibly it wasn't the past of this Princess Sophia she searched for but a future with the man she'd once professed to love. It was a ridiculous thought, of course, triggered only by the startling clarity of his dreams and his own arrogance. While it was obvious at their last meeting that desire between them still simmered, it could go no further than that. He would not allow it, and in truth she had given him no reason to believe she wished otherwise.

She had not thrown herself into his arms, declaring her undying love. She had not wept with remorse at having abandoned him. Her apology had been scarcely more than polite. Nor had she begged his forgiveness and pleaded for him to allow her back into his life.

It was the height of irony to realize that he would have indeed forgiven her and more had she returned to him within the first months after her departure, even as long as a full year. He would have understood the reasons for her choice or, at least, wanted to understand and forgive. Now, it was too late.

He had no wish to rekindle what they'd once shared. Aside from his desire to protect his family, his only real reason in agreeing to her proposal was to rid himself of her continuing presence in his dreams. In his blood. To regain that part of his soul he'd given freely and never reclaimed. He cared no more for her than for any woman whose bed he wished to share.

Still, it was odd to note how much her quick agreement to his last condition dwelled in his mind. He knew full well, aside from her first husband, there had been no other man in her life before him. Had there been others since then? Had she discovered the kind of passion she'd shared with him with another man? More than one? Fifteen months, three weeks and four days—no, six days now—was a very long time.

Certainly he had been with other women since he'd last seen her. Nameless and for the most part faceless, they had been one way he'd struggled to fill the emptiness Tatiana had left him with. Had she felt the same void?

Hardly. His jaw tightened at the thought. She had been the one to leave. The one to decide their marriage could not continue. He had had no choice in the matter. And no choice in her return.

The sounds of an approaching carriage caught his attention. He stalked to the door and stepped outside. But he damn well had choices now.

A curricle, rather too shiny to be anything but new, pulled to a halt on the road in front of the cottage. A horse tethered to the vehicle trailed behind. The gentleman, or more likely officer, he'd seen help Tatiana onto her horse after her last visit held the reins. Tatiana perched on the seat by his side, entirely too close. Matthew raised a brow. Surely that was not proper behavior for a princess or any other respectable woman.

The officer accompanying her leapt out of the carriage and hurried to help Tatiana to the ground with a familiarity that struck Matthew as far too intimate and extremely irritating.

"Good day, Lord Matthew." She cast him a brilliant smile.

"Is it? I hadn't noticed." He directed his words toward her, but his gaze focused on her companion. The man was not unattractive—some might even say handsome, in a stern sort of way. Indeed, foolish women might well appreciate his dark hair and disapproving eyes. Matt wondered how foolish Tatiana was.

She laughed. "That is scarcely the way to start such a lovely day. I do think something a bit more welcoming is in order, although a sincere *good day* is always appropriate."

"Good day," Matt said, feeling not the least bit sincere.

The officer's eyes narrowed slightly as if he didn't appreciate Matt's tone.

Tatiana ignored the palpable tension between the men. "My lord, I should like to introduce you to Captain Petrov. Captain, this is the Lord Matthew Weston."

"My lord." Petrov nodded coolly.

"Captain." Matt's voice was every bit as cold. For whatever reason, he didn't like this man, and it was obvious the enmity was mutual.

Petrov was of a similar height and breadth as Matt, with a distinctly military bearing. Nonetheless, Matt was confident he could defeat him in a fair fight if need be. The idea was surprisingly inviting.

"I thought you understood that if this ruse is to be effective, you shall have to abide by my terms." Matt met the other man's gaze. "I believe I specifically mentioned that does not include servants."

The officer's eyes darkened with anger and he took a step forward. Good. Matt's fists clenched. He would quite enjoy thrashing Tatiana's escort.

She held out a hand to restrain the officer. "Nonsense, my lord, any fool can see Captain Petrov is not a servant."

"Perhaps, Your Highness," Petrov said coolly, "his lordship is not just any fool, but a fool of astonishing proportions."

"Perhaps he is," she said brightly. "Perhaps only such a fool would agree to help me in my endeavor, and for that we can be most grateful."

"You shall quite turn my head with your compliments, Your Highness," Matt said wryly.

"However, Captain, apologies are in order. Lord Matthew is not a fool, simply annoying. It is one of his finer qualities."

"I've no doubt of that, Your Highness." Petrov stared at Matt with disdain. "Very well. I am sorry, my lord, that you are an annoying, astonishing fool."

"I too apologize for mistaking you for a mere servant when it's obvious you are little more than"— Matt crossed his arms over his chest—"a glorified coachman."

"That is quite enough." Tatiana shook her head. "I should have known you two would not get along. You are far too similar in nature to approve of one another."

"Yet another compliment, Your Highness? I'm not

certain if I should be flattered." Matt's gaze locked with the other man's and he knew full well the captain was assessing him with an eye toward combat. "Or insulted."

"The insult is mutual, my lord. Furthermore, you should understand I do not approve of Her Highness's plan," Petrov said slowly. "I think it is both foolhardy and dangerous."

"Dangerous?" Matt raised a brow. "I scarcely think gathering information for a family history is dangerous."

"The enemies of Avalonia are everywhere." Petrov's voice was grim. "As the commander of the guard charged with her safety, I would prefer she allow those trained for the position to accompany her rather than leave her protection to a single escort."

"She will have the protection of my name as well as my presence. She'll come to no harm." Matt studied the other man carefully. His reactions were overblown, even if understandable given the nature of his position, if indeed Tatiana had told the truth about her quest. The captain's attitude confirmed Matt's suspicion that her story was nothing but a fabrication. "I will see to that."

Petrov leaned closer, his voice hard and threatening. "See that you do. If she is harmed in any way I will track you to the ends of the earth and kill you with my bare hands."

Matt lowered his own voice. "Nothing would give me greater pleasure than to see you attempt to do just that."

"Stop it at once." Tatiana huffed. "You sound like small boys drawing lines in the dirt. My lord, you are being even more annoying than usual and, Captain, it is past time you were on your way."

Petrov stepped toward her. "Princess, I cannot—"

"You can and you shall." Tatiana's voice was firm. "Now, Dimitri. This discussion is at an end."

Dimitri?

"Very well, Your Highness," the captain said stiffly, nodded in a curt manner then strode around the carriage to his horse. He untied the beast, mounted and walked the animal back toward Tatiana. "I shall await word from you in London." Petrov cast Matt a last warning glance and rode off down the road.

Matt's gaze followed the officer's retreat. "He doesn't like me."

"I cannot imagine why. As always, you were most charming and thoroughly delightful. Furthermore, you made no effort to conceal your opinion of him." She blew a disgusted breath. "You need not have been quite so rude."

"Do you call all the members of your guard by their given names?" he said without thinking, watching the mounted figure disappear down the road.

"Certainly not. But I have known Captain Petrov all my life. I consider him to be a friend as well as a trusted advisor." She studied him curiously. "Surely my familiarity with *Dimitri* does not bother you?"

"I scarcely care one way or the other. I simply thought it was odd behavior for someone of your position."

She smiled smugly. "You needn't be jealous of . . . *Dimitri.*"

"I am not jealous. Merely curious."

"You sound jealous."

"Well, I'm not." His voice was sharper than necessary for a man who was not jealous. "I don't care in the least, although I daresay he might."

"Really?" Surprise crossed her face as if she'd

never before considered such a possibility. "Why do you say that?"

"It's clear to anyone with half a brain." Matt snorted in disdain. "Everything about him shows his feelings. To start with, there's his attitude toward you."

"Duty, nothing more."

"His attitude toward me," Matt said pointedly.

"Scarcely proof of anything. I believe we have already agreed you are extremely annoying. You make no effort to be pleasant. I daresay there are any number of people who do not especially like you."

"Hah." He scoffed. "If you recall, I can be extremely charming."

"I am having some difficulty at the moment remembering that," she said under her breath.

"However, we are not talking about me. We are speaking of your captain, *Dimitri*. Aside from his manner, he is given away by"—he paused for emphasis—"the very look in his eye."

"Is it like the look in your eye?" She stepped close and gazed up at him.

Matt clenched his teeth and glared. "This look?"

"Don't be absurd. That look is nothing short of murderous." She tilted her head and considered him. "Admittedly, I have seen something similar in Dimitri's eye. I have never been especially fond of it."

"No?" He stared down at her, his anger fading. He knew full well his reaction to Dimitri was irrational, probably due more to his thoughts about Tatiana before their arrival than the irritating nature of the man himself. "I should think you'd be used to it. No doubt you have seen it any number of times."

"More so in recent months," she said, still searching his gaze.

"I would have thought you'd have spent most of your life getting such looks from those charged with your protection or education or whatever else goes into the upbringing of a princess." He struggled to disregard the proximity of her body to his. How easy it would be to reach out and pull her into his arms.

"It may well be difficult for you to believe, but I have spent most of my life doing exactly what was expected of me. Without pause, without question, without argument. Aside from the odd occasion as a child, I had never done anything at all that could be considered improper until I rode in a balloon"—a teasing light sparked in her eyes—"fifteen months, three weeks and a handful of days ago."

"Five," he said absently. "It would be five days and sixteen months, if you count from when we first met."

"I believe you are wrong, Matthew," she said softly.

"I'm not. It would be five—"

"No, wrong about Dimitri. I have never seen a look in his eye like the one in yours . . . now." Her own eyes sparkled in the morning light. Green and sensual and beckoning.

"Perhaps you've simply never noticed."

"Oh, I am most certain I would have noticed." She bit her bottom lip in that way she had, endearing and entirely too provocative.

"Would you?" Bloody hell, he wanted her. Again. Here. Now. In the road, on the grass, in the cottage.

And why not? It was part of their agreement, one of his conditions. And if he knew nothing else, he knew she certainly wanted him.

Still, it would have to wait. Besides, if he could not get a grip on his unbridled lust, he would never find out what she was really up to. The only way to solve the puzzle of the Princess Tatiana Marguerite Nadia Pruzinsky of the Kingdom of Greater Avalonia was to play along with her so-called adventure.

"The question is, my lord, what do you intend to do about it?" Her voice was challenging and ... inviting.

"The answer, Princess," he said slowly, "is nothing."

Surprise flashed in her eyes, and possibly disappointment. "Nothing at all?"

"Not a thing." He grinned wickedly. "For the moment."

It was exceedingly good to realize how easy it was to keep the upper hand with her. As long as he kept his wits about him, and his desire in check, he could maintain control of the situation. It was satisfying as well to note he could no doubt have her whenever he wanted her. And this choice, along with every other choice, this time, would be his.

Matt stepped away—regardless of his resolve, distance between them was an excellent idea—and nodded at the curricle. "Your captain seems to have forgotten his carriage."

"Not at all," she said quickly. "Before you say anything, I think I should point out that, even as I have agreed to your conditions, regardless of your financial state, Lord and Lady Matthew would never travel in a wagon. It would be most unusual and attract any number of unwanted questions as to our validity."

"Do you think so?" he said mildly.

"I do." She nodded. "I firmly feel our ruse can only benefit if we travel in a suitable fashion and are properly attired. To that end, I have brought along appropriate clothing and various personal items for you as well as for myself. You may not have noticed, but your appearance is, well, somewhat—"

"Disreputable?"

"I was going to say threadbare. I do not wish to offend you—"

"I am not offended."

"No?"

"Not in the least." Matt strolled around the carriage and examined the vehicle.

Tatiana's voice trailed after him. "The garments I have had selected for you are not at all grand. I was quite specific on that point. I was assured they are really quite ordinary, but not as, oh, frayed as those you are wearing now."

"You did not choose them yourself?" The curricle was not as new as he'd first thought, and was far more suitable for city driving than lengthy journeys, but would serve adequately.

"Of course not." She sounded a bit indignant that he would suggest such a thing. "I had, well, someone I trust select them."

"Petrov?"

"It scarcely matters," she said quickly. "I am certain they'll do. I simply think the clothing, as well as the carriage, are necessary to provide the proper appearance."

"It would not do to appear improper." Two fair-sized but nondescript portmanteaus were wedged under the elevated seat at the back of the vehicle where typically a groom would perch.

"Nothing is excessive, nor is it shoddy. I do believe I have trod the fine line between prosperity and survival, and everything is most fitting—"

"For Lord and Lady Matthew," he finished, moving to inspect the horses.

"Well?" Caution sounded in her voice.

The pair of horses hitched to the carriage were well matched but not impressive. Simply good, decent beasts and precisely what a gentleman of his position might well own.

"My lord, I really feel, under the circumstances—"

"I see no need for debate."

"Really?" She studied him cautiously. "Why not?"

"Because, Your Highness, for one thing, you're right."

"I am?"

"Indeed you are." He folded his arms over his chest and leaned idly against the carriage. "Insofar as you agree with my earlier position that if we are to be convincing, we must look the part we wish to play."

She stared at him in obvious annoyance. "Do I understand you to say that I am only right when I agree with you?"

"That's it exactly."

"I see," she said carefully. "Then I think we should be off. Do you think we should be off?"

"I do indeed." He strolled to the cottage door, took the journal Ephraim had given him and a small writing case from his bag—a bag he no longer had need of, thanks to Tatiana, and tucked them both in an inside pocket of his coat. He shoved the bag deeper into the house, closed and locked the door, then returned to the carriage.

"You have no bag of your own?" she asked.

"As you have seen fit to provide all I should need, I see no need for extra baggage." He helped her into the carriage, then rounded the vehicle, climbed in and picked up the reins.

"And what of your horse and ... cart?" She glanced around. "Where are they?"

"Actually, I never intended for us to travel in a cart."

Her eyes widened in indignation. "But you said—"

"My dear princess, I never really trusted your complete agreement to my conditions. Due, no doubt, to that tendency of yours to li—"

"Misstate," she said firmly

"Regardless, I fully expected you to arrive in a suitable vehicle." He chuckled. "One far grander than this. I also expected you to be accompanied by at least a driver and a maid."

"I would have been if I had had the least suspicion you would accept them," she snapped. "And did you also expect that I would bring you an acceptable wardrobe as well?"

"Admittedly, that was a surprise. Frankly, I did not realize I had become quite so—"

"Plebeian?" she said in an overly sweet manner. "Common? Ordinary? Your appearance little better than that of a peasant?"

"A peasant." He laughed and clucked to the horses. The carriage started down the road. "I rather like that. Lord and Lady Matthew, the peasant and the princess. Ephraim would love it."

She muttered something he didn't quite catch.

He slanted her an amused glance. For once, she didn't look completely confident. "I do have to admit, however, the clothing was no more unexpected than your acquiescing to my demands to the extent that you have."

"You gave me no choice." Her brows drew together in irritation. "I needed your help and you refused to assist me without your childish conditions designed to do nothing more than put me in my place."

"Perhaps they were a bit childish. But fun nonetheless."

"Fun?"

"Great fun." He chuckled. "The most fun I've had in a long time."

"I would scarcely call it fun."

"You would if you could have seen the look on your face when I talked about my shack."

"The look on my face?" The corners of her lips quivered as if she were struggling not to smile. "Why, my lord, it could not have compared to the look on your face when I wept at having to be your wife in the fullest sense of the word." She grinned. "Surpassed only your shocked expression when I agreed. Perhaps *fun* is the correct word after all."

He laughed. "It seems we are well matched. At least in a battle of wits."

"In other ways, too."

"Oh, that you remember?" he teased. "When you forget how charming I can be."

"I remember very well." Her voice was soft, and for a moment he thought she was going to say more. After a long silence, she sighed. "Where are we going, then?"

"I had the opportunity yesterday to make a few inquiries about the names you gave me. The first—"

"Lady Hutchins?"

He nodded. Matthew already knew, of course, where to find his grandmother, last on the list. The second lady was familiar to him as well, although he had never actually made her acquaintance. And Ephraim had managed to provide information as to where the remaining woman—Lady Hutchins—might be found. "It's believed she lives near Canterbury, or did live there. She would be rather old, and her memory will probably be questionable, but we shall see."

"Why did you decide to start with her?" Tatiana said in a decidedly offhand manner. Was she as unconcerned as she seemed? "Is she the closest, or simply first on the list?"

"Both." His tone was as deceptively casual as hers. "From what I have been able to ascertain, the other two ladies in question live in the opposite direction from Lady Hutchins. It only makes sense to seek her out first."

"That does make sense." She fell silent for a moment. "Is it a far distance?"

"I expect it will take us most of the day."

"I see. Well, then, it is a good thing I thought to bring along provisions." She reached beneath the seat and slid out a large cloth-covered basket. "I think we should begin our trip with a toast to our success." She rummaged in the basket and pulled out a silver flask and two matching cups. "Will you join me in a brandy, my lord?"

"Brandy?" He frowned. "Isn't it a bit early in the day to be drinking brandy?"

"Not at all," she said blithely, carefully filling her cup. "It is an Avalonian tradition to start a journey with a traveler's toast and a brandy or two."

"Not being Avalonian myself, I believe I will forgo that particular tradition."

"Pity." She raised her cup to him. "To Lord and Lady Matthew." Tatiana seemed to brace herself, then downed the brandy in one long, impressive drink.

"To Lord and Lady Matthew." He laughed and she

grinned at him, her eyes the least bit watery, as if she were not quite used to this tradition.

She replaced the flask and cups, pushed the basket under the seat, then settled back and smiled at the road before them. "I leave myself entirely in your capable hands."

"Entirely?" He raised an amused brow. "Is that wise, Princess? Your captain, Dimitri, certainly wouldn't think so."

"Ah, but I am not of a mind with Dimitri, who is not now, nor has he ever been, *my* captain. Besides, my lord"—she cast him a wicked glance—"perhaps it is not my being in your hands Dimitri should worry about, but you being in mine."

"Perhaps." He grinned. What had he gotten himself into?

"Now, then, do tell me of your work. You said something about a new device?"

"Ah, yes, my heating system." He couldn't help but be flattered by her interest. "The idea is really quite simple. I realized that the prime element of danger, and therefore the major obstacle to overcome, inherent in . . ."

He rambled on, warming to his subject, pausing only for an occasional murmur of acknowledgment. At last it dawned on him that she had said nothing for quite some time. He leaned over to peer beneath the shadows cast by her hat and grinned.

The blasted women wasn't awed to silence by his astounding grasp of the subject nearest to his heart.

She was asleep.

Chapter 6

*T*atiana shaded her eyes against the sharp slant of the setting sun and watched Matthew stride toward the doorway of the inn.

Watching him move, taut with energy and confidence, listening to him talk, losing herself in the sea blue of his eyes were the best parts of this endless day. Indeed they were the only pleasures to be found thus far. The rest of their so-called adventure had been long and hot and exhausting. Even if she had spent most of the day either dozing or sound asleep.

He stepped into the building and she stretched and rubbed the back of her neck. Tatiana quite loved traveling, or rather she loved visiting new and exciting places. Once freed from the restrictions of mourning after Phillipe's death, she had spent much of the following year wandering through the capitals of Europe until she had discovered Paris. And a taste of blissful freedom. And Matthew. But, while seeing sights she had only read about was the height of adventure, she was not at all fond of the process of travel itself.

To her dismay, she had discovered her stomach did not appreciate travel by sea—disappointing, as there were so many places in the world one could not reach by land. Even large, steady coaches provided a measure of discomfort. It was exceedingly odd that she did not suffer similarly on horseback, although she had long thought it might be because she could control the gait of the animal. She had had no difficulties when she had ridden in Matthew's balloon either. Of course, the sensation in a balloon, as far as her experience went—which admittedly was limited to ascending and descending while being tethered to the ground by a stout rope—was far less dramatic than the rocking of a ship or rhythmic lurching of a horse-drawn vehicle.

She could not abide a carriage ride of more than an hour without her stomach rebelling in a most unpleasant way. The only manner in which she could tolerate a lengthy journey was to avoid food and to court sleep. And nothing put her to sleep faster than a substantial helping of brandy. She did not even particularly like the drink and much preferred wine or, better yet, champagne. Still, brandy provided the needed effect.

Matthew disappeared into the inn. She regretted not being able to spend these hours with him more productively, but as much as she had wanted to reacquaint herself with him and begin to work her way back into his good graces and, hopefully his heart, she knew better than to run the risk of losing whatever food she had in her on his boots.

She could probably confide this particular problem to Matthew, but there was time enough later for such personal revelations. She did hope he believed

her claim as to brandy before a journey being an Avalonian tradition and her insistence that brandy with a
midday meal, which she had barely touched, while
traveling was a custom as well. She would much prefer he think her countrymen had a few odd habits
than believe she was some sort of royal sot.

She glanced curiously around the busy courtyard.
The day was growing late and there were a considerable number of people about. It would be ever so
much better to be accompanied by a maid right now
and she did wish she had ignored Matthew's stipulation on that score. Still, she had been trying to at least
give the appearance of agreeing to his demands. Besides, she had wanted to be alone with him.

The courtyard was bounded on three sides by fa-
cades more or less two stories in height, none of
which bore the least resemblance to recognizable
forms of architecture. The structure appeared as if it
had grown and blossomed, twisted and spiraled upward of its own accord, in its own time, untouched by
the hand of man. Still, while it was not at all grand,
neither did it have a disreputable appearance. Indeed, there was a rather comfortable air about the
place, like a welcoming friend. A once ornate, now
faded sign proclaimed it to be THE JOLLY HUNTSMAN.

Not that they would be staying here, of course.
Once they had located Lady Hutchins, she, or her
family, would surely insist on extending the hospitality of their home to Lord and Lady Matthew. Such an
offer was, as Tatiana understood it, to be expected
among the English aristocracy.

Matthew appeared at the door of the inn and
started toward her. His expression was at once
thoughtful and indecipherable. She did wish she

could read the blasted man's mind. He drew closer and she recognized the gleam in his eye. She sighed to herself. Perhaps she could read his mind after all.

"Is something amiss, my lord?"

"We have a slight problem." He stopped beside the carriage. "The inn is fully occupied, but the innkeeper, a Mr. Wicklund, was willing to take a moment to answer my questions. He seems to be a fairly knowledgeable fellow, and his wife, the very vocal Mrs. Wicklund, apparently knows everything her husband does not and furthermore has an opinion on those matters and more. According to them, your Lady Hutchins is, well, dead."

"Oh, dear, that is a problem." Tatiana thought for a moment. "Is it possible that her family remembers the princess? It was not all that long ago."

"It was fifty years ago," he said pointedly. "A great deal can change in half a century."

"Even so, relations do tend to remember things like visiting royalty. It is what family legends are made of."

"Perhaps, but even if anyone in this particular family can recall those events"—he shrugged—"it scarcely matters now."

"Of course it matters," she said firmly. "Goodness, my lord, I do not think you are in the spirit of this adventure at all. Lady Hutchins's demise simply adds another element of difficulty but is by no means insurmountable."

"Your confidence is really rather charming." He leaned against the carriage in an altogether insolent manner, a slight smile lifting the corners of his lips.

"I do not know why you find this so amusing. Indeed, you should share my confidence. We have scarcely begun and nothing cannot be overcome at this point. We shall simply go to the lady's offspring and see what can be learned. Surely they have an estate in the vicinity?"

"They may well have an estate, but it is not in the area."

"No?" She narrowed her eyes and studied him. Matthew knew something he had not yet told her and was obviously holding his revelation for the right time. Fortunately for him, his annoying nature was part of his charm. She heaved a frustrated sigh. "Very well, then. Where is Lady Hutchins's family to be found?"

"It's a tragic story." He shook his head in a mournful manner. "According to the innkeeper, Lady Hutchins died more than forty years ago."

"That long," Tatiana murmured.

"After her death, her family did not fare well. It seems her husband, distraught by the loss of his wife—"

"To be expected when one loses a wife." She shook her head. "I imagine he missed her terribly. As the night misses the warmth of the sun."

"She *died*, Princess, she did not leave of her own accord. In that respect, I am certain he did miss her, although in this case it was perhaps more akin to my analogies."

"The horse and the flies?"

"Exactly. You see"—he leaned closer—"after Lady Hutchins's death, her husband turned to drinking and gaming and took up with all manner of disreputable women. This according to the innkeeper's wife, who, in spite of the passage of time, recalls Lord Hutchins wasted little time in mourning before wallowing in his bad habits." Matthew straightened and smirked. "Perhaps was not at all unhappy to bid his wife farewell."

"The beast." Indignation flowed through her. "How could he?"

"Perhaps the blame should not be laid with the husband but with the wife."

"I daresay, whatever her faults, she may well have had good reasons and the very best of intentions," she said stoutly.

"The best of intentions?" He snorted with disdain. "Scarcely an acceptable excuse. What if she did not confide in him? Or even lied to him?"

"She might have thought he would never understand the reasons for her deception and therefore would never believe how she truly felt about him. She might have realized she could never be what he wanted, what he deserved, until she had resolved her own responsibilities."

"That's absurd. If indeed she cared for him, she would have trusted him." His voice hardened. "Would have trusted that together they could resolve any problem. Together, nothing could have defeated them."

"Unless, of course, she did not know him well enough to accept that on little more than blind faith," she snapped. "She could well have been scared to put her trust in him when another man before him had so cruelly failed her."

"But he was not another man, he was her husband. And he was her husband not because of her position or title or wealth but because he loved her. And she discarded him without a second thought!"

"And because she loved him as well, it broke her heart to do so, and more, when he never took so much as a single step to find her. He can place the blame on her if that is his wish, but he let her go!"

Their words hung in the air, a palpable cloud of anger and resentment. Tatiana's gaze locked with Matt's and she stared in horror. She had not meant to say any of that. If there was any hope at all of finding what they had once shared, such outbursts were not the way to smooth the path. He was not ready for such confrontations. And neither was she.

Matthew looked as shocked as she felt. For an endless moment they could do nothing but stare.

"Yes, well, Lady Hutchins died, didn't she? And there was nothing her husband could do on that score." He cleared his throat and was once again cool and collected, his voice steady and composed. "To continue, Lord Hutchins's wicked ways proved to be his undoing. He lost his fortune, quite substantial at one time, according to the innkeeper's wife—"

"Who should know," Tatiana said, forcing a bright note to her voice. If Matthew could pretend nothing had passed between them, so could she.

"He was forced to sell his property and all his remaining assets in order to buy passage to America. He left the country with his children, two boys and a girl, I believe, just a year or so after his wife's death." He shook his head. "Neither he nor any of his family has been heard from since."

"I see." The significance of Matthew's story wiped all else from Tatiana's mind.

If indeed Lord Hutchins had been forced to sell his estate, his birthright, it would have been a last resort. In her experience, noblemen were never willing to give up their heritage unless they had no other choice. If Hutchins knew of the jewels, surely he would have sold them and saved his home. Of course, he could indeed have disposed of them and squandered the profits on wild living. But aside from the symbolic value of the Heavens, they would provide a fortune far too substantial to be lost quite as quickly as Lord Hutchins appeared to have lost his.

It was therefore logical to assume that neither Lord nor Lady Hutchins had knowledge of the jewels. Which further meant Tatiana would not have to follow this family to America. By ship. Buffeted by rolling swells and wave after wave. Across a long, heaving ocean.

"Your Highness?" Matthew's voice broke into her thoughts. "Are you all right? You look a bit green."

"A trick of the light, no doubt. I am fine." She favored him with her brightest smile. "It cannot be helped, I suppose. We shall simply have to move on to the next name."

"I'm grateful you're not too disappointed." He studied her thoughtfully.

"One has to expect a few impedimento. It is simply the nature of life. You of all people should understand that. Why, your work with your balloons has not always progressed smoothly, yet you have not abandoned it. Nothing worthwhile is ever especially easy."

"A pity, that," he said wryly. "It would be delightful if it were, at least on occasion."

"Come, now, my lord, on occasion, it is." She smiled and patted the seat beside her. "Now, then, we should probably be on our way."

"On our way where, exactly?" His brows drew together.

"Well, you said the two other ladies I wish to meet live in a direction opposite from London. Therefore, I suggest we return the way we came." She patted the seat again. "My lord?"

"Are you aware that it will be dark soon?"

"I can scarcely miss the setting of the sun."

"Traveling on these roads after nightfall is ill-advised. We shall not travel tonight."

"Do we have a choice?" She stared at him. "I had planned to stay with Lady Hutchins's family, but obviously that is not to be. Therefore, we have no option but to—"

"We shall stay here."

"Here?" She glanced around. "I thought you said the inn was full."

"It is. Now. We have obtained the last available room. One of the reasons the innkeeper was willing to so freely answer all my questions was because I paid him substantially more than his usual rate. Of course, he assures me he has given us his finest room." He held out his hand. She placed her hand in his and stepped down from the carriage.

"It has taken rather more of my resources than I anticipated, but I assume, in spite of your agreements to my"—he snorted—"*conditions* about living within my finances that you have brought along a fair amount of money."

"A coin or two, perhaps," she said casually. It would probably be better for him not to know exactly how much she had brought.

"I thought as much." He blew an annoyed breath. "Are there any of my conditions you do intend to abide by?"

"If I told you, it would spoil everything. Remember, my lord, surprise is the essence of—"

"Yes, yes, adventure. I would hate to spoil that."

He tucked her hand in the crook of his elbow and they started toward the entrance. "There is only a single bedchamber and I imagine there will be only one bed."

"We shall have to make do, then." She gazed up at him. "Besides, it is only natural that Lord and Lady Matthew share a room. I do not imagine they are the type of couple that would insist on separate sleeping accommodations. Do you?"

"Not at all. But my imagination is rather active." A slight smile played across his lips. "It does not bother you, then?"

"Not in the least," she said, ignoring a tremor of what was part apprehension, part anticipation. "I like a man with a vivid imagination."

He laughed. "That's not what I meant."

"I know what you meant. However, if you are waiting for me to swoon at the thought of sharing your room—"

"And my bed."

"And your bed." Her voice was serene, as if she were speaking of something of no consequence whatsoever and not discussing the very thing she had dreamed of night after long, lonely night. "I should think you would no longer expect hysterics from me on this subject after the last time we spoke of your so-called conditions."

"I never know what to expect of you, Princess," he said under his breath.

"And do stop calling me *Princess*. Or *Your Highness*. Someone is bound to overhear and—"

"Very well, my lady . . ."—he bent close, his lips near to her ear—"wife."

The word whispered against her skin, provocative and promising. Delight shivered through her and raised the hairs at the back of her neck. She might have to swoon after all.

Why should she not share his bed? Had she not been in his arms in her dreams every night since they'd parted? Regardless of what happened between them now, would she not always consider herself his wife? And wouldn't he always be her love?

Why should she wait until that love was returned, if indeed it ever was? It was clear that his feelings already went beyond mere physical attraction. The odd debate they had had a few moments ago proved that. He might not love her now, but he did tolerate her, and surely he liked her just a little. Still, even if he detested her, it was a fine and passionate hatred. And was there not little more than a thin line between love and hate?

"Yes," she said.

"Yes?" He stared down at her. "Yes—what?"

"Yes is the answer to your question."

"And which question would that be?" he asked slowly.

"You wanted to know if there were any of your conditions I intended to honor." She glanced up at him, pleased to note the distinct look of trepidation in his eye. "The answer, my lord *husband*, is yes."

Chapter 7

*I*t was the look in her eye he couldn't get out of his mind.

She'd cast him what he now thought of as *the look* every time he'd seen her since her return. In the stables, at her residence and his cottage, and then earlier tonight, when they had entered the inn. Even now, as she sat across the table from him in the privacy of their room, eating the meal Matt had arranged for, her dining was punctuated by the periodic directing of *the look*.

He couldn't quite describe *the look*: It was a mix of flirtation and determination. Of innocence and challenge. Somehow, she managed to peek up at him while keeping her lashes lowered. He couldn't have duplicated the maneuver if he practiced in front of a mirror for years. It was distinctly feminine and not particularly straightforward. In the section of his mind reserved for mechanics he wondered how anyone could give the impression of gazing down in a most modest manner while glancing upward in a way that could only be described as enticing. In various other parts of his body, he didn't care about the how of such a feat, only the why.

Potent. That was the word for it. The look was extremely potent. No doubt the kind of look Delilah ensnared an innocent Samson with or Cleopatra employed on an unsuspecting Marc Antony. Tatiana was probably trained from birth in the use of such looks as a national defense in time of Avalonian crisis.

A lesser man might have been taken in by it. By the seductive lure of those green eyes. But Matthew Weston, *Lord* Matthew, was more than up to the challenge of a mere look, no matter how potent or inviting or intriguing or—

"Do you not like it, my lord?"

"Like it?" He hadn't thought of it in terms of like or dislike. It did make him feel as if there never was, nor would there ever be, anyone in the world as significant to her as him, which in and of itself was suspicious. "I'm not entirely sure I trust it."

"Goodness." Tatiana huffed in annoyance. "Now you sound like Dimitri."

"I've no doubt you've given the good captain more than enough reason for distrust through the years," Matt said coolly.

"Nonsense. In point of fact, I had never even left my country until recent years. And the political climate at home was relatively calm until my father's illness."

He stared at her in confusion. "What are you talking about?"

"Concerns of security, of course. The possibility of poisoning in the food. Which I do think is absurd. No one knows who I am, nor, I suspect, would they especially care." She drew her brows together. "I asked you if you liked the food and you claimed you did not trust it. What were *you* talking about?"

"I was talking about . . ." *The look in your eye and the way it makes me forget the past and ignore the future.* He cleared his throat and adopted a lofty manner. "I think the food is excellent." The plates laid out between them were laden with roasted beef, vegetables in cream and large chunks of crusty bread, accompanied by two bottles of a rough, but tasty, red wine.

"You have not eaten much of it."

"You, on the other hand, have eaten a remarkable amount."

"Yes, I know." She sucked her middle finger and uttered a contented sigh. "It was quite, quite wonderful. I was famished."

"No doubt." He was hard-pressed to pull his gaze away from that lovely, lucky finger. "You've scarcely put anything in your stomach today unless one counts brandy."

"Brandy does not count if it is part of a tradition. Besides, I do not especially like brandy. It is such a serious drink, dreadfully heavy and intense. However, one must make sacrifices for the sake of tradition, do you not think so?"

"It depends, I should say, on the tradition."

If she was an enigma to him when they'd first met, she was a puzzle of an even more difficult nature now. Knowing now who and what she was did not serve to answer his questions but only deepened the mystery around her.

"Tradition is extremely important." She trailed her finger idly around the rim of her wine glass. In truth caressed it. His stomach tightened and he downed his wine in one swallow. "In some ways, it is the impetus that drives me."

"Oh?" He quickly refilled his glass.

She nodded thoughtfully. "It is important for a country, for a people, to have something to believe in. That is the true purpose of tradition, custom, even symbols. It is comforting to know, no matter how the world changes, some things remain the same and always will. A baby will be christened in the same manner, the same church and probably the same gown as his father and his father before him."

"I never suspected brandy played such a crucial role in the world as we know it." A teasing note sounded in his voice.

"Brandy is most important when it is one of the national products of your country." Her tone was serious, but the candlelight reflected the gleam of laughter in her eyes. "Surely you have sampled Avalonian brandy?"

"Avalonian brandy?" He chuckled. "I admit I have never so much as heard of it and I've always considered myself fairly well versed in the alcoholic offerings of the continent."

"I am not surprised. It is rather hard to find the farther one gets from Avalonia. The very best is Royal Amber, and it is extremely rare. The Royal Amber brandy served this year has been aged for nearly a century. There is only enough made each season by the monks who live in the monastery midway up Avalonia's highest mountain to meet the needs of the royal family."

"Just the royal family? The ordinary folk have to drink ordinary brandy?"

She nodded. "Ordinary Avalonian brandy is still

quite good, or so I have been told. And even for the royal family, Royal Amber is only used on occasions of great celebration and ceremony. The Feast of St. Stanislaus, Christmas and welcoming the new year, Easter, of course, baptisms, weddings, coronations. That sort of thing." She raised her wine glass to him. "It is tradition."

"I see." He returned the toast, then sipped casually. "I assume, then, it was drunk at your wedding."

She hesitated, and there was a flash of something in her eyes. Regret? Anger? No, more than likely pain. She had buried her first husband, after all, not left him, and she had probably cared for him.

"I shouldn't have asked," he said slowly.

"Nonsense." She smiled lightly and her chin raised a fraction of an inch. "You were at my second wedding. It is only fair you know about the first. The occasion most certainly required the benediction of Royal Amber brandy. It was as much a joining of two countries as two people."

"You never told me about your husband. There's no need—"

"Perhaps not. Perhaps there is every need." She leaned back in her chair and studied him for a long, silent moment. "Do you know anything of my country, Matthew?"

"Not really. I have managed to locate it on a map, but beyond that"—he smiled to lighten the mood—"I know only of its people's traditions regarding brandy while traveling."

She laughed. "There is little more to know. We are strategically located, in that part of the world shared by Russia, Prussia and Austria. While my family has ruled for centuries, they are also prone to fighting amongst themselves. This past year my father was quite ill and my cousin tried to wrest power for her own branch of the House of Pruzinsky. Thankfully, she failed. She isn't at all nice and I cannot imagine what dire consequences would result from her rule."

She took a drink and considered him over the rim of her glass. "But you were asking about my first husband."

"I wasn't really asking." It seemed somewhat petty to abruptly delve into her past. Still, if he had no other claim as her second husband, perhaps he at least had the right to know something of her first. "But I do admit to some curiosity."

"Phillipe Andre Augustus de Bernadotte was the son of the monarch of a small principality allied with Avalonia. My father and his decreed we should wed when I was but four years of age. Even though Phillipe's country was . . . well, *absorbed* is the polite, civilized term . . . by Austria before he came of age, it was decided it would still be of political benefit for the marriage to take place. So I did my duty, fulfilled my responsibilities and I married him."

"I see." He did, but only to a certain extent. Tatiana had given no clue as to how she had felt about this Phillipe. If she had cared for him. Mourned him. Loved him. Not that it was the least bit important. He was curious, nothing more.

"You might well have liked Phillipe. He was the kind of man other men tend to admire. An expert in everything he turned his hand to—riding and shooting, gaming and drinking and all those odd things men seem to enjoy. He was exceedingly charming and quite handsome. Other gentlemen liked him, but women"—she sipped at her wine—"women adored him. And he adored them."

"I see." This time he did indeed understand. "Did you?"

She stared into her glass and long moments passed by. He wasn't sure why he wanted to hear her answer, but he did even as he told himself, here and now, it scarcely mattered.

"I can't imagine in your entire life you have ever done anything so completely foolish that it haunts you forever." Her voice was low but firm.

His heart twisted. "Yes, well, once or twice, perhaps."

Her gaze flicked up to meet his. "I grew up knowing I would one day be Phillipe's wife. It was not my decision, neither was it my choice.

"Even as a boy, he had a charm and a passion for living that was irresistible. Whether I would have felt the same meeting him for the first time as an adult, I do not know. But yes, for much of my life I too adored him. I fell under his spell as a child and did not emerge from his enchantment until it was too late."

"Like a princess in a fairy story."

"Not at all." She wrinkled her nose and held out her empty glass. Matt grabbed the bottle, leaned over the table and refilled her wineglass. "In such stories, the princess, upon coming out of her enchantment and discovering the truth, would then have been rescued by her true love, or at the very least would have found a way to escape. No one rescued me, Matthew, nor did I save myself.

"I did exactly what was expected of me. What I had been trained to do." She shook her head in disgust. "It was really quite revolting, when I look back on it. I was a perfect wife, and a perfect princess. I did not chastise him, publicly or privately. I pretended I knew nothing of his activities. I ignored the whispers and looks of pity."

Matt scoffed. "I cannot believe that. Granted, you seem rather more forceful now than when we first met, but even then you did not strike me as the type of woman who would tolerate such behavior in a husband."

"That is perhaps the nicest compliment I have ever had." She favored him with an odd smile, sad and sweet at the same time. "The woman you met in Paris had taken the opportunity provided by her husband's fortuitous death to examine her own life. Not as a princess but as, well, an ordinary person, I suppose. She discovered her entire life had been spent meeting the expectations of others and in many ways that was how it should be. That was her position in life. Her fate.

"But after Phillipe's death, it seemed she, or rather I, had fulfilled my purpose and lived up to the responsibilities of my position. If my husband had not died, I am certain my life would have continued without change or question. But his death freed me, not merely from a farce of a marriage but from a state of mind. I followed the requirements of mourning and then I left my country to experience a world I had only dreamed of."

She rested her elbows on the table, laced her fingers together and propped her chin on her hands. Her eyes gleamed with intensity. "And my travels took me to Paris."

"And to me." His statement was level, unemotional, an observation, nothing more. He wasn't sure what to say and wasn't entirely certain how he felt about what she'd just said.

"And to you." She studied him carefully. "I only left you because I knew I was not, at the time, truly free of my responsibilities."

"And now?" The question surprised him. Especially since he didn't care. Refused to care. "Are you free now?"

"I will be, once I have accomplished what I came here to do."

"And what exactly is that?" He kept his voice nonchalant. Now, late in the night, with a long day behind them and a certain amount of truth already revealed, would she tell him the rest? What she was really looking for? And why had she wanted him with her?

"You know perfectly well what that is." She heaved a long-suffering sigh. "The story of the travels of the Princess Sophia, of course."

"Of course," he muttered.

She raised a brow. "What did you want me to say?"

"The truth."

"That's right. You do not believe me. It is becoming most annoying."

"Thank you." He shrugged. "As you have pointed out, being annoying is one of my finest qualities."

"Yes, Matthew, but you have now honed it to a fine art and can desist practicing." She smiled in an overly sweet manner.

He laughed. "I can make no promises on that score."

"I did not think so." She shook her head. "Do tell me, though: If you truly do not believe me, why are you helping me?"

"The adventure, of course," he said with a grin. "And the money. I need the money."

"Now I do not believe you."

"No? You have seen where I live. The clothes I wear. My work is quite costly. Have you ever met a man who needed money more than I?"

"Of course you need money." She huffed. "I just do not believe that is why you are helping me."

"Why?" He settled back in his chair and smiled slowly. "Whatever other reason could I possibly have for accompanying you?"

"You, my dear Lord Matthew, cannot get me out of your head." She pushed away from the table and rose to her feet.

"Nonsense." He snorted. "I've barely given you a second thought."

"Not a second thought?" She circled the table. "Not in fifteen months, three weeks and however many days?"

His gaze locked with hers and he got to his feet. "Not one."

"You said you missed me." She stopped in front of him and trailed her fingers lightly down his arm.

"One misses all manner of things when they are gone." He kept his voice light, as if her touch on the fabric of his jacket were not the least bit disturbing.

"I confess"—her tone was low and sultry—"I missed you."

"Did you?"

"You sound surprised."

"I am." Only a scant inch or two lay between them. He could smell her scent, subtle and erotic, feel the heat from her body, sense the rise and fall of her chest with each breath. "You stayed away rather a long time for someone who claims to have missed me."

"I had responsibilities to fulfill. Portions of my life remained . . . unfinished. There were doors I needed to close." She hesitated. "In addition, my father fell ill and it was my place to stay with him. I had no choice, but in truth I would not have left his side."

"Am I a portion unfinished, then?" He stared down at her, resisting the urge to yank her body close to his, to press his lips to hers. "A door that needs to be closed?"

"I would say matters between us are as yet unresolved. Can you not feel it in the very air between us?"

"Is that what it is between us?" He forced a light note to his voice. "I thought it was something else entirely. Distrust. Disdain. Deceit."

"Desire?" She rested her hands on his chest and he resisted the urge to flinch. She cast him *the look* and he knew he was lost. And didn't care.

"Definitely desire." He pulled her hard into his arms, cupped the back of her head in his hand and crushed his lips to hers.

She greeted him without pause, without hesitation. She threw her arms around his neck and twined her fingers in his hair. Her mouth opened beneath his and her tongue met his. He wanted to invade her, conquer her, control her. Make her his for now. Forever.

She met his desire with her own, as if she wanted to devour him as he wanted to devour her. As if she needed to mark him as hers, as he needed to mark her. As if she too had dreamed of nothing but how they were once and how they could be again.

He slid his hands down her back and cupped her buttocks, pulling her closer against the hard ridge of his erection. She ground her hips against his and he shuddered with need.

He pulled his lips from hers to taste the corner of

her mouth, the line of her jaw, the tender flesh of her neck. He could not breathe and did not care.

"I have not changed my mind, you know." His voice was harsh with unrelenting desire. "This means nothing to me."

"Nor to me." She gasped and dug her fingers into his shoulders.

With one hand and without thought, he shoved the dishes on the table aside. He lifted her onto the table and she grabbed the fabric of his coat and pulled him after her. His hands cupped her breasts and her nipples hardened against his fingers beneath the fabric of her frock. Impatiently, he pulled down her bodice to reveal her breasts, full and firm and heaving with every gasping breath. He took one nipple in his mouth with a care that required every ounce of his control. She cried out softly and her back arched upward.

He ran his hand up her leg, over her stocking and garter and found the sweet, moist promise between her legs. She was wet and wanting and gasped when he touched her. He moved his thumb to and fro in the way he remembered drove her mad. And indeed, she writhed on the table and clutched at him.

"Matthew." His name was little more than a moan. "It has been so long and I have missed you so."

It might have been the sound of her voice or something she didn't say but he heard nonetheless or perhaps simply wanted to hear, but abruptly his senses cleared and he hesitated. He wanted her, dear God, he wanted her, and thought he could well die if he didn't have her. Right here, right now.

But something—some odd, horrible hand of principle or honor or conscience—refused to let him.

"Matthew?"

No! He brushed aside whatever scruples had

reared their ugly head. Bloody hell. She'd been his wife once and there was no doubt she wanted him now. Time enough later to deal with principle or honor or conscience.

"Nothing." He worked at his trousers and she shifted on the table to accommodate him, knocking a platter to the floor. The crash reverberated through the room.

He scarcely noticed.

She reached for him. He braced a knee between her legs.

A knock sounded at the door. And they froze.

"Is everything all right in there?" The voice of the innkeeper's wife sounded on the other side of the door.

"Everything is quite fine." Tatiana's voice had an odd, strangled sound about it. She stared up at him.

"Yes, thank you." Matt stared down at her.

"I heard a crash, I did." There was a pause, heavy with suspicion. "It's my good platter in there, it is."

"A bit of a mishap," Matt called. "Nothing of any significance."

"I want to see." The demand was accompanied by what was obviously the jingling of keys. "Now."

"Bloody hell," Matt said under his voice, stumbling toward the door. He threw his shoulder against it and tried to readjust his clothing at the same time. Tatiana slid off the table and frantically rearranged her dress into some semblance of propriety.

For a bawdy house, perhaps.

She patted her hair, not that it helped, caught his gaze and nodded. He drew a deep breath and stepped away from the door.

The door flew open, banged against the wall, and

the short, round form that was Mrs. Wicklund burst into the room, a diminutive avenging angel with the fire of righteous indignation blazing in her eyes. Matt could have sworn a whiff of smoke curled up from her nostrils.

"Your lordship." Mrs. Wicklund's gaze slid from Matt to Tatiana. "My lady."

"My husband and I were just finishing supper," Tatiana said as if she didn't look like she'd been doing exactly what she'd been doing.

"That'd be my story." Mrs. Wicklund stared at the overturned platter on the floor.

"I am dreadfully sorry about that. It was an unfortunate accident, but luck was with us and the platter did not break." Tatiana stepped to the older woman's side, took her arm and firmly led her to the door. "It is lovely and I can certainly understand your concern."

Mrs. Wicklund craned her neck to see around Tatiana. "Well, I don't have none too many, that I can afford losing one."

"We will, of course, make certain you are compensated for the distress this has caused you." Tatiana glanced at Matt. "Will we not, my lord?"

He nodded eagerly. "Oh, we will, we will indeed."

"No doubt." Mrs. Wicklund cast a disgusted look at Matt's shirttail still hanging out of his pants. "I should clean—"

"Oh, but you are most certainly far too busy." Tatiana steered her through the doorway. "Why not send a maid up to take care of it when you have the chance?"

"Might be a while." Mrs. Wicklund pursed her lips but was obviously mollified nonetheless.

"We understand completely." Tatiana's sincerity

convinced even Matt. "And we do appreciate all your hard work. Why, the inn is lovely and the food was wonderful."

"Tasty," Matt said helpfully. "Extremely tasty."

Mrs. Wicklund peered around Tatiana and glared at him. She turned back to Tatiana and lowered her voice confidentially. "You've not been married long, have you, my lady?"

"No indeed. In truth, scarcely a week, all told."

"I thought as much." Mrs. Wicklund's voice took on a conciliatory note. "Watch him, my lady. Be they lords or louts, there's only one thing they want from a woman. Especially them as good-looking as your husband. And he's a randy one too, I can tell as much just looking at him."

"Good lord, my dear woman." Tatiana's voice rang with suppressed laughter. "I certainly hope so."

Matt expected indignation from the older woman but instead heard a chuckle. Mrs. Wicklund and Tatiana exchanged a few more comments, too low this time for him to hear, and the woman was on her way.

Tatiana shut the door behind her and breathed a sigh of relief. "Now, then, Matthew, shall we continue?"

Once again, something despicably honorable raised its nasty head.

"I think not," he said slowly, never regretting any words so much.

"Why not?" She stepped close and gazed up at him. "This is one of your conditions. I did agree to abide by those conditions."

Her eyes were bright, her lips red and full, her skin glowed with an inner light, her light hair was disheveled. She looked like the lush subject of a renaissance painting. A courtesan served up as a meal for the gods. Delicious and irresistible. His loins throbbed.

Of course, she did agree. . . .

"I'm not at all sure why, exactly, but I . . . we . . ." He ran his hand through his hair and blew a long, frustrated breath. "Can't."

"Oh, Matthew, I am quite certain we . . . you . . . can." She reached down and cupped the still-hard bulge in his pants.

"Tatiana!" He jerked away and glared at her. "I did not mean I couldn't in that respect! I have never had problems in that respect!"

"I did not think so." She grabbed the fabric of his shirt and drew him back to her.

"What I mean to say is . . ." He took her hands and firmly set her aside. He had to leave. Now. If he didn't, he'd finish what they started, and there was an odd feeling deep in his gut that that spelled disaster. Probably for him. "I have just remembered a . . . a . . . a task I need to attend to. Of course, how could I have forgotten? It can't wait."

"What kind of task?" She planted her hands on her hips and stared at him. "You did not mention any task."

"It's . . ." He swallowed hard. "The horses. Yes, that's it, exactly. The horses. I need to do something about the horses."

"Now?" Her voice rose in disbelief.

"This very minute." He edged to the door. "I forgot to give the stable hands specific instructions as to their care."

"They are horses. How specific do you need to be? You feed them, you groom them. It is my understanding there is nothing more to it than that."

"Oh, there's much more to it than that. They

are . . ." He groped for the words. "They're very special horses." The door, escape, was nearly within reach.

"Special?" Incredulity and confusion colored her face. "They did not look special to me, and you had never seen them before today."

"Nonetheless, they require special treatment because they are"—they are what?—"well, *special*, and I do need to see to them." He yanked open the door. "Now."

"That is the most ridiculous . . ." She gasped and stared. "Good Lord! I can see it in your face. You are scared. Of me." Her eyes widened. "Of *us*!"

"Now, that is ridiculous."

"You are a coward, Matthew Weston." She folded her arms over her chest and grinned in a smug manner. "You will fly over the rooftops, yet you're afraid of what will happen if you and I—"

"I most certainly am not," he said with the proper note of indignation. "I told you before, this"—he waved at the table—"means nothing to me. Therefore, I have nothing to fear. However, I am concerned that the horses—"

"The very special horses?"

"—will not receive the attention they deserve and we shall be forced to remain for yet another night." He stepped through the door with all the dignity he could muster and called over his shoulder, "I shall return shortly."

An unladylike snort of disbelief sounded behind him.

He closed the door and collapsed against it, as if it held back the very hounds of hell.

Blasted woman. What had she done to him?

She was his for the taking and he couldn't take her.

No, he amended the thought, he *could* if he'd wanted to. And certainly would have if not for the untimely arrival of Mrs. Wicklund. But he didn't want to. Oh his body wanted, but his mind . . .

It made no sense whatsoever, particularly since even now he still wanted her. More than he had ever wanted anyone in his life.

As much now as when they'd first met.

He drew a deep breath, pushed away from the door and strode down the corridor. He had no particular destination in mind, although he might as well check on the horses now. The very special horses. He groaned to himself. That lie was as feeble as any of hers.

He still couldn't figure out what exactly had happened tonight. He'd had no trouble when he and Tatiana were last together. Caught in the throes of passion and emotion, they'd spent as much of their time in bed as out. There'd been no odd qualms of morality then. No twinges of guilt or honor.

He took the stairs quickly and passed through the public dining room crowded with travelers unwilling or unable to pay extra for the luxury of eating privately in their own rooms.

He'd had no trouble with other women and could not recall ever deciding against proceeding with a willing partner. It was always satisfactory even if never particularly significant. He'd paid the act of copulation no more importance than the quenching of his thirst or the sating of his hunger. It was a need, nothing more.

Of course, he was not in love with those women.

The thought pulled him up short. Love had nothing to do with this. He wasn't in love with Tatiana. Not now anyway. Oh, certainly he had been once. Indeed, what they had shared in his bed was beyond anything he'd known with another female. Even he realized that was obviously due to the intense emotion they shared, as well as the physical act. With Tatiana it was lovemaking in the truest sense of the word.

Without love, with this woman alone, it seemed . . . well, wrong. Even dishonorable, to share the bed of a woman you once loved, without love.

He stepped into the courtyard and pulled a long breath. The night air was cool on his heated skin and the stars twinkled in the blue-black sky.

It was the silliest idea he'd ever heard. Love, honor, had nothing to do with lust. And the fact that he'd loved her once had nothing whatsoever to do with this. He'd trusted her once too, and look where that had left him.

He started toward the stables. He might as well check on their horses. He had nothing better to do and he had no intention of returning to their room, for the time being.

Or was it pride holding him back?

He'd vowed to himself that this time their relationship would be on his terms. He'd be the one making the decisions, making the choices.

Yet just who was choosing to seduce whom this evening?

Pride and honor. He snorted with disdain. Ephraim was right. The qualities were debilitating. Couple them with questions of love and trust, and it all became even more complicated. And conflicting.

Well, he'd have to get over that.

As for her charge that he was afraid of her, of *them*, there was nothing further from the truth. Fear would mean he felt *something* for her, and any emotions he had had ended long ago. The very idea that he was scared was as ludicrous as everything else he'd considered tonight.

He wanted her and he would have her. On his terms, in his time. His choice, not hers.

Long hours—and many pints of ale—later, Matt quietly slipped back into their room. In spite of the fact that one pint had led to two, had led to four and so on, he was still sober and clear-headed. Regrettably so.

The platter and all remains of their meal had been cleared away. A candle burned low on the table, casting its flickering light on Tatiana, asleep and unmoving on the bed.

Matt rummaged through his bag for the writing case and journal. He sat down at the table, prepared a pen and opened the book. But his gaze strayed to Tatiana's sleeping form.

She'd disrupted his life once and he would not allow her to do it again. Not to him, not to his family.

He had no answers and was no longer even sure of the questions. If one discarded all possibility of affection and emotion, nothing made sense at all. But accepting that he might well feel something beyond desire for this woman was not worth considering.

He pulled his gaze away from her and stared at the blank page before him. This was, no doubt, as ridiculous as everything else, yet his entire life seemed an exercise in absurdity at the moment.

He drew a deep breath and began.

Dear Ephraim . . .

Dear Ephraim,

First of all, I should like you to understand that while I may be writing these letters per your request, I have made no decision as to their eventual use. To ensure discretion, should this become public, I shall not use the proper names of any person or country. In truth, it is entirely possible that neither you, nor anyone else, will ever read so much as a word of what I put forth. Nonetheless, while I have never been prone to putting pen to paper, I find a need to discuss the events that have transpired today, and this writing will serve that purpose, if no other.

The princess continues to be an enigma to me. While she is forthright about some intimate details of her past, she refuses to confide in me completely. She still insists her purpose for our travels is to document the journey of an ancestor.

I must confess I now understand her reticence. Trust does not come easily to her. Admittedly, where she is concerned, trust no longer comes easily to me either. We have both suffered at the hands of those we have felt great affection for and therefore trusted. It is exceedingly ironic to consider her lack of trust in me is entirely the fault of someone else, yet my lack of trust in her is due to her and her alone.

Our first day together passed uneventfully, for the most part. We spent long hours driving from London, and Her Highness slept most of that time. I envy her that ability, as I myself have never been able to manage such a feat, but she appeared to have no trouble. Indeed, she was slumbering within moments of our departure. It is something of a pity, as I had hoped idle conversation between us would reveal at least a hint of her true purpose.

I am, however, learning a great deal about her country. She has chatted about its history and surroundings as well as its curious customs and traditions. While her descriptions sound most interesting, I must confess the people themselves might well be a drunken lot.

Still, one might find it worthwhile to visit. . . .

Chapter 8

"Good day, my lord." Tatiana favored Matthew with her brightest smile.

Matthew waited impatiently beside the carriage and glowered. "We need to be off at once. The hour is growing late and—"

"Are you always this unpleasant in the morning?"

"Yes," he snapped and held out his hand to help her into the vehicle. He assisted her in an overly brisk and highly impersonal manner, then circled the horses to take his place beside her.

"Well, now that we have settled the question of your disposition," she said sweetly, "how is your virtue this morning?"

"My virtue?" He glared. "My virtue has nothing to do with anything."

"I do apologize. *Virtue* might not have been the right word." She paused. "*Morals* is perhaps a better word."

"My morals are not in question either." He tugged on the reins and the horses started off.

"Oh, come, now, Matthew, your morals are definitely in question. In truth, when we first met I did not particularly think you had any. And yet you married me when I am most certain you have *not* married every woman you have bedded."

He stared straight ahead and a tiny muscle in his jaw tightened. "Only the princesses."

"I see." She stifled a grin. "So you only have high moral standards when it comes to women of royal blood?"

"Apparently," he muttered.

"Why did you marry me, Matthew?"

"At the moment, I have no idea." His voice was grim and quite deflated her lovely mood.

"You need not be so nasty about it."

His foul nature could be attributed to the fact that the man had had very little sleep. Or he could truly hate her, but she preferred to think he was simply tired and perhaps frustrated. She certainly was.

When he had finally returned to their room, she had pretended to be asleep. In truth, she had spent most of the night surreptitiously observing him at the table, writing something in a small notebook, probably to do with his work.

The candle flame cast him in light and shadow and she spent long hours studying the planes of his face. Not that she did not know the curve of his cheekbone, the line of his jaw or the way his eyes crinkled at the corners with concentration, by heart. After all, she had studied him every day in her mind's eye. And she could watch him forever.

"The horses look fine," she said in an attempt to engage him in some sort of conversation before she needed to observe Avalonian tradition and start the journey with a brandy. "Not particularly special, but fine."

He did not respond. Apparently, he was not inclined to idle chatter today.

She settled back against the seat and tried not to smile. As disappointed as she had been last night—and she had been extremely disappointed—it was in many ways a most satisfactory evening. Matthew's refusal to carry on was an excellent indication of the possibilities of a future together. Oh, certainly he would have continued if Mrs. Wicklund had not interrupted. Regardless of conscience or honor or anything else, he was still a man, and such things were to be expected from men. If nothing else, Phillipe had taught her that.

Matthew's reticence to pick up where they had left off was perhaps the nicest thing that had ever happened to her. It was obvious he could not simply treat her as if she were any other woman. Whether he realized it or not, he did indeed have feelings for her beyond the irritation he expressed right now and the lust he had shown last night. And regardless of his protests, she was convinced he was leery of what physical intimacy between the two of them would bring.

It made perfect sense. She had hurt him terribly and he had no reason to trust her. No reason to want her back.

But he would. Eventually.

Not because she had always gotten what she wanted in life. In truth, she had never really *wanted* anything before now. Not like she wanted this man, her husband, back.

"I do not know why you should be so disagreeable this morning," she said. "After all, I was not the one who ran shrieking from the room last night like a nervous virgin."

"I did not shriek." His voice was cold, but there might have been the tiniest glimmer of amusement in his eye.

"But you must admit you were nervous."

"I was not the least bit nervous, nor"—he cast her a pointed glance—"was I scared. I have been with women before."

"Hundreds, no doubt," she said blithely. "But that is not what frightened you."

"Then do tell me, Your Highness, as you know me so very well, what did frighten me?"

She ignored his sarcasm. "You were afraid that once we made love you would discover feelings for me you would prefer not to have."

"I have all sorts of feelings for you. None of which require discovery, as I am more than aware of each and every one, and most of which are not particularly pleasant." His voice was firm. "Anything that might have happened last night would have meant nothing beyond the immediate gratification of the moment."

"Then why did you stop?"

"The mood, my dear princess, had been shattered. I was no longer interested." His voice held a lofty, superior note.

"Hah. From what I observed, you were extremely interested."

"Appearances can be deceiving."

"Not that appearance." She bit back a grin.

"You surprise me, Princess." He slanted her an assessing glance. "I don't remember you being quite so forthcoming about such matters. If I recall correctly, you were rather . . . well, demure."

"I have put demure, and reticent as well, behind me," she said lightly, ignoring the wave of heat that flashed up her face.

In truth, she had never been so forthright in her life. But she had realized, almost as soon as she had gone, that the way she had left him—indeed, leaving him at all—was a dreadful mistake. From that instant she knew the perfectly proper creature she had always been was not able to do what needed to be done in order to claim a life for herself—with or without him. She had put a great deal of effort since then into ignoring the upbringing that had taught her to be retiring and complacent. Instead she'd learned to speak her mind and do what she, and she alone, thought best.

To her surprise, Tatiana found she liked the change in herself—indeed, liked herself—far more than she ever had. She no longer felt like a wisp at the mercy of the wind, but like the wind itself. She had a new-found sense of respect for the woman she was and realized she had not had such respect before.

Matthew was not the only incentive for her change, but he was the beginning. Perhaps it was because they had known each other as nothing more than a man and a woman rather than a princess and a nobleman. With Matthew, the barriers of position she had always been bound by vanished.

"Since last we met, I have learned to be bolder in word and deed. I have discovered the only way to achieve what one really wants is to pursue it."

"And what do you really want?"

"You," she said without thinking.

"Me?" Surprise washed across his face.

She drew a deep breath. Perhaps it was time to tell him the truth. Or part of it anyway. "Come, now, Matthew, surely you have realized that by now?"

"No." His brows drew together. "I most certainly did not realize that."

"Why else would I have come to you?"

"Admittedly, I have been curious about your true motives. However, we were together once and you tossed me aside without a second thought. Discarded me like so much excess baggage. Treated me like—"

"That is quite enough," she said sharply. She had not had considerably more sleep than he and at this moment felt every bit as disagreeable. "I am extremely tired of hearing how poorly I treated you. I know that and I have apologized. It was wrong. I was a terrible creature for what I did to you. I am truly sorry, but I will not apologize again."

"Gracious as always, Princess," he said dryly.

She stared at him, anger welling within her. "And what of you, my lord? Have you nothing to say?"

"Not really."

"No?" She stared in disbelief. "You, who swore to love me until your dying day? You did nothing to stop me from—"

"You left when I was asleep. It was the act of a coward."

She sucked in a hard breath. "It most certainly was not!"

"What would you call it?"

"Prudent. It would have been most awkward otherwise."

"No doubt. If I was awake you would have had to explain to me how you'd lied about who you really were."

"I said it was awkward!" She struggled to regain a sense of calm. "Regardless, when you awoke, you did not follow me."

"Oh, but I did, Princess." His tone was cool. "I learned where the Avalonian delegation was staying in Paris and I went there to find you. Or rather, I sought the princess's companion. Imagine my surprise when I saw you in a carriage, and a guard pointed out his princess. Her Highness. My wife. You."

She winced. "I am certain that was most upsetting."

His head snapped toward her and his eyes widened. "Upsetting? You think it was simply upsetting?"

"I said *most*."

"Yes, well, it was indeed *most* upsetting." Sarcasm colored his tone. "Rather on a par with the cut of a jacket being a bit off or the gait of a horse being not quite right. Most upsetting, indeed." He snorted with disgust.

"Still, I should think, at this point, you would be . . . well"—she met his gaze directly—"beyond it."

"Beyond it?" He glared. "I am beyond it. I have put it, all of it, firmly in the past."

"Then why do you keep bringing it up?"

"I . . ." He narrowed his eyes and stared at the road before them. "You are driving me mad, Princess."

"Good! You are the most annoying man I have ever met and I cannot imagine what I was thinking to come back to you."

"*You* have come back to *me*?" He raised a brow. "I thought I was incidental. I thought you came to England to write the history of a long-dead relative."

"That too!" She crossed her arms over her chest and stared unseeing at the passing countryside.

Why on earth did she bother? He was indeed the most irritating man in the world. Still, he was also the only man in the world who triggered such depths of emotion and passion, anger and excitement, the only man who made her feel that life itself was not worth living without him.

Annoying creature.

Long minutes passed with only the sound of the horses' hooves and the crunch of the carriage wheels on the road to break the silence. Tatiana had already told him more than she had planned. It was not her intention to tell him she wanted him. Or cared for him. Or loved him. At least not yet.

"So, what you really want is me," Matthew said with a chuckle in his voice.

She refused to look at him.

"I daresay that puts a whole different light on the matter." His voice was smug and she bit back a sarcastic reply. "I don't recall ever having been pursued by a princess before."

"You are not being pursued," she said curtly.

"Chased, then."

She clenched her teeth. "Not at all."

"Hunted?"

"Only if I had a weapon," she muttered.

He laughed, and she turned toward him indignantly. "I am so pleased, my lord, that I could lighten your mood."

"You have not merely lightened my mood, my dear lovely princess, you have quite lifted my outlook on life itself." He grinned, a self-satisfied smirk that made her want to hit him. Hard. More than once.

"Does this mean you will be more pleasant in the morning?"

"I shall be more amenable morning, afternoon and night."

Without warning, he wrapped his free arm around her, slid her against him and kissed her firmly. He drew back and stared into her eyes. "See what happens when one tells the truth?"

"I do," she said, her voice oddly breathless.

"Anything else you wish to tell me?"

"Yes." She stared up at him and swallowed hard. "That was quite, quite nice."

He studied her for a moment, then laughed and released her. "You do not trust me, do you, Princess?"

She folded her hands in her lap and smiled. "Nor do you trust me, my lord."

"Yet another instance in which we are well matched."

"I agree." She reached beneath the seat. "And we should seal our agreement."

"Ah, the traditional Avalonian traveler's toast." He chuckled. "Very well, today I will join you."

She pulled out the flask, poured two cups and handed him one.

"To a safe and successful journey," he said, lifting his mug.

"Excellent, Matthew." She smiled. "Now you are in the spirit of the adventure."

He took a deep swallow and gasped.

"Do you not like it?" She studied him closely. His face was an interesting shade of scarlet.

"It's . . . it's"—his eyes watered and his voice was strangled—"rather, well, thick, isn't it? And oddly flavored."

"Do you think so?" She stared down into her cup. "I have heard it is an acquired taste."

"Acquired under force, no doubt." He studied the contents of his own cup with what could only be called morbid curiosity. "Your people actually drink this voluntarily?"

"Then you do not like it." Odd that she should feel

so disappointed, as she had never been overly fond of the drink herself.

"I didn't say that. But you're right, it's an acquired taste. It just takes some getting used to, that's all."

"Probably." She shrugged, squinted her eyes closed, held her breath and downed her drink. She opened her eyes to find Matthew staring with a bemused expression. "Is something amiss?"

"No." He stared at her curiously. "You really don't like it, do you?"

"Not at all."

"Then why—"

"Because it is part and parcel of being Avalonian. The heritage of my people. A traveler's toast is tradition." She was almost beginning to believe the lie herself. "And Avalonian traditions call for Avalonian brandy." That much, at least, could be true. "Do you not understand?"

"I do understand. Completely." His gaze was thoughtful. "I was just wondering, though, how far one would really go for tradition."

Chapter 9

*T*he sun had just dipped below the horizon when at last Matthew and Tatiana arrived at her London residence.

The butler and who knew how many servants had, no doubt, observed their arrival but were well enough trained not to raise so much as a single brow. Nonetheless, Tatiana was certain belowstairs would buzz with gossip over the princess's absence and subsequent return with a handsome man by her side and not even a maid in sight as chaperone. Scandalous behavior, they would whisper, but what can one expect from a foreigner? Tatiana bit back a grin at how scandalized they would be if they suspected even a morsel of the truth.

A handful of assorted servants stood at a discreet distance in the shadows of the foyer, probably with hopes of overhearing every word she and Matthew exchanged.

"I do not understand why you have brought me here rather than your cottage," she said in a low voice and tried not to yawn. The journey to London was uneventful as far as she knew. At least nothing, save brandy at midday, had awakened her.

"I have a few things to take care of in the city this evening, therefore this is much more convenient." Matthew's circumspect tone matched her own. "And I think it would be best if you arranged for a proper coach and driver for the continuation of our travels."

"Really?" She raised a brow. "And what of your conditions? Living on your finances and all that?"

"Silly, wasn't it? You were right, my conditions were simply to put you in your place. It will be much more comfortable to travel with a coach and driver, especially as the next lady on your list resides at Effington Hall, another full day's drive from here. Besides, if we were truly married, what is yours would be mine as well. You may consider it a portion of the dowry I never received."

"I see," she said, brushing aside an odd touch of displeasure at his change of heart. "I suppose I may bring a maid as well?"

"I think not." He shook his head and leaned closer. "I have not abandoned all my conditions and I rather like the idea of sharing the privacy of a coach with you and you alone."

Delight shivered through her at the wicked note in his voice. "Do you, my lord?"

"I do indeed. If, of course, you can stay awake." He grinned. "I shall see you next week, then." He turned to go.

"Next week? What do you mean?" She grabbed his arm. "We are not leaving tomorrow? You are not staying here?"

"I daresay that would not be at all proper."

"Nonsense. This is a huge house, fully capable of accommodating another guest. There is a veritable army of servants, and I do—"

"*And* I have business to attend to that may last well into the night. And tomorrow, there is work I must get back to," he said firmly. "Unless, there is some reason why the delay of a few days would create difficulty with your history writing."

"Not at all, my lord." She met his gaze directly. "Princess Sophia's story has waited half a century thus far; a few more days scarcely matter. Take all the time you require."

"Excellent. Then the Princess Tatiana shall reside here with her retinue of retainers and shall attend to whatever royal details need attending to. Next week"—promise flashed in his eyes—"Lord and Lady Matthew shall be on their way."

"It is not precisely what I had in mind."

He laughed, then took her hand and drew it to his lips. "My dear princess, I imagine, or hope, that you are not used to being the pursuer, and I have rarely been the object of pursuit." He brushed his mouth across the back of her glove. "However, it is my experience that the chase is not nearly as satisfying when it is too brief, the prize won too quickly or too easily. I should hate for your satisfaction to be either quick or brief."

"Matthew!" Her eyes widened and her face burned.

"You are even more lovely than usual when a blush is on your cheeks." He grinned. "And your mouth is shut. You make it tempting to give the servants something more to talk about."

He turned over her hand and placed a kiss in the center of her gloved palm. A wave of pure desire spread from his touch and she wanted nothing more than to drag him up the stairs and into her bed.

"Sleep well, my princess." Matthew released her and headed for the door.

"In a week's time I could change my mind, you know," she called after him. "I could decide the prize is not worth the effort of the chase."

His all-too-smug voice drifted back to her. "You won't."

He chuckled, and was gone before she could so much as utter an appropriate retort.

She laughed to herself. She could wait another week, and it might well be a good idea to give him time to dwell on what had passed between them and what had not. And what lay ahead.

"Your Highness?" Katerina's amused voice sounded from the shadows.

"Yes?" Tatiana absently pulled off her gloves.

The change in Matthew since she had admitted wanting him was at once wonderful and frightening. She was not quite sure how, but he had used her admission to wrest the upper hand in their relationship. Even if he did not know all her secrets, he now knew the most important. Still, for the first time since their reunion she felt that glorious thrill of anticipation that came from knowing that the man you wanted, wanted you.

"Given the expression on your face, I gather all is going well with your Lord Matthew." Katerina stepped into the foyer.

"He is not *my* Lord Matthew." Tatiana handed her gloves to Katerina, then pulled off her hat and pelisse, passing them both to the other woman, who handed them to a maid. "But he soon will be."

Katerina laughed. "I did not doubt it for a moment, Your Highness."

"And you, dear friend"—Tatiana hooked her arm through Katerina's and they strolled into the grand salon—"how have you fared since yesterday? I cannot imagine it has been easy putting up with your cousin for any length of time, given the temper he was in when I left."

"In truth, Dimitri has not been at all difficult."

"Really?" Tatiana sank down onto a soft sofa, all the more delightful given the long carriage ride. Of course, they would continue their travels in a far more comfortable coach. A very private, closed coach. Pity she would have to sleep through most of it. "Is he still sulking, then?"

"I wouldn't be at all surprised; however, I cannot say. He is not here at the moment." Katerina perched on the sofa beside her, a vague expression of unease flitting across her face.

Tatiana ignored it. It was not unusual for talk of Dimitri to prompt such looks, particularly when the captain's views clashed with his princess's. "I would ask him to join us for dinner, but I thought we could eat privately in my rooms. I am famished, of course; I do wish I could eat when I travel."

"The brandy still puts you to sleep, then?"

"Thank goodness. However, I have been wondering . . ." Tatiana drew her brows together. "Katerina, do you think . . . is it possible that Avalonian brandy is, well, not very good?"

"I cannot imagine such a thing." Indignation rang in Katerina's voice. "I have never cared for it, but I am not a connoisseur of brandy. I understand it is an acquired taste."

"It scarcely matters, I suppose." Tatiana leaned toward her friend. "I have all sorts of interesting things to tell you. Most of which I prefer not be over—"

"Forgive me for interrupting, Your Highness"—reluctance showed in Katerina's eyes—"but you should know, Dimitri is no longer in London."

"Where is he?" Tatiana asked, ignoring an immediate sense of unease. "He did not follow me, did he?"

"No." Katerina drew the word out slowly.

"Please tell me he has a rendezvous with a woman in Paris or an assignation with a lady in Vienna."

"I would like nothing better than to tell you just that, but"—Katerina winced—"he has returned to Avalonia."

"What?" Tatiana sprang to her feet, Katerina a split second behind. "How could he?"

"He thought—"

"I know exactly what he thought." Tatiana clenched her fists and paced the room. Katerina followed at her heels. "He thought he would scurry home to tell my father I am looking for the Heavens with a man of questionable reputation—"

"I understood Dimitri had determined your Lord Matthew was of admirable character."

Tatiana waved away the protest. "Of course he did, but they do not like one another. You should have seen the two of them. Like dogs growling over a bone. Who knows what Dimitri will tell my family about him?

"Furthermore, Dimitri thinks my quest is both ridiculous and dangerous, although frankly what I have seen of England thus far does not seem especially hazardous. He refuses to allow me to live my own life if it conflicts with what he thinks is a proper life for a princess. And I refuse to allow him to dissuade me from what I want." Tatiana swiveled and nearly ran into Katerina. "Swear to me you will not tell him or anyone what I am about to say."

"I promise." Katerina's eyes widened.

"I do not want to be a princess. I want to be a wife."

For a long moment Katerina stared silently. "I wondered when you would admit it aloud." A weak smile curved her lips. "I have suspected as much since Paris."

"You have? I thought I hid it rather well."

"You forget, Your Highness, I have known you all my life." Katerina studied her carefully. "Then your search for the Heavens really is nothing more than a ploy to be with your Lord Matthew."

"Not at all. My purpose has always been twofold." Tatiana thought for a moment. "If I can return this treasure, this symbol of the monarchy, I will have done something truly worthy for my country. I will have no qualms, no self-reproach, about abdicating my position."

"You would do that?"

"I would. Or rather, I will." It was a relief to at last say it out loud.

"You have considered all the ramifications of such an act?" Katerina's gaze met hers. "Succession and other matters?"

"I have thought of little else. But in truth, in the scheme of royal succession, I am"—she shrugged—"superfluous."

"Princess! How can you—"

"Come, now, Katerina, even you can see the reality of my position. Unless, God forbid, there was a tragedy of untold proportions and the lives of my father and bothers were lost, I would never succeed to the crown. And that is as it should be.

"I am good for nothing more than forging a strategic alliance for Avalonia through marriage, and that is out of the question." Her voice was firm. "I married once for my country, and once was quite enough.

"But I will not be able to find the Heavens if Dimitri comes back with an edict from my father demanding my return. I will have no choice." She turned and resumed her pacing. "Blast Dimitri anyway. He could not trust that I—"

"It's not quite as simple as trust, Your Highness. Matters have changed, and your safety—"

"I am perfectly safe."

"—is very much in question now." Katerina drew a deep breath. "We have learned that your cousin is in England."

"Valentina?" A heavy weight settled in the pit of Tatiana's stomach. "That does complicate matters."

The Princess Valentina was beautiful and brilliant, and as cold as she was lovely. The daughter of the present king's younger brother, Valentina had always believed she would be a better ruler than any of her cousins, all of whom would have to die without issue for Valentina to legitimately succeed to the throne.

The princess was older than Tatiana and had recently been exiled from Avalonia for her nefarious activities aimed at overthrowing the rightful ruling branch of the House of Pruzinsky. The woman was a widow twice over and Tatiana was not alone in suspecting Valentina was behind the untimely end of inconvenient spouses. Yet, while Valentina took great delight in fomenting unrest among the people of Avalonia to further her own cause, she had not stooped so low as to have her uncle or cousins removed from this life. Not yet anyway.

There was a time when Valentina's name alone would have triggered unease and even fear in Tatiana. Indeed, as a child, she had always suspected the older girl was something of a witch. A suspicion that only deepened with age, Valentina's beauty and the unscrupulous way she used it to maneuver men.

It was a surprise, and more than a little gratifying, to note that the thought of Valentina no longer prompted fear but rather caution, determination and the conviction, deep inside her, that Tatiana might well now be a match for her formidable cousin.

"Does he think she is in England for a reason," Tatiana said slowly, "or is this nothing more than coincidence?"

"Given Dimitri's reaction when he learned of your cousin's whereabouts, I am certain he does not think her presence in this country is innocent. He left at once for Avalonia."

"Did he? That is most unusual. If he truly thought I was in any kind of danger, he would never leave the country. I cannot imagine . . ." At once the truth hit her, and she narrowed her eyes. "Does he have men following me?"

Katerina shook her head. "I do not know. However, I would not be surprised."

"Nor would I. He has probably had someone following me all along." Tatiana gritted her teeth. "How dreadfully annoying."

"Your safety is his responsibility," Katerina said pointedly. "You cannot fault the man for doing his duty."

"I can," she sighed in resignation. "But I will not. However, Dimitri's absence and Valentina's presence does change everything." Tatiana sank into a chair, propped her elbows on the armrests and laced her fingers together. "There are several reasons why Valentina might be in England."

"She has nowhere else to go?" Katerina said wryly and sat on the sofa.

"Nonsense. She has a great deal of money, she can go anywhere. Her presence could indeed be coincidence."

Katerina snorted her disbelief.

"Granted, none of us believe that."

"She could be hunting for a new husband and considers England fertile ground as yet unplowed. Or she could . . ." Katerina shook her head helplessly.

Tatiana's gaze met her friend's. "Or she could know the Heavens of Avalonia are lost and possibly somewhere in England."

"And she could further know that is exactly why you are now here," Katerina said softly.

Tatiana groaned and slumped back in the chair. "How could she have found out? Only a handful of my family's closest advisors know about the jewels."

"Yes, but was not a trusted councilor of your brother's found to be in league with the princess? Is it not possible he knew about the jewels?"

"Possible and probable." Tatiana rubbed her forehead. "Damnation."

Katerina gasped. "Your Highness."

"Forgive me. Desperate times call for desperate words, and that was the best I could think of at the moment."

"If that was the best . . ." Katerina murmured.

"It does not bode well, does it?" Tatiana cast her a weak smile. She straightened in the chair and drew a deep breath. "There is little I can do about Valentina until I know exactly where she is and what she is planning.

"As for Dimitri, even at top speed, he cannot possibly travel from London to Avalonia in substantially less than a fortnight. I have at least a month to find the jewels and—"

"Win back your lord?" Katerina teased.

"Exactly."

"I suggest, Your Highness, at this point it might well be wise to tell him the truth."

"I should, I suppose." Tatiana drummed her fingers on the armrest. "It will come as no surprise. He has not believed my story from the beginning. He does not trust me."

"And do you trust him?"

"I do not know. I want to. I will confess, I agreed wholeheartedly with Dimitri's insistence on keeping my quest for the jewels from Lord Matthew. I thought it was wise at the time and it may still be." Her gaze met the other woman's. "You see, at first he appeared somewhat reluctant to accept my money. You recall those ridiculous conditions of his about living on his finances?"

Katerina nodded.

"I thought it was a result of both his own pride and his desire to make my life miserable. Now he seems more than willing to make use of my fortune."

"Perhaps he no longer wishes to make your life miserable?"

"One can only hope," Tatiana said under her breath. "I want to trust him, and indeed my heart longs to believe in him. But my head refuses to ignore the fact that I have truly known the man for barely more than a week. While I am confident he is a man of honor and principle"—she grimaced—"we both know my heart has not always been as discriminating as my head."

"But you are both older and wiser now."

"Is one ever wiser when it comes to matters of the heart? I cannot allow my emotions to dictate my actions." She shook her head. "Lord Matthew is a clever man, and as such is not interested in balloon flight in and of itself."

"That is clever."

"He is not so foolish as to believe there is any true future in flying."

"Extremely clever."

"He also realizes there is potential profit to be made from balloons, or rather, as he prefers to call them, aerostats."

"It does sound nicely scientific that way."

"Or scientifically pretentious," Tatiana scoffed. "It is a characteristic of men, I suspect, to make their toys sound legitimate. Regardless, his desire is to earn enough money to invest in shipping and thereby make his fortune."

"Admirable I would say."

"Indeed it is, but . . ." She paused, not at all liking the way this would sound. "For a moment, consider the possibility—remote, I am sure—that a man wanting to make his fortune, even a man of honor, might well consider, or at least be tempted—"

"To take a fortune in jewels should it drop into his lap," Katerina finished. "Oh, dear. Perhaps you are right to be cautious."

"Or perhaps I am simply a fool who has still not learned how to determine those she cannot trust from those she can." Tatiana shook her head. "My instincts tell me he is a good and honorable man. I would trust him with my life without a second thought, but the future of my country lies with the Heavens, and that I cannot place in jeopardy."

"So you will continue to play this game of secrets?"

"I do not see another choice, and I dearly wish there was one. He is not exactly as I remember him; he is far more serious, but he is exactly what I want." She took her friend's hand. "I feared, in this past year, that I might have made a grave error. That it was a mistake to care for him once and to continue to care for him. He is annoying and arrogant and he has the most irritating habit of bringing up my past crimes.

"But I know I have never felt so . . . so right as I do with him. As if I were only half alive before him. And now I feel as if I can do anything if I am by his side. Reach out and grasp the stars in my hand, if I so wish. It is quite remarkable. Time and separation have only strengthened my feelings for him. Even without his balloons"—she grinned—"he makes me feel as though I could fly."

Katerina laughed. "It is most gratifying to see you in love."

"And with love"—Tatiana rose and pulled Katerina to her feet—"is it not said all things are possible?"

"Indeed it is. But, as you well know, love alone is not enough"—Katerina's gaze searched her princess's face—"without trust."

"I do wish you had not mentioned trust."

"And honesty."

Tatiana wrinkled her nose. "I am not nearly as fond of honesty as I am of love."

"But is it fair to—"

"Probably not." She shook her head. "It does get

more and more complicated, does it not? With Valentina about, I cannot in all conscience keep him completely unaware. He deserves some warning. Not that I think she is truly dangerous—"

Katerina raised a brow.

"At least allow me to lie to myself on occasion."

"Lying to yourself may well prove a greater danger than your cousin."

"Perhaps. However, I will think of something to tell Lord Matthew." Tatiana shook her head. "When he left, I thought we had all the time in the world; now there is no time to waste. We must think of a way to lure him away from his work. Or perhaps"—an altogether excellent idea popped into her head—"we need not get him away from his work at all." She crossed the room to a small writing table and sat down.

"You have quite changed the subject." Katerina studied her suspiciously. "Are you going to tell him the truth or not?"

"Don't be absurd," Tatiana said without thinking and pulled open a drawer, searching for paper and pens. "I cannot possibly tell him the truth about everything."

Katerina narrowed her eyes. "You cannot?"

"What I meant to say is that I cannot tell him the truth *yet*," Tatiana said quickly. "I will when the time is right."

"I understand your hesitation about the Heavens. However"—Katerina pinned her with a firm gaze—"there are other matters, other truths, he should know."

"Possibly."

"Is it not past time?"

"Probably." Tatiana cast her friend an irritated

glance. "I do so hate it when you play the part of my conscience."

Katerina adopted a prim manner, but her eyes twinkled. "It is my job, Your Highness."

"Indeed it is, and you do it far too well." She sighed with resignation. "I will tell him what he should know—"

"What he deserves to know," Katerina said firmly.

"Of course. At the first opportunity. But . . ." Tatiana hesitated for a long moment. "I must confess, I am somewhat afraid of how he might react. I do not think I could bear it if he was angry, or worse, did not care."

"Still . . ."

"Yes, yes, I know. And I shall make every effort to inform him of the facts, although I have no idea how." She shook her head. "How do I tell a man I did not carry out my promise to annul our marriage? What words do I use to tell him he is still my husband?

"And I am, in truth, Lady Matthew."

"You are in remarkably good spirits, all things considered." Ephraim sat with his feet propped up on his desk, a cigar in one hand, a whiskey in the other.

"I am, Ephraim." Matt's position mirrored the other man's. "I am indeed."

The hour was late, but neither man was in the mood to retire. They were the only two left in the *Messenger* building and Matt could well understand his friend's fondness for spending his evenings here in the solitude of this place where the silence late at night reverberated deep in a man's soul. A reverent temple to the gods of mechanics and progress.

"I'm sorry I could not uncover anything that might be useful to you." Ephraim puffed thoughtfully on his cigar. "Aside from recent unrest in Avalonia, apparently resolved at this point, there is little else I could find. And that's really only interesting if one looks at the factions involved."

"Oh?"

"Apparently members of the royal family of Avalonia are not especially fond of one another. It seems while your princess's branch of the House of Prune-something—"

"Pruzinsky."

"That's it. Anyway, while they have been the rightful rulers for the last few centuries, various and assorted relatives have regularly challenged them for power." Ephraim snorted with amusement. "It's almost a tradition."

"Probably triggered by the brandy."

"As for this Princess Sophia, there's not much I can tell you that you don't already know." Ephraim drained the rest of his glass and eyed the bottle on the desk. "Ignoring small skirmishes, minor uprisings and the like, the last major insurrection in Avalonia was half a century ago. The princess's husband was killed and she fled to England with her daughter. A few months later she married the Earl of Worthington and spent the rest of her days living in a castle somewhere in the country." With an air of regret, he turned his attention away from the bottle and toward his friend.

"There's little of interest after the marriage. Lady Worthington's life was pretty sedate, from what I hear. No scandal, no intrigue—"

"No murder?"

"Not a thing." The publisher shook his head in disgust. "The woman rarely left her castle."

"And before her marriage?"

"Again, nothing you don't know. You're already aware that the lady was sheltered by several families. Then she met the earl, married him and that's it. She died about twenty years ago. As I said, there isn't much to tell."

"That's what I thought."

Ephraim studied Matt over the end of his cigar. "You still think *your* princess is up to something, don't you?"

"More than ever." Matt thought for a moment. "Do you know what happened to the daughter?"

"That one was easy. The daughter married a viscount. Beaumont, I believe. The current viscount is her son."

"Really? For some reason I was under the impression they were all dead." Matt took a sip of his whiskey, then a puff of the cigar, relishing the mix of flavors. "One would think, if one were indeed writing a family history, that the first people you would go to would be family."

"Keep in mind I've had little time to look into this, but I did learn both the mother and son have been out of the country. I have not yet determined when they are expected to return, or, indeed, if they already have."

"And this history is so pressing, so urgent, it could not wait?"

"It does make one wonder." Ephraim grinned. "I'm damn proud of you for thinking of it. We'll make a journalist out of you yet."

"Don't count on it, my friend. What little I've written thus far is the work of an amateur."

"I want the story, not the words. Words can be edited."

"Don't expect to get either. I plan on remaining an

amateur." Matt considered the whiskey in his glass and wondered if it was yet time for a refill. "You, Ephraim, have your gaze set too firmly on reality for me. I want to see the possibilities in the distance, not the facts of the here and now. I've enjoyed the feel of a ship and the sea beneath me, and a gondola and the open sky and who knows what lies ahead."

"On that score, how goes the work? Will you be able to make enough progress in the coming week to . . ."

For a long time they discussed the progression of Matt's work, the possible contenders for the prize, the mysterious group sponsoring the design competition as well as the latest political scandals and life in general. They talked late into the night of matters both noteworthy and trivial until Ephraim's bottle was empty and Matt's cigars little more than lingering blue smoke and scattered ash.

"You never did explain one thing." Ephraim squinted at the other man. "Why are you in such a bloody fine mood tonight?"

"This morning," Matt corrected.

"This morning, last night, the day after tomorrow." Ephraim studied him with the kind of suspicious stare seen only on the faces of men who have shared a long night and a great deal of drink. "There is something you have not told me."

"Indeed there is."

"Well, aren't you going to tell me now?"

Matt grinned.

"Not for publication." Ephraim heaved a sigh. "All I do these days is work, you know. I have to live vicariously through you. The least you can do is share your exploits. If I had a princess, I'd share with you."

"You're right. It's only fair. Very well." Matt

paused for dramatic effect. "She wants me, Ephraim, she said it herself. She wants me."

"Wants you? You mean . . ."

Matt's grin widened.

Ephraim blew a long, low whistle. "Oh, that is good. She wants you. Bloody hell. Some men have all the luck." Ephraim planted his elbows on the desk and propped his chin in his hands. "And what do you plan on doing about that?"

"Why, old friend, I'm going to do what any man who finds himself in my position would do." Matt leaned back, puffed on his stub of a cigar and blew a perfect smoke ring toward the ceiling. "I'm going to let her have me."

Chapter 10

"*D*id you miss me?"

Tatiana's voice registered somewhere in the dim recesses of Matt's mind, but he paid it no heed. She was in his head as often as not these days, although her face, her form, her voice did not usually intrude when he was deep in thought.

"My lord"—impatience colored the words—"I asked if you missed me."

Matt jerked his head up and stared at the figure in the stables' entry, for a moment not entirely certain if she was real. He shook his head and squinted against the sunlight behind her. "What are you doing here?"

"That is not at all the greeting I had hoped for." Tatiana sauntered into the stables.

"Nonetheless, that is all the greeting you shall get." He drew his brows together. "Especially as you've not answered my question. Once again, what are you doing here?"

"I shall answer your question when you answer mine." She located a battered stool, similar to the one he sat on if not quite as steady, dusted it off, then pulled it up to the table, seating herself across from him. She folded her hands and rested them primly on the rough wooden surface. "Did you miss me?"

"No," he snapped.

"Come, now, Matthew." She rolled her gaze toward the heavens. "I do not believe you for a moment. Surely you missed me a bit? Perhaps as the horse—"

"Why are you here?"

"Oh, dear, I quite forgot. It is morning and you are never at your best in the morning. You shall have to work on that."

He drew a deep breath for calm. "Indeed I shall. Now, then—"

"Well, *I* missed *you*."

"As charming as that is to hear, I must admit to a certain amount of skepticism. It's been but two days since we parted. I would think you would not miss me for at least fifteen—"

"Matthew." Her voice was cool and controlled, in the manner of a reproachful governess. "First of all, you have apparently forgotten but you did promise to be more agreeable in the morning. You are not at all pleasant to be with at this time of day. And secondly," her eyes narrowed, "you have no idea whether I missed you or not. Not yesterday, nor the day before, nor the months before that. For all you know, I might have been pining away, counting the hours, the days—"

"The year," he said pointedly.

"—until I could return to you. Now, if you bring up the subject again for anything other than rational discussion—which I might consider, although I am not inclined to at the moment—I shall be forced to have Captain Petrov, *Dimitri*, shoot you."

"Hah!" Matt got to his feet, braced his hands on the table edge and loomed toward her. "He can't shoot me. This is my country, not yours. He would be hung for it."

"Nonetheless, he is my subject. He will do as I command regardless of the legal ramifications. Furthermore, he would quite enjoy shooting you. He would consider it a pleasure." She slipped off her stool and mimicked his stance. "As would I!"

His gaze locked with hers and for an endless moment they glared at one another. Her lush green eyes flashed in the shadows. Wild tendrils of golden hair escaped from their knotted confinement to tease her cheeks and dance along the lines of her lovely neck. Her breasts heaved enticingly with every breath. She was magnificent and damn near irresistible.

He tried to ignore the racing beat of his pulse in her presence. The dryness of his mouth. The tightness in his chest. It was lust, of course, simple desire, perhaps even anticipation, but nothing more complicated than that. Still, whatever the cause of the tumult in his stomach and elsewhere, he was hard-pressed to remain annoyed when she fixed him with the erotic promise of those eyes.

"Very well, Your Highness, I *may* have missed you for a moment."

"I thought you might." She grinned in a knowing manner.

"And?"

"I *may* have missed you for a moment as well." She hopped back on the stool. "As for why I am here, I have been doing a great deal of thinking."

He sat down with a resigned groan. "I'm not at all sure I like the sound of that."

"I have come to fetch you so we may be on our

way." Tatiana's tone was casual and he didn't trust it
for a minute. "I have decided my work cannot wait."

"I thought a few days wouldn't matter."

"I had forgotten that the anniversary of the birth of
the Princess Sophia is fast approaching and I did
wish to have this history compiled before then." The
explanation flowed from her lips smoothly. Far too
smoothly. As if it had been rehearsed.

"Really?" He raised a brow. "When?"

"Next month," she said without hesitation.

"What day?"

Indecision flashed in her eyes.

He smirked. He was right. This was another lie.

"The fourth." She smirked right back. "I am certain
it is the fourth."

"Regardless"—he nodded at the papers and assorted paraphernalia spread across the table—"I too
have work that cannot wait."

"What exactly are you doing?"

"I told you. I am trying to develop a type of heating system, really more of a method than a—"

"Yes, yes, I believe you mentioned that." She
waved impatiently, her gaze skimming across the
mechanical bits and pieces on the table. "But it seems
rather complicated and I must confess I do not quite
understand."

"I explained much of this on the way to Canterbury." He fixed her with a pointed stare. "You found
it so fascinating you were compelled to sleep
through it."

"I do that in carriages," she murmured. "However,
I am fully awake now and would very much like to
hear about your efforts."

"Very well." He shrugged in an offhand manner as
if he didn't care one way or the other but he did. "As

you know, a balloon can be inflated by the simple process of building a fire and funneling the resulting hot air into the balloon. Here, let me show you."

He reached for the papers covering a good portion of the tabletop. Every free inch of the large sheets was jammed with sketches and notations. He found the one he wanted, then stepped around the table to her side, smoothing the drawing out in front of her.

"You can see what I mean." He pointed out the various elements, accompanied by a cursory explanation. "The problem occurs when one tries to keep the balloon aloft as the air cools."

"That much I do know."

"In the past"—he pulled out another drawing to illustrate his words—"a fire on a grate beneath the balloon has been employed, but that requires carrying a great deal of fuel."

"Which is why many of your balloonists, aeronauts, have turned to hydrogen," she said.

He nodded. Even now, it was exceedingly pleasant to note she had taken the time during their separation to acquaint herself with his interests. She had definitely thought of him. Perhaps she had missed him after all.

"Yes, but hydrogen carries with it an entirely new set of problems, including production and its combustible nature. Ultimately, the length of an ascent is limited.

"Hydrogen can only be created on the ground and it's a massive and tedious process. But heating air is child's work."

"Still you do need a fire."

"Indeed. However, the question that now arises is just how great a fire is necessary. If one wants to reduce the size of the fire, the best way to do that is to use a substance that burns at a hotter temperature. Oil burns hotter than wood, as do spirits, alcohol, and so forth. I have experimented with a number of possibilities. What I propose to do is fill the balloon itself—"

"Aerostat," she said sweetly.

"Aerostat with hot air in a conventional fashion. Then keep it aloft by burning something far more convenient to carry. Look here." He shuffled through the assorted papers until he found the one with his most current design. "While it is still necessary to have a heating area larger than that provided by a single flame, I have determined binding several containers together, each burning independently with its own fuel source will produce the desired effect."

She glanced up at him. "Will it work?"

"It has worked, although not as well as I would like. I am still tinkering with the valves, as well as the fuel. I have tried a number of combinations. Types of oils, various spirits—"

"Spirits? You mean brandy? Such as Avalonian brandy?"

He laughed. "That would, no doubt, be an appropriate use for Avalonian brandy."

Her expression fell. "You really do not like it, then."

"Nothing of the sort," he said quickly. "You yourself said it was an acquired taste. I simply have not acquired a taste for it yet."

"I have an excellent idea." She beamed up at him. "While I do have a bottle or two with me now—"

"Traveler's toast?"

"Exactly. We brought quite a lot with us to England."

"With your entire retinue traveling and toasting,

you must go through quite a bit of the stuff," he said wryly.

"Tradition, Matthew. However, as it may prove of use to you, I will send someone back for more. While we wait, you can direct the packing of"—she waved her arm in a wide gesture—"all this."

"Packing?"

"You said yourself you could not leave your work. Therefore, I have arranged for your work to accompany us."

He shook his head in confusion. "What are you talking about?"

"In addition to the coach and driver—your suggestion, I might add—I have brought a wagon and footmen to assist you."

"You have what?" He strode to the open door and out into the morning sunlight.

A private traveling coach of a modest size stood in the dirt drive. A large wagon drawn by a stout team of horses waited nearby. Several saddled horses were tethered to the cart. The woman he'd seen with her the other day stood patiently beside the vehicle. A half dozen or so servants lounged about and straightened respectfully at his appearance.

"Now there is no reason why we cannot be on our way." Tatiana came up behind him. "Although judging by the clutter surrounding your work, it will take hours to actually begin our travels."

His disbelieving gaze moved from coach to wagon to servants and finally settled on Tatiana's expectant face. Matt wasn't certain if he was annoyed by the arrangements she'd made without so much as a by-your-leave, or impressed with her determination. She was certainly not the same reserved creature she once was.

"Before you protest," she said quickly, "do keep in mind you said you no longer had any difficulties using my resources."

"This is not a simple question of cost." He chose his words carefully. "I have no idea how such things are done in Avalonia, but we are in England. Our next stop is Effington Hall. The woman we wish to speak with is the matriarch of a powerful and extremely wealthy family. You simply cannot call on such a woman with a balloon—"

"Aerostat."

"—in tow. It's presumptuous. Rude. And very, very odd."

"Rather like gypsies of the sky, I would think."

He shook his head. "A romantic image, but nonetheless—"

"Sometimes, my dear Lord Matthew"—she heaved a long-suffering sigh—"I do wonder which of us has the true spirit of adventure. This is the first real adventure of my rather staid existence, while you have traveled to exciting places and sailed the seas and flown the heavens. You constantly take the most horrendous risks with your very life yet you are at once overly proper, terribly conventional and even a bit stiff. Not at all as I remember you."

"I most certainly am not stiff or proper," he said, ignoring how very stiff and proper he sounded. "I simply think—"

"I think you should listen to me." She crossed her arms over her chest. "When I realized that time was running short, I wrote to the Lady Helmsley mentioned in the princess's letter, only to discover she was now the Duchess of Roxborough, and the dowager duchess at that." She frowned. "Were you aware of this?"

"Yes."

"And you did not mention it?"

"I was going to."

"Well, it is of no consequence, I suppose. I had the letter dispatched to Effington Hall and received a reply last night."

He stared, hard-pressed to believe the lengths she had gone to. "Did you? And precisely what did you say?"

"I explained my mission, stating I was sanctioned by the royal family of Avalonia to write a history of Princess Sophia's travels and wished to speak to her."

"And she believed you?"

Tatiana's brows drew together. "Of course she believed me. You are the only one who does not believe me."

"Go on."

"I further explained that my husband's work was at a critical point and he could not leave it. And I could certainly not travel without him."

"And she said do come and bring his balloon and whatever goes along with it." Sarcasm dripped from his words.

"Something like that," Tatiana said firmly. "More along the lines of Lord and Lady Matthew are cordially invited to Effington Hall and it will be a great delight to see Lord Matthew's daring work at close hand." Her eyes narrowed. "She further stated she looked forward to seeing you again."

He resisted the urge to squirm. "Did she?"

"Whatever did she mean by that?"

"I have no idea."

"You do not lie as well as I do, my lord. You should probably give it up altogether."

"Forgive me if my skills are not as great as yours."

He blew a long breath. "Very well. The dowager is acquainted with members of my family. I may well have met her as a child, although I don't specifically remember."

"Matthew!" Her eyes widened with surprise. "Why did you not tell me?"

"Because it's of no real significance." He adopted his best no-nonsense manner. "It scarcely matters."

"Do not be absurd. Of course it—"

"Nonetheless," he cut in. He had no wish to continue this particular topic. "As you have contacted the dowager and made all the arrangements, I suppose there is nothing to be done but bow to your wishes. Very well, we will be off as soon as we complete packing the wagon."

She cast him a brilliant smile. "I knew you would see it my way."

"I don't see that you left me any choice."

"Leaving you a choice would be extremely foolish." She stepped close and smiled up at him. "And I am not extremely foolish."

"Tell me, Princess." He stared down at her with a rueful smile. "What is the urgency behind all this? What are you really after?"

"Nothing more than what has been lost." She gazed deep into his eyes, and for a moment he longed to accept what he saw there. "You still do not trust me, do you, Matthew?"

"No more than you trust me," he said softly.

She laughed, turned and walked away, joining the lady he suspected was her companion. The woman she had pretended to be when first they'd met. Tatiana signaled to one of the servants and spoke to him for a moment, no doubt sending him back to town to fetch the bottles of brandy.

He shook his head at the absurd thought. How ironic if it turned out Avalonian brandy, *her* Avalonian brandy, was just what his endeavors needed.

Another footman approached him in a respectful manner. "My lord," the man said with a brisk bob of his head, "where do you wish us to begin?"

"In here." Matt led the servant into the stables and pointed out what was needed and what could be left, urging caution and care.

Within moments the building and yard were alive with activity. Matt personally directed the folding of the vast yards of fabric that comprised the body of the balloon itself and the careful packing into a large, lined wicker trunk he had adapted for that very purpose. He issued a few more instructions and observed long enough to see that the men Tatiana had brought were excellent workers and could be trusted.

He caught himself studying her as well. She had an air of dignity about her but was nonetheless approachable. She moved with an effortless grace that stirred something deep within him. And her laugh rang through the late morning air like a song.

Why hadn't he gone after her?

The question took him by surprise. He'd never particularly considered it before. At the time, he was too lost in his own anger, sense of betrayal and, yes, self-pity, to take action. Certainly, once he'd learned she was a princess, it was logical to conclude her involvement with him was nothing more than a royal lark, despite their marriage. He'd been spurned by the woman he loved—his *wife*, no less—and he would not crawl after her like a pathetic dog. He cringed now at the memory. Had he really been that arrogant? That proud? That stupid?

He should have followed her. Tracked her to the

ends of the earth, if need be. Demanded to know from her lips if all they'd shared had been a lie. If she'd ever loved him. If she loved him still.

Would he follow her today?

He pushed the question aside. He had no time to consider it now; there was far too much to accomplish. It would take well into the afternoon to pack his equipment securely. Still, he could not dismiss the question altogether.

He collected his plans and diagrams, rolled them up, then carefully tucked them in a paper tube. Trying not to dwell on whatever feelings he'd had or might have still for Tatiana left his mind free to dwell on what this visit to Effington Hall might well mean.

He'd accepted they would travel there eventually, but he wasn't entirely prepared to do so yet. The Effington estate was far too close to Weston Manor for comfort. Logically, he knew the possibility of running into one of his brothers was slim. After all, he'd not seen any of them in the years since his return to England. Yet the closer he was to home, the greater the chances.

Home.

The very word caught at his heart. Perhaps—he stared into the shadows of the stables—it was time to go home. In that, Tatiana might well have been right. And indeed, wasn't his desire to protect his family as much a part of his willingness to go along with her quest as the woman herself?

At some point soon he would have to confront her about her interest in his grandmother and his family. He would have to force the truth from her, whatever it was. And with truth, perhaps, would come trust. And forgiveness.

He understood now why she'd left, but not the

manner of her leaving, nor why she'd stayed away. And he might never understand why she'd annulled their marriage.

Of course, if he had followed her . . .

He winced at the thought. As many mistakes as she had made, as many painful blows as she had dealt him, weren't his just as significant? Even, possibly, as painful? If he could not forgive her, how could he expect her to forgive him?

The question of trust, or lack of it, still lay between them. It would have to be resolved before . . . before what?

He didn't know what she really wanted, any more than he knew his own mind. Or his own heart.

That was the crux of it all, wasn't it?

For a mere six days in his life he had loved this woman, this princess, then spent the next fifteen months, three weeks and four days trying to forget everything about her.

The sound of her laughter echoed faintly in the distance.

Was it now time to at last accept that, in truth, he never had?

Chapter 11

$\mathcal{M}$att followed the liveried footman through the endless corridors of Effington Hall, and wondered vaguely if Tatiana's adventure was in truth nothing more than an endless journey.

The trip here had taken longer than expected. Effington Hall was a day's carriage ride from London, but they'd been unable to leave yesterday until well into the afternoon. While the coach was capable of acceptable speeds, the wagon was inexorably slow, and Tatiana insisted they travel throughout the night. Fortunately, while some of the servants had returned to London with Tatiana's companion, more than enough accompanied them to provide respite for the coachman and wagon driver.

As for Matt's lascivious inventions toward his former wife, the intriguing prospect of something intimate between them in a closed carriage gave way to the reality of traveling with this particular princess.

A scant quarter of an hour after they'd toasted the beginning of their journey, the woman fell asleep and stayed asleep until they'd stopped to refresh the horses. The toast was repeated and shortly thereafter, that, combined with the rocking motion of the carriage, no doubt, lulled her back to sleep. It was unusual, of course, but he'd heard of other people similarly affected. So much for encounters of an intimate nature in a coach. Still, they would have tonight.

He was beginning to be a bit concerned over her penchant for the brandy. Yet she didn't appear to feel any ill effects, and when they'd supped at the inn she'd had nothing save wine. Perhaps it was no more than obligation to a bizarre custom that kept her drinking the foul liquor.

Still, he did note the servants accompanying them did not take part in her toast. Tatiana quickly, and rather curiously, informed him the men were English, not Avalonian, and therefore had no such customs.

Matt envied them, as he was compelled to share her toast and had not yet developed a taste for her country's drink. He was fairly certain he never would, as the flavor of the liquor was not at all pleasant, with an odd aftertaste he could not place. He wisely thought not knowing the exact origin of Avalonian brandy may well make the stuff more palatable. He was wrong.

They had arrived at the Effington estate today a scant hour before sunset. Matt had been immediately approached by a groundskeeper, who'd said arrangements had been made for him near a lake. It was close enough to the house to be convenient, yet far enough away to allow him to work undisturbed. A large tent had been set up and Matt had spent the time since their arrival overseeing the unpacking of his equipment and instructing the Effington servants as to the arrangement of his things. Having men about eager to assist him was a luxury he could certainly get used to.

Luxury was apparent everywhere he looked, and for the first time in years he realized he rather missed the finer things in life. Still, there was no going back. If he wanted the life wealth made possible, he would have to earn it himself. Even if he reconciled with his family. Even if he married a princess.

That too was an idea that lingered in his mind more often than not these days. As recently as a week ago he would not have considered the possibility of a future with Her Highness. Now he couldn't help but wonder if fate had brought them together again because together was where they should be.

He followed the footman past any number of Effington ancestors, who stared forbiddingly down at him from paintings lining the walls as if they knew of his and Tatiana's deception.

She was right: He neither lied as well as she, nor was he as comfortable with deception as she appeared to be. It was one thing to fool Mrs. Wicklund and her husband about their marital status, but quite another to deceive the dowager duchess. He suspected their ruse would feel disconcertingly like lying to his own grandmother. She had never taken that well, nor, he wagered, would the dowager.

He'd hoped to convince Tatiana to reveal her true identity to the elderly woman. After all, a dowager duchess would not be overly intimidated by a princess.

But he'd not seen his *wife* since their arrival. Their assigned rooms in what was apparently a guest wing of the huge house were joined via a dressing room, but she had already gone downstairs when he'd returned.

He'd changed to evening clothes as quickly as possible. The idea of leaving Tatiana alone with a frail old woman, matriarch or not, sent a chill down his spine. Who knew what tale Her Highness might spin? Until he found out exactly what this princess was up to, fragile elderly women were probably not entirely safe.

At last, Matt was shown into a large parlor, empty save for Tatiana.

"Good evening, my lord." She stepped toward him with a welcoming smile, then paused. Her eyes widened. "I must say I have never seen you looking quite so . . ."

"Respectable?" He grinned.

"Exceedingly respectable." She considered him for a moment, her gaze assessing the deep blue coat, crisp white shirt and snug dark trousers. He resisted the urge to tug at his suddenly too-tight cravat, perfectly tied thanks to the assistance of a valet sent to help him dress. "And exceedingly handsome as well."

The compliment, coupled with the look in her eye, was at once pleasant and disconcerting. It had been a long time since he'd had the reason or the means to dress in attire this fine. "Whoever selected this clothing had excellent taste."

"I would not have had it otherwise." Even the satisfied note in her voice did not detract from the impact of her own appearance.

Her gown was a sea green in color, of some sort of fabric that shimmered when she moved, and cut low to reveal the creamy swell of her breasts. Far too revealing, although admittedly he would have appreciated it on another woman. But Tatiana, at least for the moment, was his wife.

Tonight, a voice whispered in the back of his head.

He took her hand and lifted it to his lips. "And you are looking exceptionally lovely this evening."

"You shall quite turn my head, my lord." Her green eyes gleamed with promise and there was a blush on her cheeks.

"Will I?" His gaze locked with hers. "To what end, I wonder?"

"To whatever end is desired." She tilted her head and cast him *the look.*

A wave of desire so strong it caught at his breath rushed through him.

Tonight.

"My dear Lord Matthew, how delightful to see you." A voice sounded from the doorway.

Matt and Tatiana stepped apart quickly as if they'd been caught doing something untoward. As one they turned toward the entry.

A diminutive woman stood in the doorway, the twinkle in her blue eyes belying the regal manner of her bearing. This was obviously the Dowager Duchess of Roxborough. He knew full well she had to be approaching eighty years of age, yet she looked considerably younger.

"Your Grace." He bowed, and out of the corner of his eye noted Tatiana staring. He nudged her as surreptitiously as possible. She shot him a startled glance, then thankfully understood and dropped a stiff curtsy.

"Your Grace," Tatiana echoed.

Matt bit back a grin. His princess was not used to

deferring to anyone, but right now she was no princess. She was his wife.

"I am so pleased to see you again." The dowager held out her hand. "It has been far too long, Matthew."

He stepped to her at once, took her hand and raised it to his lips. "I'm afraid, ma'am, you have me at a disadvantage. I do not recall meeting before."

"Of course you wouldn't. You were a mere child. Your grandmother brought you and your brothers here for a visit so many years ago I cannot say for certain when it was, but I distinctly remember what an enjoyable time your family had with my own grandchildren." The old woman shook her head and sighed. "It is exceedingly odd, as one progresses through life, that it is often easier to remember what happened twenty years ago than the incidents of yesterday."

The dowager turned her attention to Tatiana. "And you must be Lady Matthew."

"Your Grace," Tatiana said and bobbed another curtsy.

"Come, now, my dear, we do not stand on ceremony here, particularly when it concerns members of the family. And whether Matthew realizes it or not, I quite consider him to be in the wide circle of family that encompasses close friends. His grandmother is one of my oldest and dearest friends and I have always thought of her with the affection one reserves for a sister." Her gaze slid back to Matt. "We correspond quite regularly. Did you know that?"

"No, I wasn't aware of that." The cravat around his neck seemed to tighten.

"Yes, indeed. Often enough to know that you"—

she pinned him with a firm gaze—"do not. In point of fact, even with my spotty memory, I am certain she has written that she has not heard from you in many years. Am I correct, Matthew?"

"Possibly." The neckcloth was definitely getting tighter.

"Furthermore, she has never mentioned your marriage." The dowager studied him. "I would wager a great deal she is unaware of it. Would you take that wager, Matthew?"

"Probably not." He resisted the urge to tug at his cravat and wondered if the lady would let him strangle to death before her very eyes.

"Your Grace, Lord Matthew has been extremely busy in recent years." Tatiana stepped forward. "He was at sea, and now with his work with aerostats—"

"Ah, yes, the balloons." The dowager nodded in a knowing manner.

Tatiana slanted Matt a quick look. "You can certainly understand how time would simply slip through his fingers."

Matt cast Tatiana a grateful glance for her defense.

"He truly has the best of intentions," Tatiana continued. "But you do understand how men can be when it comes to matters like correspondence."

"That, my dear," the dowager said firmly, "is why they have wives."

Tatiana smiled weakly and Matt wondered if she too felt an invisible noose around her neck.

"There is never an excuse for thoughtlessness or discourtesy. However, I suppose when there has been a rift in the family, such things are to be understood and forgiven." She fixed Matt with a pointed look. "Do I make myself clear, Matthew?"

"Yes, ma'am," he said quickly, even though he wasn't entirely certain what he had just agreed to or what the dowager expected of him.

"Excellent." Her Grace nodded. "I gather, from appearances when I walked in, you have not been wed for any length of time?"

"Indeed, it has not been very long," Matt said.

Tatiana nodded. "Not at all."

"Barely a week," Matt said.

"Little more than a year," Tatiana's voice sounded in unison with his.

He stifled a groan. How convincing would their deception be if they couldn't agree on how long they had been married?

"I see," the dowager said slowly.

"No, Your Grace, I am quite sure you do not." Tatiana stepped forward.

"My love." A warning sounded in his voice. "Tatiana."

She ignored him. "Shortly after we were wed, more than a year ago, family obligations forced me to return to Avalonia. Unfortunately my husband was unable to accompany me. It is only recently that I have returned to England and Matthew."

"And you have done so to write about my old friend, the Princess Sophia."

"Precisely." Tatiana flashed him a triumphant smile. "But more importantly to return to my husband."

"Indeed." The dowager studied her for a moment, then nodded as if satisfied. "We have a great deal to discuss. About your princess as well as your husband."

"I am quite looking forward to it." Tatiana beamed at the older woman, who returned her smile.

At once Matt had the oddest sensation of being excluded from something of great importance. Unease settled in the pit of his stomach.

"Excellent. Please excuse me for a moment." Her Grace turned and stepped into the foyer, signaling to a servant.

Matt moved to Tatiana and bent to speak low into her ear. "This will not work."

"Nonsense," she said quietly. "It is progressing beautifully."

"I do not like lying to her."

"We are not lying. We are simply not revealing everything."

"It feels like lying."

"Well, it is not. We have not said a single word that is not essentially true." She sighed. "Besides, Matthew, the essence of a good lie is that it is based in truth. You would do well to remember that."

"I don't care how much basic truth there is in it, I refuse to lie to her."

"Then I alone shall lie to her," she said quickly. "Will that ease your too-busy conscience?"

"No," he snapped. "Whether I like it or not, I am part of this deception. However, I will make a bargain with you. You tell me the truth right now, and then I will decide whether or not to continue with your charade."

"The truth?"

"Yes."

"Which truth exactly?" she said slowly.

"What do you mean, which truth? How many truths are there to choose from?" He narrowed his eyes. "Or should I say, how many lies?"

"One or two." She bit her bottom lip. "Or more."

"I want all of it, Tatiana. Why you are here. What you want. Everything."

"What if you do not like what you hear?"

He clenched his jaw. "Then I shall not be disappointed, as I do not expect to like it."

She met his gaze defiantly. "And if I do not confess all?"

"I shall tell the dowager who you really are. Regardless of your true purpose, I suspect that will hinder your efforts."

"Very well, you leave me no choice. Obviously, now is not the time, but I am willing to explain all tonight when we are alone." She raised a shoulder in a careless shrug. "I had planned on telling you everything soon at any rate."

He straightened and stared down at her. "You are, without a doubt, the most—"

"Matthew, if you would be so good as to accompany me in to dinner." The dowager stepped back into the room.

"I would be honored." He hurried to her side, praying he and Tatiana had kept their voices low enough to keep their discussion private.

"It shall only be the three of us tonight." Her Grace took his arm and smiled up at him. "I quite look forward to a long evening of conversation. It should be most interesting."

Not nearly as interesting as later tonight would be. Matt forced an unconcerned smile and uttered his first real lie of the night. "I do hope so, ma'am."

If indeed there was an underlying topic of conversation at the dinner table that continued even after the meal was finished and the trio had retired to a large drawing room, it was the importance of family.

The dowager spoke at length about the various

members of the impressively large, and apparently ever-increasing, Effington family. Tatiana was grateful none of the Effington relations were in residence at the moment. She would never be able to remember the endless number of names and titles."

The older woman went on about Matthew's family as well, obviously making it her mission to reacquaint him with the lives of his brothers. Tatiana realized Matthew's name on the note she had sent was the reason why the dowager had responded so quickly and so graciously. Now the discussion gave Tatiana a fascinating glimpse into the past of the man she loved.

He was the youngest of four sons of the Marquess of Stanwick and had no sisters. His mother had died shortly after his birth and his father within the past few years, while Matthew was still serving at sea. Unfortunately, Her Grace did not specifically bring up whatever had caused the rift between Matthew and the rest of the Weston family, but from what she did say, or perhaps what she did not, Tatiana had the distinct impression whatever had happened was by no means insurmountable. Judging by the expression in Matthew's eye, he may well have come to the same conclusion.

Was it pride, then, that kept this man from returning to those people he had once cared for? Or was it fear? Tatiana certainly understood that kind of fear. It clutched at your heart and kept you from turning to the one you loved because you feared opening your heart might destroy you. Whether she wished to or not, tonight she would face that fear with Matthew. One way or another, the past between them would be resolved. Could she help him resolve his own past?

"I am sorry, my dear." The dowager cast Tatiana an apologetic smile. She and Tatiana sat on a small sofa. Matthew had settled into the chair closest to the older woman. "Matthew and I have quite monopolized the conversation with talk of his family and mine. Now I should like to hear something of your background."

"There is very little to say, Your Grace." Tatiana picked up her glass of sherry and sipped, ignoring the apprehensive glance cast her by Matthew.

"Your note said you were from Avalonia. Do you have family there?"

The essence of a good lie is that it is based in truth. Tatiana smiled pleasantly. "I do indeed. My father and my brothers all reside in Avalonia."

"Is that it, then?" The dowager raised a curious brow. "No aunts, uncles, cousins, grandparents?"

"Regretfully, I have very few other relations. A handful of distant cousins, nothing more." Tatiana took another sip of wine and met Matthew's gaze over the rim of the glass. Tonight she would tell him everything. And tonight they would at last—

"What a pity." The older woman studied her thoughtfully. "Yet surely you have some blood connection to your country's royal family?"

Tatiana struggled to keep her composure.

"Why do you say that, ma'am?" Matthew asked quickly.

"Why, my dear boy"—the dowager's brows drew together—"she bears a startling likeness to the Princess Sophia. Unless my memory is far worse than I suspected, it's quite remarkable."

"Do I?" Tatiana forced a light laugh.

Tatiana had seen portraits of the princess, of course, but most were painted when Sophia was a child or young girl. Tatiana had never noticed anything more than a vague family likeness and no one else had ever commented on the resemblance. "I suppose, then, I should confess."

Matthew breathed a subtle sigh of relief.

"There is a distant connection between my family and the royal family. Through my father, I believe." She ignored the flash in Matthew's eye. "In truth, that is one reason why I am so eager to tell her story. It seems a terrible disservice to allow this lady—a hereditary princess, no less, who had the courage to take her child and flee her country, with little more than the clothes on her back—to fade into obscurity.

"I want to know everything about her. Did she share confidences? Talk about the past? Her fears and her hopes?" She leaned closer to the older woman. "I want to know where she went and who she spoke to. Did she take long walks or morning rides? I want to see the places she saw and even the very room she stayed in.

"Frankly, I consider it"—she raised her chin a notch and her voice rang in the huge dining room—"a sacred trust."

Matthew snorted.

Tatiana cast him a threatening glare and he hesitated, then coughed and grabbed his glass of cognac. He took a gulp and gasped.

"Forgive me." His voice was convincingly breathless. "I had something caught in my throat."

"We can only be grateful you did not choke to death," Tatiana said in an overly sweet manner.

"I suspect fate is saving me for something far more painful," he muttered and drained the rest of his drink.

Tatiana smiled. "One can only hope."

"Fate has brought you home," the matriarch said

firmly. "How long has it been since you were last at Weston Manor, Matthew?"

Matthew had the grace to look chagrined. "Ten years or so."

"And in all that time you have been too busy to write?" Her Grace fixed him with a chastising look. "My dear boy, one is never too busy for family. When all is said and done, the only people one can count on in this life are those people you are related to by bonds of blood or bonds of marriage or, if you are extremely lucky, bonds of friendship."

Matthew blew a long breath and nodded slowly.

"And, as Weston Manor is less than a day's drive from here, especially given your wife's quest, this is indeed the perfect opportunity for you to reestablish those bonds."

"Your family home is that close?" Tatiana stared in surprise. "Her Grace is right. You cannot possibly let this chance slip by."

"I most certainly can." His voice was firm. "There is much about my relationship with my family you are not aware of."

"Nonsense." The dowager snorted in a most unladylike manner. "You would be rather shocked, I think, to learn just how much I do know. Old ladies have little else to do with their time than gossip and meddle. I know a great deal about the lives of those who touch my life, because I make it my business to know.

"I know of your wild youth and I know of the trouble between you and your father that led to your departure. Furthermore, I know, as I am confident you do not, that at the end of his life he very much regretted his actions."

"Did he," Matthew said softly.

"He did indeed. And your brothers would be most happy to welcome you home." Her Grace heaved a heartfelt sigh. "Matthew, you are, what? Six and twenty?"

He nodded.

"You have the luxury of a great portion of your life still ahead of you. Do not waste it." She shook her head. "Do not get to my years with regrets and no time left to make amends. Go home, Matthew."

"I . . ." he heaved a sigh of surrender. "I will consider it."

"Do you have regrets, Your Grace?" Tatiana said without thinking.

The dowager raised a brow. "My dear young woman, that is a most impertinent question."

Heat flashed up Tatiana's face. "I am sorry. I did not—"

"Do not apologize." Her Grace chuckled. "I rather like impertinence. As for regrets . . ." She folded her hands on her lap and thought for a moment.

"I have known many women through the years who regret that over which they have no control, primarily that they were born women. They long for the public power and authority denied them by virtue of their gender. But I have discovered that in many ways the power of women is far greater than that of men." She cast Matthew a wry smile. "Do forgive me, my lord, I know how this must shock you."

"Not at all." Matthew laughed. "I confess, I expected as much from you, ma'am."

"As well you should." The dowager nodded primly, then continued. "It is a private power, a private influence, and a wise woman wields it carefully. My own regrets do not concern that which I could not control. As for that which I could . . ." She fell silent for a long moment. "There are paths I did not take in my life, choices I did not make that I regretted when I was younger. But I realized with the passage of years the paths I chose and the choices I made were indeed the best ones. So no, my dear Lady Matthew, in truth I have no significant regrets.

"And what of you? Although you are far too young to have any regrets of any consequence."

"Oh, but I do." She wasn't sure if it was the kindliness and candid nature of the elderly woman or simply that Tatiana had never spoken of important matters with a woman of experience, but the words tumbled out of their own accord. "I regret I have spent much of my life doing what was expected of me. It led me to a disastrous marriage with a man who could not be trusted and who, in truth, did not care for me."

A startled expression crossed Her Grace's face.

"Oh, not Lord Matthew," Tatiana said quickly. "I was wed once before, a marriage arranged by my family. I regret I had neither the courage nor the strength to control my own fate and I regret that I failed to see how my husband's weakness might be the result of my position in life."

"Oh, my," the dowager said, her blue eyes bright with interest. "Sometimes it's a blessing to talk about all those things one never speaks of aloud." She placed her hand on Tatiana's. "Do go on, my dear."

Matthew's eyes widened and his mouth opened as if he were about to protest, then snapped shut, and he stared with the stunned fascination of one who is watching a house go up in flames or a shipwreck upon a shore. And is helpless to to prevent the disaster.

"Very well, I shall." Tatiana sqaured her shoulders.

"I regret that parts of my life have made me suspicious and unable to fully trust now those people I should. I regret some of the decisions I have made with my head, even if they were rational choices, and not trusting my heart. Always. And I regret the fear that still keeps me from doing those things I should have done long ago. And . . . and . . ." She sat back in her chair and blew a long breath. "And I believe that may be it."

"That may be enough," Matthew murmured.

"I must say that was quite impressive." Her Grace smiled knowingly. "You do feel better now, don't you, my dear?"

"Yes, actually, I do." Tatiana had been taught from birth, regardless of the circumstances, not to reveal her thoughts and feelings. Now a fresh clean sensation of freedom and relief swept through her. She grinned at the dowager. "In truth, better than I have for a very long time."

"Excellent." The dowager beamed.

Matthew smiled in an absent manner. She had no idea what he might be thinking. He should be pleased. After all, everything she had said was true. Still, there was no reading his mind.

"Your Grace, I wonder if we might now discuss the Princess Sophia?" There was no time like the present to begin, and, with Valentina in the country, no time to waste.

"I do hope you do not think it rude of me, Lady Matthew, but the hour is late and I am beginning to feel somewhat fatigued. I should prefer to put off any discussion of the princess until tomorrow, perhaps, or even later in the week."

"Later in the week?" Tatiana kept her voice level and unconcerned.

"Indeed. Several members of my family were in residence here up until a fortnight ago. Lord Matthew's presence provides me with the perfect opportunity to call them back. I sent out informal invitations the moment I received your note and I expect the guests nearest to Effington Hall to arrive as early as tomorrow. Why, no one would speak to me again if they knew Lord Matthew and his balloon were here and I had allowed them to miss it. In addition, my grandson and several other relations have recently visited Avalonia. I'm certain they would enjoy the opportunity to discuss their activities there with you."

"That would be lovely," Tatiana lied. She would much prefer not to speak with anyone who might recognize her, although she had not been home since shortly after her brother had left Avalonia for England early in the spring.

"I think a ball is in order. Nothing extensive, mind you, a small gathering. No more than fifty guests or so, probably less than a hundred all told, mostly family, could be managed by the end of the week. Oh, say, three days from now. You will stay, of course?"

"Of course," Matthew said, his polite smile belying the reluctance in his eye.

"Of course." Tatiana nodded. As much as she did not want to waste the rest of the week, the time would give her the opportunity to fully explore Effington Hall and its grounds. If the Heavens were here, this was her chance to find them.

"Excellent." The elderly woman beamed. "I do so love impromptu entertainments, and I confess I will use any excuse. I rarely travel to London these days and the country can be frightfully dull. Most of the time, I rather prefer it that way, but at the moment, I am oddly restless." She pulled her brows together in a considering manner. "I have no idea why, but there you have it." She squeezed Tatiana's hand and met her gaze. "It may well be that whole issue of regrets. I shall not live forever and there are any number of things I have yet to do."

She pulled her hand away and turned toward Matthew. "And I fully expect you to help me accomplish one of them."

"Me?" Apprehension flickered in Matthew's eye.

The dowager nodded. "You and your balloon."

"My balloon?" he said slowly

"Aerostat," Tatiana added.

"In your wife's note I was given to understand you are at a point in your work where it will be necessary to inflate the"—she cast a quick smile at Tatiana— "aerostat. It should be quite exciting. I was hoping you would give me the honor of a ride." She smiled, and a far-off look appeared in her eye. "I do regret that I have never had the opportunity to fly."

"The honor would be mine, Your Grace."

"Excellent. And to seal our bargain, I have something of a treat in store." She picked up a bell and rang. The butler appeared in the doorway immediately. The dowager nodded and the servant disappeared, to return almost at once bearing a tray with a decanter and three filled glasses. "I have been saving this for years, and tonight is indeed the perfect occasion."

The butler offered the tray first to the dowager, who selected a glass, then to Tatiana and Matthew in turn. Tatiana had no idea what the beverage might be, although the deep, dark red-brown color looked familiar.

The dowager raised her glass to Matthew. "To family and friends"—then directed her glass to Tatiana—"and to those who have newly joined our company."

All three brought their glasses to their lips. In that instant before the liquid touched her mouth, Tatiana recognized the sharp, unmistakable scent of Avalonian brandy. At once she realized if she drank it she would soon be asleep and there would be no opportunity for confession to Matthew and no chance of anything much more delightful. But the dowager was offering the brandy in honor of Lord and Lady Matthew, and it would be most impolite not to accept it. Tatiana had little choice.

She squinted her eyes closed, held her breath and drained the glass.

"Avalonian brandy," Matthew said in much the same manner one would say *hemlock*. As much as Tatiana did not like the drink, it was still not at all pleasant to hear Matthew speak of it as if it were poison.

"Oh, my." The dowager gasped and held her glass out to study its contents. "I did think brandy got better with age."

"It's supposed to," Matthew muttered.

"Do you think it's gone bad? The taste is distinctly . . ." The lady licked her lips and her nose wrinkled.

"Foul?" Matthew said.

"Odd." Her Grace stared down into her glass. "The princess sent it to me years ago. I understand it's rather rare."

"It's very difficult to get outside of Avalonia," Tatiana said.

"Thank God," Matthew said under his breath.

"I rarely drink spirits other than wine or sherry or champagne, of course. Perhaps a cognac on special occasions. The odd glass of whiskey now and then during the winter. A sip of gin . . ." She held the glass to the light and scrutinized its contents. "But is brandy supposed to taste like this?"

"I believe it is." Tatiana was beginning to wonder if Avalonian brandy was any good at all. At least as the rest of the world judged brandy.

"It's an acquired taste," Matthew said pointedly.

"And no doubt difficult to acquire. This may well explain why after all these years in this house, in which there are a fair amount of spirits regularly imbibed, it has not been drunk." The dowager leaned toward Matthew. "I believe there are quite a few bottles of the stuff still in the cellar."

The dowager brightened. "We could serve it at the soiree. In honor of Lady Matthew. It would be perfect."

"And you would get rid of it." Matthew grinned.

"Is it really that bad?" Tatiana asked, staring at her empty glass.

"No, my dear." The dowager rose to her feet, Matthew and Tatiana following suit. "But as Matthew says, it is obviously a taste that must be acquired."

Tatiana sighed. "And I have never truly acquired it."

"That is not, necessarily, a bad thing." Matthew grinned down at her. Something in his look, amusement or perhaps even affection, caught at her heart and her gaze locked with his.

The look in his eye changed, deepened, and desire now stared at her. A wonderful, tremulous sense of anticipation settled in her body.

She stifled a yawn.

"I shall bid you both good night," Her Grace said.

"I am more than ready to retire. However, if you are not"—she turned to Matthew—"we have an excellent library and a billiards room. Along with a gentleman's lounge, those are the only rooms where the smoking of cigars is permitted. Many of the Effington men like the foul-smelling things. Do you, Matthew?"

He shrugged in an offhand manner. "On rare occasions."

"Well, there are supplies in both rooms if you consider this occasion rare." The dowager chatted on about the quality of the offerings in the Effington library and the enjoyment of the game of billiards and Tatiana was not certain what else. In a few short minutes, she would have to tell Matthew everything and in many ways she rather welcomed it. He could be of great assistance in her search for the jewels. He would certainly understand her affliction brought on by travel. As for the rest, well, the truth about the state of their marriage could no longer be put off. She should have told him long ago.

The dowager turned to Tatiana and took the younger woman's hands. "I have quite enjoyed this evening, and I do so look forward to speaking with you about the princess."

"As do I, Your Grace," Tatiana said.

"I shall see you tomorrow, then." Her Grace started toward the door and called back over her shoulder. "And do put that young woman to bed, Matthew, she is falling asleep on her feet."

Tatiana yawned.

Matthew moved closer and studied her carefully. "You *are* falling asleep."

"Not at all." She forced a bright note to her voice

and blinked hard. She had never particularly tried to counteract the effects of the brandy—indeed, she had always welcomed the respite it brought—but tonight she very much wanted to remain awake. She stepped to Matthew, placed her hands on his coat and slid them up and around to the back of his neck. "Besides, I have far too much to accomplish tonight to sleep."

"Oh?" His brow raised in a wicked manner and he drew her body close to his. "And what do you have to accomplish?"

"Well . . ." She brushed her lips back and forth across his mouth and his arms tightened around her. She could feel the heat of his body through the layers of their clothing and pressed closer, wondering if he could feel the throb of her own body in response. Her eyes drifted closed and she savored the warmth of him. She sighed. "Well . . ."

"If you do not stop that, we will not make it to our bed," he growled against her ear.

"I have much to tell you. I promised." She rested her head on his chest and sank into his embrace. It was as if she were in a dream, at once familiar and exciting. And indeed, had she not had this dream so many times before?

"I'm sure you do." Matthew sounded oddly distant and resigned.

She snuggled closer against him.

Without warning, he scooped her up into his arms and started toward the door and the corridor beyond.

Her eyes snapped open. "What are you doing?"

"Exactly as the dowager instructed." A wry smile quirked the corners of his mouth. She wanted to touch his lips, but it required far too much effort. "I am putting you to bed."

"Excellent." She closed her eyes and curled against him, then summoned all her strength and lifted her head. "Alone?"

"It appears that way."

"Pity." She sighed.

"My sentiments exactly." He shifted her weight in his arms and started up the stairs.

Tatiana struggled to open her eyes. "Not that it would mean anything to you."

He chuckled. "Nothing at all."

"Just lust?"

"Nothing more."

"You are lying, Matthew." She smiled with a wonderful sense of contentment. He did care. She knew it. "My lord husband."

"Your Highness. My lady . . ." He paused for a moment, then she felt him sigh in surrender. "Wife."

The next thing she knew, he was placing her on the bed in the room that adjoined his and . . . leaving. She struggled to prop herself up on her elbows and stared after him.

"You are not staying?"

He paused at the door to the dressing room. "Not tonight."

"But tonight . . ." Tonight, what? She could not find the words. Tonight was important . . . why? She could not . . . of course. "You called me your love."

She couldn't make out his face in the shadows, but she could hear his smile. "A slip of the tongue."

She sank back onto the bed with a sense of joy she had not had for a very long time. "You do not lie as well as I do, Matthew."

"Thank you."

"I have to tell you . . . everything. You really should . . . know." But she could not grasp what *everything* was. What did she have to tell him? What did he have to know? A moment ago it had seemed so urgent; now it scarcely mattered.

In her fogged mind only one truth surfaced. "You hate my brandy."

He laughed softly. "I confess, it isn't exactly to my liking."

"It is an acquired taste, Matthew." She rolled onto her side and curled her hands under her cheek. And murmured in the last second before sleep claimed her, "As am I."

. . . and, in truth, Ephraim, I am as befuddled by her as much now as ever.

I must confess, she makes me smile and I have laughed more in recent days than I had thought possible. While I am not happy with the deception she has woven around us, nor do I as yet trust her intentions toward my family or her true purpose, I have found myself beginning to believe in the woman herself.

It is an exceedingly odd admission, given both our pasts and our current circumstances, yet when I look into her eyes, I see a depth of affection and, indeed, a truth, that I am hard-pressed to disregard. It catches at my breath and melts my resolve and I forget my own intentions.

I began this adventure of hers determined to remain in command of my emotions, of my heart, as it were. I swore to myself that my agreement to accompany her was for the prime purpose of the protection of my family and only incidentally to resolve what was still unsettled between us. I can now admit, to you and perhaps to myself, there was an element of retribution as well. Do not think poorly of me at this confession, old friend. I have still retained that sense of honor you find so inconvenient. I did not plan to wound her as she had injured me; however, I fully intended not to especially care when next we parted. To be unconcerned and aloof when we bid one another farewell, as surely we must. She is a princess and I am the disinherited youngest son of an English marquess, as unsure of his future as he is of his own dreams.

Knowing this, I would be a fool to fall under her spell again, yet I cannot seem to prevent it. It is as inevitable as my next breath and the beat of my heart.

She loves me, Ephraim, I am certain of it. As certain as I am that I feel the same. It is the nature of such emotion to be optimistic and so, no matter how foolish, for now I live only in the moment. And in her laugh and her smile.

I know not how this farce of ours will play out. I have no clue as to the true purpose of her quest, nor what will happen should she succeed. Or, perhaps, should she fail.

Fate has thrust us together once again, but to what end?

Somewhere in the far distance, where the gods that rule such things reside, I hear the faint sound of laughter. . . .

Chapter 12

Tatiana was indeed an acquired taste and, God help him, he had acquired it once and, it now appeared, acquired it for life.

Matt strode back toward Effington Hall, his step determined but his heart lighter than it had been in more than fifteen months. He grinned to himself. It was past time to admit there hadn't been a week, a day, a minute when the thought of Tatiana hadn't lingered in his mind. His feelings about her had never changed. Not for a moment. And he was confident, no, he *knew* she felt the same.

Oh, certainly last night hadn't turned out as he'd expected. He still did not know what his princess was up to, nor how his family entered into it. But her long list of regrets had revealed much about her life and her choices and, more importantly, how she felt now. It would not be easy to put the past behind them, and he refused to consider what marriage to a princess might mean for his future, but for the moment, all he wanted was to clear the mistakes between them. And take her in his arms.

He'd slept later than usual this morning and she was still abed when he'd checked on her. It was apparent now that it was not the rocking of a coach that lulled her to sleep but that foul drink with which she began every trip. Perhaps she had some sort of fear of travel. Odd, since he'd never believed she feared much of anything.

Matt had spent the day assembling the various fittings, riggings and myriad of other components required to get his balloon airborne. His experimentation was for the most part complete. While his system worked in principle, in practice each effort proved the need for additional modification. Still, he was confident that it was nearly perfected and he was planning to take the balloon up in an hour or so. The sky was overcast but did not threaten rain and he did not anticipate any particular problems. Even now, eager Effington servants were funneling hot air into the taffeta body. He grinned at their enthusiasm. Ballooning was not quite as fashionable as it once was, but it still held a fascination for most people. If he didn't win this competition, he could always go back to selling balloon rides in Paris parks and make his fortune in that manner. Of course, by then he could well be too old to care.

And he did have a princess to provide for.

His step slowed. Matt was not a man of means. If he and Tatiana remarried—and indeed it seemed they headed toward that end—what then?

He'd never concerned himself with the question of supporting her. Their time in Paris had been far too short to consider the realities of life, and then he'd had no idea of her title. Their time together now was an adventure, nothing at all like his usual way of living. Wasn't she, in fact, paying for their travels? Why, she had provided the clothes that were on his back at this very moment.

Even if he managed to win the funding needed to invest in a ship, his finances would not be substantially improved for a long time. Tatiana was a blasted princess. She was used to luxury. To palaces and places like Effington Hall. Not cottages that were little more than shacks.

The hall loomed in the distance and he could make out figures seated at a table on the terrace.

Perhaps the idea of spending the rest of his days with her was as absurd as the fairy story he'd likened her life to. Perhaps he should simply let her go when the time came and be grateful they'd had the chance to resolve the past. Perhaps her decision to leave him in Paris, disregarding the manner of her leaving, had been the wisest decision for them both.

Matt drew closer to the hall, following a gravel path dividing a formal garden. Tall boxwood mazes flanked the gardens. Tatiana waved from the terrace and he responded with feigned enthusiasm, his light-hearted mood gone.

There was nothing to be done now. It was entirely possible he was mistaken about her feelings and her return was prompted by no more than her need for assistance from an Englishman. It was possible he was simply a convenience. And possible as well that she had no intentions toward him beyond sharing his bed.

"My lord," Tatiana called and waved again from the terrace. "Will you join us?"

He skirted a fountain and continued along the gravel path to the broad stone steps of the terrace.

"Good afternoon, Matthew." The dowager duchess waved at an empty chair. "Do sit down and tell us how your aerostat is progressing today."

In spite of his now dour mood, Matt smiled. He appreciated the older lady's use of the proper term, and while he'd never admit it to Tatiana, in his own mind he did tend to refer to the aerostat as nothing more exotic than a balloon. "Quite well, thank you, ma'am."

Tatiana poured a cup of tea and handed it to him. Her fingers touched his and electricity sparked between them. His gaze jumped to hers and his breath caught at the emotion simmering in her green eyes.

"I can just see it from here." The dowager shaded her eyes and stared out in the general vicinity of the lake. "Do you see it, my dear?"

Tatiana reluctantly pulled her gaze from Matt's and followed the dowager's gaze. "I think so." She squinted and held her hand out to block the bright late-summer sun. "That is it, is it not, my lord? That bright yellow blob?"

"If you can see it, it should no longer be a blob," Matt said, scanning the distance. He spotted it, noting the inflation was nearly completed. "Once it's fully inflated it will be tied down. I plan to go up in it in a bit—tethered to the ground, of course."

"Oh, Matthew, may I come?" Tatiana's eyes sparkled with excitement. "It has been such a long time."

"Indeed, far too long." Were they talking about his balloon or something entirely different? And far more important?

"I do understand how perhaps today is not a wise choice—the sky is far too gray—but"—Her Grace leaned closer—"you will take me soon, will you not? Preferably before any of my family arrives."

"You fear they might forbid you to go up because of the potential danger." Matt nodded sagely.

"My dear young man. No one forbids me to do anything I wish to do. Why, the very thought is absurd. No, I am simply afraid that once the numerous members of my family arrive, they will monopolize your time and I shall not get to fly at all." She smiled. "I should then be most unhappy."

Matt chuckled. "I shall make certain, Your Grace, that you get to fly."

"I thought you would. Now, enough fun for the moment. It is time for more serious matters." She turned to Tatiana. "Do you prefer to ask me questions about Sophia or should I simply ramble on until you are bored?"

"I cannot imagine being bored, Your Grace."

"Very well. Let me think. It was a long time ago, 1760-something. The exact date eludes me." The dowager settled back in her chair in the manner of a master storyteller. "The old duke was still alive. My husband was the Marquess of Helmsley then. Sophia's mother, then the Queen of Avalonia, was a friend of my mother's, although I have no idea how they were acquainted. At any rate, if memory serves, the queen gave Sophia the names of three ladies who could lend her their assistance.

"She and her daughter arrived in England with very little." Her Grace shook her head at the memory. "It was really quite sad. She had some clothing and trinkets, the type of sentimental odds and ends one might grab as a keepsake. I recall she had a small portrait of her husband. He'd been killed only recently."

The dowager gazed off into the distance and the long-ago. "It was apparent she'd loved him a great deal, yet, for the most part, she kept her feelings to herself. We became firm friends during her stay here—of course she had no one else—and she once told me mourning was a luxury she could not indulge. She could not allow her personal sorrow to cripple her. She had a child, his child, to protect, and that was paramount to her.

"She remained here, oh, let me think." Her Grace paused to gather the years. "A month or so, I believe. Sophia was extremely restless, and rightly so. She'd had no word from Avalonia and feared she could have been followed by her family's enemies. She felt compelled to move from one location to another. That's why she stayed so briefly with Lady Hutchins, barely more than a week." She glanced at Tatiana. "Pity she is no longer with us. She might be able to tell you more."

"I cannot imagine how difficult this must have been for her. Forced to flee with nothing more than a handful of keepsakes. The princess had spent her life surrounded by the finest things, clothing and jewels and whatnot. What a shame she had to leave it all behind." Tatiana's comment was offhand, but something in her manner caught Matt's attention and he studied her carefully.

"Indeed, she had no more than a single bag with her and no jewels that I was aware of." The dowager thought for a moment. "A ring, I think. Perhaps a necklace as well. I don't recall more than that, although she was not penniless." She cast them an apologetic smile. "I fear I can tell you little else. Soon after leaving Effington Hall, she met the Earl of Worthington and married him. He was considerably older than she, but I think she had had love and was now looking for a safe and secure home for her and her daughter. The earl died, oh, ten or fifteen years later and left her quite well off.

"Sophia and I saw each other a time or two after her marriage, but she rarely left Worthington Castle. I always thought she considered it her haven and was therefore reluctant to stray far from its gates. We corresponded sporadically until her death, twenty years ago now." The dowager shook her head. "I must say, it's depressing to note how many people in this story are no longer with us. Such is the curse of a long life, I suppose. And in truth"—she smiled—"I am willing to bear it."

Her gaze met Tatiana's and her voice was firm. "When you write this history of yours, speak well of her courage. I have never met another woman, and only a handful of men, with her strength of character and depth of determination. I have often wondered if that is why she spent the long years after her marriage and the earl's death in relative solitude. If she had exhausted her reserves of strength and valor and now had to concentrate on the simplicities of an ordinary life." The lady chuckled. "A rather fanciful notion, I suppose."

"Not at all," Matt said thoughtfully. "I can see your point. It makes a great deal of sense."

"You are a charmer, Matthew." The dowager had the look of a grandmother about to ruffle the hair of a small child, and Matt braced himself. Thankfully, she did no such thing. Her gaze slid to Tatiana. "Last night you mentioned seeing her rooms. I believe she had a suite in the guest wing, but in this my memory fails. It could well be the rooms you and Lord Matthew share, as those are the best-appointed rooms in that wing. However, they have been refurbished once or twice since Sophia's stay.

"She did spend a great deal of time out-of-doors, though, always on foot, and never went out of sight of the hall. She was far too cautious for that."

"Of course, she would be." Tatiana nodded.

"By the look on your face, I fear I did not give you what you wished for. I hope you are not disappointed?"

"Not at all, ma'am." Tatiana shrugged as if it were of no consequence, but Matt noted a touch of concern in her eyes. "I am merely trying to tell her story. Nothing more."

Her Grace turned back toward Matt. "Well, perhaps your grandmother can add to the story."

Matt winced to himself. "Perhaps."

"Your grandmother?" Tatiana said slowly. "I fear you have me at a disadvantage, my lord. What does your grandmother have to do with this?"

The dowager turned to her in surprise. "My dear, in your note you said you were retracing the travels of the princess and wished to speak to the three women who helped her. Lady Hutchins, whose demise you had already learned of, Lady Cranston and myself. Lady Cranston is my dear friend Beatrice. Matthew's grandmother."

"Your grandmother?" Tatiana's voice was level.

"My father's mother." Matt smiled in an apologetic manner.

"I cannot believe you did not tell her this." Her Grace drew her brows together in a chastising manner. "Although I suppose I can well understand your reluctance."

"You can?" Matt said and hoped her reasons would be good ones.

Tatiana's eyes narrowed slightly. "You can?"

"It's obvious." The dowager settled back in her chair and studied him for a long moment. "In spite of your naval exploits and your daring in the skies, when it comes to matters of family, you, my dear boy, are a coward."

"I most certainly am not." Indignation sounded in his voice. The dowager was right, of course; even if he was not about to admit it to anyone other than himself.

"That is obvious." Tatiana's expression was cool, but anger etched every line of her body.

"Matthew, you are afraid to return home. You are afraid to face your family and admit your actions as a youth were reprehensible. You are further afraid you will not be forgiven." The older lady's voice was firm. "And that is what you fear most."

"I said I would consider going home," Matt said under his breath.

"And I must beg your indulgence, Your Grace." Tatiana rose to her feet. Matt stood at once. "I feel it is necessary to return to my room and write down what you have told me." She cast the dowager a genuine smile. "A faulty memory is not always the result of age."

"Do be off, then, my dear. We will speak more later."

"My lord." Tatiana turned to him. "Would you be so kind as to accompany me for a moment? I should like to speak with you."

"I thought you might," he said.

"Good day, Your Grace." Tatiana nodded pleasantly, cast him a lethal glance and started toward the doors leading into the house.

"I wouldn't dawdle if I were you, Matthew," Her Grace said with a smile.

"In truth, ma'am, dawdling seems like a prudent idea."

The dowager chuckled. "She is extremely angry with you and I would not provoke her further. I have given her a logical reason why you might not have mentioned your relationship with Lady Cranston, but it's not entirely the correct one, is it?"

"Not entirely, no." Matthew grimaced and tried not to feel like a schoolboy caught in a prank.

"I thought not. I further think there are secrets between the two of you which you would do well to reveal."

"A few minor items, perhaps."

She raised a brow.

"Very well, hers are more than likely quite significant. However, mine," he said pointedly, "are minor."

"She did not seem to think your grandmother especially minor."

"She is not used to someone else having secrets."

"There is a fascinating story here, is there not, Matthew?"

"I don't know if *fascinating* is the right word."

"She loves you very much, I think. I can see it in the way she looks at you." The older woman studied him carefully. "Probably as much as you love her."

"Yes, well, sometimes, Your Grace, love may not be enough."

Tatiana pushed through the French doors leading into the main corridor off the terrace and headed toward the stairs.

Had she ever been so furious? Why, even Phillipe's infidelities had not angered her this much. No doubt because she cared so much more for Matthew. And perhaps because she expected deceit from her first husband but never from her second.

A tiny rational voice in the back of her mind noted Matthew had not really done anything so terribly consequential. In truth, he had said nothing that wasn't true, he simply had not told her everything. But the anger that gripped her ignored that fact. He had essentially lied to her the exact same way he claimed she lied to the dowager! How dare he?

She started up the stairs and heard his hurried footsteps approaching.

"Tatiana." He was right behind her.

She ignored him.

"Tatiana, wait."

She reached the top of the stairs, swiveled toward the guest wing and marched down the corridor.

"Will you let me explain?"

"No," she snapped without looking at him. "You are a liar, Matthew."

"And you, of all people, would recognize a liar when you saw one."

She clenched her teeth. "And not a very good liar, at that."

"Hah! I fooled you, didn't I?" His voice rose indignantly. "Besides, I have done nothing more than you have. In fact, I have done far less. My lie was a simple omission. You have concocted this entire Lord and Lady Matthew farce for God only knows what nefarious reason—"

"It's not nefarious!"

"How would I know that?"

"You should"—she faltered over the words—"trust me."

"Trust you?" He sputtered with indignation. "I should trust *you*?"

She reached the door to her room and grabbed the handle.

"Why in the name of all that's holy should I ever trust you?"

She spun toward him. "Because, you annoying creature, I love you. I have always loved you."

"You left me!" He glared down at her. "I married you and you discarded me and—"

"Oh, do sing another tune, Matthew. I am quite tired of hearing that one!" She shot the words without thinking. "I came back not because you married me, but because *I* married *you*. I promised to love you forever, and I meant it. Because I am, in truth, your wife and I will always be your wife." She yanked open the door. "Because I want nothing more than to be your wife." She stepped into the room and whirled back to face him. "Although at the moment I have no idea why!"

She slammed the door in his face. The room reverberated with the satisfying sound. She stared at the still-quivering door and clenched her fists. How could she be so foolish as to love him? He might never be able to forgive her for the past. He would probably have difficulties with the very idea of a princess for a wife. He was stubborn and arrogant and he did not even lie well.

But dear Lord, she did love him. And more, she needed him. She had never been as alive as she had been with him. He was as necessary to help her survive life as Avalonian brandy was to help her survive travel. And just like the brandy, no doubt, an acquired taste.

And God help her, she had acquired it.

Well, at least she had told him. Not that he understood. But in the matter of their marriage, at least, she had confessed. More or less. Enough to ease her own conscience anyway.

She heaved a sigh, brushed her hair away from her eyes and turned away from the door.

And froze with shock and more than a little fear.

Chapter 13

"*D*amn it all, Tatiana!" Matt slammed open the door from the dressing room and strode into her bedchamber. "I was not finished. And you still have a great deal of explaining to do."

She stood before the door to the hall and stared at him, her eyes wide with—what? Fear? Blasted woman, he didn't mean to scare her.

"Tatiana." He stepped toward her and stopped short at the scene before him.

The room had been ripped apart as if a tempest had swept through and upended it. Drawers were torn from chests and hurled aside. Clothes had been flung wildly across the floor and over furniture.

He blew a long, low whistle. "Bloody hell."

No corner of the room was untouched. The mattress had been pulled from the bed and tossed, the bedclothes scattered. The carpet was shoved into a rumpled heap. Even paintings had been torn from the wall and thrown onto the floor.

"I don't remember you as being this untidy."

"I did not do this." She planted her hands on her

hips. "Why would I do this? Obviously someone was . . ." She sucked in a hard breath, then dashed across the room to a writing desk. Its drawers rested precariously on one another, writing papers strewn about like fallen leaves. Tatiana dropped to her knees and pawed through the paper on the floor. "Do not stand there staring at me as though I were a lunatic. Help me."

"I rather enjoy staring at you as if you were a lunatic." He picked his way through the debris, trying not to step on various articles of clothing and whatever. He stepped to her side and squatted down beside her. "What are we looking for?"

"The letter. The one from Sophia to her mother."

"I don't see anything that looks like a letter."

She rocked back on her heels. "Neither do I. Damnation. I know it was here. I was looking at it just this morning. It has been stolen."

"Why would it be stolen?"

She paused, and he wondered if he was finally going to get the truth. "Because it is the only clue I have."

"To what?" he said sharply.

"I cannot tell you here."

"You mean you won't tell me here." He was hard-pressed to restrain his anger. His justifiable anger. "I have had quite enough of your—"

"No, you annoying man, it is not that I will not tell you. At this point not telling you would be extremely foolish. However, as I do not know who did all this"—she waved at the surrounding disorder—"I do not know who to trust—"

"You can trust me," he said grimly.

"Hah. As you are so very trustworthy," she scoffed. "I did not mean you. I meant the vast number of people who live and work in this house. Someone could be listening at the keyhole at this very moment."

His gaze flicked to the door and he half expected to see a shadow move in the gap between the door and the floor.

"A valid point." Matt stood. "Very well." He grabbed her hand and pulled her to her feet. "Let us be off, then." He started toward the door.

She hurried to keep up with him. "Where are we going?"

"Trust me," he snapped.

"Always," she shot back.

He half pulled, half dragged her behind him, retracing their steps back the way they had come. Along the corridor, down the stairs, through the hall, out onto the terrace and past the table where the dowager still sat.

Matt nodded politely but didn't break his stride.

Tatiana gasped a fast greeting. "Your Grace."

"Do have fun, children." The dowager waved gaily as if they were off for a picnic lunch.

He slowed a bit descending the terrace's stone steps to accommodate Tatiana, but he wanted nothing to impede their progress. He was at last going to learn what she was hiding, and he was not about to risk that she might think better of it.

"Where are we going?" She gasped.

"To the balloon." He sped up on the gravel walkway. "The one place I can guarantee we will not be overhead."

"Excellent idea." Her voice was breathless. "But must we run?"

"We are not running," he said, his tone clipped and

determined. They circled the fountain and continued down the path toward the broad expanse of lawn that stretched endlessly toward the lake. "We are proceeding at a speed designed to ensure I have you where you can speak freely before you have the opportunity to change your mind."

"I shall not change my mind, but, Matthew, I cannot—" She stumbled behind him.

He turned on his heel, scooped her up in his arms before she could hit the ground and continued without so much as a momentary pause.

"Matthew." She stared at him. "Surely you do not intend to carry me all the way to the balloon?"

"Surely I do," he said firmly.

"It is rather a distance, and you shall be exceedingly tired."

"I shall survive." He slanted her a quick glance. "It will be well worth it."

"I do hope so."

It might well have been his single-minded concentration, but they reached the balloon in no time. It was fully inflated, tied to the ground with a series of stout ropes.

He tossed Tatiana unceremoniously into the balloon's wicker gondola, ignored her muffled "Ooph" and muttered comment and turned to study the scene.

Something didn't seem right, although he couldn't say what exactly struck him as odd. A fire still burned in a pit dug nearby, and the funneling device used to direct the hot air sat on the ground. His tools and various other pieces of equipment were neatly arranged under the protection of the tent canopy. But there wasn't a servant in sight. Perhaps that was it.

"There were half a dozen men here when I left. There should be at least one or two still here."

"Obviously they were called away. Is that bothersome?"

"Not really."

It wasn't a concern, given that all he and Tatiana would do was simply ascend while remaining tethered to the ground. He could certainly handle that alone and indeed had done so uncounted times before. Still, there was something here that bothered him. Probably nothing more than apprehension over Tatiana's long-awaited revelation.

He shook off the feeling and climbed into the basket, running his gaze and his fingers over the ropes, lines, connections and hundred other tiny points where a problem could occur.

He nodded at the far side of the basket. "If you will untie those ropes at the same time I unfasten these, that will even the pull on the basket from the balloon and allow us to ascend in a relatively level manner."

"I am not an idiot, Matthew. I do remember." She huffed. "And this particular chore is not overly complicated. I think I can manage it."

He glanced at her. "I hope you also manage to remember not to untie the thickest rope. That's the line keeping us tethered to the ground."

She cast him a look of disgust and he bit back a grin.

Within moments they were rising smoothly in the gray sky. Matt watched the thick roll of rope on the ground, linking the craft to a stake driven deep into the earth, uncurl easily without the knotting or kinking that could cause a hazard later. The rope would allow them to go up approximately eighty feet, high enough to test his equipment, although for this quick flight he was not planning on testing anything. And high enough to avoid any possibility of eavesdropping.

They had ascended to a height of about twenty feet. Everything was proceeding as it should. Matt's gaze skimmed once more over potential problem areas. One could never be too careful. A fall from even this height would kill them.

"Now, then." He turned toward Tatiana and crossed his arms over his chest. "I'm ready."

"Very well." The wooden rail that rimmed the wall of the basket came to just above the small of her back and she rested against it, grasping the rail in either hand, as comfortable in manner as if she traveled in balloons every day.

"Go ahead." He stared at her expectantly.

"I am thinking." She pulled her brows together in a considering manner. "I am indeed trying to follow the path taken by the Princess Sophia when she was in England."

"I have determined that much," he said wryly. "Why?"

"Well . . ." She paused. Her reluctance at this point was disquieting. Apprehension trickled through him. He had never believed what she was doing was dangerous in any way. At most he thought her quest was regarding something of a scandalous nature. Until the destruction of her room. Abruptly he realized how serious this might well be.

She drew a deep breath. "But when I said I was writing a history of the princess's travels, that was not entirely accurate."

"No?" He widened his eyes in feigned surprise. "Imagine my astonishment."

"Perhaps it would be easier to start at the beginning."

"How refreshing."

She ignored him. "As a hereditary princess of the Kingdom of Greater Avalonia, I am permitted to wear the Heavens of Avalonia. Indeed, I am charged with the care and protection of the Heavens."

"The care and protection of the heavens?" He raised a brow. "Why not the sun and the moon as well?"

"The sun and the moon as well as the stars are indeed part of the Heavens."

He studied her. "Precisely what are you talking about?"

"The Heavens of Avalonia is a set of precious jewels. Specifically, it is comprised of a large opal representing the moon, an equally large ruby for the sun and four slightly smaller, perfect diamonds—"

"The stars?"

"Exactly." She nodded. "They are set in a wide gold cuff and traditionally worn by the queen in the absence of a hereditary princess. Otherwise, it is one of the duties of my office to safeguard the Heavens. It is a tradition hundreds of years old."

"A tradition? Like Avalonian brandy?"

"Not exactly." She wrinkled her nose. "This one is much more pleasant and, well, legitimate. At any rate, I have worn the cuff for state events and ceremonies all of my life. It is only recently that it was discovered that the Heavens, which neither I nor anyone else had ever questioned, was fake.

"My brother Alexei learned of this quite by accident, in papers hidden away somewhere, I believe. The jewels disappeared during a time of great upheaval in my country's history, half a century ago. My grandfather was king and had a replica of the cuff created. He and the queen both died within a few years of the disappearance of the Heavens and the mere fact that it had vanished and been replaced died with them. It was a closely guarded secret and even my immediate family was unaware of it. The counterfeit is quite an excellent copy, but then I suppose it had to be."

"I see," he said slowly. "And all this happened fifty-some years ago?"

She nodded.

"At around the same time your Princess Sophia fled to England with little more than an infant, a bag of clothes and—"

"The heritage of my country."

"Are you certain?"

"No. It is entirely possible Sophia did not take the jewels. Even if she had, I am confident her motives were honorable. It was, after all, her sacred duty to protect them. But her flight from Avalonia coupled with the disappearance of the Heavens is too great a coincidence to ignore."

"A ruby, an opal and four perfect diamonds." Matt shook his head in disbelief. "Set in gold."

"I rather suspect by this time they have been taken out of the cuff. A handful of gems is much easier to hide than a wide gold bracelet. Besides, the gold is really not significant."

"Of course not," he said wryly. "The jewels alone must be worth a fortune."

"Indeed, they are priceless, but their value cannot be measured in terms of money." Her gaze met his, dark green—no, emerald—and intense. "According to legend, Avalonia will stand as long as the Heavens. They have been in my country for centuries and are a symbol of the right of my family to rule."

"It all makes a horrible sort of convoluted sense. Your ridiculous story about writing a family history—"

"It was not ridiculous."

"And why you wanted to be known as Lady Matthew instead of an Avalonian princess."

"Exactly." She nodded, obviously pleased that he understood. "If someone knew about the jewels, they would never tell a princess. However, they might well inadvertently reveal something to Tatiana Weston, a mere scholar."

He stared at her for a long moment. "I thought your original story about writing a family history was ridiculous, but this one is even more absurd."

"Regardless, it is absolutely true," she said staunchly.

"Oh, I believe the story." A gust of wind buffeted the basket and he gripped the rail on either side of him, bracing his feet to accommodate the sway. "What I don't believe is that you seriously planned to travel to the homes of three elderly women, engage them in conversation over tea, whereupon they would promptly tell you where a fortune in jewels is hidden."

"I did not think it would be easy," she snapped.

"I'm certain you didn't. I'm equally certain you planned to take advantage of their hospitality to search their homes."

She clenched her jaw and turned her head to stare off into the distance. "It could have worked."

"It's the second most foolish thing I have ever heard you say." He shook his head. "These are all honorable women from honorable families. They are not part of your Avalonian political intrigue. All they have ever done is to help a lady in need. You would do best just to tell them the truth."

"Possibly," she said grudgingly.

"While I shall never understand your thinking, I do realize how, to a mind like yours, your plan could seem reasonable. What I don't understand"—he chose his words carefully—"is why you didn't tell me."

"Why I did not tell you." She repeated his words slowly, as if she were struggling to find an acceptable response.

"That's the question." He was certain he wouldn't like the answer. "Why?"

"Why?" Her gaze snapped back to his. "I could not trust a man I had known less than a week with the future of my country."

"But you could marry a man you'd known less than a week."

"Indeed. But"—she shook her head—"that was different."

"How?"

"That was my life, my future, not my country's."

"Did you honestly think I was so desperate for funding I would take your jewels for myself? That I had no sense of honor? That I was a thief?"

"No," she said without hesitation. "But I could have been wrong and I could not take that risk."

He pulled his gaze from hers and stared unseeing over the treetops. He was angry, yet he was hard-pressed to fault her.

"Would you have done differently?" Challenge rang in her voice. "If you had been in my position, would you have put your country's fate in the hands of someone you barely knew, no matter how much you cared for him?"

He looked at her and blew a long resigned breath. "No."

"No?" She narrowed her eyes suspiciously.

"No." He shrugged. "Because I could not put the fate of a family I had not spoken to in a decade in the hands of someone I had known less than a week and was now certain was lying to me. No matter how much I cared for her."

"Oh." She stared for a long moment. "How much do you care for her?"

He shook his head and uttered a short laugh. "More than I ever thought possible."

"Something else in which we are well matched. It cannot be mere coincidence." She smiled slowly. A smile of promise and invitation. "Perhaps it is past time we do something about it?"

He grinned with surrender. Damn it all, he wanted her, and she wanted him, and maybe the future could take care of itself. "It would be wrong if we didn't."

Pity there wasn't room to do much of anything. The basket was designed for function and smaller than the gondolas on most balloons. Circular in shape, the bulk of the center section was taken up by his heating device. A narrow walkway, less than a yard in width, ran between the mechanism and the outer wall of the basket. Leather pouches for storage were affixed to the wall. There was barely room for two people to pass.

Yet within a moment they were face-to-face.

He braced his feet instinctively to adjust for the movement of the balloon. In the back of his mind he noted the wind was a bit brisker than he'd realized. Not a particular problem, but something to be aware of.

Tatiana gazed up at him. "I quite believe you would like to kiss me."

"Is it the look in my eye?"

"Most certainly the look in your eye." She slipped her arms around his neck. "Among other things."

Her lips met his and he gathered her close against him. The basket swung sharply with a hard gust of wind and he barely noticed it, far more intent on the feel of her mouth, pliant and welcoming under his.

"Matthew." She looked up at him. "I think it would be best if we were to descend." She swallowed hard. "At once."

He laughed and pulled her closer. "Come, now, Princess, if I recall, you quite enjoyed being up amidst the clouds. Surely you've not developed a fear of heights?"

"Heights is not what I fear," she murmured.

He studied her carefully. It might have been nothing more than the effect of the late afternoon light. The day had been gray and overcast with no sun to speak of, but the color of her face was odd. A pasty shade of white. Not at all normal.

"Are you quite all right?" Concern sounded in his voice.

"Fine. Really, quite"—she smiled weakly—"fine."

No not white. Green. He'd seen that color before. On board ship on those rare occasions when someone unused to the rigors of the sea succumbed to mal de mer.

"You're sick, aren't you?"

"I do not travel well." She drew out of his arms and turned away, leaning on the basket rim for support.

"Travel? You don't travel at all. You simply move from place to place in a constant state of slumber brought on by . . ." At once he realized the truth. "You drink that awful brandy to put you to sleep because travel, or rather motion, makes you ill. I should have known." He laughed. "I daresay that traditional traveler's toast is nothing but fabrication to keep me from discovering this little problem of yours."

"It is a most unpleasant problem and not something I prefer to discuss. Furthermore, I am glad you find it amusing, although I doubt you will be laughing for long."

"No, of course not." He stifled a grin. "You are feeling unwell and it's not at all gallant of me to make light of your problem."

"It is not your gallantry that will change your mood." An odd note sounded in her voice. "I believe, Matthew, we may be in trouble."

"In trouble?" At once, he looked upward at the balloon looming over them but saw nothing untoward. He glanced at Tatiana and followed her gaze. She stared downward, and only now did he note the treetops rushing past beneath them.

His stomach clenched. "Well, this is indeed enough to foul anyone's mood."

He leaned over the side of the basket. One end of the heavy tether rope was still firmly attached to the basket. He could spot the other end dancing in the breeze below them.

"Damnation." He stared in disbelief. "I watched the rope uncurl and saw nothing untoward. I can't believe I missed this."

"Apparently we were far too busy with my confession to notice."

He straightened and studied her. "I checked to make certain that line was staked firmly to the ground not half an hour ago. Given that, and the state of your room, I gather there is more you have yet to tell me."

"Yes, of course, but are you not going to do something?"

"There really isn't much I can do at the moment. We seem to have caught a current of air that is taking us in a northwesterly direction at a rather brisk rate of speed."

She glanced uneasily over the side. "Should we not, well, land?"

"Would you have us land in the trees?" He shook his head. "We shall have to wait and watch for a pasture or a wide clearing of some sort."

"Are you certain we can wait? Will not the balloon descend when the air cools?"

"Of course. However"—he smiled in a confident manner—"as that is precisely what I've been working on, there is no need for concern."

Tatiana eyed the odd-looking contraption in the center of the basket with obvious skepticism. "I thought you had said it still needed adjustment."

"Adjustment, yes, but minor." He studied the combination of padded bottles, bindings and supports with pride. "Those containers are filled with a mix of oil and spirits. Lighting several of them will supply enough lift to avoid the trees."

He nodded at one of the leather pouches hanging on the basket. "You will find a brimstone match in that pouch."

She stuck her hand in the nearest pouch and shook her head. "This is empty."

"That's odd. Well, no matter." He squatted and gazed at the bottom of his heating system. Tucked within the supports, for situations precisely like this, was a flint box. "I much prefer matches, but this will do."

"Good." She sank to her knees, folded her arms against the rail, closed her eyes and rested her head on her arms. "Do let me know what happens."

He cast her a quick look of sympathy. Poor woman. He'd never experienced such problems himself, but he could well understand her distress. It would be best to get her back on solid ground as soon as possible, but the balloon was already starting to drift lower, and without additional lift they could well crash into the trees.

"This is quite unsettling," she said, as if talking more to herself than to him. "Especially as it did not happen when last I was in your balloon."

From another pouch, he selected several of the thick wicks he had fashioned to fit his bottles. Normally, the wicks would already be mounted in the containers but today he had not planned anything more than a quick ascent, short and simple and private. He'd considered not even inflating the balloon today given the low cover of the clouds. Even so, at the moment, he was grateful he'd filled the bottles.

"Although we never flew freely like this, did we? I do not recall ever going farther than the end of a rope. It is an entirely different sensation altogether."

Fifteen bottles were arranged in a circular cluster, somewhat broader in diameter than a wine bottle. Once he inserted the wicks, he planned to light the five that comprised the innermost section. He could see a clearing in the distance and they would not need much additional heat to provide the lift necessary to reach it.

"And the winds in Paris always seemed so calm." She moaned.

He tugged a bottle free from its carriage and it nearly flew out of his hands. Unease gripped him. The bottle was far lighter than it should have been. He jerked out the cork, leaned over the side and carefully upended the bottle. No more than a drop trickled out. Quickly he checked the rest of the containers. Each and every one had been drained.

"This just gets better and better," he said, more to himself than to her.

"Matthew?"

"In a minute."

He needed to think, calmly and rationally. And while he fully expected Tatiana to be calm and rational as well, who knew how the turmoil in her stomach would effect her ability to be either calm or rational? Now was not the time for emotional outbursts.

They were not in dire straits yet, but their situation was not particularly good. They were moving at a high altitude, at a brisk speed and he had no idea exactly where they were. They could be miles from Effington Hall or literally just down the road. The balloon was descending, but slowly; that was in their favor. On the other hand, the sun would soon set, and that presented their biggest problem.

"Matthew?" Tatiana's voice rose.

If he didn't put the balloon down before dusk, there would not be enough light to land safely.

"Do any of your Avalonian traditions involve luck?"

"None that come to mind." She scrambled to her feet, grabbing the rail with one hand and clutching her stomach with the other.

"This would be the appropriate time to invent one."

"Why do we need luck?"

"We have no fuel to heat the air in the balloon and we are descending. However, we are also moving quickly. If we are extremely *lucky*"—he blew a frustrated breath—"we will travel fast enough to miss the trees below us and land in the clearing beyond."

She stared at him as though he were insane. "No fuel? Why not? Is that not, well, stupid?"

"It would be if I had planned on traveling across the country," he said sharply. "All I had intended to do was go up and come back down, never straying farther than the end of a rope. This, my dear princess, can be laid firmly at your feet."

"My feet?" Her eyes widened with indignation. "This is your balloon. I have nothing to do with it."

"The fact that my bottles have been emptied, when I filled them myself, means the fact that the tether was not secured, something else I checked personally, is no accident. Coupled with the destruction of your room and the missing letter means someone else is looking for your blasted jewels. And if you had seen fit to tell me the truth before now, I would have taken the proper precautions." His voice rose. "As it is, we do not even have bags of sand on board for ballast."

"I am not to blame because you are unprepared!"

He gritted his teeth. "I am not unprepared for what was planned, only for the circumstances we now find ourselves in."

"Perhaps they can put that on our gravestones!" Her voice was sharp, edged with anger and probably fear. "If they can find our bodies!"

"They'll find our bodies, upright and walking," he said with a hard confidence he didn't entirely feel. "All we need is a bit of luck. You don't, by any chance, have a flask of that foul brandy hidden away on you?"

She cast him a look of disgust.

"Let me think." He ran his hand through his hair and voiced his thoughts aloud. "If we continue along the course we are now on, given the slow rate of our descent at the moment, we shall crash among those trees. Possibly a good hundred yards or so from that clearing." He pointed to the tree line in the distance. "If we could get a bit of lift, it might enable us to reach the clearing, whereupon I could release the air and bring us to earth."

She squinted into the distance. "It is not a very big clearing."

"It scarcely matters. We probably won't make it." He stared up at the balloon. There had to be something he could do. "I can think of no way to increase the lift. We have only the necessities on board and nothing we can discard."

"You could jump," she said in an overly sweet manner. "Fling yourself over the side to save me. It would make you a national hero in my country."

"Posthumously, of course."

"That goes without saying."

"Then it would certainly be well worth it," he said absently, still studying the balloon. "I think I shall pass, but I am grateful for the offer."

"Can you not get rid of all of this nonsense?"

"What nonsense?"

She gestured at the mechanics in the center of the basket. "This."

"I most certainly cannot." He huffed with indignation. "This *nonsense*, as you call it, represents a year's worth of work."

"Come, now." She grabbed the bottle closest to her with both hands and yanked it from its support. "It is extraordinarily heavy and would probably do the job well."

"I don't care." He snatched the bottle from her. "I had those bottles made to my specifications. They are irreplaceable."

"Matthew." She stepped to him and grabbed his jacket with both hands. Determination shone on her face. "I will not lose my life or yours because of some silly bottles. They are delightful, I suppose, but they are still only glass and cork wrapped in—whatever you wrapped them in."

"Padding and rubber," he said without thinking.

"The genius is not in the bottles but in the creation. You created all this and you can do so again. They are most certainly replaceable." She fisted her hands in the cloth and pulled tighter. "*You* are not. And, my lord husband, I vow I shall not let you rest in your grave for a single moment if we end our days together without truly being, well, together."

"Indeed." His gaze slipped from her eyes to her inviting lips and back. "That would be a shame."

"I did not mean that." In spite of her obvious fear, the corners of her lips curved upward. "Or rather, I did not mean that alone."

"That alone is more than enough reason to live. Very well." He sighed, disengaged her hands and handed her the bottle. "Be my guest."

She cast him a heartfelt smile and heaved the bottle over the side.

If there was any difference at all, it was negligible. They tossed another bottle, and another, until more than half of them had vanished into the trees below.

They had not gained any significant altitude, but they were no longer dropping.

"Will we make it or should we toss the rest?" She looked at him in the way of women who are fully confident in the abilities of their companions.

"Of course we'll make it." The lie came without hesitation.

It was only in the last few minutes that the true desperation of their situation had struck him. He had always thought of himself as a man who accepted the realities of life, even his own death, and it was not in his nature to panic. Yet the thought of Tatiana's possible demise filled him with a desperate dread and an absolute determination to ensure her survival—even if he had to rip apart this aerostat, and all that went with it, with his bare hands.

"You *still* do not lie well." She cast him a resigned smile.

"I do not lie at all." He grinned. "Or rarely." He caught her hand, pulled her close, twirled her around until her back rested against his chest and pointed. "I do believe, Princess, that we might just make it to the clearing."

"Then what?"

He wrapped his arms around her and rested his chin on the top of her head. "Why, then it's easy.

"We just have to survive the fall."

Chapter 14

"Survive the fall?" Tatiana swallowed hard. "What do you mean, *fall*?"

"A misstatement." She felt him shrug behind her. "*Drop* is what I meant to say."

"Oh, *survive the drop* sounds ever so much better."

"It will be as controlled as possible." Matt's voice was cool and calm. If the man was frightened, he certainly did not show it. Of course, she was scared enough for them both. "I have done it any number of times before."

"Well, I have not." She grimaced. "Besides, I do not believe you. And should you not be doing something?"

"I am. I'm determining exactly when to start letting air out of the balloon. At the moment I am calculating the distance . . ."

He continued, and as much as she wanted to listen to him, it was impossible to concentrate on such matters as speed and altitude, although admittedly every time he rambled on about his heating system or those annoying bottles of his, her mind tended to drift. It was not that she was uninterested. But so much else occupied her mind these days that there was no room left for the intricacies of his work. It was difficult to pay attention to anything that did not involve recovering the Heavens and reclaiming the affections of her husband.

Right now all she wanted was to be safe and sound and firmly on the ground with Matthew by her side, and she did not care what process he took to get her there.

"All right, then." He spun her around, kissed her hard and fast and released her. "Now stand out of the way, and be prepared to sit down and grab tightly to the ropes." He stepped in close to the mouth of the balloon, reached up and did something she couldn't see. "I'm going to start releasing the air through a valve. The wind might make this a bit rocky."

He glanced at her and raised a brow. "I must say, though, you're looking better. This sort of thing must agree with you."

"Terror always tends to put color in my cheeks." She grimaced. "Although I admit, I have quite forgotten about my stomach."

"Excellent." He grinned. "Now hold on."

She gripped the rim of the basket and braced herself.

He was wrong about the wind. They were not buffeted any more now than before. But they did seem to be dropping rather quickly. The word *fall* was definitely appropriate, although *plummet* was even better.

"Damnation, I must have miscalculated." Matthew muttered a few colorful oaths and moved quickly to toss the remaining bottles overboard.

Tatiana couldn't help but peer over the edge of the

basket, even as she knew it was probably a mistake. The trees below were rushing past them and drawing closer at the same time. It was a dizzying sight that matched the sensation in her stomach.

"Get down and hang on," he yelled.

At once she slid down to sit on the base of the basket and looped her wrists around ropes stretched from the railing to the floor. She pulled her knees up, planted her feet against the bottom of Matt's contraption, closed her eyes and prayed. A moment or an eternity later she heard the sickening sound of leaves and branches against the bottom of the basket. Her heart beat wildly in her chest and she thought of all the things she had never done. All the things she had never done with him. And she promised herself, if they survived, she would do everything in her power to make certain she and Matthew spent the rest of their lives together.

And prayed the rest of their lives lasted rather longer than the next few minutes.

The sound of rushing leaves beneath her vanished and a moment later they dropped quickly but smoothly. Perhaps they would survive after all.

Just then the basket lurched horribly to one side. The awful sound of snapping branches filled the air. The basket tumbled downward ever faster. Matthew's voice rang out in the bedlam and she realized she was screaming. Chaos filled her senses, terror gripped her and she clung for dear life. Time lost all meaning. It stretched a second or a lifetime. Without warning, there was a sharp jerk and all movement stopped. The cessation of motion was as terrifying as everything else.

Cautiously, she opened her eyes. The basket slanted at an odd angle. She was in the higher end and peered around the contraption in the center to Matthew's body, crumpled in a heap below her.

"Matthew?"

"Yes?" The word was as much a groan as anything else.

"Are you—"

"Don't move," he said sharply, then carefully untangled himself from the ropes, lines and debris surrounding him. He moved in a gingerly manner, but every motion shifted the basket and struck fear into her heart.

"Matthew?"

"Hold on," he snapped. He struggled to his feet, leaned over the edge of the basket and . . . vanished.

Matthew!" she screamed.

An odd chuckle greeted her cry. A moment later, his head popped up from outside the basket. He grinned with obvious relief. "It's all right. We're on the ground."

"Are we?" She struggled to stand, but the basket still swayed. "It does not feel overly solid."

"Well, I am on the ground. You are still dangling from the trees." He reached out his hands. "Come on."

She scrambled to the lower end of the basket and fairly threw herself over the side and into his arms. "Oh, Matthew, I thought surely we were done for."

He held her tightly against him. "I must admit, for a moment there, I thought the same."

She buried her face in his chest. "I should not like to lose you like this."

"I should not like to lose you at all."

For a long time he held her and she wondered that in the midst of all this, she could think of nothing more than how very much she loved him.

"However, we are in something of a pickle now." He heaved a heartfelt sigh and released her.

As one, they looked upward. The basket, or rather what was left of the basket, dangled at a precarious angle a scant few feet above the ground, its ropes and lines hung up in the trees. Above them, in the deepening twilight, long stretches of taffeta hung in ghostly strands, pale and ethereal against the branches.

Her heart sank for him. "Oh, Matthew, your balloon. It is ruined."

"Yes, well, that's that, then." His words were clipped as if it did not matter. "We did the best we could. We hit at the very edge of the clearing. Another ten feet or so . . ." He shrugged. "It couldn't be helped. It's entirely my fault. I should have checked the tether and the fuel again before we went up. Furthermore, I know better than to ascend at all without someone on the ground to assist in cases of difficulty." He shook his head. "I have been exceedingly stupid and should be grateful that we managed to survive at all."

"Can you rebuild it?" she asked hopefully.

"Look at it, Tatiana." He grabbed a section of the wicker and yanked. It came away easily in his hands. "There are gaping holes in the basket; the basic structure of the thing was weakened by our slide down the trees. It cannot be rebuilt, only replaced. As for my heating system . . ." He waved angrily at the tangled mass of ropes and wires now settled on the downward slope of what remained of the basket's floor. "There's little there that can be salvaged. And the balloon itself . . ." He shook his head. "It is hopeless."

"Surely you can start over?"

"I have invested everything I have in this. I don't have the funding to start over."

"But with the money I had planned to pay—"

"I'm not going to take your money. Did you really think I would?"

"Why not?" She laid her hand on his sleeve. "It is only money. I certainly do not care about it."

"I do!" He shook off her hand and moved a few steps away, gazing out into the distance. "It may well be difficult for you to understand, but I have a desire to succeed on my own. Make my fortune with my own two hands. It's an absurd idea, I know, and in my youth I would have scoffed at the very thought of it. But now"—he shook his head—"I don't know. I should never have spent these last years on something as absurd as balloons, *aerostats*, anyway. There's no future in flight of this nature. You're at the constant mercy of wind, there's no way to sustain altitude for any length of time and there are a myriad of other problems I can't even begin to list.

"And even if I were to win this ridiculous competition—out of the question now, by the way— it would only provide me with the funding to invest in a ship. Not purchase, simply invest."

"Matthew." She had never seen him like this. Her heart twisted at the sight.

"There comes a point in your life, Princess, when you have to take stock of who you are and what you've done." He turned back to her. "I am the youngest son of a man whose wisdom and affection I did not appreciate until it was too late. I am a man who is not afraid to fly but fears facing his own family. I am a dreamer with nothing left of his dream but tattered wicker and a handful of torn taffeta." He laughed harshly. "I am six and twenty and I have little to show for my years upon this earth. I am nothing more or less than a fool."

Abruptly anger, swift and unreasonable, surged through her. "You are indeed a fool, Matthew Weston. I cannot believe I did not see it before."

He stared with surprise. "Your sympathy is overwhelming."

"You do not need sympathy, you need to be shaken. Or smacked. Or hit over the head. I shall not waste my sympathy on you." She planted her hands on her hips. "Poor Matthew. All he has done with his life is flown the skies in search of a dream. Certainly it was not a practical dream—indeed, some might say it was absurd—but most people do nothing about their dreams. Most of us live the lives that have been laid out for us, the lives others expect of us, without regard for our own desires. For what, in our hearts, we truly wish to do.

"You have been extraordinarily lucky that you have been able to follow your heart. You would do well to remember that. Success is of little consequence. It is not always the destination that is important, but the journey. Have you not enjoyed the journey of your life thus far? Have you not been satisfied in and of yourself with your choices?"

"For the most part," he said slowly.

"Then you have nothing to complain about." Her voice rose. "Certainly you have not made your fortune, and perhaps you never will. Does it truly matter?"

"I must confess, poverty has lost a certain amount of its appeal." His manner was wry and she could not see clearly in the growing darkness, but she suspected there might be a hint of a smile on his lips.

"You shall simply have to come up with some other way to make your fortune. You are a clever man. I have no lack of confidence in your abilities."

"You don't?" There was no doubt of his smile now.

"Not for a moment," she said loftily. "In addition, I have decided to rescind my offer. I shall not pay you so much as a shilling for our adventure."

"You most certainly will." He laughed, grabbed her arm and pulled her into his arms. "You called it a dowry, if I recall."

"You said you would not take my money."

He gazed into her eyes, a faintly wicked smile on his face. "I have changed my mind. I want what is rightfully mine."

Her heart thudded in her chest. "And what, precisely, is that?"

"The woman I married." He nuzzled the side of her neck. "In my bed."

She drew a long, shuddering breath. "You have no bed here."

"No?" His lips moved to the base of her throat, and delight shivered through her. "I had not noticed."

She closed her eyes and let her head fall back. "Nor had I."

Her hips pressed to his and she could feel the hard evidence of his desire. It might have been the relief of survival or the ongoing tension between them or simply impatience to at last join her body again with his, but she could wait for him no longer. "Here, Matthew, now."

"Now?" His words teased against her skin. "Here?"

"Yes." She struggled to hold on to a coherent thought.

"I don't know." He feathered kisses along her neck and pushed her dress off her shoulder. "It scarcely seems appropriate."

"You are a most annoying man." She gasped out the words, conscious only of his touch on flesh now overly hot and far too sensitive.

"We should make a fire first." His hands slid down to caress her bottom, his lips murmured against her skin.

"We have always had a fire." Her lips met his and her hands slipped around the back of his neck, drawing him harder against her. His arms tightened around her, her breasts flattened against his chest, her hips pressed tighter to his.

They sank to their knees on the hard ground, still locked in an embrace. Desire, need and the long nights without him gripped her with an urgency that could not be denied. Her mouth opened to his and his tongue met and mated with hers. She wanted to taste him. Drink of him. Consume him.

Without warning, he pulled away and stood.

"Matthew!" Indignation and frustration rang in her voice.

"Patience, Princess." He stepped away from her, grabbed a low-lying tree limb and pulled himself to perch on a branch.

"What are you doing?" She scrambled to her feet.

"Catch this."

The rustle and ripping of fabric sounded in the twilight, and the next moment a large piece of taffeta drifted over her head. She struggled to free herself and heard the soft "*Oof*" as Matthew jumped down from the tree.

"Allow me." He pulled the taffeta from her, tossed it carefully on the ground, then bowed in an overly dramatic manner. "Your Highness, our bed awaits." Abruptly, his tone sobered. "It has waited a very long time."

"Far too long," she said softly. Without another word, she turned away and slipped out of her clothes.

It was odd to be fully undressed out-of-doors, as if the lack of walls and ceiling unfettered one's spirit just as the lack of clothing unfettered one's body. It was a glorious feeling of freedom and, here and now, most appropriate. As if they were part and parcel of the grasses and trees around them. As if they were not separate from the earth but one with it.

"Princess?"

She turned to him and caught her breath.

As if he were Adam and she were Eve.

What remained of the lingering twilight cast an ethereal glow about him. He was as wonderful, as magnificent as she had remembered.

He held out his hand. She took it, and together they lay down upon the taffeta, face-to-face. For a long moment they did nothing but stare into one another's eyes. The urgency between them had vanished, replaced by deep, unrelenting need and the certain knowledge that they had all the time in the world. At last, his lips met hers, gently, with a tenderness that stole her heart. His kiss deepened, and she moved closer to press her body against his.

His fingers trailed lightly along the side of her leg and up over her hip to her waist, and she shivered with anticipation. His hand slipped to cup her breast, and she gasped at the heat of his touch. He drew his lips from hers, and she rolled onto her back, pulling him with her. He took her nipple in his mouth, and she wanted to cry out with delight. His tongue toyed and teased first one, then the other, until she could scarcely remember to breathe, and still the anticipation mounted.

His hand caressed the rounded curve of her belly

and slipped lower, to the curls at the joining of her thighs. She swallowed hard. He slipped his hand between her legs and slid over that most sensitive place that only he had ever paid heed to. His fingers slid slowly and deliberately into her and his thumb rubbed to and fro over the point that encompassed all her desires, her needs, her wants. The world around her faded, vanished. She knew nothing, cared for nothing, save the rhythm of his caress and the throb of her body in return. Sweet, agonizing tension built within her, well remembered and too long denied.

But it was not enough.

"No." She pushed his hand away and pulled him onto her. "I want . . ."

"I know," he murmured. He braced his knees on either side of her legs and guided himself into her, filled her, joined her. At long last, two again were one. And she knew a welcoming bliss that went beyond simple pleasures of the flesh.

There was a joy in her soul.

They moved together in a harmony she had never forgotten, as natural as the setting around them, as right as forever. She urged him on, faster and deeper, as if the very act alone would bind them together always. Her body tightened around him. He groaned against her and she met his thrusts with hers, his passion with her own, two bodies too long denied now together in perfect union. Perfect accord. Perfect love.

She strained against him, reveling in the feel of his heated flesh and the strength of his hard, muscled body against her own. The sharp edge of ecstasy coiled tighter within her, as if again, together, they flew. Higher and swifter toward release. Freedom. Bliss. She ached for it as much as she wanted this joining with him to never end. She wanted eternity.

Without warning, her body exploded with his and she tumbled in a glorious spiral of sheer sensation. She screamed softly and her back arched upward to meet his final thrust. He shuddered against her and gasped as if in pain. As if in ecstasy.

And they were one. As they were once. As they would be forever.

He collapsed against her and rolled to his side, taking her with him in his arms. For a long time they lay unmoving, wrapped in each other's arms. The clouds had cleared and stars twinkled in the night sky. Tatiana willed her breathing back to a normal pace, her heart to a normal beat. Still, there was something so absurdly wonderful about lying out-of-doors, gazing at the stars without so much as a stitch of clothing on, the man you loved equally naked by your side, that made her want to giggle with the sheer joy of life itself.

Beside her, Matthew chuckled. "There is something extremely uncomfortable under this fabric, digging quite painfully into my side."

"Do you mind?" she said with a grin.

"Not in the slightest." He propped himself up on one elbow and gazed down at her. "I have missed you."

"As the horse misses the flies, no doubt."

"Not at all." His tone was abruptly serious. "As a man misses the woman he loves."

Her heart leapt, but a voice in the back of her head urged caution. She adopted a lighthearted manner. "You do have a way with words when your lust has been sated."

"Oh, my lust is nowhere near sated." She could see his wicked grin in the starlight and desire stirred again within her.

"Excellent, my lord, after all"—she reached up and pulled his lips down to hers—"where would be the adventure in that?"

"Are you comfortable?"

"Quite." She snuggled against him.

They were wrapped in strips of taffeta salvaged from the wreckage, more than enough protection against the cool summer night. Matt rested against the trunk of a tree, tightened his arm around Tatiana and smiled into the small fire he'd built, a major accomplishment in the dark. He'd managed to locate the flint box in the remains of the balloon. He'd also spotted a road from the air and was fairly certain he could find it in the morning. From what he'd seen before the sun had set, it was something of a miracle they'd survived. Even if Tatiana didn't have a specific custom for luck, they'd had some today.

But their luck *had* run out in other ways. His balloon and all of his work were destroyed. He had no idea exactly where they were. And apparently there was someone rather nasty, given the tampering with his equipment, looking for his princess's jewels.

"I am hungry, though."

"I shall request a tray sent up at once." He snapped his fingers as though signaling to a servant.

She laughed. "Roast of beef would be good, I think. No, strawberries would be even better. Yes, I do believe I have a taste for strawberries. And perhaps champagne."

"What? No, Avalonian brandy?"

"No." She shuddered. "Definitely not. I shall certainly never develop a taste for it." She paused for a moment. "In truth, now that I think about it, while I can recall seeing people drink the Royal Amber brandy, I am not certain I have ever seen anyone drink Avalonian brandy."

"There is a reason for that." He chuckled. "Now, as it does not appear we shall be seeing that tray anytime soon, perhaps we can fill the empty hours with the continuation of the confession you started some hours ago."

"I'd scarce call it a confession," she said in an offhand manner. "More of an explanation."

"Very well, then. Explain."

"Let me think. I told you about the Heavens?"

"Um-hmm."

"And their importance?"

"That too."

"Did I also mention that I have a horribly wicked cousin who believes her branch of the family should rule Avalonia and will do anything to achieve her ends?"

"No." He shook his head. "That you did not mention."

"Then I probably failed to tell you she was behind the recent unrest in my country."

"Indeed." He sighed. "Anything else?"

"Nothing of significance." Tatiana paused thoughtfully. "Unless you consider the fact that she is currently in England to be significant?"

"Significant? Yes, I believe I would consider that significant." He thought for a moment. "How dangerous is this cousin of yours?"

"She has been exiled for her traitorous acts, she did

try to overthrow the rightful government. I doubt if she has ever killed anyone personally, although I would not be surprised to learn she has had someone else do her evil deeds for her. She is a widow twice over and both husbands died quite mysteriously." She fell silent for a long moment. "However, one was extremely aged and the other extremely foolish and the rumors of her involvement in their deaths could be nothing more than gossip. Still, both husbands were extremely wealthy."

"I do hope that is not a family trait? Disposing of husbands for their money?"

"You need not worry." She nestled closer against him. "You have no money."

"At last, a benefit to poverty." He smiled.

Not that it really mattered. He stared into the fire. He was no longer her husband, even if his heart told him otherwise. Even if she felt the same. Why had she said earlier today that she was his wife and would always be his wife? He wondered idly how difficult a royal Avalonian annulment of a French civil wedding would be to undo.

Not that they could or would. Not that they had any future together whatsoever.

"Matthew," she said, "what was the first?"

"The first what?"

"You said today my plan was the second most foolish thing you had ever heard me say. What was the first?"

"Oh, let me think. There have been so many, it's difficult to remember the first."

She laughed.

"I believe, Princess." He placed two fingers under her chin and turned her face toward his. The firelight danced over her features and reflected in her eyes. "The most foolish thing was when you said you'd marry me."

"In that, my lord, you have never been more wrong." She gazed into his eyes and his heart caught. "That was the most intelligent thing I have ever done."

"It cannot work between us."

"Why not?

"You are a princess and I am a failed aeronaut living on a seaman's pension with no prospects and no future."

"What if I were not a princess? What if I were to give up my position?"

"What if the sky were to rain gold coins?"

"I am serious, Matthew." Her gaze searched his. "Would you have me if I were no longer a princess?"

"I would have you if you were a frog," he teased.

"I said I was serious." She pulled away from him, wrapped her arms around her knees and stared into the fire. Long moments passed. At last she sighed. "Do you recall when I told you about Phillipe?"

"Vividly."

"Phillipe's nature was . . . how shall I say it? *Weak* is the best word. He did not take well to being the husband of a princess." She turned her head toward him and rested her cheek on her knees. "He had no real duties, no particular interests—outside of other women, of course."

She smiled wryly and he wondered if the pain this man had caused her was indeed past or if a touch would linger always. Anger on her behalf swelled within him.

"I have often wondered if another man, one with a stronger sense of purpose or a stronger sense of himself, would have fared better. Would have carved a place for himself at court that was something more than merely the husband of the princess.

"But then I wonder as well if any man could remain unchanged. We expect the wives of kings to be subservient to their husbands, in truth, their sovereigns. But a man in that strange office of spouse to royalty . . ." She shook her head. "I think it must take a man of extraordinary strength to survive unscathed. I suspect you might manage it."

"You shall quite turn my head, Your Highness," he teased.

She laughed softly. "To what end?"

He grabbed her hand and pulled it to his lips. "To whatever end is desired."

Her gaze caught his, and even in the firelight he could see determination in her eyes. "I shall not put another man in that position."

His heart clenched. Of course she couldn't. And he could never live as nothing more than a royal consort.

"However, I would give up my title and all that goes with it, and gladly, for a man I loved."

"But a man who returned your love would never ask such a thing. We are who we are, Tatiana. Nothing can change that."

"We are who we are *inside*, Matthew." Her gaze bored into his. "The rest of it—Her Highness, his lordship, wealth, poverty—it is all trappings and, in truth, of no real consequence. A king can be just as unhappy as a pauper."

"Indeed." He grinned and drew her back to his side. This discussion was fraught with all kinds of dangers and he dared not risk a confrontation about the future, hers or his, at the moment. Because, at the moment, he might not have the strength of purpose she saw in him. "But the trappings of a king are ever so much more enjoyable than those of a pauper."

She laughed softly and he wondered if she was as relieved to end this discussion as he.

They spoke on and off of various things through the long hours. The dowager's ball was planned for two days from now, and Tatiana worried whether those Effingtons who had recently been in Avalonia would recognize her by name if not by sight. She spoke of her brothers and her father and her home, and even managed to get him to speak of his own family. And she promised to tell Her Grace the truth. They talked late into the night until Tatiana fell asleep in his arms.

Matt found it impossible to rest. Impossible to do anything save stare into the fire and consider all that had happened and all that was yet to come.

His ballooning days were over and the realization did not especially distress him. It was great fun, but he'd never had a grand passion for it. It was little more than a means to an end and as close as he could get to skimming over the waves on board ship. Yet he had no desire to return to sea. If there was a passion within him, it was for the business of shipping itself. There was something uniquely exciting about the arrival of a ship fresh from foreign ports with exotic goods and visitors. The very thought of dispatching men and their vessels to the four corners of the world fired his blood. The idea of nurturing, of building a shipping fleet—no, a shipping empire—was as exhilarating as anything he'd found at sea or in the sky.

He had the heart of a businessman. He chuckled to himself. If his father were alive, he'd no doubt be scandalized publicly. But privately the old man would probably be pleased. And it was past time

Matt did something about it. Perhaps the place to start was with a small shipping firm, eager for a man of his unique experience. He could get a job as a—he shuddered—clerk for now, but he'd watch his money, invest carefully and someday he'd own the place. It wasn't much of a plan, but it was solid and smart, and he had no doubt he could succeed.

Still, a clerk could scarcely be married to a princess.

He stroked Tatiana's hair in an absent manner and contemplated everything she'd said and everything she hadn't. When all was said and done, it came back to one thing, and one thing only.

Whether she'd give up her life for him wasn't as important a question as whether or not he'd let her.

Chapter 15

*T*atiana sat on her bed, pillows propped behind her head, and stared at her aching feet. She was rather amazed they were not the size of Matthew's balloon.

Poor Matthew. He had indeed lost everything he had worked for, yet after that one outburst, he had appeared to take it all in stride. As always, she did so wish she could read his mind.

It had taken them the better part of the day to make their way back to Effington Hall. Thankfully, Matthew had an excellent sense of direction and managed to find a road he had seen from the air. Eventually they met a group of riders sent from the hall to find them.

The dowager had been extremely concerned, particularly after the discovery of the disarray in Tatiana's room, and was most relieved to see them alive, although she was somewhat appalled at their condition. Both Tatiana and Matthew were disreputable in appearance, their clothes torn and ragged, Tatiana's slippers in tatters. Her Grace was also clearly disappointed by the destruction of Matthew's balloon, and insisted on sending servants and a wagon with him at once to recover the wreckage.

Tatiana had slept through the remainder of the day, waking long after dark and only because a maid had arrived at her room with a light supper. Too tired to rise, she had had the girl place the tray on a table near the door. But a quarter of an hour had passed and Tatiana now eyed the offering. Were those strawberries? She glanced at her feet and back to the food. She certainly could not lay here forever, as delightful as that sounded. And in truth, she *was* rather hungry again. And strawberries? She did long for strawberries. Besides, it would be most impolite not to eat what someone had taken the trouble to send up to her.

She stretched her legs, pointed her toes, then flexed her feet back toward her head and winced. Her ankles were unbearably stiff. She swung her legs over the side of the bed and gingerly attempted to stand. Her feet felt like stumps, her legs were wooden and she wondered if they would support her at all. Cautiously she took a step and groaned. Every muscle in her body ached. From her shoulders to her toes, there was scarcely an inch that did not scream in protest. Not surprising, really. She and Matthew had fallen from the sky, after all.

She gritted her teeth and hobbled slowly across the room, grabbed the tray and made her way back to the bed. She set the tray on the side table, then collapsed face first onto the deep, cozy mattress. She could well lie like this, unmoving, unthinking, forever. Still, strawberries beckoned.

With a resigned sigh, she rolled over and struggled to sit up. Surely she would feel better tomorrow if she lived that long. Tomorrow was the dowager's ball, and even while Tatiana was reluctant to meet those Effingtons who had recently visited Avalonia, she was quite looking forward to the ball itself. She was not, however, eager for the discussion she could no longer avoid with Her Grace. Matthew was right. This was an honorable woman who deserved to be treated honorably. She deserved the truth.

Tatiana plucked a strawberry from the bowl heaping with the luscious fruit. She took a bite and savored the delightful flavor, the lovely taste of warm summer days. It was something of a relief to have decided to tell the dowager all.

And a decided relief to have told Matthew everything. Of course, she was fairly certain he did not understand the true status of their marriage, although she could argue that she had indeed told him. Perhaps not in a clear and concise way, but she had said it aloud nonetheless. Of all the things she had kept from him, that was the most difficult to reveal. She picked up another strawberry and sucked on it thoughtfully. She was convinced he did care for her and possibly had never stopped, but there was something in his manner last night that was vaguely unnerving. She could not put her finger on exactly what it was and was sorely tempted to attribute it to her own state of mind.

Still, what did she expect? Indeed, if he was the kind of man willing to do nothing with his life save be the husband of a princess, or even the kind of man willing to take her money, he would be an entirely different man from the one she loved.

Did he mean it when he said a man who loved her would never ask her to give up her crown for him? It scarcely mattered. It was not his choice to make.

A knock sounded at the dressing room door and her heart caught.

"Yes?"

The door opened and Matthew poked his head in. "I was wondering if you were awake or if you were going to sleep through the rest of the night. You were so deeply asleep when I returned, I suspected Avalonian brandy may be involved."

She laughed. "There was scarcely any need for that. I could well have slept for a full week." She waved at the tray. "Would you care to join me?"

"Strawberries?"

"I simply snapped my fingers." She grinned.

He laughed. "As did I." He vanished for a moment, then pushed the door open, a bottle of champagne in one hand and two glasses in the other.

"Champagne?" She raised a brow. "What if I had been asleep?"

"I would have had to drink it myself. Drown my sorrows, and all that." His hair was damp, as if he'd just bathed. He wore a long, silk dressing gown and, she suspected, nothing underneath. He sauntered toward the bed, a decidedly wicked gleam in his eye. "You have saved me from a devilish headache in the morning, and for that I am grateful."

"How grateful?"

"Eternally grateful." He reached the bed and handed her the glasses. She held them out to him and he opened the bottle.

"Are you trying to seduce me?"

"Don't be absurd." He filled the glasses. "The plan was to allow you to seduce me."

"And are you so confident that I will?" She sipped the wine and studied him.

He thought for a moment. "Yes."

"I see." She downed the rest of her champagne, set the glass aside and scrambled to her knees, all painful twinges forgotten. He finished his drink, placed the glass beside hers and stepped closer. She grabbed the tie at his waist. Her gaze met his and she pulled the sash slowly free. The gown loosened and opened. She was right. He had nothing on underneath. Her gaze followed the smattering of dark hair on his chest and the trail it led downward. A slow throb of desire started somewhere low in her midsection.

"My." Heat rose in her cheeks. "You are confident."

"Thank you." He laughed and reached for her.

"Not yet." She brushed his hand away.

He raised a brow.

She leaned close until her lips were but a breath away from his. "Tonight, Matthew, I am in charge of . . ." She pushed the dressing gown off his shoulders and it fell softly to his feet. "Sailing the heavens."

"Are you?" Amusement sounded in his voice.

"You expected seduction, my lord"—she sighed the words against his lips—"and seduction you shall get."

He drew back in mock horror. "And what of my virtue?"

"I think we settled the question of your virtue long ago." She rested her fingers lightly on his chest and traced slow, lazy circles. His muscles tightened beneath her touch. "Matthew?"

"Yes?" Her fingers drifted over the flat of his stomach and he sucked in a sharp breath.

At once, she had an amazing sense of power and she bit back a smile. "As we were discussing virtue"—her touch moved lower still—"do you think I am overly eager?"

"Overly eager?" His voice was strained.

"A tart?" Her hand brushed against his erection and he jerked and grabbed her hand.

"What are you doing?"

"Why, Matthew." She pulled her hand free. "I am simply trying to prove your confidence in me well placed." She closed her fingers around him. He was at once steel and velvet, rock-solid and soft as silk. "Now, do cooperate and allow me to seduce you."

"Very well." He smiled slowly. "I am at your mercy, Princess."

"Indeed you are," she said softly. Her hand tightened around him. He groaned low in the back of his throat and closed his eyes. "So, are you going to answer my question?"

She stroked back and forth along the hard shaft. His jaw clenched and his breath was shallow.

"Question?" he murmured. "What question?"

"Do you think I am a tart?"

"Good God, I hope so."

She leaned forward and flicked her tongue across the hollow of his throat. "Do you?"

"I quite like tarts, pies, cakes, that sort of thing."

"Matthew." She ran her lips lightly across his chest and he grasped her shoulders. "That is not what I meant."

He grinned, but he did not open his eyes.

"I do not want you to think . . ." She drew a deep breath and straightened. "It has been a long time, and I did not . . ."

His brow furrowed and he opened one eye. "You are not finished, are you? I am scarcely seduced yet. Why, I am barely more than compromised."

"No, no, of course not. I just wanted to say . . . that is, I need to tell you . . ."

His other eye opened and suspicion sounded in his voice. "What? Is there something else you haven't told me?"

"Not really. It is only that I . . . I have been with no one else since I was last with you."

"You mean since last night?"

"No, you annoying man." She rolled her gaze toward the ceiling. "I meant since I was last with you in Paris."

"Oh." He nodded thoughtfully. "Excellent. Now, then, Your Highness"—he closed his eyes and lifted his chin—"I am once again all yours. Do with me as you will."

She stared at him for a moment. "You do not seem overly surprised. I was under the distinct impression you thought Dimitri and I were not merely friends."

He shrugged. "A jealous assumption on my part, nothing more. I soon realized I was mistaken." He pulled her hand back to his chest. "Now, then . . ."

"Matthew," she said slowly.

He sighed and opened his eyes. "You're not very good at this seduction business. What is it now?"

"Have you?"

"Have I what?"

"Been with other women?"

What might have been panic flickered in his eyes. "Well, I did serve on board ship, and sailors in port are notoriously—"

"That is not what I meant, and you know it." She could almost see the gears and workings of his mind desperately searching for an acceptable answer, and at once she realized the truth.

He blew a long breath. "Yes."

Anger and disappointment washed through her, even as she knew her reaction was unreasonable.

"How could you?" She pushed him away, slid off the bed and stalked across the room.

"What do you mean, how could I? What did you expect me to do?" he said indignantly, a rather impressive feat for a naked man. "I was unencumbered, if you recall. Abandoned by a wife who could not wait to rid herself of an unwanted marriage, with no prospect of ever seeing her again. I had no intention of either pining away or of remaining celibate for the rest of my days. Did you expect me to?"

She whirled toward him. "I expected a certain amount of mourning for me!"

"That's how I mourned!"

"How long did you wait until you took another woman to your bed, Matthew? A day? A week?"

He paused, and indecision flashed across his face.

She gasped. "You did not wait so much as a week?"

He crossed his arms over his chest. "In point of fact, Tatiana, I have no idea how long I waited. I spent much of the months after you left in a steady state of inebriation and those days are rather fuzzy in my mind. I cannot honestly tell you how soon or how many women there were after you."

"That is most comforting," she snapped.

He strode toward her, the look in his eye distinctly unnerving. "I was the one in need of comforting, if you recall."

She stepped back. "I have apologized—"

"Not well, and not nearly often enough, but I am willing to concede the point. You are sorry and I accept that, but I am not about to beg forgiveness for anything I might have done after you left me." He grabbed her and yanked her into his arms. "Do you understand?"

Her eyes widened and she stared up at him. She could not recall anyone ever chastising her in as firm or threatening a manner. She swallowed hard. "I think so." But was that not one of the very reasons she loved him? To Matthew she was first and foremost a woman, not a princess. Desire, hot and urgent, surged through her. "Shall I continue my seduction, then?"

He picked her up and strode toward the bed. "You don't seem to understand the basic principles of seduction."

"No?"

"No," he said firmly. He stood her on her feet beside the bed and anticipation trickled through her. "The beginning of a good seduction does not lie in confession or recrimination, but in a kiss."

He suited his actions to his words, pulled her close with one arm and cupped her chin in his hand. He pressed his lips to hers, gently, as if this kiss were their first. She relaxed against him and her mouth opened to his. His tongue traced the rim of her lips, then delved deeper in a leisurely, lazy exploration.

His hand drifted lightly along her jaw and down the column of her throat, his fingers trailing over the sheer fabric of her night rail to the valley between her breasts. He traced circles around her nipple until it puckered and hardened. She strained against his hand, wanting, needing more, but he acknowledged her only with a deepening of his kiss.

His fingers caressed the underside of her breast, then slipped downward in an agonizingly slow manner along her side. She bit her lip, wanting to cry out with the sweet torture. The room around them vanished and she existed only in the reality of his touch.

His fingers whispered over her hips and around to

her thighs and over the curls between her legs. She wanted to rip away the delicate fabric of the nightgown, wanted to feel him against her without barrier. His hand slipped between her legs, the sheer material at once abrasive and exciting against her. He fingered the point of her yearning for long moments through the dampened material, and she whimpered with need.

Without warning, he stepped away. She gasped, but before she could say a word, he pulled her night rail over her head and tossed it to one side.

"That was an excellent beginning," she said in a strangled voice.

"Indeed it was." His voice was barely steadier than hers.

"Now what?"

He scooped her into his arms, laid her on the bed, then stood beside her and surveyed her as a general might a battlefield. "Now"—he climbed onto the bed and knelt between her legs—"close your eyes."

"Is that a principle of seduction as well?"

He leaned over her, his blue eyes dark as a wild storm, a wicked smile on his lips, and kissed her eyelids closed.

"For tonight, yes." His voice was a growl in the back of his throat.

His lips whispered kisses over her face, her throat and continued downward. He took one nipple in his mouth and teased and tasted with teeth and tongue until she moaned and grasped his shoulders. He caught her wrists in one hand and held them over her head, thrusting her breasts upward, like an offering to a conquering army. There was nothing she could do, and she reveled in her helplessness and his power over her. He moved from one breast to the other, and she thought surely she would die with the pleasure of his touch.

His hand danced over her stomach and lower, to the juncture of her legs. He caressed the top of her thighs, but did not approach that part of her that throbbed and ached for his touch. She arched upward, desperate for his touch, and dimly, through a haze of arousal, heard him chuckle softly. The blasted man knew exactly what he was doing to her. It was torture.

It was exquisite.

He pulled her wrists down to hold them against her stomach and shifted his position on the bed. His hand slid between her legs, parted her and held her open for him. She felt the warmth of his breath and gasped.

His tongue flicked over her, caressed her, encircled her. The sensation remembered in her dreams. *Sailing the heavens.* She moaned and struggled against his grip, but he held her wrists tight. Tension tightened within her until she was lost in the throb of her body and the skill of his touch. She cried out his name and abruptly he drew back and released her wrists.

Her eyes snapped open. "Matthew!"

"Tatiana." His voice was heavy with passion and his lips claimed hers. He supported himself with one hand and guided himself into her with the other. And restraint vanished between them.

She wrapped her arms around him and arched upward to meet his thrusts with the wanton eagerness of the tart she was only with him, always with him. He invaded her, filled her, consumed her. And she consumed him in return. Two bodies, one soul. As they always should have been. As they were meant to be.

They moved together higher and faster, to the edge of madness. Sweet and awful and forever. And she strained against him and he plunged deeper and harder until he groaned and his body shook and her own climaxed in blinding, magnificent release that stole her breath and her senses and her self.

Sailing the heavens.

A glory and a wonder and a joy, to be found with him, and him alone.

For a long time, neither moved. Then he shifted to her side, raised his head and stared at her, a bemused expression on his face.

"Excellent job, my lord," she said softly. "You do indeed know the basics of seduction. Practice, no doubt."

His expression sobered. "If I had known or suspected or even hoped that you would ever return, I—"

"No." She reached to quiet his lips with hers. "I cannot blame you for what may well be my fault. However . . ." Gently, she bit his lower lip. "You shall restrict your activities to only one tart in the future."

"A royal tart?"

In answer, she slipped her hand between them and caressed him. He gasped and grabbed her hand. "I can certainly see the benefits to that."

He anchored her legs with his and kissed her thoroughly. "Surviving death puts rather a remarkable edge on everything in life, don't you agree?"

"I do indeed. However, edge or not, it is rather more comfortable in a bed."

"We should try a bed more often."

"Very often."

"As often as possible."

"More often," she said and met his lips once again.

She had had doubts, before her return, as to
whether coming back to him might not be a horrid
mistake. She had had doubts as well over her plan to
renounce her title. It was a drastic step, requiring a
great deal of thought and consideration.

But every minute spent with him, in his arms, in
his bed, simply in his company dispelled those mis-
givings. She knew, with a certainty she'd never
known before, that this was where she was meant to
be.

It was not mere happenstance that had brought her
to Paris some fifteen-odd months ago. No simple impulse that caused her to escape the bonds of her position that day. No odd chance that led her to a park
and an English charmer with a balloon.

No, Matthew Weston was her fate.

Now she just had to convince him.

"If this is a small, intimate affair, I should hate to see
Her Grace's idea of a grand occasion." Matt leaned
close to Tatiana's ear. "Granted, it has been a significant length of time since I was present at any ball
whatsoever, yet this seems rather a crush to me."

"Nonsense, Matthew." Tatiana's gaze skimmed
over the crowd. "I cannot imagine there are more
than a hundred people here. Why, it is scarcely large
enough to be called a ball."

Matt studied her curiously. His princess was in her
natural surrounding. Wealth. Nobility. Power.

Her eyes sparkled, and excitement sounded in her
voice. When they'd changed from the carriage to the
larger coach, Tatiana had taken the opportunity to increase her luggage as well. And well worth it. The
gown she wore tonight was deep and blue and made
of fabric so insubstantial it clung like gossamer to

every curve. It was scandalously low and he tried not to frown forbiddingly when he glanced at her overly exposed cleavage. She was tantalizing and inviting and delicious, and he would wager he was not the only man here who thought so.

She looked, in truth, every inch a princess.

"I must admit, I am quite impressed with how quickly Her Grace's staff has put this all together. Particularly, so far from the city."

"It's ridiculous that the dowager decided to go ahead with it at all. Rather a lot of trouble for nothing." A waiter presented them with a tray bearing glasses of champagne. Matt handed one to Tatiana and took one for himself. "The balloon was the true attraction, and it's gone."

She shook her head in a gesture of feminine disgust. "You really do not understand anything about women, do you?"

"Apparently not, as I have no idea what you are talking about."

"It is obvious, my dear Lord Matthew." She spoke as if he were a small child incapable of understanding even the simplest concept. "The dowager duchess has a strong belief in the importance of family. As you are the grandson of her dear friend, she considers you an honorary member of this particular family. All this is to welcome you back into the fold."

"This is not my fold." He frowned and took a sip of his drink. "And I am not back in it."

"Come, now, all prodigal sons say that."

"I am not a prodigal son, nor do I plan on becoming one."

Tatiana sipped at her wine and cast him an overly innocent gaze. "You did promise to visit your grandmother and your home."

"I did not promise to visit. I promised to *consider* visiting. However, as we are discussing promises . . ." He narrowed his eyes. "Didn't you promise to tell Her Grace the truth about who you are and what you're looking for?"

"I do believe, my lord, that, just like you, I promised to think about it." She fluttered her eyelashes at him. "You are such a good influence on me."

"Tatiana." The woman would drive him mad in no time.

"Oh, do stop looking at me as if I have done something reprehensible. I have indeed decided to confess all. I simply did not have the opportunity today."

He raised a brow. "Too busy searching Effington Hall, were we?"

"Not at all." She bristled. "I was too busy preparing for this evening, as was she. I shall bare my soul to her tomorrow. If that is acceptable to you. I may even give up dishonesty altogether, if that should make you happy."

"Blissful." He raised his glass to her. "To your vow of honesty, then."

"Unless, of course, the situation truly calls for its opposite." She smiled in an all-too-regal manner and turned her attention back to the milling crowd. "I have no idea who is whom here. I am somewhat surprised there was no receiving line, nor were we announced upon our arrival, although I suppose this is not a formal affair."

"No, this is one of those small, family gatherings."

"Do you know any of these people?"

"I should, I suppose, but I entered naval service when I was sixteen, still a bit young for occasions like this." He shook his head. "I don't know a soul."

"Well, the tall gentleman standing near the dowager is her grandson, Thomas, the Marquess of Helmsley," a feminine voice sounded behind them.

Matt and Tatiana turned at once. An attractive woman with a mass of unruly blond curls and spectacles perched on the end of a pert nose smiled at them.

"Do forgive me, but I could not help overhearing. Or rather, I suppose I could help it, but it would not be nearly as much fun." She held out her hand. "I am Lady Helmsley, Thomas's wife. I gather you are Lord Matthew Weston."

"Lady Helmsley." Matt drew her hand to his lips. "Allow me to present my wife." He bit back an inadvertent grin. "Lady Matthew."

"You are the scholar from Avalonia." Lady Helmsley's eyes sparkled. "Her Grace told me all about you and your quest to learn of the travels of a princess. It must be fascinating."

"Oh, indeed it is," Tatiana said blithely. "One never knows what kinds of things one can find with just a bit of searching."

Matt snorted, then effected an odd cough and smiled apologetically.

Tatiana shot him a quick, scathing glance.

"Do you see the couple conversing with the dowager duchess?" Lady Helmsley nodded at a tall, dark-haired gentleman accompanied by a lovely blonde, also with spectacles. "That is Viscount Beaumont, and his wife, my sister Jocelyn. No one knew it when they wed, but he is your princess's grandson. In truth, he has a legitimate claim to the title of prince, although he chooses not to use it. I'm certain you will wish to speak with him about her."

"I had hoped to, but I had heard he, as well as his mother, were not in England at the present time." Tatiana's tone was offhand, but her gaze on the couple was intent. That was obviously the cousin she had never met, and Matt wondered if her newfound promise of honesty would extend to *him*.

"His mother has returned to London and is planning a small reception next week." She leaned close to Tatiana. "We shall make certain you are invited. That will be the perfect opportunity for you to meet her and inquire about the princess.

"Lord Beaumont and my sister returned from Avalonia only recently, as did Thomas and my brother, Richard. There have been some political difficulties there in recent months, but apparently all is resolved now." The lady cast Tatiana a curious glance. "But then, you, no doubt, are far more familiar with the situation than I."

"I have been away from my country for a rather long time, my lady," Tatiana said smoothly. "Unfortunately, I am not as well versed with the political climate as I should be."

Matt raised a brow but held his tongue.

"I'm not certain any of us are." Lady Helmsley shrugged. "I consider myself quite well read, yet even I am not as informed as I should be. However, Lord Beaumont is most up to date on current affairs in your county. He will be a fount of all kinds of interesting information." Lady Helmsley beamed at Tatiana. "I cannot believe the stroke of luck that has brought you here."

"Nor can I." Tatiana smiled pleasantly.

"The world is a remarkably small place," Matt said, trying not to grin.

"Isn't it, though?" Lady Helmsley tucked her arm through Tatiana's. "Now, then, my dear, you must meet everyone."

"I would like nothing better." There was a gleam in

Tatiana's eye that did not bode well. What was she up to now? She handed him her empty glass. "Would you be so good as to fetch me another? I find I am rather parched."

"Certainly." He leveled her a discreet warning glance. "I shall join you in a moment."

"Excellent." Lady Helmsley nodded, then steered Tatiana away. "I think we have a great deal in common. I write a bit myself. Nothing as complicated as the history of a royal family. Stories, really, not at all serious, but great fun. . . ."

Stories? He snorted to himself. If Lady Helmsley only knew she wasn't the only one experienced in spinning stories. He downed the rest of his champagne, then nodded at a passing footman, who relieved him of both empty glasses.

"Your wife is lovely."

"Thank you." Matt turned with a grin. "I think so." His smile froze.

He stared at a man of his own height and build, with eyes the color of his and hair nearly the same shade. A man who was almost a mirror image. Not quite a twin.

His breath caught and blood roared in his ears. "Stephen?"

Absolutely a brother.

The corner of Stephen Weston's mouth quirked upward. "Have I changed that much?"

"No." Matt stared in disbelief. "Not at all." Without thinking, he reached out and clasped his brother's hand in both of his. "I would have known you anywhere."

"Come, now, Matt, is that all I get after ten full years?" Stephen pulled him into a hard quick hug, then held him out at arm's length. "You look good. The life of an adventurer suits you."

"An adventurer?" Matt laughed. "Hardly that."

"No?" Stephen raised a brow. "What would you call a man who first served in His Majesty's Navy, then turned to sailing the skies?"

"Something of a fool, actually," Matt said wryly.

Stephen laughed and slapped him on the back. "Damn, I have missed you." He nodded toward a row of French doors on the far side of the ballroom. "Come on, there's a terrace out there where we can talk. It's too bloody crowded in here for my taste."

He started toward the doors, Matt trailing a step behind. At once he was struck with a sense of familiarity. Stephen was older by barely a year and Matt had spent most of his childhood at his brother's heels.

"Besides, we can have a cigar." Stephen glanced back over his shoulder. "Of course, if you don't like cigars . . ."

Matt grinned. "I have been known to indulge on occasion."

A few minutes later, the brothers leaned on the stone balustrade overlooking the Effington grounds. Stars glittered overhead and strategically located candelabras cast circles of light. Stephen's cigars were excellent and Matt puffed appreciatively, grateful for both the quality of the tobacco and the reprieve from more serious matters the simple act of lighting up cigars provided.

"So . . ." Matt drew a deep breath.

"You are wondering what I am doing here." Stephen grinned. "The Dowager Duchess of Roxborough is not above meddling to suit her purposes. I'd wager she had a note written and on its way to us before you did more than bid her good day. She thinks it's time to put the past to rest."

"She's made no secret of her opinion."

"And we agree."

"We?"

"We. All of us." Stephen puffed on his cigar. "Alec—you do realize he is the marquess now and head of the family?"

Matt nodded.

"He, James, grandmother and I are in accord on this." Stephen cocked his cigar at his brother. "Grandmother was pleased, by the way, to learn of your marriage."

"Was she?" A heavy weight settled in Matt's stomach.

"Yes, indeed. Quite pleased. She is not as spry as she used to be and much crankier than she once was. One of her favorite themes is the lack of females at Weston Manor."

"So none of you have married?"

Stephen flicked an ash over the side of the terrace and shook his head. "No one has managed to leg-shackle us yet. Of course, Alec, as the title holder, is the most in demand, but he is barely one and thirty, with plenty of time to wed and sire an heir. And neither James nor I are in any particular hurry." He grinned in a slightly wicked manner. "We are having entirely too much fun."

Matt laughed. Stephen joined him, then sobered. "It has been far too long, little brother, and you have been missed."

"I have missed all of you as well." Emotion swelled within him and he puffed quickly to disguise it.

"That's good to hear." Stephen studied the glowing end of his cigar. "Alec and James wanted to come with me tonight, but we decided I should come alone." He met his brother's gaze directly. "We didn't know what kind of reception we'd get. If you had yet forgiven us."

"If I had forgiven you?" Matt started with surprise. "What was there for me to forgive?"

"We did nothing at the time to stop events between you and Father from unfolding as they did." Stephen chose his words with care. "We have talked about our lack of action through the years and it weighs heavily on us."

Matt stared for a long moment, then laughed.

"I'm glad you find this amusing," Stephen said dryly.

"Not amusing, exactly, simply ironic."

"Oh?"

"You see, I feared the reception I would get if I ever dared set foot in Weston Manor again." Matt chuckled. "I was concerned that you had not forgiven me."

"Not forgive you? Now, that makes no sense whatsoever."

"Perhaps." It had made perfect sense to Matt for the better part of a decade. For the first time in his life he was glad to learn he was wrong.

"You know, Matt, someone rather wise once told us you would come home when the time was right."

"Who? The dowager duchess?"

"No." Stephen smiled. "Father."

A sense of loss so great it was almost physical slammed into Matt. For a long time he could do nothing but stare out into the night.

"I was such a fool," he said under his breath.

"Not at all." Stephen's voice was thoughtful. "You were the youngest of four sons. And so much like Father it was inevitable you would not get along."

"I regret—"

"Of course you do. As did he. But he bore you no ill will. In fact, he knew, in general, where you were at any given moment, what battles your ship was in, what your duties were. He kept track of every promotion, every honor. I'm not sure how he managed any of it, but he did."

The back of Matt's throat ached.

"We all had our disputes with him, Matt. More and more as he, and we, grew older. You were simply the most unyielding, the one who refused to compromise—"

"The stupidest."

"Give me a chance. I was going to say that."

Matt blew a resigned breath. "But I am the only one he threw out."

"Threw out? I was under the impression you walked. Or rather ran."

"Semantics, brother." Matt grinned. "Let us say it was a mutual parting of the ways."

"Agreed. So . . ." Stephen puffed on his cigar, tilted back his head and blew a long stream of smoke into the air. "When are you coming home?"

Chapter 16

"*I* have a cousin in Avalonia named Tatiana." Viscount Beaumont kissed Tatiana's hand and smiled. "It's a beautiful name."

"Perhaps that is why it is so common in my country." Tatiana laughed lightly.

"Perhaps." The viscount studied her for a moment. "I have the strangest feeling we've met somewhere before."

"Really?" She considered him curiously, then shook her head. "It is probably nothing more than the belief I have noted among the English that all foreigners look alike. Besides, my lord, if we had met, I am quite certain you would remember."

A startled expression crossed Beaumont's face, then he grinned. "Indeed I would, my lady."

"If you will forgive me"—she peered around him and waved to an imaginary acquaintance—"I see someone I promised to speak to."

"Of course." His pleasant smile belied the puzzled look in his eye. "We can talk again later, perhaps."

"I shall look forward to it." She nodded and

walked away, knowing full well his gaze followed her.

Of course she looked familiar. She looked exactly like his grandmother. Tatiana would not be at all surprised if there was not a portrait of Sophia hanging somewhere right next to the one of her husband she had brought with her from Avalonia. A portrait Beaumont had probably seen throughout his life.

She accepted a glass of champagne from a waiter and casually glanced back to see if Beaumont still watched her. He had turned away and was speaking to his wife. Tatiana sipped thoughtfully.

So this was the cousin who had helped her brother Alexei calm the mood of the people in Avalonia. From what Alexei had written in his letter, Beaumont wanted no part, or at least no significant part, of his hereditary title. That attitude might well make the viscount a powerful ally for her in the future. However, the future was not her immediate concern.

She searched the room for her husband. She had last seen Matthew, accompanied by another gentleman, going out the doors leading to the terrace. Perhaps he was still there.

This was the first time she had been introduced to a group of people as his wife. It was disconcerting not to be treated with the deference usually accorded her as a princess, yet it was also rather refreshing. When gentlemen kissed her hand and gazed into her eyes this evening, the object of their attraction was the woman before them, not the title. Even so, she was surprisingly ill at ease at being publicly proclaimed Tatiana Weston, Lady Matthew. She might lie better than Matthew, but her conscience apparently worked as well as his. Even if the title and the name were both legitimate, she could not ignore the feeling that she was deceiving everyone she met.

Worse, these Effingtons were a remarkably friendly and candid group. Unlike most noble families of her acquaintance, these people seemed to enjoy one another's company. In truth, they appeared to actually *like* each other. It was most disconcerting and provoked the oddest twinge of envy. Certainly, she loved her father and brothers, but the time they spent together was surrounded by the pomp and ceremony of office. Dinners were state occasions, balls were public events, a few hours on horseback were significant undertakings, even a picnic outing involved a full entourage and advance planning.

Would she miss the trappings and accoutrements of a royal life? A life spent always in the light of public scrutiny and private pressure? A life of princely wealth and personal power?

Of course she would. She would be the worst kind of fool if she did not. Tatiana did not especially look forward to living on Matthew's income. However, she did have substantial personal wealth that would remain hers regardless of her position, even if there was an excellent chance Matthew would not accept it. Well, she would not dwell on that possibility now.

Thus far, Lady Helmsley—or Marianne, as she had insisted Tatiana call her—had introduced her to what was possibly every Effington in existence. She would have no trouble remembering the current Duke and Duchess of Roxborough—they were a duke and duchess, after all—but the myriad of other faces, titles and names of children, grandchildren and cousins could not possibly be committed to memory without extensive study. She would much prefer having

Matthew at her side during all this. Even if the man did not know these people personally, he was familiar with the family itself. Besides, that annoying sensation of dishonesty still plagued her. At least with Matthew here, she would have his looks of disapproval and the double meaning of his comments to distract her from any nagging feelings of guilt.

She reached the row of French doors and stepped out onto the terrace. Stars twinkled above and candles set in elaborate candelabra flickered on a more earthly plane. The night was warm, the breeze gentle and the faintest floral scent lingered in the air. All in all, it was the perfect setting for a romantic assignation or an illicit rendezvous. She couldn't resist a wicked smile. If Matthew was not now on the terrace, it would be a fine idea to find him and accompany him here.

She moved away from the doors. "Matthew?"

"Oh, he left quite some time ago. With his brother, I believe." A voice sounded from the shadows.

Tatiana's blood froze. The champagne glass slipped from her hand and shattered on the stone terrace.

"It must be the night for family reunions, do you not think so . . . Your Highness?"

Tatiana drew a deep breath, marshaled all her courage and forced a cool, unconcerned note to her voice. "What are you doing here, Cousin?"

"What? No pleasantries? No declarations of how very much you have missed me? No pretense at affection? How disappointing." The Princess Valentina sauntered out of the shadows. "But as to your question, I was invited."

Tatiana raised a brow. "I doubt that."

"Very well." The older woman shrugged. "The

gentleman I am with was invited. He is some sort of distant relation to these Effingtons and really quite boring, but he does prove useful. This gathering was most fortuitous as well, and I understand I have your presence to thank for that, although I had already convinced him that it would be the height of disrespect not to pay a visit to the dowager duchess."

Tatiana folded her arms over her chest. "Why are you here?"

"For the exact same reason you are here, dearest cousin." Valentina shook open her fan and waved it before her face as if she were discussing nothing more important than the latest bit of royal gossip. "What a pity the fabled Heavens of Avalonia are missing. And for such a long time too. Such a shame for the country and, especially, for the ruling branch of the House of Pruzinsky."

"I have no idea what you are talking about."

"Oh, do cease the pretense, Tatiana, you know exactly what I am talking about. However, if you insist, I shall play your silly game." She heaved a sigh of boredom. "I know the Heavens have disappeared. I know this was only discovered recently. And I further know their disappearance dates back to Princess Sophia's leaving Avalonia some fifty or more years ago."

"You should be in prison," Tatiana said coldly.

"My, that was certainly abrupt and most impolite. Not at all like you." Valentina shook her head. "Prison would not agree with me."

"Yet prison is where I shall make certain you end the rest of your days."

"I will not pack my bags just yet." Valentina snapped her fan closed. "Where do you think you are? You have no authority here. I doubt these English are even remotely aware of events in Avalonia. However, do not think I have not taken precautions. It would be the height of foolishness not to, particularly with our cousin, the viscount, and his charming wife here. Did you know I have met her? It has been quite a chore avoiding her this evening, yet I have managed it. Have you met them?"

Tatiana nodded.

"Beaumont is quite attractive and every bit as annoying as the rest of you. I can lay my current situation, in part, at his feet."

"It is not his fault you failed in your attempt to seize power."

"My, my." Valentina winced. "It does sound so harsh when you say it that way."

"Forgive me." Sarcasm dripped from Tatiana's words. "I do so hate to sound harsh about such things as treachery or deceit or treason."

"Yes, well..." Valentina waved the comment away as if it were of no significance. "These things happen when one is fighting for a cause."

"The only cause you have ever fought for is yourself."

"And is there a better cause? My welfare goes hand in hand with my country's. It is an attitude you fail to understand." Valentina shook her head in a disparaging manner. "You are so sanctimonious and noble, but it is that very misplaced sentimentality that will spell the end of Avalonia. It is a weakness that cannot be afforded. Neither your father nor your brothers nor, I would imagine, *you* have any idea how to take a country in the precarious position of Avalonia's into the future. How to ensure its survival and prosperity."

"And you do?"

"I know when you speak of the great rulers of history, those who led powerful countries and created vast empires, the word *nice* is rarely ever used."

"Then obviously you are suited to rule," Tatiana snapped.

Valentina raised a brow. "My, the little princess has at last developed a bite. I wondered why they sent you to find the Heavens."

"No one sent me." Tatiana drew a deep breath. She knew better than to argue with Valentina. "You stole the letter from my room."

"*Stole* is not entirely accurate. In point of fact, that letter belongs as much to me as to you. It was, after all, written to our grandmother." Valentina shrugged. "I simply arranged to have it delivered to me. It has told me nothing I did not already know, but if you found it useful, I suspect so shall I."

"And you sabotaged Lord Matthew's balloon." Tatiana narrowed her eyes. "Or should I say you *arranged* the sabotage."

"One does what one can. I was really rather surprised to see you here at all. You and his lordship must be extremely lucky. I was certain you would end up in France somewhere or the channel or, better yet, dead. A shame, of course, but unavoidable." She studied the younger woman curiously. "Who is he, this Lord Matthew of yours? He is quite handsome."

"He has nothing to do with any of this."

"I doubt that. I'd wager he has a great deal to do with all of this." She smiled slowly. "I must say, you are full of surprises. You have always been such a dear, sweet, unassuming thing. The perfect little princess. I would never imagine you to be traveling around England pretending to be the wife of a lord and hiding your true identity. I wonder what all these charming people would think if they knew you were deceiving them."

"I am not deceiving them. I have simply not seen fit to reveal facts that scarcely matter." Tatiana raised her chin slightly. "Regardless, I suspect my identity would be of far less interest to them than yours. Particularly to Viscount Beaumont."

"Perhaps. But by the time you return to the ballroom I shall have, reluctantly, taken my leave. My only real purpose tonight was to greet the relation I have not seen for ever so long and see what I might possibly do to impede her progress.

"Besides, you can scarcely reveal me without revealing yourself. For whatever reason, you do not wish to do that. And I have followed your lead as well. I too am using a name I have no particular claim to." Valentina tossed back her head and flipped open her fan. "Allow me to introduce the Contessa de Bernadotte."

A primal, urgent and almost uncontrollable urge to tear the other woman's throat out gripped Tatiana. For an endless moment, she struggled against it. She drew a steadying breath.

"Phillipe always did prefer his cheese and his wine well aged." Tatiana kept her expression cool, her voice level. "I had no idea that preference extended to women as well."

Shock widened Valentina's eyes, then she laughed. "Well said, Cousin. I am impressed. You have indeed changed. But then, I suppose an unfaithful husband of, to be blunt, legendary exploits will do that to a woman. Even a princess."

"One is either strengthened by the fire or consumed by it." For the first time since their encounter began, confidence filled Tatiana and she smiled. "I was not consumed."

Valentina hesitated, her gaze assessing. "Not yet."

Tatiana wanted to laugh with the odd satisfaction of being equal to this woman. "Not ever."

"Perhaps I have misjudged you. What a pity, to have discovered it at this late date. We could have been powerful allies."

"Never." Tatiana shook her head. "But we could have been family."

"Family?" Valentina shuddered in an exaggerated manner. "Like these Effingtons? I should scarce survive the sheer boredom of it. However, husbands are an entirely different matter." She eyed Tatiana thoughtfully. "I wonder if your Lord Matthew is as . . . oh, what is the word? *Proficient*, I think, as Phillipe was."

"In truth, dearest Valentina, he is much, much better." Tatiana turned on her heel and started toward the doors.

Valentina grabbed her arm and jerked her around. "I shall find the Heavens, and when I do"—her voice was low, threatening, evil—"I will return them to Avalonia and claim the crown for myself. After all, she who returns the heritage of the country will be a hero to her people and will have earned the right to rule. There is much to be said for tradition, dear cousin." She smiled, and the starlight reflected wickedly in her eyes. "And I will not allow you or your Lord Matthew to stop me."

"No, Cousin." Tatiana shook off her arm. "I will not allow you to stop *me*." She strode toward the doors, not bothering to look back, half expecting Valentina to call out or even shoot her. She pushed open the doors, trying to ignore the trembling of her hand and the quivering in the pit of her stomach.

She spotted Matthew almost at once and made her way through the crowd toward him. Out of the corner of her eye, she noted a few odd looks, a speculative glance or two. Surely no one had heard her encounter with Valentina. If they had, someone, Matthew or possibly Beaumont, would have interceded. It was probably nothing more than an overactive imagination and some strange lingering effect of the confrontation with her cousin.

Or the realization that the stakes had just been raised to staggering proportions.

The meeting with Valentina realized her worst fears. Until now, she could fool herself into believing that her cousin's presence in England was a coincidence. It was imperative that Tatiana find the Heavens, if they could be found at all. Valentina could well claim the throne if she recovered the jewels. Indeed, simply by making their absence public in Avalonia she could undermine the rule of Tatiana's father and her brother's succession to the throne.

She reached Matthew's side and took his arm. "Matthew—"

"Tatiana." His voice was firm. "Allow me to introduce my brother, Lord Stephen." The man beside him stepped forward, and Tatiana tried not to gape. One would never confuse him for Matthew at this distance, but the similarity in appearance between the men was startling.

"My lady." Lord Stephen caught her hand and raised it to his lips. "I cannot tell you what a pleasure it is to meet you. My family has been consumed by curiosity over what kind of temptress had managed to snare him." Stephen smiled Matthew's smile. "Now I can see she is exquisite."

"Your manner is as polished as your brother's, my lord." She cast him a genuine smile and reclaimed her hand. "I can see the resemblance between you is not limited to appearance."

Stephen laughed, then sobered and glanced at his brother. "Are you . . . ?"

"Indeed I am." Matthew cleared his throat in that way he had when he was reluctant to tell her something. "Her Grace would like to speak to us in the parlor. It seems we are the subject of gossip."

"Gossip?" Tatiana held her breath. "What kind of gossip?"

Matthew's gaze met hers, his smile wry. "Apparently there is a rumor spreading through the room that you and I are not . . . married."

"That you and Matthew are simply posing as man and wife," Stephen added.

Relief washed through her and she laughed.

Stephen's brows pulled together. "My dear, this charge is not at all humorous."

"Oh, I don't know, Stephen," Matt said mildly. "There is a certain element of ironic amusement to it."

"I am sorry, my lord. You are right; this is nothing to laugh about." She shook her head and tried to adopt a more serious tone. "It is simply not what I expected. Shall we go see Her Grace, then?" She smiled up at Matthew.

"Indeed we shall." He held out his arm. She took it and he leaned close, his voice low. "You aren't the least bit worried, are you?"

"Not about this. I have a great deal to tell you. Besides, we have already survived your balloon." She couldn't stifle a grin. "Scandal is the very least of my concerns."

It was as close as Matt ever wanted to get to a tribunal or court of inquiry.

The dowager sat regally on a sofa, flanked by her daughter-in-law, the duchess, on one side and Lady Helmsley on the other. The duke himself leaned against the mantel with an expression of amused curiosity. His son, the Marquess of Helmsley, Thomas, stood nearby.

Matt and Tatiana stood before the ladies, Stephen a step behind in a silent, but appreciated, position of support. He braced himself for what was ahead, even as an odd sense of relief filled him that, at last, the pretense would be over.

"My dear Lady Matthew," the duchess began. "An unpleasant rumor has come to our attention. It is being said that you and Lord Matthew are, well—"

"Now is not the time for subtleties, Katherine." The dowager waved her silent. She pinned Tatiana with a firm gaze. "While we consider ourselves broad-minded about the relations between adults, we do not appreciate deception in our own home."

Tatiana didn't so much as flinch. She was serene and composed and every inch a princess. Matthew marveled that no one could see it but him.

The dowager studied her for a long moment, then smiled. "You are this man's wife, are you not?"

"Indeed I am, Your Grace." A slight smile tilted Tatiana's lips. Matt's stomach clenched. She had promised to confess everything, and this was not exactly what he'd had in mind.

The dowager nodded. "I assume the facts of this marriage are not generally known, am I correct?"

"You are." Tatiana's tone was as composed as if she were discussing something as undisputed as the rising of the sun. "We were wed in Paris last year. I have the documents to prove it, if that is required."

Matt stared at her in shock. "Tatiana," he said, without thinking. "She didn't ask if we wed but if you were my wife."

"My hearing is excellent, my lord." Tatiana cast him an innocent gaze.

"You swore there would be no more *misstatements*." His voice rose and he forgot they were not alone. "Isn't there something else you wish to say?"

Tatiana thought for a moment, then shook her head. "Not on this particular matter."

He gritted his teeth and bent closer to her, aware every gaze in the room was intent upon them, but no longer caring. "What about the annulment? The dissolution of the marriage?"

She sighed. "Matthew, I told you I was your wife and would always be your wife."

He stared at her in confusion. "What?"

The dowager cleared her throat. "And I suspect, Matthew, she has the papers to prove it."

Tatiana cast the dowager a brilliant smile and the elderly woman grinned back.

Matt shook his head. "I don't understand any of this."

"Understanding will come, my boy," Her Grace said coolly. "Now, then, there are a few other matters I should like to discuss. Ladies," she addressed the women sitting beside her, "I shall trust you to lay this nasty rumor to rest."

The women exchanged glances, then stood with obvious reluctance.

"I assure you, you will miss nothing of significance

by leaving." The dowager chuckled. "And should anything of great interest transpire, I will inform you both."

"Thomas, Lord Stephen, ladies." The duke stepped to the door and waited.

"I always knew they were married," the duchess said sotto voce to her daughter-in-law as they passed from the room. "You could tell by looking at them."

"Yes, but wouldn't it have been delightful"— Lady Helmsley cast a wicked grin at Matt from the doorway—"if they weren't?"

"I'm still not sure why we needed to be here," the marquess muttered to his father. "We haven't said a word."

"Only our presence was required, my boy, not our opinion," the duke said wryly. "Scandal is not official unless it is acknowledged by the gentlemen in attendance with the loftiest titles. It is an odd rule of life you would do well to accept, as it is perpetuated by the wives"—he cast the dowager an affectionate grin—"and mothers of those with the loftiest titles who are truly in control of this world."

"Indeed we are," the dowager said with a chuckle, and the duke closed the door firmly in his wake.

Her Grace directed her attention back to Matt and Tatiana. "As much as I am certain I would find the explanation of what has transpired between the two of you fascinating, it is no doubt none of my concern." She gestured for Tatiana to sit in a chair to her right. "Not that that would particularly stop me, but at the moment there are other issues of concern. Don't you agree, Lady Matthew?"

Tatiana settled in the chair and considered the question. After a long moment she met the dowager's gaze. "Yes."

"I thought you would." Her Grace folded her hands together primly in her lap. "Now, then, it's past time for you to tell me exactly what you are looking for"—she smiled pleasantly—"Your Highness."

Chapter 17

"Do you know everything, Your Grace?" Tatiana said with a smile.

"Not everything, Your Highness. But I have the means to discover what I don't know. In addition, I have a son who is a duke with excellent connections. What I do not know, he does or can find out."

"I do apologize if my deception has offended you in any way," Tatiana said slowly. "That was not my intention."

"I never imagined it was." The dowager studied her carefully. "You look far too much like your aunt for it to be a coincidence. Therefore, I made certain assumptions, and my son managed to confirm them for me." She leaned toward the younger woman. "If one is going to meddle, it helps to have powerful relations."

Tatiana smiled. "So I have always believed."

"Why are you asking about Sophia's travels?" The older woman's eyes sparkled with interest. "I am fairly confident you have very little interest in writing a history of your family."

Tatiana paused.

"Your Highness, I would not have sent the others from the room if I were not committed to keeping your secret. My son is the only one who knows who you are." The dowager's voice was firm, her manner honorable. "I am astute enough about the affairs of the world to know there was a good reason for a princess to conceal her identity."

"She didn't trust you," Matthew said coolly. "She doesn't particularly trust anyone."

"Sometimes, Matthew, that is extremely wise." She turned toward Tatiana. "You do not know me, my dear, therefore it seems rather foolish for me to simply ask for your trust and expect to receive it. However, do consider that your aunt trusted me. And, as immodest as it sounds, she did not regret it."

"No, I do not think she would." Tatiana drew a deep breath. "Did Sophia ever speak to you about the Heavens of Avalonia?"

"Do keep in mind the annoying problem I have with my memory, but to the best of my recollection, it does not sound familiar." Her Grace shook her head. "What are the Heavens of Avalonia?"

"Jewels, Your Grace," Matthew said. "Large and priceless. An opal, a ruby and four flawless diamonds originally set in a wide, gold cuff. I'm certain you would remember if you had seen, or been told, of them."

"I should think so." Her Grace's eyes widened. "Flawless, you said? Oh, my, yes. That I would remember. One never forgets jewels, particularly if they are large or perfect."

"Their value is far greater than any monetary amount. They are a symbol to my people of the right to rule Avalonia. Of Avalonia's very right to exist. It was not until recently that we learned they had been replaced by nearly perfect copies. It appears they vanished at the same time Sophia left the country."

"I see."

"Their guardianship is a charge of my position as hereditary princess. But I must confess, until now, recovering them was very much a personal quest."

"And now?"

"Now," Matthew said, "someone, more than likely a cousin of hers who wants to claim the throne for herself, is also on the trail of the jewels. We suspect she was responsible for the wrecking of Tatiana's room and the tampering with my balloon."

"Actually, Matthew"—Tatiana met his gaze—"it is no longer mere suspicion. It was Valentina. She was here tonight."

"What?" He started toward the door.

"Do not bother. She has gone by now. I met her on the terrace. She said she had impeded my progress and I now understand what she meant."

"She started the rumor about you and your husband?" the dowager said. "But why?"

Tatiana shrugged. "Perhaps to force me to reveal my title. I thought—admittedly a mistake—that it would be easier to inquire about Sophia and the Heavens as a simple scholar. I see now that Matthew's insistence that I am dealing with honorable people and should therefore be honest with them has merit."

"Complimentary as always, Your Highness," he said under his breath.

She ignored him. "However, it is more likely, as she was unaware that Matthew and I are truly married, that she assumed if our deception was uncovered we would no longer be welcomed here or at the home of the next lady on the list."

"But she has no idea that lady is my grandmother, does she?" Matthew asked.

"*I* had no idea," Tatiana said pointedly. "The woman mentioned in Sophia's letter was a Lady Cranston, not Stanwick."

"My grandmother was married more than once," Matthew said. "Her first husband was Lord Cranston. Her second was my grandfather."

"Sophia stayed at Weston Manor because Beatrice resided there for a considerable time before her marriage." Her Grace chuckled with the memory. "Another interesting scandal long since forgotten."

"Oh?" Matthew said.

The older woman paid him no heed. "This is all fascinating, Your Highness, and explains a great deal. You are certainly welcome to look throughout the house for your jewels, a room-to-room search if you wish—if, of course, you have not already done so." Laughter sparked in the old lady's eye.

Matthew raised a brow. Tatiana smiled weakly.

"I am fairly certain, though, after this length of time, if they have not yet been found, they are in all likelihood not here. I can recall no stories through the years of anyone finding jewels, nor can I recall abrupt, unexpected and unexplained wealth among relations or guests or servants."

"I am beginning to think Sophia would not have been so foolish as to hide them where she could not watch over them." Tatiana blew a long breath. "When Matthew and I began this, I confess the search for the Heavens was not well planned. I simply hoped that all would work out. In truth, the purpose of my quest was deeply personal and the jewels were little more than a convenience." She slanted a quick glance at Matthew.

Tatiana rose to her feet and paced before the sofa. "Since learning of Valentina's presence in England, I have spent much of my time studying the letter Princess Sophia wrote to her mother. I was doing so the morning before it was stolen.

"She mentions your help and the assistance of the other ladies. It is apparent she trusted the three of you greatly." Tatiana cast the dowager an appreciative smile. "She also writes of duty and heritage and honor. Sophia wrote that heritage is the tie that binds the past to the future. I paid no heed to those words at first, but now I wonder if her writing may be an oblique reference to the Heavens. I know it was a very long time ago, but have you any idea what she meant?"

"None whatsoever. Although there could well be another explanation, Your Highness." Her Grace's voice was gentle. "Sophia was quite private about her concerns. There was an air of determination about her even as she seemed burdened with an awful sorrow. Understandable, given all she'd been through. Her words may well be more reflective of the upheaval in her life than anything else."

Tatiana heaved a heartfelt sigh. "I am beginning to fear the jewels are lost forever."

"It is not nearly time to give up yet, child. It is entirely possible Beatrice knows more than I. Sophia did stay with her for more than a month, I believe. It was during that visit she met and married Lord Worthington."

"And then moved to Worthington Castle, essentially exiling herself from the rest of the world." Tatiana spoke more to herself than the others. "But Alexei searched there and found nothing. He is convinced the jewels are not there."

"You have not spoken to Lord Beaumont about this, have you?" the dowager asked.

Tatiana started with surprise. "No, of course not."

"He is your cousin and Sophia's grandson." Her Grace paused to press her point. "He could be a great deal of help."

"Possibly, but"—Tatiana shook her head in as firm a manner as possible—"I do not wish to involve anyone else at this point. In my brother's last letter he wrote that he is confident the viscount had never heard of the Heavens until Alexei told him." She sat down on the edge of the sofa and met the dowager's gaze. "I cannot help but think that the fewer people who are aware of my search, the better the chances for success. Just revealing the loss of the Heavens would give Valentina an advantage in Avalonia I fear to consider. It is a weapon already in her hands, but I am confident she will not use it, nor will she give up looking for the Heavens, until I do. Or until the jewels are found."

"Then you have little time to lose. You should leave for Weston Manor at once." The dowager rose to her feet. Tatiana followed suit. "Given your brother's presence at your side tonight, my lord, I gather you have gotten over your reluctance to return home?"

"Indeed I have, ma'am." Matthew grinned. "And I am most appreciative of your assistance in that regard."

Her Grace snorted. "Come, now, my boy. Call it

what it is. Meddling, plain and simple." She cast him a smug smile. "And most successful. Now, if you will excuse me, I shall return to my guests."

Matthew quickly stepped to the door and opened it for the elderly lady.

"I shall leave the two of you alone." Her Grace paused in the doorway and leveled a firm gaze at Tatiana. "I suspect you have much to discuss."

"As for you . . ." She leaned toward Matthew and lowered her voice. "Sometimes, my boy, love is indeed enough." The dowager turned and swept from the room.

"What did she mean?" Tatiana said.

Matthew closed the door slowly and deliberately, as if he needed time to pull his thoughts together. It did not bode well.

"Why didn't you tell me?" His voice was level and cool. She hadn't the slightest idea what he was thinking.

She stifled the immediate urge to pretend she had no idea what he was referring to as well. "I did."

He scoffed. "When?"

"Well . . ." She bit her bottom lip and thought for a moment. "Any number of times, I just can't recollect exactly, at the moment."

He raised a brow. "Odd, how they seem to have slipped your mind."

"Now I remember." She nodded firmly. "When I discovered your deception regarding your grandmother—"

"My deception?"

"I distinctly remember saying then that I was your wife and would always be your wife."

"I thought you were being sentimental."

"Sentimental?" She planted her hands on her hips

and stared. "If I remember the circumstances of that conversation correctly, the pervasive sentiment was not undying love and affection."

"Yes, well . . ." He waved away her comment and stepped toward her. "You should have told me long before then."

"I've called you *my lord husband*. Several times, I believe."

"I considered it nothing more than sarcasm."

"Well, it certainly is now." She blew a frustrated breath. "I tried to tell you, Matthew. The day you brought up the annulment, I attempted to say something then, but you did not want to discuss it."

His eyes narrowed. "I did not want to discuss the annulment of our marriage, not the fact that you did not have it annulled at all."

"That makes no sense whatsoever."

"It makes perfect sense." He paused. "Or perhaps it doesn't, but you know what I mean nonetheless."

"I knew this was how you would react," she huffed. "You are angry, are you not?"

"Angry?" His brows pulled together. "Of course, I—"

"I knew it. For fifteen months and so forth and so on, I knew this would be your response." She pointed a finger at him. "This is exactly why I did not tell you, although, in truth, I did tell you."

"You did not," he snapped. "And what is thrown about wildly in the course of an argument does not count as a legitimate announcement of something as serious as the state of a marriage."

She tossed back her head. "In your country, perhaps."

"In any country where men and women are forced to live together!"

"You are not being forced to do anything! Nor have you ever been forced to do anything including marrying me!"

"No, indeed. I did that of my own free will. I married you because I wanted to make you my wife." He moved closer. She stood her ground. "You are my wife. Apparently you have always been my wife, and with luck you shall be my wife until my dying day."

"Which could well be any moment if you do not tell me right now you are not unhappy about this!"

"I am not unhappy about this. I am bloody blissful!"

"But you are angry with me?"

"Not, I'm not angry. I am beside myself with joy. Ecstatic! I can hardly control myself. Look, Tatiana." His mouth stretched into a bizarre showing of teeth. "I am so happy I can scarce contain my smile!"

"That hardly counts as a smile," she scoffed. "I have seen better smiles on the faces of condemned prisoners."

"Oh, were they married too?"

"Only if they were very, very lucky!"

"Well, I consider myself very, very lucky!"

"Why?"

"Because I'm still married to you! And I love you! And . . . and—that's why!"

"Hah! How can you expect me to believe that?"

"Because . . ." A wild, desperate light showed in his eye. "Damn it all, Tatiana, what do you want me to say? Because it's true?"

"I do not know." And in truth she was as confused as he. "You just said nothing thrown about wildly in the course of an argument carries any weight."

"Yes, well . . ." His brow furrowed and he looked

like a drowning man grasping at a fraying rope. "I lied."

"You lied? Matthew Weston? Lord Honesty? I doubt if the rest of us mere mortals can accept such a concept."

"It's true, and I shall say it again." He raised his chin in a gesture she recognized at once as her own. "I lied. Or perhaps"—he thought for a moment—"I did not lie so much as I merely omitted a few pertinent facts, misstated a bit, dissembled somewhat."

She stared in disbelief. "You are making fun of me."

"Not at all." He stepped closer to her. "I am simply turning the tables on you."

"You are an annoying man."

"And you . . ." He jerked her into his arms. His blue eyes glared down at her intensely. A slow grin spread across his face. Slightly wicked. Quite wonderful. "Are my wife."

His lips crushed hers in a kiss hard and powerful. A kiss of possession. Of reclamation. Of reunion. And she responded in kind to possess, to claim, to reunite.

An endless moment later, he raised his head from hers. "I too have a confession to make. I have lied before."

"Oh?" She struggled to catch her breath.

"Indeed." He kissed her again. "When I said I had missed you only as the horse misses the flies about his tail, that was a misstatement."

"Was it?" She sighed.

"It should have been more as the fox misses—"

"Oh, do stop that, Matthew." She slid her arms around his neck and stared into his eyes. "Are you angry that we are still married? Or worse, disappointed?"

"No," he said without so much as a heartbeat of hesitation. "I am shocked, of course. It's rather difficult to go from not married to married in the blink of an eye without benefit of ceremony." His arms tightened around her. "Beyond that, I feel . . . grateful, I think. As if we have been given a second chance."

Her breath caught. "Then you are not going to insist on an annulment? I know it is extremely difficult in England, but in Avalonia, as I am a member of the royal family, it would take little more than a decree from my father. Although there would be rather a lot of explaining to do. And quite frankly, I would much prefer to explain why I have a husband I have never mentioned rather than why I want to get rid of one."

"No, I don't want a dissolution of our marriage." He shook his head. "I never wanted that."

"Are you certain?" She couldn't hide the concern in her voice. "You married a companion to a princess, not a princess."

"This is going to be extraordinarily difficult, isn't it?" His gaze searched her face.

She hesitated. "I do not know."

"There is a great deal to consider."

"I have spent more than a year considering it." Tatiana drew a deep breath. "Matthew, I fully intend—"

"Stop," he said firmly. "This is not the time for irreversible decisions. I don't want you to make promises—"

"Matthew, I—"

"No matter how well-meaning, you may not be able to keep."

"I have no intention—"

"Listen to me. Until the question of the Heavens is resolved, the question of our future cannot be. You cannot consider abandoning your family and your country in a time of crisis, and crisis for Avalonia indeed lies ahead if Valentina is merely a fraction of what you say she is. There will be time enough later to consider what is to become of us." He grinned down at her, but there was an odd shadow in his eyes. "For Lord and Lady Matthew."

"Lord and Lady Matthew," she said softly. "I quite like the sound of it after all."

"Do you?" He raised a brow. "It does not have the ring of Princess Tatiana."

"It has a lovely sound all its own." She beamed up at him and wondered if he could see the love for him in her eyes. "A sound made all the sweeter as it is a sound for two."

A discreet knock sounded at the door. It opened almost at once and Lord Stephen poked his head in. "I hope I am not interrupting."

Tatiana reluctantly moved out of Matthew's embrace, but he kept an arm around her.

"Actually, you are indeed interrupting," Matthew said wryly. "So if you would be so good as to come back later . . ."

"I would like nothing better." Lord Stephen stepped into the room. "But for some absurd reason we are to be off at once. I have been informed, by no less a personage than the duke himself, that we need to return to Weston Manor without delay."

"Tonight?" Matthew said

Lord Stephen nodded. "If we leave now, we shall be home by dawn."

"It is for the best," Tatiana said, pushing aside a stab of disappointment at the realization that they would spend this night in a carriage instead of a bed. And one of them would be sound asleep.

Lord Stephen looked from his brother to Tatiana

and back. "There is something far more interesting than a simple question of scandal here, isn't there?"

Matthew chuckled. "Yes, I suppose you could say that."

Lord Stephen's eyes narrowed. "Are you going to tell me what it is?"

Matthew cast her a questioning glance and she nodded. "He is family, after all, my lord."

Lord Stephen struck a lofty pose. "Indeed I am. You can scarcely be more family than I."

"Very well, then." Matthew drew a deep breath. "Tatiana is actually a princess of the royal House of Pruzinsky of the Kingdom of Greater Avalonia. She is searching for the priceless jewels that symbolize the right of rule and were lost some fifty-odd years ago, but there is a wicked princess also searching for the jewels, and whoever finds them first may well ultimately rule the country." He huffed a short breath and glanced at Tatiana. "How was that?"

"Concise yet accurate." She grinned. "Well done."

Lord Stephen stared in obvious disbelief. "Your wife is a princess?"

"Born to the position." Matthew nodded.

"And there is a wicked princess as well?" Lord Stephen said slowly.

"She is unfailingly wicked." Tatiana nodded firmly. "It is her fault Matthew's balloon was destroyed, and we barely escaped with our lives."

"I see." Lord Stephen's eyes widened slightly. "And there are jewels as well? Priceless, you say?"

"Oh, you can't put a value on such things." Matthew glanced at Tatiana. "Can you, my love?"

"No, indeed." She shook her head. "One can never put a price on heritage and tradition."

"Oh, and Stephen"—Matthew smiled at his

brother—"did we mention Grandmother might well hold the key to all this?"

Lord Stephen stared in obvious confusion. "Our grandmother?"

"The very one." Matthew nodded.

Lord Stephen stared suspiciously for a long moment, then a grin broke on his face. "Matthew, you haven't changed a bit. That is an outstanding story." He laughed. "Good job, Brother. I daresay I didn't know you had it in you."

Matthew traded glances with Tatiana.

"You had me until that part about Grandmother." Lord Stephen shook his head and chuckled. "Imagine, that eminently proper lady involved in anything as absurd as missing jewels and wicked princesses."

"Imagine." Matthew grinned and accompanied Tatiana to the door. "However, we do need to be off. We can talk more about all of this in the carriage."

"Oh, certainly." Lord Stephen winked at Tatiana. "I can scarcely wait to hear more about the evil princess and the priceless jewels."

"It may well be even more amusing than you suspect," Tatiana said with a smile.

"I have no doubt of that. *Princess*." Lord Stephen snorted. "That is the best part. Matthew wed to a princess."

"Not at all, that's just the beginning. I suspect you'll be hearing all sorts of interesting things." Matthew opened the door and allowed Tatiana to proceed, then glanced back at his brother. "By the way, Stephen, do you recall ever hearing anything of a scandalous nature about Grandmother and Grandfather?"

Chapter 18

*T*he sun was still low in the sky when Matt at last caught sight of Weston Manor.

It hadn't, of course, changed at all. The manor sat precisely as it had sat for nearly a century and a half, sprawled at the end of a gravel drive like an overfed cat lounging in the warmth of the day. He had always seen it like this, even though he now recognized the design of the house was not at all sprawling but precise and formal, with its central portico flanked by symmetrical wings. The early morning light cast a warm glow upon the pale stone walls; the rows of many-paned windows stacked on top of one another for two soaring floors glittered in the sun. Still, regardless of his knowledge and appreciation of architecture and style, the manor struck him now, as it always had, as short and plump and comfortable.

Home.

The word echoed in the back of his mind, the sight of the manor itself evoking a rush of emotion he had not expected.

"You should probably awaken her." Stephen

stretched and yawned on the seat across from Matt. "We will be at the door in a few minutes."

Matt glanced down at Tatiana and grinned. His wife was curled up at his side, asleep as always.

His wife. That too evoked emotions he did not expect.

He loved her, of course, that was no longer in question, if indeed it had ever been. Throughout the night, in those few moments when he and Stephen were not talking of the years apart, his thoughts turned from recollections of the past to speculation about the future.

A very uncertain future.

He could not live the kind of useless life her first husband had. Even if he were willing to try, he knew she would never allow it. He knew as well, from what she had said and what she had implied, she was willing to give up her crown for him.

How in the name of all that's holy could he ever allow that?

It wasn't a matter of forfeiting some insignificant title. She was a princess. A member of the royal family and third in line to rule Avalonia. She would not merely be giving up an office but her country. And her people. And her family.

She might well love him enough to sacrifice everything, but he loved her too much to let her.

"So she really is a princess?" Stephen said with a note of awe in his voice.

Matt pushed his thoughts aside for the moment and forced a light chuckle. "Indeed she is."

"And all the rest of it: the missing jewels, sabotage of your balloon, Grandmother's involvement—"

"Don't forget the wicked princess."

"I would never forget the wicked princess."

Stephen smiled in a rather wicked manner of his own. "Is this wicked princess at all attractive?"

Matt laughed softly. "As far as I know."

"I wouldn't mind a princess of my own." Stephen wagged his brows in a lascivious manner. "I should be more than willing to take her off your hands should she make an appearance here."

"She has already had two husbands," Tatiana murmured. "Neither of whom survived the marriage."

"Ouch." Stephen winced. "Scarcely seems worth the effort."

Tatiana opened her eyes and gazed up at her husband. His breath caught.

"Oh, I don't know, Stephen," Matt said. "The right princess is well worth the effort."

She smiled and shifted to sit upright. She glanced at Stephen, who straightened in his seat at once. "And the wrong princess can be deadly."

"Sounds entirely too hazardous to suit me." Stephen shook his head. "I shall simply have to avoid princesses in the future as anything other than"—he thought for a moment, then grinned—"sisters."

The carriage rolled to a stop amid their laughter and the trio disembarked. Stephen and Tatiana started up the front steps but Matt lingered behind. For a long moment he stood before the house and gazed upward.

A myriad of childhood scenes flashed through his mind. At one time he would have thought all his memories would be bad. But here and now, the reminiscences that held him motionless were of happier times. He remembered how, even as a boy, Alec took the position of heir to the title somberly but still managed to run faster, ride harder and take more risks than anyone else. Or how James, with his nose always in a book, made use of his literary skills to convince his brothers there were fairies living in the garden and goblins in the woods. Or how Stephen delighted in turning James's stories into reality, and thus created tiny fairy footprints under the gardener's finest blooms and goblin dens under the stone creek bridge.

Then there was Matt, who took risks like Alec and spun stories like James and joked like Stephen. And ultimately rebelled against it all.

And there was his father, who was beloved when Matt was a child, detested when Matt was a youth and mourned when it was too late.

"It's not as daunting as you think," Stephen said softly.

"Probably not." Matt shook his head and grinned wryly. "It's probably worse."

For the second time in as many days, Matt was not only willing to admit he was wrong, but glad of it.

Alec and James greeted him like the long-lost brother he was, their welcome every bit as warm as Stephen's. There were no awkward moments between the brothers, no silence fraught with unsaid charges. No recriminations, no accusations, no censure. It was not as if they'd never parted; all had grown and changed with the years. But rather, having been apart, they could appreciate who they were now and the bond that joined them.

Tatiana had watched the reunion with obvious amusement, then excused herself, pleading a need to rest. A falsehood, of course. The woman never slept better than she did in a carriage with a glass of Avalonian brandy in her.

Now the brothers had gathered in the Weston library. It was a room designed by gentlemen for the comfort of gentlemen, and it too had not changed. A circle of well-worn leather chairs was arranged near the fireplace, each flanked on either side by small tables specifically placed to accommodate glasses or whatever else might be necessary. The chairs were extraordinarily comfortable and the company unequaled. It was not yet noon, but each brother held a glass of good brandy in one hand and a cigar in the other. A pale blue haze hung like a halo above them, distorting the light from the tall widows.

Damnation, it was good to be home.

"I am sorry about your balloon," James said. "I was quite looking forward to taking flight with you."

Stephen nodded. "As was I."

"We all were. However, that's neither here nor there at the moment." Alec studied his youngest brother. "The real question is, what will you do now?"

"And an excellent question it is, too." Matt raised his glass in a toast.

"But do you have an excellent answer?" James asked.

"Or any answer at all?" Stephen chuckled. "I daresay I'm still looking for one."

Matt took a long sip and considered his plans. He wasn't entirely sure his brothers would appreciate having a clerk in the family. "I am seriously considering gainful employment."

"No." Stephen feigned a shocked gasp. "Not that."

"Yes, indeed." Matt nodded in mock solemnity. "When this business of Tatiana's is resolved, I plan to return to London and seek a job with a shipping firm."

"A shipping firm?" James said. "It doesn't sound

terribly exciting, unless you're planning on returning to sea yourself."

"Not on a regular basis, James, although I shall not rule out an occasional voyage. Oddly enough, I do find the idea of commerce exciting." Matt blew a smoke ring into the air to drift lazily upward. "I have no idea why, mind you. There are no particular business skills running through the family."

Alec pointed his cigar. "Actually, Matt, Father was rather intrigued by business. He continually made investments, most of them sound. He seemed to have a gift for it and a bit of a passion as well."

Stephen nodded smugly. "See? Didn't I say you were just like him?"

Matt laughed. "If he had a gift for investment, then I do hope so. My plan at the moment, such as it is, is to earn a living beyond my pension for investment purposes while simultaneously learning the business of shipping. Admittedly, it will take some time. But"—he shrugged—"time is the one thing I have in abundance."

Alec frowned. "I certainly understand wanting to learn about the business that interests you. I find that admirable and quite wise. What I don't understand is why you don't simply start a firm yourself or purchase an existing firm."

"Money, dear brother. The only true purpose of my venture with balloons, if indeed I had a purpose at all, was to earn enough with my designs to invest in a ship and thereby make my fortune."

"That was a plan?" Disbelief rang in James's voice.

"Yes, well, it doesn't sound like much of a plan now, but it made a great deal of sense at the time." Matt thought for a moment. "Or perhaps it was unreasonable then too and was nothing more than an excuse. It was great fun, you know. Flying above the earth. Tinkering with machinery." He grinned at Stephen. "And women love balloons."

"I should get one myself, then." Stephen raised his glass to his brother.

"Stephen," Alex said firmly. "You didn't tell him everything you were instructed to, did you?"

"I didn't have the time." Stephen shrugged. "One minute we were being interrogated about the validity of Matt's marriage, and the next we were being shown the door. Add to that Matt's story about princesses and missing jewels and, well"—he shook his head—"everything else paled in significance."

Matt looked from one brother to the next. "What did he fail to mention?"

Alec and James traded glances. Alec's gaze met Matt's. "It's not necessary for you to find employment to supplement your income."

"Come, now, Alec," Matt said. "I knew you wouldn't be especially happy at the idea of a Weston as a lowly clerk, but I am the youngest and have always been well aware that I have no expectations."

"Matt," James said. "There is money available for you."

Matt shook his head firmly. "I am not going to take your money. I have long decided that I wanted to succeed on my own."

"There are moments, little brother, when our elders drive me quite mad." Stephen heaved a long-suffering sigh. "What they are trying to say—poorly, I might add—is that unbeknownst to us until long after you'd left, Father did indeed have a gift for investment in all kinds of things. Ships—"

"Far Eastern trade," Alec said.

"Plantations in the West Indies," James added.

"And any number of other interesting ventures. The point is, while the estate and Weston Manor are Alec's, Father made sure the rest of us were well provided for." Stephen grinned.

"Each of us has a substantial legacy." Alec smiled.

James chuckled. "Beyond substantial."

Matt stared at his brothers. "I was notified of Father's death. Why wasn't I told of this?"

Once again, the brothers traded glances.

"There was a stipulation." Alec studied his brother. "You were not to have your share until you came home. Father made it clear that—"

"I would come home when the time was right." He glanced at Stephen. "He did mention that much."

Stephen shrugged.

"I must say, this is an unexpected turn of events." Matt leaned back in his chair, puffed at the cigar and stared up at the coffered ceiling. It was at once odd to note he had typically gazed upward in much the same way during any number of dressing-downs, and ironic to realize he had returned to the same setting to receive his father's final gift.

He did indeed want to make his own way in life, and had his brothers simply come up with a plan to give him money, he never would have taken it. But this was different. This was from his father. The very fact that his father had thought of him at all, and had in the end treated him no differently than his brothers, was a gift far beyond a monetary legacy.

And that he had to come here to get it was his father's way of saying he was welcome home.

Matt looked at Alec. "Substantial, you say?"

Alec nodded. "Quite."

Matt met James's gaze. "Enough for a ship or two?"

"Perhaps a small fleet," James said.

Matt glanced at Stephen. "I'd be a fool to turn it down, wouldn't I?"

"Actually," Stephen said in an offhand manner, "*fool* is putting it kindly."

"Then I really have no choice." Matt grinned.

"Few of us truly do in life, Matthew." A familiar voice sounded from the doorway. "The difficulty is in accepting it."

At once Matt and his brothers were on their feet. His grandmother, Beatrice, the Dowager Marchioness of Stanwick, stood in the doorway, as unchanging as the house around her. She was not quite as tall as he remembered, but tall for a woman nonetheless, and even though she leaned on a cane, her bearing was still elegant. Matt stepped forward to greet her.

"Grandmother." He took her hands in his and kissed one offered cheek, then the other. "I have missed you."

"It is nice to be missed," she said in a stern tone. "Although an occasional letter would have been far nicer."

She pinned him with an unyielding gaze and he resisted the urge to shift his weight from foot to foot.

"However"—she allowed a grudging smile to crease her lips—"I can well understand how the exciting life of an adventurous young man might preclude such things as courtesy."

"I am sorry, Grandmother." Matt smiled weakly, feeling rather more like a ten-year-old boy than an adventurous anything.

"I'm sure you are at the moment. Now . . ." She glanced pointedly at Stephen, who immediately moved to shift an upholstered chair hidden in the shadows against the bookshelves, to the circle of male seating. The stiff-backed, tapestry-covered chair, with its delicate wooden arms, was as startling a contrast in this masculine domain as the elderly lady herself. A minute later, she settled comfortably in the chair.

"This is quite an honor, Matt," Alec said with a grin. "The library's not Grandmother's favorite spot."

"On the contrary, Alec, I quite like this room. I always have. I simply believe that in a household such as this, even if you and your brothers are away more often than you are here, there should be places reserved for the primary entertainment of men and women. This room I have graciously granted to you and your bothers. Besides"—she wrinkled her nose—"the foul odor of cigars is ever-present here."

At once four cigars were stubbed out. James stepped to the side windows, Stephen to the rear windows and both men simultaneously threw up the sashes. Alec pulled a large lace fan from a drawer in a table, obviously kept there for just this purpose, and handed it to his grandmother.

"Now, then, Matthew, do sit down and stop towering over me." She smacked the chair next to her with the fan. "I hate it when men tower over me. It is most disconcerting."

Matt sat obediently.

Her gaze skimmed over the other men. "The rest of you can sit as well."

They sat without question, and Matt bit back a smile.

"I don't know what you are smirking about." She swatted his knee with her fan. "They have one and all at least written when they've been in London or elsewhere."

Out of the corner of his eye, he noted Alec nudge James and Stephen stifle a grin. And for a moment he was indeed no more than ten years of age.

"Now, then, Matthew." Grandmother folded her hands in her lap and fixed him with a steady stare. "As you have failed to keep me apprised of the events in your life, I want to hear all about them now. From the day you left the manor, through your years at sea, at war, with your balloons—and finally your marriage. I want you to relate every fact, every detail."

"Everything?" Matt asked uneasily. "It will take rather a long time."

"Then you should begin at once." Grandmother nodded.

"As the two of you shall be occupied for a while"—Alec got to his feet, James and Stephen following his lead—"I shall take my leave."

"I think not, Alec," Grandmother said firmly. "You, above anyone else, as the head of the family and the title holder, should learn about your brother's life."

Alec reluctantly returned to his seat. James and Stephen exchanged glances, then started toward the door.

"You are not excused," she said, without so much as a single look in their direction. The brothers turned without pause and retook their seats.

Grandmother could always do that: see what the boys were doing without looking. Alec was barely six when their mother had died, and their grandmother had raised all four of them with the help of an ever-changing series of haggard governesses. She once told Matt it was impossible to raise male children without a firm hand, a lesson he'd wondered at the time if she'd learned from rearing his father.

"Proceed, Matthew." Grandmother nodded. "You may consider it a form of verbal letter-writing. And you have a great many letters to write."

Chapter 19

Lady Stanwick remained silent for a long while after Tatiana's tale about the Princess Sophia.

Tatiana glanced at Matthew, who shrugged helplessly. He was certainly not going to interrupt the musings of his formidable grandmother. Tatiana tried not to smile. She had never imagined him to be intimidated by anyone, let alone an elderly, silver-haired woman.

Matthew had spent the better part of the day in the library with his grandmother and his brothers, relating the last decade of his life in great detail. During dinner, his brothers had seized every opportunity to tease him about one childhood incident or another. Tatiana herself had learned a great deal about her husband. Unfortunately, she had not had the chance to speak to him privately about what he might have told his family about her. She did hope it was not as entertaining as some of his other tales.

In truth, she had had no private time with Matthew at all since the secret of their marriage had been revealed. Now that he had had time to get used to the truth, they needed to discuss the future. *Their* future. He had been adamant about postponing any such discussion until the question of the Heavens was resolved. Still, she had caught him studying her tonight at dinner with an expression that was at once thoughtful and resigned. It was most disconcerting.

Now Tatiana, Matthew and his grandmother had retired to a well-appointed parlor that was quite obviously a favorite of the older woman's. Tatiana and Lady Stanwick sat in matching chairs, Matthew perched uncomfortably on a nearby sofa. His brothers had been told in no uncertain terms that they were not to be included in this particular conversation. Tatiana suspected the men were more relieved than annoyed by the exclusion.

"Her Grace thought you might be of great help," Tatiana said in an effort to pull the older lady from her reverie.

"Her Grace did, did she?" Lady Stanwick snorted in disdain. "At least *I* can remember those days. My memory is as sharp today as it was fifty years ago." She favored Tatiana with a slightly wicked smile. "I can remember all sorts of interesting things about Her Grace that I am certain she'd rather not have anyone know. Although admittedly"—she chuckled—"the duchess can probably say the same about me. Precisely why we both keep our lips sealed."

Tatiana laughed.

Matthew cleared his throat. "The Princess Sophia, Grandmother?"

"Yes, of course." Her brows drew together with her memories. "Sophia and I became friends when she was here. Both of us had lost husbands, and it drew us together. Even after she married, we corresponded regularly until her death." She cast Matthew a chastising look. "She never failed to write, and wrote an excellent letter. Sophia was well aware of the need to keep in touch with those she cared about."

Matt smiled weakly and tugged at his cravat as if it were suddenly too tight for him.

Lady Stanwick turned her attention to Tatiana. "But I am sorry, Your Highness, Sophia never mentioned your Heavens or jewels of any sort. She was an extremely private person, but we did talk rather a lot. She stayed here for several months and I think she needed someone, another woman, to talk to. I know I certainly did at that particular time in my life.

"Sophia talked more about the people she had left behind than anything else. Her late husband, of course, her parents and her brothers. She spoke at length about Avalonia as well, almost as if it were a person rather than a country. She was certain she'd never return there, and while I believe she was resigned to her fate, it was a matter of great sorrow to her." Lady Stanwick shook her head. "She talked a great deal about the importance of tradition and the need to pass one's heritage on to one's children."

"Heritage is the tie that binds the past to the future," Tatiana said under her breath.

Matt raised a brow. "Do you think that means something significant? Or is it mere sentiment?"

"There is nothing *mere* about sentiment, Matthew," Lady Stanwick said sharply.

"I do not know what to think." Tatiana blew a long breath. "It's to be expected that she would speak often of what she had lost. It is only when we start looking beneath the surface that her words seem at all cryptic. I do not know if we are giving her comments meaning she did not intend."

"She was deeply concerned for the future of her daughter," Lady Stanwick said. "But she could at least control that. It's precisely why she married Lord Worthington. Of course, he was quite head over heels for her, and I believe she eventually developed a certain fondness for him as well. As least her letters never indicated otherwise."

"Did she regret it, I wonder?" Tatiana said without thinking. "Leaving her country and family and position behind?"

"I don't know. She never spoke of regrets." The older woman's eyes narrowed in an assessing manner. "Of course, she had no choice initially. And by the time the insurrection in Avalonia was laid to rest, she had already married Lord Worthington. She once told me she felt as though she'd had to make a choice between the past and the future and she chose the future. In many ways, her choice was a source of great sorrow to her. She took her position very seriously." Lady Stanwick's gaze met hers. "As I am certain do you, Your Highness."

"Indeed," Tatiana murmured.

Lady Stanwick smiled pleasantly. "You are a hereditary princess as well, are you not?"

Tatiana nodded.

"She is third in line for the throne," Matt said.

"Only if my brothers were to die without issue, my lady," Tatiana said quickly. "While neither of them are yet married I cannot imagine such a thing happening."

"Of course not." Lady Stanwick studied her for a long moment. "What exactly are your intentions toward my grandson, Your Highness?"

"My intentions?" The question caught her by surprise.

"Good Lord, Grandmother, what kind of question is that?" Matthew glared at the woman. "I am not a sweet young virginal female who needs protection. Tatiana is my wife. I would say her intentions are honorable."

"Matthew." Lady Stanwick addressed her grandson, but her gaze never left Tatiana. "I believe I have left my favorite fan in my rooms. It matches my dress. My maid will know exactly where it is. Would you run up to my room and fetch it for me?"

"I most certainly will not. However, I shall be more than happy to have a servant bring it to you." Matthew rose and started toward the door.

"No, Matthew," his grandmother said sharply. "I would appreciate it if you would get it for me. Personally."

"Absolutely not." Matthew crossed his arms over his chest. "I know what you're up to, Grandmother, and I will not permit it."

"You are being terribly rude, Matthew." Tatiana's gaze locked with the other woman's. "Lady Stanwick has made a reasonable request and I think you should comply with it."

"You don't know what she's trying to do," he said firmly.

"Come, now, dear boy," Lady Stanwick said coolly. "She knows exactly what I have in mind."

"And it is understandable." Tatiana flashed Matthew a reassuring smile. "Go on."

Matthew's gaze traveled from his wife to his grandmother and back. "If you are certain?"

"I am."

"I shall not be long." He turned and strode from the parlor.

Silence hung in the room for a long moment. Tatiana knew Lady Stanwick's only concern was for her grandson. As was Tatiana's.

"This marriage can never work." Lady Stanwick pressed her lips together in an unyielding manner.

Tatiana drew a deep breath. "There are difficulties, of course, but—"

"Difficulties?" The old woman scoffed. "*Impossibilities* is a more accurate term.

"You are young, Your Highness, and you have a great deal to learn about the world. There are only two kinds of men who can be married to a woman in your position. Men who do not love you but rather love power and position and privilege. And men who love you to the exclusion of everything else. Men who love you better than they love themselves. They have no pride, no strength, no sense of themselves. Frankly, such men are not worth loving in return. They are little better than lapdogs."

"Matthew is hardly a lapdog."

Lady Stanwick heaved an annoyed sigh. "Of course he isn't. A man like my grandson cannot possibly survive in your world. He is not cut out to be a consort for a princess."

"I do not intend him to be." A hard note edged Tatiana's words.

Lady Stanwick considered her for a tense moment, then nodded slowly. "But can you give it all up, Your Highness?"

"Yes."

Sympathy showed in the older woman's eyes. "You will pay a dreadful price. I know, my dear; I watched your aunt pay it.

"She lived her life in quiet resignation. She retired from the world when she married Worthington, spending the rest of her days in that drafty old castle of hers. She scarcely left it at all, either before the earl's death or after. And when her daughter married, she lived there alone save for her stepson."

Lady Stanwick shook her head. "While Sophia never officially abdicated her title, she did so in her heart, and in many ways it destroyed her."

"But when Sophia gave up the life she knew, she was escaping. She was running away from danger and pain and despair." Tatiana leaned toward the other woman. "I am running toward the man I love and cherish with all my heart. Anything I give up for him is not a sacrifice; it is nothing more than a burden if it keeps us apart."

"It sounds so noble and selfless in theory. But can you really give up your title and family and country for my grandson?" Lady Stanwick settled back in her chair and studied her intently. "And can you live with yourself afterward?"

"Yes," Tatiana said without hesitation. "I have given this a great deal of thought for a very long time. In many ways I have no choice." She smiled ruefully. "I have tried, but I cannot live without him. I am well aware of all that I will lose, but it pales in comparison to what I will gain."

"Oh, dear." Lady Stanwick sighed. "You are very much in love. Such love ends as often in tragedy as it does in joy."

Tatiana laughed. "Well, then there is at least half a chance."

Lady Stanwick fell silent, her fingers plucking at a thread on the arm of the chair. "He loves you, you know."

"I am confident of it."

"A great deal, I suspect." She raised her gaze to meet Tatiana's. "So much so that he would be willing to accompany you back to Avalonia."

Tatiana shook her head. "I would never allow that."

"Never?"

"No," she said firmly. "I would never allow Matthew to be less than what he is. A mere husband rather than a man."

"I see." Lady Stanwick chose her words with care. "You would not allow him to give up his life for you, yet you believe he will permit you to give up your life for him?"

Tatiana lifted her chin. "I have no intention of asking his permission."

Lady Stanwick raised a brow. "I'm not sure if that calls for applause or censure."

"Perhaps"—Tatiana smiled—"what it really requires is prayer."

Tatiana leaned against the window frame in the rooms she and Matthew were to share and stared out into the night. Her chat with Lady Stanwick had given her a great deal to think about. Oh, not about relinquishing her title. She had wrestled with that dilemma some time ago. It was the other points Matthew's grandmother had made that gave her pause.

Would he indeed be willing to return to Avalonia with her? To live by her side in that odd position accorded to men who marry women of power? It scarcely mattered. Her jaw clenched. She would not allow it. She acknowledged that Matthew was not Phillipe and she had no doubt Matthew would manage to make a useful life for himself at court. But in spite of the strength of character he possessed, she was afraid of turning him into something less than what he was. Something less than the man she loved.

A lapdog.

And Lady Stanwick did not believe Matthew would accept her decision to give up her title. Not that Tatiana planned to either ask him or tell him until the deed was done.

It was a simple matter, contingent more upon the will of her father than anything else. He could well refuse to accept her abdication on paper, although in practice she had no intention of living the rest of her life in Avalonia. She could arrange everything when she returned home with the Heavens.

If she found the Heavens.

She blew a long, frustrated breath. No one Sophia had trusted had even heard of the Heavens. According to Alexei, Beaumont knew nothing of them either. It was unreasonable to expect that Sophia's daughter was any more knowledgeable than her grandson.

Valentina would use the loss of the jewels to foment unrest. Alexei had just managed to restore confidence in the throne and the House of Pruzinsky, but was it enough to deflect any new threat by their cousin?

And how could Tatiana abandon her country if that should happen?

"You were gone by the time I came back," Matthew said behind her. "I never did find that fan of hers."

"She already had it," Tatiana said absently. "It was tucked beneath the arm of the chair."

"I should have known." He enfolded her in his

arms, pulled her back against him and rested his chin on the top of her head. "Are we looking at anything in particular?"

"Nothing." She sighed. "Everything."

"Everything?" Matthew shuddered, but his voice was light. "You make it sound so dire."

"Sometimes it feels dire."

"You're worried about finding those blasted jewels of yours, aren't you?" he said softly.

"Yes." It was not a complete lie. It was indeed one of the things she worried about.

"You will have the opportunity to talk to Sophia's daughter. An invitation arrived this afternoon for a reception she's giving in London to mark the marriage of her son and his betrothed."

"No doubt we have Her Grace to thank for that," Tatiana said wryly. "I fully expect she told the viscount everything."

"I wouldn't be surprised. She and my grandmother follow their own rules. Probably why they're friends."

"That and blackmail."

"It is a two-day drive back to London from here. We shall have to begin, again, first thing in the morning. Does it strike you this adventure of yours consists of nothing more than traveling from one end of England to the other?"

"It does seem that way."

"Although I suppose we are fortunate that my balloon was destroyed before I could try your Avalonian brandy as a source of fuel. We have more than enough for the journey."

She wrinkled her nose. "It is not very good, is it?"

"No, my love, it isn't." He paused for a moment. "But I suspect it is highly flammable."

She smiled and rested her head back against his chest, letting let his warmth soak into her.

"How bad will it be if your jewels aren't found?" he said quietly. "Your family has thwarted Valentina before."

"And I have faith in the ability of my father and brother to do so again. But the absence of the Heavens gives her a powerful weapon."

"That's not all that's bothering you though, is it?"

She thought for a moment. "When I started this quest, the Heavens were an important symbol to my people, of course, but they were a personal talisman for me as well. I thought"—she searched for the right words—"if I could return them to Avalonia I would earn the right to live as I chose because I had, in some measure, lived up to the expectations set for my life. By finding the Heavens I would somehow fulfill my obligations to my title and my heritage. I would have earned my freedom."

"Your freedom?"

"You could not possibly understand, Matthew. You are perhaps the freest, most unfettered man I have ever met."

"You're just saying that because you like a man who teaches you to fly." His voice held a teasing note and she laughed in spite of herself.

"That is it, of course. You know me far too well."

"Not at all, Princess. I daresay you will always be able to surprise me."

"And is that a good thing?"

"I'm not entirely sure. Tatiana . . ." he hesitated, as if uncertain of his next words. "If you don't find the Heavens, will you claim that freedom you seek?"

"The Heavens were a crutch. Nothing more than an excuse. A substitute, if you will, for courage. And yes." She twisted in his arms to face him. "I will claim that freedom."

His gaze searched hers. "Do not do anything in haste."

"Matthew." She gazed into his blue eyes and her melancholy lifted. He was her match. Her fate. She had found her way back into his life and his heart and she would not allow the Heavens or anything else on earth to pull them apart. "It has taken me more than fifteen long, lonely, disheartening months to know where my destiny lies and find the courage to claim it." She drew his lips down to hers. "I will not lose that courage again."

"Now, my love"—her words murmured against his lips—"once again, teach me to fly."

The return to London was uneventful. Stephen accompanied them. Tatiana slept.

Upon their arrival, they moved into the sizable townhouse Matthew's brothers shared when their duties or interests took them to London. There was a distinctly male air about the place, and Tatiana suspected their grandmother rarely, if ever, visited. Indeed, the servants seemed rather surprised by Tatiana's presence.

Tatiana then paid a brief visit to Katerina. There had been no word from Dimitri or Avalonia and neither woman was certain if that was a blessing or a portent of disaster.

Tatiana should have gone to meet Sophia's daughter at once, but she could not bring herself to do so. She and Matthew were on a holiday of sorts and she hated to see it end. Whether Lady Beaumont knew about the jewels or not, Tatiana and Matthew's adventure would be over. She would have to return home to face her family and her future. The thought was at once exciting and terrifying. And nothing would ever be the same again.

She and Matthew relived their time together in Paris without the secrets that had separated them before. She learned of his childhood and his days at sea. He shared his thoughts and feelings about the past and, better, the future. She told him of her life before Phillipe and after. She talked of her country and her people and her private joys and fears. They spoke of books and art and they disagreed as often as not. And even their disputes were glorious and passionate and ended in each other's arms.

As much as she believed these days with him were but the beginning of their life together, she sensed an odd desperation in Matthew's manner and look and touch. It was vague and elusive, and when she tried to speak of it he laughed off her concerns and teased her about not enjoying each moment as it came.

He was, as always, a poor liar.

And she could not shake a terrible sense of foreboding.

Chapter 20

"*N*ow, this, Matthew, is indeed an adventure." Tatiana cast her gaze over the crowd milling through the elegant London townhouse.

"An adventure?" Matthew sipped his champagne. "Hardly. This is an obligatory social event of the kind I have been fortunate enough to avoid up until now. The room is stuffy, the men obviously bored and the ladies overly curious." He shook his head mournfully. "Apparently I have failed you, if you consider this to be the height of adventure."

"Nonsense," she said, still scanning the gathering. "I feel as though I were a spy or something equally exciting. Here under false pretenses. Using an assumed name." She flashed Matthew a smile. "Not that it is assumed, of course; it simply feels that way."

"Well, there is a world of difference between a royal princess and the mere wife of the youngest son of a marquess." His tone was dry and cynical, and she glanced at him.

He too studied the crowd, his expression cool,

even uninterested. His tone was probably of no significance.

She turned her attention back to the crowd. Viscount Beaumont and his wife were easy to spot, although they seemed to have eyes only for each other. The depth of their feelings was obvious and her heart melted at the sight. She wondered if people would think the same of her and Matthew someday, if someday ever came. She noted the presence of the Duke and Duchess of Roxborough, the Marquess and Marchioness of Helmsley and others she had met at Effington Hall.

She and Matthew had presented their invitation upon their arrival, but had managed to avoid the receiving line. Tatiana wished to observe Sophia's daughter, the Dowager Viscountess Beaumont, Natasha, before approaching her.

At the moment, Lady Beaumont stood on the far side of the room, exchanging words with guests and surveying the scene with a satisfied smile. She was taller than Tatiana, with a graceful bearing, still-lovely face and figure and appeared considerably younger than her fifty-some years. It was obvious, even to the untrained eye, that this woman had the blood of royalty flowing in her veins.

Lady Beaumont's gaze drifted over the gathering, meeting Tatiana's briefly, then continuing. A scant second later, the lady's eyes widened and her gaze snapped back to Tatiana's. She stared for a shocked second, then a slow smile spread across her face. A smile of acknowledgment and welcome.

"Matthew," Tatiana said in an aside to her husband. "I am going to speak to Lady Beaumont."

"I'm going with you."

She shook her head. "It is not necessary."

"Are you mad?" He scoffed. "Necessary or not, you've dragged me across half of England. One way or another, this is the end of your search, and I have no intention of missing it."

"Matthew." Her voice was firm.

He was just as firm. "Don't bother to protest. I am your husband. Lord and master and all that."

"You can be so annoying," she muttered.

"It's one of my finest qualities." He plucked her empty glass from her hand and passed their glasses to a nearby footman, then took her elbow and steered her toward Lady Beaumont.

"I have the most horrid feeling of turmoil in my stomach," she said quietly.

"Nerves, my love." He glanced down at her. "A brandy would settle your stomach or at least provide false courage. Have you ever had brandy that wasn't made in Avalonia?"

"No, never. Brandy holds no particular appeal."

"I can see why."

They reached Lady Beaumont, but before they could say a word, the older woman grasped Tatiana's hands in hers and kissed her on both cheeks.

"My dear cousin, I would have known you any-where." Her gaze skimmed over Tatiana's face. "The resemblance is extraordinary. You are as lovely as my mother was."

A flush spread up Tatiana's face. She was not entirely sure what she expected, but the affection in her cousin's greeting warmed her heart. "It is good to meet you at last, Lady Beaumont."

"My dear, Your Highness, do call me Natasha. We are cousins, and there are not so many of us that we can afford to be standoffish." Natasha cast her a brilliant smile, then turned toward Matthew, offering him her hand. "And you are obviously the Lord Matthew Weston."

"A pleasure to meet you, my lady." Matthew took her hand and brushed a polite kiss across it.

"Natasha, Cousin," she said firmly.

"Natasha." He smiled and glanced from one woman to the other. "I gather from your greeting, you know precisely why we are here."

"Of course." She laughed. "Surely you didn't think Her Grace could resist sending me a note with every detail."

Tatiana's brows pulled together. "Does everyone know?"

"Dear me, no." Natasha shook her head. "The duke is the only one who knows all—besides his mother and myself. Even my son is still unaware of who you are. I can scarce believe you are finally here. I was just telling my father that the world is filled with wonderful possibilities, and then you appeared."

"Your father?" Matthew's brow furrowed with confusion.

Natasha nodded toward a small portrait on the wall beside her. It was no more than nine inches square, displayed in an elaborate carved and gilded frame.

"It is the painting Sophia carried with her from Avalonia, is it not?" Tatiana stepped closer and examined the portrait.

"Indeed it is. Her husband, my father."

"I had no idea he was so young." The man staring back at her could not possibly be much older than

Tatiana was now. He was handsome and dashing and had an air of confidence about him, if as he were invulnerable.

"This was painted a few months before his death. The portrait was at Worthington Castle until recently." Natasha laughed softly. "I used to speak with him, or rather his portrait, often when I was a child, and it appears to be a habit I have failed to break."

"It must have been difficult for your mother to haul this across Europe." Matthew moved to Tatiana's side and peered closely at the frame. "It looks rather cumbersome."

"Oh, this is not the original frame. My mother carried the painting rolled up." Natasha nodded at the work. "She had the frame made for it sometime later."

"It scarcely matters, my lord," Tatiana said, pushing aside a touch of annoyance at Matthew's continued fascination.

"Probably." Matthew's brow furrowed. "Admittedly, I don't know a great deal about the presentation of art, my lady, but the frame seems too heavy in scale given the size of the painting."

"Do you think so?" Natasha crossed her arms over her chest and considered the portrait. "I'm not sure I've ever noticed that."

Tatiana stifled her growing impatience and forced a pleasant note to her voice. "I think it looks most appropriate."

Matthew ignored her. "The balance seems off somehow." He reached out and ran his fingers along the carved frame. "The molding is far too wide and the carvings . . ." He leaned closer and his eyes widened so slightly no one but Tatiana would have noticed. He straightened and met Natasha's gaze. "The carvings are extremely interesting."

"I have always thought so." Natasha directed her words to Tatiana but kept her gaze on Matthew. "You have an extraordinarily clever husband."

"It can be a most annoying quality," Tatiana said sweetly.

He glanced at her and grinned. "I'd wager it won't be nearly as annoying in a moment."

Natasha laughed. "I believe we should continue this discussion in private."

"Just the two of you, I think," Matthew said. "I am feeling rather pleased with myself right now and I'm certain that will make me that much more annoying."

"If that is possible." Tatiana's gaze shifted from her husband to her cousin and back. "I have the distinctly unpleasant feeling that there is a joke you both find most amusing, yet I am not in on it."

"Then obviously it's time you were included." Matthew took her hand and drew it to the frame, then guided it over the carvings. "Observe, Princess."

She studied the whorls and curves and angles of the intricate design and started to pull her hand away when her gaze caught on the shape of a half moon. At once the complicated pattern became clear. She stared in disbelief.

Heritage is the tie that binds the past to the future.

The frame was a series of stars and moons and celestial bodies. She caught her breath and snapped her gaze to Matthew's.

He bent to speak low into her ear. "I believe, Your Highness, you have found your Heavens."

"I couldn't simply give them to you," Natasha said. She and Tatiana sat on a sofa in a small library just off the main rooms. "No, that's not entirely true. I could have given them to you, and I fully intended to do so if you had come to me."

Tatiana stared at her in confusion. "I was told you were traveling and not in England."

Natasha's brow furrowed for a moment. "I returned a few weeks ago. Of course, I was not in the city." She shrugged. "It scarcely matters, I suppose. You are here now and I am more than willing to at last fulfill the promise I made to my mother."

"Promise?"

"I should explain." Natasha paused to gather her thoughts. "Although my mother had put Avalonia and the life of a royal princess behind her, she still held the responsibilities of that position close to her heart. When she left Avalonia, her mother, the queen, insisted she take the Heavens for safekeeping. All that nonsense about Avalonia standing as long as the Heavens and the right to rule and whatnot.

"But the queen also gave her a letter that seemed to relieve her of that charge, implying the Heavens were not as important as our lives. My mother was never forced to make that choice, and to this day I don't know what decision she would have made. At any rate, she made me vow that upon her death I would be the guardian of the Heavens until such time as a legitimate guardian, a hereditary princess of Avalonia, came to claim them and return them to their rightful home. I'm afraid they were removed from the gold cuff and I have no idea what might have happened to that."

Natasha relaxed against the back of the sofa and smiled. "I cannot tell you how relieved I am to at last be able to fulfill that promise."

"No more relieved than I. I feared the Heavens

were lost forever." Tatiana shook her head. "So the jewels are in the frame."

"That's what I have been told." Natasha wrinkled her nose. "Apparently, there is a piece of the carving that fits perfectly into a corner and conceals a hollow area where the jewels are hidden."

"But you've never seen them yourself?" Tatiana said with a growing sense of unease. "Then you cannot be certain they are still there."

"I suppose not." Natasha shook her head. "You don't think—"

"I think"—Tatiana rose to her feet—"we should look for ourselves."

"I think that is an excellent idea."

Tatiana clenched her fists and tried not to scream in frustration. Was the blasted woman everywhere?

Valentina stepped from behind the curtains. "I think we should all look."

Natasha stood and stared at the newcomer. "You must be Valentina." She studied her curiously. "I must say, you don't look all that wicked."

"What did you expect? Horns protruding from my head?" Valentina sniffed haughtily and glanced at Tatiana. "You have been telling tales about me, Cousin."

"Do forgive me for engaging in idle gossip," Tatiana said. "In truth, *wicked* hardly seems a strong enough term for treason or a multitude of dead husbands—"

"Scarcely a multitude. No more than two, unless I have miscounted. And their deaths were a tragic co-incidence, nothing more." She looked at Natasha. "I know it is impossible to imagine now, but would you believe our dear cousin used to be quite shy and retir-ing? And much better mannered than she is now as well." Valentina lowered her voice confidentially. "Why, the perfect little princess I knew would never masquerade as the wife of a man she was not lawfully wed to."

"In truth, Cousin, some things do not change." Tatiana couldn't resist a smug smile. "I am indeed married, and have been for well over a year."

"A marriage your family is unaware of?" Valentina's eyes widened. "You simply overflow with one amazing revelation after another."

Tatiana ignored her. "How did you get in here?"

"You are intent on knowing all the petty details, aren't you?" Valentina shook her head. "Your predictability is certainly unchanged. Very well." She sighed. "I observed you talking and realized, from the so-easy-to-read expressions on your faces, your conversation was significant enough to seek privacy. I guessed you would use this room, as it is the most convenient—an excellent guess, I might add—and slipped in here before you."

"I didn't see you amidst the crowd." Natasha studied her thoughtfully. "And furthermore, I don't believe you were invited."

"And yet here I am, in spite of that omission on your part. The gentleman I am with was invited." She nodded at Tatiana. "Yes, it is the same gentleman I accompanied in the country and now, as then, he is dim but useful. I am certain I have committed some horrible social faux pas by my presence and I shall be banned from polite society forever. So be it. Now"— her tone hardened—"I suggest we proceed to do exactly what the two of you had proposed before I so rudely interrupted."

"I think not." Tatiana folded her arms over her chest.

"In fact, I believe this discussion is at an end." Natasha stepped toward the door. "I'm certain my son will be most interested in detaining you until the authorities can be notified."

Valentina scoffed. "By all means, notify whomever you wish. I have done nothing in this country that could be deemed illegal."

"Hah!" Tatiana glared in disbelief. "You stole my letter, ransacked my room and tried to kill me."

Valentina shrugged. "Trifles. And you can't prove it."

"Perhaps you are wickeder than you appear," Natasha murmured.

Valentina smiled modestly. "Thank you."

Natasha and Tatiana traded glances, then the older woman again started toward the door.

"Wait, Cousin." A note of sincerity sounded in Valentina's voice and Natasha paused. "I scarcely think it is necessary to involve others in what is essentially a matter among the female members of the family. I find men do tend to muck things up more often than not, especially husbands. Besides, if you take another step"—Valentina pulled out a dueling pistol from the shawl draped over her arm—"I shall have to do something regrettable."

"Come, now, Valentina, are you not being overly dramatic?" Tatiana scoffed. "I doubt you will really shoot us."

"My dear cousin, I have no intention of shooting you. That would be most unpleasant and possibly quite messy. However, the firing of this pistol will alert the men I have positioned in the other rooms." She glanced at Natasha. "I fear they were not invited either."

"Quite all right." Natasha smiled weakly.

"My men will then proceed to shoot your"—she snorted—"*husband* and"—she nodded at Natasha—"your son."

Tatiana's stomach twisted, but she refused to let so much as a flicker of fear show. Her gaze met and locked with Valentina's. Tatiana knew full well her cousin was more than capable of doing exactly what she threatened. She further knew Valentina's recent failure to seize power less than two months ago had left whatever supporters she still had disorganized and scattered. It was a risk, but the chance that Valentina was lying was probably greater than the possibility that she was telling the truth.

The woman Tatiana had been once trembled at the thought of the consequences if she was wrong.

The woman she was now knew there was no real choice.

"Very well," she said coolly. "Fire your pistol."

Natasha gasped.

"I will, you know" Valentina's voice was cold, but there was a glimmer of uncertainty in her eye.

At once, Tatiana knew she was right. "I doubt it. You have no *men* waiting for the signal to shoot anyone. Furthermore, I strongly suspect, aside from your escort tonight, you are alone."

Valentina shook her head and heaved a sigh. "It does not sound very clever, does it?"

"Rather absurd, if you ask me," Natasha said under her breath.

"No one did," Valentina snapped and turned her attention back to Tatiana. "I must say, I liked you a great deal more before your ordeal by fire or whatever it was you said. It would be ever so much easier if you would simply do as I ask. You may not realize it, but I am a desperate woman and have no qualms about doing whatever it is I must. And as you apparently do not fear for the life of your husband"—she leveled the pistol at Tatiana—"perhaps you fear for your own."

Tatiana ignored the fear that did indeed grip her heart. "You will not shoot me."

"Oh, dear cousin, I am afraid this time you are wrong. I will indeed shoot you." Her eyes narrowed in a nasty manner. "And I shall quite enjoy it."

"Nonsense." Natasha stepped in front of Tatiana. "There's no need for that."

"What? Would you rather I shoot you?" Valentina snorted with disdain. "Are you mad, or has that air of nobility you all display addled your brain?"

"Not at all," Natasha said sharply. "If you want the painting, you may have it."

"The frame," Valentina corrected.

"Of course." Natasha nodded.

Valentina moved to the door, opened it a crack, then peered out. Tatiana took the opportunity to whisper into Natasha's ear. "Surely you're not going to give her the Heavens?"

"Of course not," Natasha said. "But I think our chances are better of saving the jewels and ourselves in the midst of a crowd rather than alone."

"I do hope you are right," Tatiana said softly. "Because in here only the two of us are her targets. Out there it is everyone."

Natasha murmured a low obscenity Tatiana couldn't quite hear.

"Ladies, if you please." Valentina nodded in the direction of the door and draped her shawl over her arm to cover the pistol. "After you."

Natasha and Tatiana obediently filed out, Valentina a step behind and positioned between them.

Tatiana searched the milling crowd for Matthew. She wasn't sure if she wanted him to come to her rescue or stay as far away as possible. She was fairly certain that Valentina would indeed shoot someone if provoked and Natasha's idea that their chances were better in the crowd might well miscarry. Still, Tatiana had no better plan.

"Now, then, let us walk casually over to the painting, as if you are doing nothing more than showing it to me. And I think a smile is called for," Valentina said softly. "Try to look as if you are having a lovely time. After all, we are all family."

Tatiana forced a smile through clenched teeth. They were but a few steps from the portrait and the Heavens. She had to think of something. Anything.

The trio stopped before the painting.

Valentina stared at it as if transfixed.

Tatiana and Natasha traded glances.

"Take it down," Valentina said in a hard tone.

"The painting?" Natasha asked.

"Yes," she snapped. "It is not large. Take it down and the three of us will walk toward the door." The corners of her mouth curled upward into the approximation of a smile. "I may not have men in the room, but I do have a carriage waiting."

Tatiana scoffed. "You will not make it that far."

"Oh, but I will if I create a diversion just as I leave." Her gaze met Tatiana's. Hate gleamed in the older woman's eye and her voice was cold. "I shall let you consider what that might be."

Tatiana's blood froze and at once she realized

Valentina did indeed plan to shoot someone. More than likely Tatiana herself.

Natasha reached to remove the portrait from the wall. Surely someone would notice what they were doing? Valentina watched Natasha intently. Tatiana took the opportunity to discreetly peer around her. She spotted Matthew speaking with Beaumont and his wife. All three were looking in her direction, concern on their faces. Matthew started toward her.

"Help her," Valentina ordered.

Tatiana had no choice. She turned to assist Natasha.

"Tatiana," Matthew called and all hell broke loose.

Valentina whirled toward Matthew's voice, the shawl slipping to the floor.

A male voice yelled, "She's armed!"

A woman screamed. Matthew was but a few yards away, Beaumont at his heels.

The pistol in Valentina's hand fired.

For a moment it was as if the world itself had stopped, frozen in time.

Tatiana's breath caught. A shocked expression colored Matthew's face. Natasha's gaze met with hers, and understanding flashed between them. She released the painting and Tatiana swung it with all her strength.

It smacked Valentina hard across her shoulder and the side of her head. The pistol flew out of her hand and she staggered forward. At once, strong hands grabbed her.

The portrait thudded on the floor, a chunk of the frame skidding across the polished wood.

A small, dark velvet bag lay half out of the hole in the gilded frame.

Chapter 21

$\mathcal{F}$or an endless moment no one moved.

Tatiana and Natasha traded shocked glances, then dropped to their knees beside the frame. Matthew hunched down beside them.

"Do go on, my dear. I can't stand it a moment longer." Natasha's eyes gleamed with excitement.

Tatiana stared at the velvet bag, wanting desperately to know if the Heavens were inside and terrified they were not.

"Go ahead, Princess," Matthew said in a low voice meant for her ears only. His gaze caught hers and he smiled with encouragement. "It's the end of your quest. Your adventure."

Something in his tone caught at her heart. No doubt it was nothing more than the emotion that gripped her at knowing that he was right. Whether the Heavens were here or not, this was indeed the end of her search.

She nodded and her gaze caught on a wet stain on his jacket. "Good Lord." Without thinking she touched it. Blood smeared on her fingers. "Matthew, you've been shot!"

"I noticed that." He looked at the spot and grimaced. "It hurts like hell. But it's not bleeding overly and I think it simply grazed me." He grinned at her. "I fear I shall live."

"Do not joke at such a time."

"I told you once I had no intention of losing my life in the immediate future. I have not changed my mind." The smile remained on his face but there was a look in his eyes she couldn't decipher and his gaze searched hers as if he were committing it to memory. Abruptly, a chill raced up her spine. "Now"—he nodded at the bag—"go on."

"Wait." Natasha stood and gestured to her son. Beaumont moved to her side at once. "Do see if you can get the crowd to back away. I'm not certain it's wise to let everyone see this."

"Of course." He glanced at the frame. "So they were here all along. And you never told me."

"In truth, dear boy"—Natasha's voice was firm— "it was none of your concern."

Beaumont cast her a long-suffering look and stepped away. He spoke to a few of the closest spectators, who herded the bulk of the gathering toward more food and drink. Only a handful remained in an observant half circle: Beaumont and his wife, the duke and duchess, Lord and Lady Helmsley and Lord Stephen. Valentina stayed as well, restrained now by footmen.

Tatiana turned her attention back to the portrait and drew a deep breath. She grasped the exposed velvet and pulled it gently. It caught and she tugged a bit harder. The bag slipped out of the hole.

She picked it up and her hand trembled. The pouch was no longer than the span of her hand, tied with a silken cord, and with a weight that indicated it was not empty. She fumbled with the cord, but her fingers would not work properly.

"Allow me." Matthew took it from her, untied it and tipped the bag into her hand.

The sun, the moon and the stars tumbled onto her palm.

There was a collective gasp from those around her. Tatiana could do little more than stare.

The ruby flashed blood red in the candlelight. The opal glowed with an unworldly iridescence. The two gems were oval in cut, perfectly matched in size, about the length of her thumb from the joint to the tip. The four diamonds were half the size of the colored gems, round and obviously perfect. Fire shot from the centers of the jewels with the slightest movement of her hand.

Matthew emitted a long, low whistle. "So those are the Heavens. Quite impressive, and bigger than I expected. Rather gaudy as well, don't you think?"

A half dozen pairs of indignant female eyes turned toward him.

"My dear young man." Natasha's tone was adamant. "There is no such thing as a gaudy gem."

"Nor can it ever be too big," Lady Beaumont said.

"Not if it's genuine," the duchess added. "His grandmother has apparently failed somewhere in his education."

"I think they are wonderful," Tatiana said softly, still staring at the jewels in her hand. They winked up at her with a life all their own.

And a promise.

Their return would not ensure a peaceful reign for her father and eventually her brother, but their presence would be an asset. Nor could their return guarantee her family's acceptance of her decision to relinquish her title or even ease the inevitable uproar that would greet her choice, but their recovery had given her the courage she needed to proceed with her plan. Not because she had found the Heavens, but because she had looked. Her fist closed tightly around the jewels.

Matthew stood, took Tatiana's free hand and assisted her to her feet.

"What now, Your Highness?" His gaze bored into hers, blue and intense, and she wondered if she would ever know what he was thinking.

"Now?" She shook her head. "I am not certain."

Matthew opened her hand and returned the jewels to the velvet pouch that had protected them for more than half a century. He tied the bag, put it in her hand and covered it with her other hand. "Take them home, Princess."

There was something in his voice that caught at her heart. She searched his gaze with a growing unease.

"He's right, Your Highness, it is time to return home." Dimitri's voice sounded behind her. She gritted her teeth at the sound. The adventure was indeed over. She straightened her shoulders and turned to face him.

"Oh, dear God, let my eyes be failing." Valentina groaned. "Please, tell me I am not seeing the terribly noble, always sanctimonious Captain Petrov."

"Your Highness." Dimitri bowed curtly to Valentina. "It is a pleasure to see you again as well."

He nodded sharply at the contingent of men at his heels. At once four stepped to Valentina's side and relieved the footmen holding her.

Valentina raised a brow. "Surely you do not think you have any authority here. We are in England, not Avalonia."

"Indeed we are, Your Highness." Dimitri pulled a rolled paper from his coat. "However, this document, duly signed by the proper British and Avalonian authorities, authorizes me to return you to Avalonia or to place you on the first ship bound away from these shores."

"I should have known. Very well." Valentina shrugged as if it were of no consequence. "I hear France is nice this time of year."

"How did you get that so quickly?" Tatiana studied the captain suspiciously. "You could not possibly have traveled to Avalonia and back this fast."

"I did not," Dimitri said. "I received the warrant authorizing the detention of the Princess Valentina—"

"I knew I recognized her." Lady Beaumont nudged her husband.

"—in the same dispatch in which you received the letter from your brother. It was a precaution at the time, as no one knew where the princess might appear." Dimitri turned to Valentina. "There is a carriage waiting, Your Highness."

"I had grown rather tired of England at any rate. The parties are as dull as the men. And I am perfectly capable of leaving under my own power." She cast the men holding her a scathing glare. Dimitri nodded and they released her.

Valentina looked at Tatiana and smiled ruefully. "I underestimated you, Cousin."

"Cousin?" Lady Helmsley said.

"I shall not make that mistake again." Valentina nodded in a regal manner to her escort and the group left the room, leaving behind a trail of questions.

"Captain," Tatiana said, "why have you returned to London?"

"When I learned of the incident with his lordship's balloon"—Dimitri cast an accusing look at Matthew—"I realized Valentina was a far greater threat to you than I had first imagined."

Tatiana narrowed her eyes. "And you knew this because you had men following me."

Dimitri's voice was resolute. "I could scarcely leave otherwise, Your Highness."

"*Your Highness*?" Beaumont said to his mother. "Was this none of my concern as well?"

"Try not to sound so put upon, Randall," Natasha said in an offhand manner. "It was not my secret to reveal."

Tatiana pulled in a steadying breath. "I do apologize. I thought concealing my identity would make it easier to find the Heavens—"

"The Heavens?" the duchess said to the duke.

"The jewels," her husband said. "I will explain all later."

"And in that I was wrong." Tatiana smiled at Matthew. "I should have trusted that those who helped my aunt in her time of need were honorable and good and would assist me in finding the Heavens as well."

"She was looking for missing jewels?" Lady Helmsley said to her husband. "What a wonderful adventure."

"Perhaps you can write about it, my dear," Lord Helmsley said.

"Just think," Lady Beaumont said to the viscount. "They were right under our noses all along."

"Indeed they were." He stared at Tatiana. "As was she. I realize it now, you bear a striking resemblance to my grandmother. That's why I thought we had met."

"Forgive me, Your Highness." Dimitri stepped closer and lowered his voice. "I must insist on leaving for Avalonia immediately. It is imperative that the Heavens be returned to their rightful place without delay."

"Yes, of course." Tatiana glanced at the bag holding the Heavens for a long moment, then shifted her gaze to Matthew. At once, she knew her course was clear. "Captain, you have served my family and our country well. There is no one I trust more. Therefore"—she held out the bag to him—"I charge you with the care of the Heavens. Take them home, Dimitri."

Shock colored Dimitri's face. "Your Highness, I cannot possibly—"

"Of course you can. I shall make the journey back to Avalonia sometime soon to speak with my family, but for now I would much prefer to stay here." She lifted her chin. "With my husband."

"Your husband? You married him?" Dimitri's gaze shot to Matthew. "Him? But Your Highness, he . . . he . . . he flies!"

Lord Stephen snorted. "Not anymore."

Tatiana sighed with exasperation. "Nonetheless, he is my husband and I will stay with him."

"No." Matthew shook his head. "You won't."

Tatiana stared at him. "Matthew."

"Come, now, Your Highness, the return of the jewels won't be nearly as significant if Captain Petrov brings them back instead of you." Matthew's voice was light, as if he were discussing something of no more significance than the weather. "You should go with him. It is, as you have so often said, your duty to safeguard the Heavens."

She shook her head. "I found them. I have fulfilled the responsibilities of my title and I see no barrier now to giving it up." She ignored the gasps of those behind her. "The only title I wish is that of Lady Matthew."

"Don't be absurd." Matthew scoffed.

A cold hand seemed to squeeze her heart.

"It was great fun, this adventure of yours. I cannot tell you when I have had a more enjoyable time. I have to thank you for that and thank you for Paris as well. But it is past time to face the realities of life." Matthew shrugged. "You're a princess. I'm the youngest son of a marquess. Even in children's stories that's not a suitable combination."

She stared into his blue eyes, as cool and unconcerned as his tone. "What are you saying?"

"I'm saying it was a lark, Princess. For both of us. Granted we went a bit too far, but"—he grinned— "we were carried away. Passion and all that. A grand passion, I might add."

"It was more than that." An odd desperate note sounded in her voice.

"Was it?" He raised a brow. "Are you sure?"

"Yes." Her voice rose.

"Perhaps. For a moment. Or rather six days. Not even a full week. Oh, I admit I was upset when you left me in Paris. Pride probably more than anything else, but eventually I came to my senses and realized it was for the best." He shook his head. "You said once that I married a companion to a princess, not a princess, and you were entirely right. I never would have married you if I had known who you are. And, in truth, if you were who I first believed you to be, well, by now I probably would have grown tired of you. I don't think I'm well suited for marriage, and especially not marriage to a princess."

She grabbed his arm. "I will give up my title."

"For me? Don't." He studied her curiously. "How can you possibly do that and be happy? You have lived your entire life for your country and your family. You cannot turn your back on all that as easily as you once turned your back on me."

"Matthew, I—"

"And I certainly have no intention of trailing after you like a well-trained puppy. I may not have done much with my life thus far, but it has been my life. I would not do well as the consort of a princess." He shrugged off her hand. "Besides, you told me you would not put another man in that position. Why, I'd probably have a mistress myself in no time."

She sucked in a hard breath. "I do not believe you."

"Believe me, Princess." His gaze bored into hers. "Get your annulment. You should have done it a year ago. Whatever we might have had once no longer exists. You have your life to lead and I have mine. It's as simple as that."

She struggled to remain calm. "But you said you were happy that we were still married."

"Of course I said that I was happy we were still married. Would you really have shared my bed if I hadn't?"

She stared at him in disbelief. Anger and pain flashed through her. She didn't know what to think. What to believe.

He lowered his voice and smiled wickedly. "And you did share it exceedingly well."

Without a moment's thought, she cracked her hand hard across his face. The sharp sound of the slap resounded in the room. Her hand stung with the blow.

"I daresay, Your Highness"—he caught her hand and drew it to his lips—"you do that exceedingly well too."

She snatched her hand away. Tears burned the back of her throat, but she refused to let them fall. How could she have been so wrong? About him. About them. About everything.

"Captain," she said, still staring at the amused expression on Matthew's face, "you are right. We should be off at once."

"Of course, Your Highness," Dimitri murmured.

She drew a steadying breath and turned to Natasha. "I cannot thank you enough for all you have done to keep the Heavens safe through the years."

"My dear cousin." Natasha took her hand and met her gaze. "I have done nothing save keep my knowledge to myself. But perhaps I should have said or done something long ago."

"Not at all." Tatiana forced a smile. "You did exactly what was expected of you. Regardless of the circumstances of your life, the blood of the House of Pruzinsky flows in your veins as it does in mine and with it comes obligations and duties. I shall not lose sight of that again."

"My dear child." Natasha pulled her close, her voice for Tatiana's ears alone. "You have a great deal of courage and I suspect you will need it. Do not let your responsibilities to position blind you to the obligations owed to yourself. Even a princess has the right to happiness."

"But apparently for a princess, Cousin," Tatiana said softly, "happiness is as difficult to grasp as the heavens above." She pulled away and turned to the small group still gathered, avoiding any glance at Matthew. "Thank you all. I shall never forget your kindness." She nodded at Dimitri. "Captain."

"Your Highness." He stepped to her side and they started toward the door, Dimitri's men following.

She held her head high and spoke in a low voice. "Is everyone staring?"

"Indeed they are, Your Highness," he said softly.

"Then we shall have to show them how insignificant that unpleasant incident was." She wanted to cry, to weep, to throw herself in her friend's arms and sob until she could no longer think or hurt or feel. But she was a princess and such things were not allowed.

"And was it, Your Highness? Are you all right?"

They approached the door and a butler opened it without hesitation. Princess Tatiana Marguerite Nadia Pruzinsky of the Kingdom of Greater Avalonia paused and looked back at the small group of Effingtons and Beaumonts and . . . Westons. She nodded, favored them with her most regal and blinding smile perfected by generations of princesses well versed in the art of keeping their feelings to themselves.

"Dimitri," she said quietly through the smile that reached no farther than her lips. "I shall never be all right again."

She was every inch a princess. And as fine a liar as ever. Her expression was every bit as false as her stories. Her smile, every bit as meaningless.

And his heart broke at the sight of her.

Tatiana turned toward the door and swept out of the room and out of his life. Forever.

"That may well have been the stupidest display I've ever seen," Stephen said at his side. Matt wondered when his brother had joined him in a silent gesture of brotherly support.

"Not at all, Stephen." Matt swallowed hard. "But it was the most difficult."

"That's what I meant." Stephen shook his head in disgust. "It's obvious how much you love her."

"He's right, my lord." Natasha stepped closer and gazed up at him with a look of pity. "You really are something of a fool."

"A noble fool," Lady Beaumont added, moving to her mother-in-law's side. "But a fool nonetheless."

"Well, if we can see that"—the duchess joined the trio—"perhaps the princess will see it as well?"

"I don't think so." Lady Helmsley shook her head and took her place beside Her Grace. "She was far too overset to see much of anything. It's obvious he hurt her deeply." She shot Matt a scathing look. "You were quite despicable."

"Pardon me for pointing it out, ladies." Matt glared indignantly at the four women confronting him like an army of angry Amazons. "But this really is none of your concern."

"It is now, my lord." The duchess wagged her finger at him. "You played out this drama in front of us. You cannot now complain about the reviews."

Lady Helmsley folded her arms over her chest. "And none of us especially liked the ending."

"I know I had to fight back tears." Natasha sniffed. "As much as I wanted to smack him myself."

"It was horribly sad and quite nasty." Lady Beaumont's eyes narrowed. "And I think we should do something about it."

"No," Matt said sharply. He glanced at the respective husbands and, in two cases, sons as well, of the ladies confronting him and knew from the identical expressions on the faces of the duke, the marquess and the viscount, and more from the way each and every one refused to meet his eyes, that he could expect no help from that quarter.

He drew a deep breath. "Ladies, I well appreciate your concern, but I cannot allow you to interfere." He met Natasha's gaze. "Tatiana was willing to give up her title because she was afraid of what being nothing more than a consort to a princess might do to me. She said she would not put a man she loved in that position."

His gaze shifted to Lady Beaumont. "She has a great sense of the responsibility of her position, to her country and to her family. It's what spurred her to search for the Heavens. It's part of her very nature."

He turned to the duchess. "You understand such things, Your Grace. Can such a woman truly abandon the duties she was born to, has lived her entire life for, without losing her soul in the process?"

Matt's gaze locked with Lady Helmsley's. "You told us you write stories, my lady. Can you write an ending for this that will satisfy us all? I cannot.

"In the name of love, she would give up all she is for me." He struggled to find the right words. "If I love her in return, how can I allow her to do so?"

For a long time no one said a word. As one, the ladies stared at him, a tear in more than one eye, a tremble on more than one lip. It would have been quite satisfying if he hadn't meant every word he said and didn't feel so wretched about it.

"You have apparently done the impossible, Lord Matthew," the duke said over the head of his wife. "You have succeeded in silencing a group of ladies I know full well to be stubborn and opinionated. And rarely silent. You are to be congratulated."

Matt smiled wryly. "Thank you, Your Grace. Ladies." He nodded at the women still lined up before him, the once-formidable group now firmly on his side. "It was an honor to have"—he paused—"incurred your wrath."

He glanced at his brother. Stephen nodded. The brothers made their farewells and a moment later headed toward the door.

"Surely there is something . . ." Lady Beaumont murmured behind them.

"Let it be, Jocelyn," Natasha said softly. "He is right and it may well destroy him."

"I must say, little brother, I am impressed," Stephen said in a low voice. "Those ladies would have done anything for you in the end."

Matt chuckled. "Women are always moved by sentiment. It is in their nature."

A footman let them out the door. They stood on the front steps for a moment. Matt pulled in a few deep, refreshing breaths of cool evening air. Not that it lessened the catch in his throat or the weight in the pit of his stomach or eased the numbness of his heart.

"Was she right, Matt?"

"Was who right about what?" An overwhelming weariness washed through him. He could not believe he had truly sent her away. This time she would not be back. He had made certain of it. And he suspected it would take a lot longer than fifteen months, three weeks and four days to recover. It would take the rest of his life.

"The one who said this might well destroy you?"

"That's a question for another night, Stephen." Matt forced a grin. "Right now, we'd best do something about this arm of mine. It throbs like the dickens. After that, I propose we make it our mission to sample every decent and every not-so-decent tavern in London."

Stephen eyed him cautiously. "To ease the pain?"

"In my arm, Stephen. Only in my arm."

"Of course," his brother muttered in obvious disbelief.

It was pointless to put off Stephen's question. Matt already knew the answer.

Natasha was wrong when she said losing Tatiana might well destroy him.

It already had.

. . . and indeed, Ephraim, as I have related the details of the princess's adventure, the significance is not in the miles we traveled, or even the importance of finding of what was lost.

If I had your gift of words or the skills of Byron or Keats, I would call it a journey of the heart, but I am a man whose mind is more attuned to the intricacies of mechanics or the nature of seafaring or, one hopes, the solidity of business, and such expressions seem to me overly sentimental and silly.

But it is, in truth, the emotion of it all that has caught me in its grip. Until her, love had always seemed an ethereal sort of thing, elusive and ill-defined. Not something you could hold and feel. Now I know it does indeed have substance, for it lies heavy at the bottom of my heart and the pit of my stomach and in the weight of my step.

It was that vile emotion that made me do what I thought was best. How could I allow her to sacrifice so very much? Her family and her country? Love would not permit it.

So she is gone.

And I am left to wonder if again I have made a mistake. I did not follow her when I should have, and now I know I cannot.

We have come full circle, she and I.

She is once again my wife, and I am once again alone.

Chapter 22

SIX WEEKS LATER...

*E*phraim closed the journal slowly and tossed it on his desk. He stared at the book for a long moment, then raised his gaze to Matt's.

"You're a wicked man, Matthew Weston."

"Am I?" Matt raised a brow. "Why is that?"

"You let me read all this"—he waved at the journal—"but I know full well you will never allow me to publish it." He heaved a sigh of frustration. "You are the worst sort of tease, Matt."

Matt chuckled. "My apologies."

"Why did you let me read it at all?"

"Well, I did write it for you," Matt said lightly. He paused for a moment, then met Ephraim's gaze. "You are my closest friend and the only one who knows everything about Tatiana and myself. I seem to need someone to talk with about all this."

"Very well," Ephraim said gruffly. "But it is only because we are friends that I will overlook your taunting me with something my readers would salivate over and make me a wealthy man in the process." He leaned forward, rested his elbows on the desk and clasped his hands. "Although, while it would certainly boost circulation, I daresay no one would like the ending."

"The ending does reek."

"So . . ." Ephraim drew the word out slowly. "What do you plan on doing about it?"

"Well, I thought I'd rewrite it. Or add an epilogue." Matt settled back in his chair and wished he had thought to bring cigars. "It's been more than six weeks since she left. I spent the first two weeks drinking at a steady rate here in London."

"Here?" Ephraim huffed with annoyance. "I wasn't even aware you were back."

"Apologies, old man. My brother did the honors with me this time. At any rate, two weeks," he said pointedly. "That's about how long it would take her to travel from here to Avalonia. I spent the next two weeks at Weston Manor, still drinking, but not nearly as much, and feeling extremely sorry for myself. And thinking about"—he paused—"*my wife* every minute of every day. Wondering how she was faring. If she'd delivered the Heavens to the great acclaim of her family and people. If indeed she was still my wife at all or if she'd had her father nullify our marriage.

"And I've spent the last two weeks coming to the realization that I cannot live my life without her."

Ephraim studied him for a long moment. "And?"

"And." Matt spread his hands in a wide gesture of inevitability. "I'm going to Avalonia. I'm going to be the consort of a princess, if that is what's necessary to have the woman I love in my life."

"Then you were wrong to send her away?"

"No." Matt got to his feet and paced before the desk, trying to pull his thoughts into words. "That was the best thing I have ever done. I couldn't ask her to sacrifice her life when I was unwilling to sacrifice mine."

"And now you're willing to sacrifice yours?"

"Yes, actually, I am." He ran his fingers through his hair. "I have the means now to do whatever I wish. I do not intend to be merely the husband of a princess. Surely I can find something useful in government or commerce." He grinned. "I could become the minister of the fleet."

Ephraim's brow furrowed. "I believe Avalonia is landlocked. It has no fleet."

"Then I'll build a fleet. Of balloons, perhaps. Or I'll find a place to invent odd, useless devices like systems to heat air with oil and brandy. Or I'll learn all I can about the distilling of spirits and dedicate the rest of my life to the improvement of Avalonian brandy. God knows it could use improving."

"And it won't bother you? Being nothing more than a husband?"

"Certainly it will bother me, but being without her bothers me more. Frankly, Ephraim, I don't know that I can do this. She told me once that she thought it would take a man of extraordinary strength to survive being a spouse to royalty. She thought I could manage it. But"—he met the other man's gaze—"she never asked me."

"Of course, you never asked her to give up her crown either."

"No, I didn't."

"Perhaps for the same reasons."

"I hope so." Matt paused. "She might well hate me, you know. I said some pretty vile things to her."

Ephraim shrugged. "You'll have to grovel. Apologize profusely. Maybe even beg. Women love all that."

"How would you know? I thought you lived vicariously through me."

"I have picked up a few pointers along the way. Women can be quite forgiving if one is repentant enough. Of course, I've never dealt with a princess." He frowned. "She wouldn't have you shot, would she?"

Matt laughed. "There's a definite possibility."

"I still can't believe you are going through with this." Ephraim shook his head. "Are you sure you're not making a mistake?"

"No, I'm not sure about anything beyond how I feel about her. I have had six long weeks to think about this, and following her now may well be one of the biggest mistakes of my life. Second only to not going after her the first time she left me. But Ephraim"—he picked up the journal and stared at it—"she was willing to give up the life she's known for me. Can I do any less for her?"

Ephraim studied him for a long moment. "You were wrong, Matt. You have quite a way with words. Why, if I were a woman, I'd fall right into your arms."

Matt laughed and tossed the book back onto the desk. "Then we can only thank God you're not. I prefer my women substantially more attractive, with considerably less facial hair than you."

"You always have had discriminating taste. Now"—he picked up the journal—"what am I supposed to do with this?"

"Save it for the future. Perhaps I'll let you publish it someday."

Ephraim's face lit and Matt grinned. "The day when the sign overhead says CADWALLENDER AND SONS WEEKLY WORLD MESSENGER."

"I shall count the minutes," Ephraim said wryly, then opened a drawer and tossed the journal inside. "I nearly forgot about this." He pulled out a letter and handed it to Matt.

"What's that?" Matt scanned it quickly.

"It's from the consortium sponsoring the design competition you were supposed to take part in. They pulled out. Apparently they've decided to put their money into steam power. Seems they think there's more of a future in steam than in flight." Ephraim took the paper back and tossed it into the drawer. "Can't say I blame them."

They chatted for a few more minutes, then Ephraim stood and grasped Matt's hand. "When do you leave?"

"In the morning. Right now I am headed to my workshop and the cottage. I have not been there for some time, and I want to clean out the rest of my things, as I'm relinquishing the lease. Most of what I've left is worthless, but there are some things I want to take with me."

"For that fleet of Avalonian aerostats you'll be building?" Ephraim grinned.

"Of course."

Ephraim laughed, then sobered. His gaze met Matt's. "I do wish you luck, old friend."

"I shall certainly need it." Matt smiled ruefully. "She is my fate, Ephraim. I just pray I can convince her."

There wasn't as much here as he'd thought.

Matt glanced around the stables. He'd always chosen tools and supplies sparingly, his choices limited by his budget. Most of his work things had been transported with the balloon to Effington Hall and then on to Weston Manor. He hadn't accumulated much in recent years. What few personal possessions he had now resided in a bag he'd dropped by the stable door.

He wondered if he shouldn't be a bit melancholy at the realization that he had nothing of worth to show for his life thus far. Still, between the aerostats and naval service, he'd gained knowledge and maturity and confidence in the ten years since he'd left home. And he'd thoroughly enjoyed life in the process. Regardless of what the future held, he looked forward to it.

He moved to the table where he'd spent long hours tinkering with various mechanisms, toying with odd ideas. It struck him that he did rather like working with his hands, and if he did nothing else in Avalonia perhaps he could put that skill to use. After all, as the husband to the princess, his official duties would probably be minimal.

Could he indeed carve out a life for himself at her court? Or in her country? He ran his fingers idly along the edge of the table. He didn't know, but he had to try. And more, he had to succeed.

"Did you miss me?" Tatiana's voice sounded behind him.

His heart thudded and he forced a light note to his voice. "I scarce noticed you were gone."

"You are a bad liar and a truly annoying man, Matthew Weston." Her tone was casual, as matter-of-fact as a discussion on the quality of the roads outside his door.

"Those are my finer qualities." He drew a steadying breath and turned to face her.

She meandered into the stables and glanced around curiously, as if there were nothing of any significance between them. As if they had parted yesterday and under the most pleasant of terms. As if they barely knew one another.

"Why are you here?"

"I just told you." She prowled in a wide circle around him, exhibiting an unlikely interest in the stalls and structure of the stable, and he was forced to turn with her movement. "You are an exceptionally poor liar."

"I think we've established that," he said cautiously. "It's not necessary to repeat it."

"It bears repeating." She paused to consider him. He noted she kept the table between them. A barrier of sorts, but for whose protection? He had no idea what she was thinking. What she wanted. It could well be she was here to crush his hopes, destroy him as thoroughly as he had hurt her. He couldn't blame her. He well understood that particular desire and recognized the irony.

Her words were slow and measured. "I have had a great deal of time to think since we last spoke."

"About that, I want to—"

"Stop," she said sharply, and he thought he heard a slight tremble in her voice. "It is my turn to say what has to be said. You had your say six weeks ago."

"Six weeks and four days, to be precise."

She stared suspiciously at him for a moment, as if she didn't believe he had kept track. "The first two weeks after you . . . after *I* left, I slept, for the most part. Travel and all that."

"Of course." He held his breath. "And then?"

"Then, when I reached home, it was decided it

would be best if the disappearance of the jewels and their recovery was not made public. Any claim Valentina might make could never be substantiated. The Heavens will be reset in a new gold cuff and no one will be the wiser as to their disappearance."

"No one will be the wiser?" Anger on her behalf surged through him. "That's bloody unfair. You found the blasted things. You risked your life, and mine too, for that matter. You should get the credit for their return. You should be hailed as a hero. They should parade you through the streets on their shoulders."

"I would not know what to wear," she murmured, her eyes wide with surprise.

"It's what you are, you know. A hero. Or rather heroine."

She swallowed hard. "Thank you."

He shook his head. "You are as brave as you are lovely, and any country worth its salt should recognize that and treat you accordingly."

"I did not realize you felt so strongly about it. You scarcely seemed to notice the importance of my quest."

"Yes, well, I can be something of an idiot."

"Indeed you can." She considered him carefully. "An annoying idiot, if I recall."

"Regardless, I still think you should have received recognition for what you've done."

"I did not do it for recognition."

"I know, I know." He huffed a short breath. "You did it out of a sense of duty to your position. Responsibility to your country and all that."

"Of course, that was part of it." She paused, choosing her words with care. "But I told you once before, I did it for you as well."

"For me?" He furrowed his brow. "You mean what you said about earning your freedom?"

"Exactly. Now, however"—she shook her head—"I have discovered I did not really do it for you at all. You were the impetus, the excuse, but in truth, I did it for myself."

"I see." He wasn't sure he completely understood, but it scarcely mattered. She was here, and that might well be enough. He forced an offhand manner, as if he didn't care if she'd given up her title or not. "And did you then claim your freedom?"

"I have discovered an odd thing about freedom, and about royal titles as well. Freedom is relative and very much a state of mind. An attitude.

"As for my title, one may abdicate power or the throne, but, at least in my country, one is born to a title and retains it always. Sophia was a princess all of her life, as is Natasha, even if neither of them choose to use the designation. And it appears I will always be a princess."

"And will you choose to use the designation?"

"I have not yet decided." She studied him for a moment, biting her lower lip. His stomach clenched. "I should finish my story."

"Of course." He forced himself to be patient. It was next to impossible. He wanted to know why she was here and if she was still his wife. He wanted to beg her forgiveness, plead for her understanding. He wanted to hold her in his arms, in his bed, in his heart. Instead, he waited.

"After my father and my brother and I had agreed on the fate of the Heavens, it was time to decide my fate. No, that's not precisely true, it was time for *me* to decide my fate." Her fingers picked at a rough gash on the table. "I told them about you, that we were

wed. And I further told them"—her gaze rose to his—
"that I had every intention of remaining married to
you."

Even in the dim light he could see the determined
spark in her eye. If she was at all tentative or apprehensive a moment ago, there was no sign of it now.
Giddy relief washed through him and he wanted to
grin like the idiot he had admitted to being.

"I noted your bag by the door." Her eyes narrowed. "Are you returning to Weston Manor?"

"Not at the moment." He forced a casual note to
his voice. "I've heard Avalonia is nice this time of
year. I thought I might visit."

"Why?"

"It seems Avalonia is where my wife is." His gaze
met hers. "Where my heart is."

"I see." She shook her head. "But I believe your
wife would never allow you to be placed in the position her first husband was in."

He gritted his teeth. "I believe my wife needs to
understand I am not her first husband. I am nothing
like her first husband and I am tired of her thinking,
for so much as a moment, that I could be." He planted
his palms on the table and leaned forward. "Furthermore, I have no intention of following in the footsteps
of her first husband."

"And how would your wife know that?" She
mimicked his stance and glared. "Did you not tell
her that all you had shared was meaningless? That
she was great fun but you never should have married her? And that you were only interested in sharing her bed?"

"Of course. I said all that and more. But . . ." He
searched for the right words, then threw up his hands
in frustration. "I was lying!"

"Why did you have to choose that moment to do it so well?"

"Because I had to make you believe me! Because I couldn't let you give up your life for me!"

"You are so annoyingly noble." She sniffed. "It took me far too long to realize it was all an act. One I should make you pay dearly for. You humiliated me in front of those very nice people."

"Those very nice people you actively deceived," he said pointedly. "Besides, you hit me. Excessively hard, I might add."

"Not nearly hard enough," she snapped.

"Perhaps you can have your captain shoot me?"

"Do not for a moment think he did not offer," she said loftily. "And do not think for a moment I did not seriously consider it. Dimitri was quite disappointed when I forbade him to kill you."

"I should be grateful for that much, then."

She smacked her hand on the table. "You should be grateful for more than that! I am! You and I have found something few people ever do. Do you not understand, Matthew? I refuse to let your misguided nobility keep us apart. My life as a princess, or a peasant, is not worth living without you in it."

"And mine is without you? I'm willing to go to Avalonia and be your blasted lapdog, if that will keep you in my life. Damn it all, Tatiana, I love you. I have loved you from the moment you went up in my balloon. From the moment I saw the tilt of your smile and the spark in your green eyes. From the first lie to the last, I have loved you. And I love you now!"

"Then do stop screaming at me!"

"I am not screaming! I am . . ." He stopped abruptly and blew a long, frustrated breath. "Stark . . . raving . . . mad."

"I suspected as much." The corners of her lips twitched as if she were about to laugh. His heart leapt.

He stared at her for a long moment. "Can you forgive me?"

"Never." She shrugged. "Perhaps. Possibly. Someday. Years from now."

"After a great deal of groveling, I imagine?" He raised a brow. "Begging, beseeching, pleading and so forth as well, no doubt?"

"Without question."

"And how long do you expect the groveling, begging, beseeching and so forth would continue?" He started around the table toward her.

"A lifetime should do." She cast him *the look*, and any lingering doubt he had vanished.

"I see. Exactly where will I be doing this groveling, begging and beseeching?" He reached her and pulled her into his arms and back into his life

"Do not forget the so forth." She stared defiantly up at him.

"I would never forget the so forth." He bent and kissed the hollow of her throat. "The so forth has always been my favorite part. Now, where?"

"I should think a man who wants to make his fortune in shipping would need an ocean." She tilted her head and frowned thoughtfully. "England is on an ocean, is it not?"

"Indeed it is. However, I had planned to go to Avalonia."

"That will never work, Matthew." She widened her eyes innocently. "There is no ocean."

"Regardless, I—"

"It is the nicest gift you could ever offer, but"—she shook her head—"I do not wish to live the rest of my life at court like a fish in a glass bowl. I do not want my husband—"

He opened his mouth to protest and she held her fingers against his lips to stop him, "Even though I know he is nothing like my first husband"—she rolled her gaze heavenward—"to be subjected to constant observation and scrutiny and, whether he likes it or not, comparison and inevitably gossip. However, I cannot tell you I will not miss my family and my country. To do so"—she flashed him a wicked smile—"would be a lie."

"And there will be no more of those."

"Of course not, my lord," she said pleasantly. "Unless, of course the situation warrants it."

"And you do it so much better than I."

"Indeed I do. Do you remember when I said the essence of a good lie was that it be based in truth?" She slid her arms around his neck and gazed into his eyes. "I realized you were lying when you said you had only pretended to be happy about our marriage to have me in your bed. But I had been willing, and did indeed share your bed long before then."

"That's pretty feeble," he said slowly. "You were convinced I was lying because of that?"

"Well, you are an honorable man, and . . ." She paused and heaved a resigned sigh. "No, I was convinced you were lying because I couldn't bear to think otherwise."

His arms tightened around her. "Thank God."

She stared at him for a moment then smiled smugly. "You want to kiss me now, Matthew. I can see it in the look in your eyes."

"I want to do considerably more than kiss you." He grinned wickedly. "And that too you should see in my eyes."

Her eyes widened with delight and her mouth opened and before she could say a word he pressed his lips to hers in a kiss of passion and reunion and the sure and certain knowledge that no matter what adventures they would encounter in the future it would be a future they met hand in hand.

He drew back and smiled down at her. "So you are still a princess?"

"I prefer the title of Lady Matthew but yes, I shall always be a princess." She reached up and nibbled on his lower lip. "Your princess."

Desire rose within him and he wondered how exceedingly uncomfortable the stable might be. And how exciting. "My very own princess. Imagine that."

"And your very own wife."

"I rather like that." He drew her lips back to his. She was back and he would never let her go again. "Indeed, I like that a lot. It has a nice ring to it.

"Her Highness," *for now and forever*, "my wife."

Six Tips to Planning the Perfect Wedding...

WITH A LITTLE HELP
FROM AVON ROMANCE

Everyone knows that a great love story ends with "happily ever after"... and that means a perfect wedding. But before you get to the Big Day, you have to iron out the details ... picking out a dress, getting the right flowers.

Oh, and there's that little matter of finding the groom.

Now, take a sneak peek as these Avon Romance Superleader heroines ... as created by these talented authors—Cathy Maxwell, Victoria Alexander, Susan Andersen, Jennifer Greene, Judith Ivory and Meggin Cabot—go about finding that husband-to-be.

TIP #1:
IT HELPS IF YOU GET ENGAGED
TO THE RIGHT PERSON TO BEGIN WITH.

*When Anthony Aldercy, the Earl of Burnell, has the bad manners
to fall in love with someone other than his fiancée, he does everything in his power to change his own mind! But pert, pretty
Deborah Percival unexpectedly captures his heart in*

The Lady Is Tempted

BY NEW YORK TIMES BESTSELLING AUTHOR

CATHY MAXWELL

July Avon Romance Superleader

He turned—and for a second, Deborah couldn't think, let
alone speak.

Here was a Corinthian. Even in Ilam, they'd heard of
these dashing men about Town. Every young man in the Valley with a pretense to fashion aped their casual dress. But the
gentleman standing in Miss Chalmers's sitting room was the
real thing.

His coat was of the finest stuff, and the cut fit his form to
perfection . . . as did the doeskin riding breeches. His boots

were so well polished that they reflected the flames in the fire, and the nonchalantly careless knot in his tie could only have been achieved by a man who knew what he was doing.

More incredibly, his shoulders beneath the fine marine blue cloth of his jacket appeared broader and stronger than Kevin the cooper's. And his thighs were more muscular than David's, Dame Alodia's groom's. Horseman's thighs. The kind of thighs with the strength and grace from years of riding.

He was also better-looking than both Kevin and David combined.

He wasn't handsome in a classic way. But no one—no *woman*—would not notice him. Dark lashes framed eyes so blue they appeared to be almost black. Slashing brows gave his face character, as did the long, lean line of his jaw. His lips were thin but not unattractive, no, not unattractive at all.

Then, he smiled.

A humming started in her ears. Her heart pounded against her chest . . . and she felt an *unseen* pull toward him, a *connection* the likes of which she'd never experienced before from another human being.

And he sensed the same thing.

She *knew*—without words—that he was as struck by her as she was by him. The signs were there in the arrested interest in his eyes, the sly crookedness of his smile.

Miss Chalmers was speaking, making introductions, but the sound of her voice seemed a long distance away. ". . . Mrs. Percival, a widow from Ilam. This is our other guest, a great favorite of mine, Lor—"

The gentleman interrupted her, "Aldercy. Tony Aldercy."

*Women never said no to Lord Matthew Weston, but he never
met one he'd wanted to say, "I do" ... until he impetuously
married a beautiful woman named Tatiana. So imagine
his shock when he discovered his marriage bed empty,
his bride gone ... and his wife was of royal blood!*

Her Highness, My Wife

BY **VICTORIA ALEXANDER**

August Avon Romance Superleader

"If you are to be my wife, you are to be my wife in the
fullest sense of the word."

"But surely you cannot expect me to—" Tatiana caught herself and stared. "What do you mean *fullest sense of the word*?"

"I mean my wife has to live on my income." Matthew's
grin widened. "It's extremely modest."

"I see." She bit her bottom lip absently. There were benefits
to being in close quarters with him. He certainly could not ignore her presence in a—she shuddered to herself—cottage.

"And I have only one horse and he is better suited to pull—"

"A carriage?" she said hopefully.

"It's really a wagon." He shook his head in a regretful manner she didn't believe for a moment. "In truth, more of a cart."

"To go along with the shack, no doubt." She would put up with his living conditions, castle or cottage scarcely mattered as long as she was with him.

"And there will be no servants," he warned.

"Of course not, given your modest income," she said brightly. "Is that it then? Your conditions?"

"Not entirely." He studied the apple in his hand absently.

"Really? Whatever is left? You do not mean—" She widened her eyes in stunned disbelief. "You cannot possibly believe—" She wrung her hands together and paced to the right. "Surely, you do not expect that I—" She swiveled and paced to the left. "That you—that we—" She stopped and turned toward him. "That you think I would— Oh Matthew, how could you?" She let out a wrenching sob, buried her face in her hands, and wept in the manner of any virtuous women presented with such an edict.

"Good Lord! Your Highness. Tatiana." Concern sounded in his voice and she heard him step closer. "I didn't mean—"

"You most certainly did." She dropped her hands and glared at him. "*This* is exactly what you wanted. Was there a moment of regret over your beastly behavior?"

"There is now." He glared down at her but held his ground.

"Ha. I doubt that. Your intentions with this and every other of your ridiculous conditions was to shock me and, furthermore, to put me in my place. These stipulations of yours, especially the last one." She shook her head. "Did you really believe for a moment I would fall to pieces at the idea of sharing your bed? I am not a blushing virgin. I have been married."

"To me." His eyes narrowed dangerously. "Or have I missed another marriage or two?"

"Not yet," she snapped. "But the day is still young."

TIP #3:
THE PROOF IS IN THE KISS!
IF THAT FIRST KISS
IS AT THE ALTAR,
YOU REALLY ARE IN TROUBLE . . .

*Tristan MacLaughlin is sent to protect vulnerable dancer
Amanda Charles from the crazed man who is stalking her.
At first Amanda thinks MacLaughlin is overbearing—
and overwhelming—but she soon discovers
the unleashed passion in his arms.*

Shadow Dance

THE CLASSIC ROMANTIC NOVEL

BY SUSAN ANDERSEN

September Avon Romance Superleader

Tristan yanked her forward and kissed her. And, if before
that instant Amanda had thought he stood aloofly by and
observed life from the sidelines, she discovered then that she
was mistaken. For there was nothing detached about his hungry mouth moving over hers, nothing aloof about the powerful grip of his arms on her back as they pressed her forward

into the heat of his body, or in his blunt fingers, tangled in her hair, grasping her skull. There was nothing detached at all, and his intensity laid to waste her powers of reasoning.

He had pulled her to him so quickly, she had hardly had time to react. Automatically, she raised her hands to push him away. But, for just an instant, she was caught up in the contrast of how things as they appeared to be and as they actually were could be so devastatingly different.

For instance, MacLaughlin's mouth appeared hard and stern, but, Lord help her . . . it was soft. Strong. Hot. But not hard—not hard at all. The only remotely harsh element of his kiss was the heavy morning beard of his unshaven jaw, abrading the tender skin of her face.

Having hesitated for even that brief an instant, she forgot exactly to which it was she had been going to object. Being manhandled again, maybe? Um. Something like that. She didn't remember and she didn't care. Any objection she might have raised was swamped beneath a wave of sensation.

Tristan's mouth kept opening over Amanda's. Restlessly, he slanted his lips over the fullness of hers. When she didn't open to him immediately, he raised his head, stared into her eyes for a moment, and then came at her from another direction, using the hand in her hair to tilt her face to accommodate him. He widened his mouth around her lips and then slowly dragged it closed, tugging at her lips.

She didn't even think twice. Amanda's lips simply parted beneath his, and Tristan made a wordless sound of satisfaction deep in his throat.

His tongue was slow and thorough. It slid along her bottom lip and explored the serrated edges of her teeth. Releasing his grip on her head, Tristan pulled her closer into the heat of his body, moving his pelvis against her with suggestive need. His tongue rubbed along hers. Nerves Amanda hadn't even known she possessed flamed to acute, throbbing life. Her tongue surged up to challenge his and she arched against him, sliding her arms up to wrap tightly around the strong column of his neck, plunging her fingers into his crisp hair. She was aware of every muscle in his body as he pressed against her.

Murmuring soft sounds of excitement, she raised up on tiptoe, lifting her left leg with an agility borne of years of dancing, to hook the back of her knee behind his hard buttock.

Tristan groaned and kissed her harder, aroused nearly to a frenzy. Meaning only to lean her against a support, but misjudging the distance from where they stood, he slammed her up against the wall of the apartment and rocked against her with slow, mindless insistence. One large hand slid slowly up the leg locked around his hip, stroking from knee to thigh, pulling her closer into him before it eased beneath the high-cut leg of her leotard to grip her firm, tights-covered bottom with wide splayed fingers. "Oh, lass," he breathed into her mouth, and then, unable to bear even that slight separation, he kissed her harder, his mouth hungry and a little rough against hers.

Amanda tightened her grip around his neck and kissed him back, following his lead exactly.

He was frustrated by the tights and the one-piece leotard she wore. She looked smashing in it, but it protected her flesh from invasion like a high-security alarm system.

TIP #4:
MAKE SURE YOU AND THE GROOM SHARE
COMPATIBLE HOPES AND DREAMS . . .
REMEMBER, THERE'S MORE TO MARRIAGE
THAN A GOOD CHINA PATTERN!

Susan Sinclair is strong, capable, and can deal with anything—
after all, everyone tells her so a million times a day!
Surely she can handle a man like Jon Laker . . . even if
she melts into a puddle every time he comes around.
After all, she "got over" Jon a long time ago—didn't she?

The Woman Most
Likely To . . .

BY JENNIFER GREENE

October Avon Romance Superleader

When Jon realized his heart was beating like an overheated jackhammer, he stopped dead, determined to head back home and forget this nonsense. If Susan was in the area, then she was staying at her mother's. He could call her. And if she'd wanted him for something critically important, she could have—and would have—said something on the spot. It was stupid to think that he had to track her down this second . . .

He was halfway to the marina, when he spotted her. Her hands were in her pockets, her hair kicking up in the breeze; she was ambling near the docks, toward the beach, heading for nothing specific, as far as he could see.

He charged forward until he was within calling distance. "Suze!" An out-of-breath stitch knifed his side. His shop keys were still dangling from his hand. "Susan!"

She turned the moment she recognized his voice. From that angle, the sun slapped her sharply in the eyes, where he was in shadow, so he could clearly see how she braced, how she instinctively stilled. "Honestly, Jon, you didn't have to run after me."

"I figured I did. It's not like you go to the trouble of tracking me down more than once in a decade. What's wrong?"

"Nothing."

He wasn't opposed to wasting time on nonsense. But not now, and not with her. "You didn't show up at my place to discuss the weather."

"There's definitely something we need to talk about together. But it's not an easy subject to spring into. I can't just . . ."

"Okay. So. Let's sit somewhere."

"Not *your* place."

God forbid she should trust him after twenty-two years. As if he'd jump her if he caught her alone . . . well hell, come to think of it, he had. But only a few times. And only when she'd wanted to be jumped. And that hadn't happened in a blue moon because they'd both spun out of control the instant someone turned the heat up—and then they'd both been madder and edgier than fighting cats afterward.

Even the best sex in the universe wasn't worth that.

It came close, though.

*Stuart Aysgarth might be the Viscount of Mount Villiars—
and he might consider himself extremely important—
but that doesn't mean he is above the law . . . and
Emma Darlington Hotchkiss is determined he honor
his debt to her. And nothing—not even seduction—
will change her mind!*

Untie My Heart

BY JUDITH IVORY

November Avon Romance Superleader

There was nothing innocent in how his finger continued over the curve of her jawbone to her neck, taking the hem of her dress down her tendon all the way to her collarbone. His eyes followed his finger to the hollow of her throat, where at last he hesitated, paused, then—thank goodness—stopped. She shivered involuntary, tried to speak, but ended up only wetting her lips, dry-mouthed.

The path his finger had traveled left a tiny, traceable impression down her neck to her clavicle, a trail so warm and particular it seemed traced by the sun through a magnifying glass.

"You," he said finally, then paused in that soft, slow way he had that was mildly terrifying now under the circumstance, "are a very hard woman to frighten, do you know that?"

She blinked up at him. "I can assure you, you're doing a good job. You can stop, if that was the goal."

He laughed. A rare sound, genuine, deep, though she definitely didn't like his sense of humor, now that she heard it. For a second more—with him leaning on both arms, his shoulders bunching, pulling at his shirt where they held his weight—he hovered over her, surveying her in that very disarming way again. Then he stood up completely.

Good God, was he tall. From her angle, his head seemed to all but touch the ceiling.

He stared about them, perplexed for a moment, as if he'd lost track of what he was doing, then seemed to remember. And he backed up.

To take a gander at his handiwork, it seemed. Over her knee she watched him withdraw two feet to the window sill and sit his buttocks onto it, his back flattening the lace curtains. There, he crossed his arms over his chest, tilted his head, and viewed her incapacitation from this new angle.

He then said, "Do you know, I think I could do anything to you, absolutely anything, and there would be nothing you could do about it."

"What a cheerful piece of speculation," she said, a little annoyed.

"Save complain. Which you do very well."

She shut her mouth, advising herself to take John's advice and be humble. Or at least quiet.

Mount Villiars laughed again, entertained by his own iniquitous turns of mind. "And whatever I did, afterward, I could hand you over to the sheriff, and, even complaining, he'd just haul you away." The sarcastic jackanapes shook his head as if in earnest sympathy. "Such is our legal system and the power behind the title of viscount. I love being a viscount. Have I mentioned that? Despite all the trouble that arrived with my particular title, I find it's worth fighting for. By the way," he added, "I like those knickers."

Lou Calabrese never dreamed she would be left behind when her boyfriend ran off with a bimbo! And when she is accidentally stranded with that same bimbo's sexy, stubborn Hollywood hunk of an "ex" she learns that sometimes the surprise wedding of the year turns out to be your own!

She Went All the Way

BY MEGGIN CABOT

December Avon Romance Superleader

"Sorry," he said. "I don't really watch movies all that much." For a moment. Lou forgot she was the victim of an attempted murder and a helicopter crash, and gaped at Jack—Jack, the moviestar—as if he'd just done something completely out of keeping with his manly image, such as order a champagne cocktail or burst into a rendition of "I Feel Pretty."

"You're an *actor*," she cried, "and you're telling me you don't really watch movies all that much?"

"Hazard of the trade," Jack said lightly. "The magic of Hollywood doesn't hold much allure when you know all the secrets."

Lou shook her head. Oh, yes. They were definitely in Bizarro World now. No doubt about it.

"Maybe," Jack ventured, as if he hoped to change the subject, "we should build a fire."

"A fire?" If he'd suggested they strip naked and do the hula, Lou could not have been more surprised. "A *fire?* What do you think *that* is?" She pointed at the burning hulk of metal a dozen yards away. "What, you're worried when they start looking for us they won't be able to spot us? Townsend, I don't think they're going to have any problem."

"Actually," he said, in the politely distant tone he reserved, as Lou knew only too well, for incompetent waiters and crazy screenwriters, "I was thinking a fire might warm us up. You're shivering."

She was, of course. Shivering. But she'd hoped he wouldn't notice. Showing weakness in front of Jack Townsend was not exactly something she wanted to do. It was bad enough she'd been unconscious in front of him. The last thing she wanted was for him to think she was afraid . . . or worse, uneasy about their current situation—that she was stuck in the middle of nowhere with one of America's hottest Hollywood idols. She had had more than enough with Hollywood idols. Hadn't she lived with one for eight years? Yeah, and look how *that* had turned out.

She was certainly not going to make that mistake again. Not that she was about to do anything as foolish as fall in love with Jack Townsend. Perish the thought! So what if he seemed to be concerned about her physical comfort, and had saved her life, and oh, yes, looked better in a pair of jeans than any man Lou had ever seen in her life? *Are we having fun yet?* Right there was reason enough not to give him the time of day, let alone her sorely abused heart. Besides, hadn't he had the very bad taste to, until recently, date Greta Woolston? There had to be something wrong with a man who couldn't see through that vapid headcase, as she knew only too well.

It was as she was thinking these deep thoughts that she noticed Jack had stood up and wandered a short distance away. He was picking up sticks that had fallen to the ground, branches that, too heavily laden with snow, had fallen to the earth.

"What . . ." She started as he leaned down and hefted a particularly large branch. The back of his leather jacket came up over his butt, and she was awarded a denim-clad view of the famous Jack Townsend butt, the one women all over America gladly shelled out ten bucks to see on the big screen.

And here she was with that butt all to herself.

In the middle of Alaska.